Dragoon

Evan Ratke

Published by Evan Ratke, 2018.

For my parents.

Printed in the United States of America

ISBN 978-1-7321156-0-6 (E-book)

ISBN 978-1-7321156-1-3 (Paperback)

First Edition 2018

10 9 8 7 6 5 4 3 2 1

Edited by Jamie Fueglein

Cover Illustration by Margaret Peyton

PHASE 1: MARATHON

Winter of the 31st Year of Marathon

40th Year after the Reform

1st Year after the Marathon-Carthage War

1: SEAN

Sean Halley didn't expect to start the day by watching someone get their eyes cut out, but he conceded that such experiences were part of the job. Twenty-four years old with unkempt dirty blond hair and a slender agile frame, he came around with a gentle tap in the dark, his lungs overflowing with frosted air. The joints across his body were weary, his shoulder afire as it planted on the damp cement floor, his back stabbing him in retaliation for being forced against the concrete wall for so long. Little more than a walk-in closet, the room where he'd spent a few hours sleeping, or at least trying to sleep, was inescapably cold. Dirt fertilized the walls and floor, sticking to his skin. The building's air had been infused with the smell of rust, leaving a stinging sensation in his nostrils and a bad taste in his mouth since he'd arrived. It was as if the structure had been disassembled and reassembled with old spare parts many times over, with each replacement piece bringing a new layer of corrosion to the air. Darkness held a heavy weight over the tiny space, but faint-yellow from the hallway snuck under the door, guiding his tired eyes to the exit. The tap came again, soft and reserved on the other side of the door, as if the person knocking was afraid to wake him. "Mr. Halley," a voice whispered, so low he almost didn't hear. "You're wanted back in the interrogation room, sir."

"Yes, thank you," he mumbled back through the door, speech still claimed by exhaustion. Dizziness fought him as he used the wall to pull himself up and reach for the doorknob. *Well, back to the grind.*

Sluggish, Sean made his way into the halls of the Serenity Station. With his hand, he rubbed the pronounced scars that disfigured the left side of his face with a spider-web pattern. Even after a year the marks still burned whenever he woke, a searing feeling that made his face tick until the pain lessened. Dressed in a black winter jacket, black pants, black boots, black socks, and black gloves, he strove for an impression of irrelevance as he sought out his destination. Situated fifty miles north of the city of Marathon, the Serenity Station acted as a clandestine forward operations outpost for the city. Built twenty feet below ground, the garrison consisted of two extensive hallways and a third shorter hallway that sat between the two, giving the whole base an H-shape. Sean walked from his accommodations at the far end of the left side hallway, known to the more long-term occupants of the Serenity Station as East Hall. His breath glowed yellowish-white in front of him, a black switchblade hung from its clip on his belt, the tap of his boots echoed down the hall, signaling the one who waited on him. Dimly lit by the low ceiling's generator-powered lights, East Hall was by no means an improvement over his room. Grime coated every inch of the black floor and walls. The air was murky with particles of clay and dust he could see floating in the light's yellow rays. The Serenity Station reminded him more of a building that had not been entered for decades and only recently excavated, rather than a base constructed a mere two years ago. The outpost certainly hadn't been cleaned in over a year.

Passing several black doors on both sides of the hall, all of which were shut, he turned right at the corner and headed down the small connecting hallway at the building's center. Veering left at the end of the middle hall, he arrived on the right side of the station, West Hall. The interrogation room was the first door around the corner. A soldier belonging to Marathon stood guard at the entrance. Two or three years younger than Sean, the man was outfitted with a dark blue tactical suit and helmet, dark blue body armor, boots, and gloves. Trembling in his combat gear, he held his T-05 Combat Rifle at his chest. Colored black with a black strap attached and capable of semi or full automatic function, the T-05 was made with a purposefully bland design, its lack of memorable features meant to deceive those who'd never come across the weapon before into thinking the rifle was not dangerous, which it most definitely was. A single slug could take a person's head off. The door opened as Sean approached. The soldier kept his eyes on the wall as he held the knob. Sean nodded to the guard as he went through the doorway, but the man didn't so much as return a look in response to his thankful gesture. Immediately the entrance was sealed behind him, as if the soldier were afraid to keep the hallway exposed to the room any longer than necessary.

Barely illuminated by a single light on the ceiling and overrun with the acidic air of the station, the room was no larger than a small storage unit. Dark red and brown liquid flooded the center of the floor. Sean stepped to the edge of the puddle, nostrils assaulted by the room's unique fragrance of feces and urine. A black chair sat in the pool, facing the door. Bound tight with wire at the wrists and ankles, arms stretched behind the back of the chair in a no doubt painful position, was a person, the prisoner, dressed in a ragged winter coat, pants, and boots. The prisoner's clothes were so pale and dirty from wear Sean still couldn't tell what color they'd originally been. He imagined this person had worn the same outfit for the last few years at least. Each article of clothing was stained with streaks of blood. The detainee's head was slumped forward and covered with a dark red and black bag, his breathing crisp, soft, as if trying to convince anyone who entered he was asleep. *Sorry.*

The quivering started as Sean reached down and removed the detainee's bag. Around the same age as Sean, the man's face was swelled with enormous red gashes and black and purple marks, his eyes two times larger than they should've been, unable to open. Red drops fell with every shiver of his head. A piece of red duct tape shielded his mouth. The expression underneath the curtain of his wounds was seized in a tormented collaboration of pain, fright, and rage.

Sean wasn't sure where to begin, what was left to interrogate, though that didn't stop him. With a single pull, he ripped the tape from the prisoner's mouth, leaving it on the floor with the bag. Crossing his arms, he began to speak to the prisoner, his voice firm yet sympathetic. "We gave you the night to decide. What's it going to be, Jason?" When Jason's silence was the only reply Sean got, he said, "Trust me, none of us want to start this whole thing all over again. And I know you don't either. You've been in this chair for twelve hours; in your condition, you won't make it another twelve. So for your sake, tell us what we need to know. Do that and we'll get you patched up, food and water, even a shower."

He received a response, but not the one he desired. "You'll kill." Jason's head wobbled; he only managed a murmur, as if even the weakest form of communication required concentrated effort. "You'll kill her, if I tell you where."

Sean sighed with disappointment. "You've been saying that since we put you in here, I don't want to hear that excuse again. Working for the Cavaliers is a death sentence." He winced. "Believe it or not, you're safer here with us."

"Fuck you people," Jason mumbled, his spark of anger minor but noticeable. The door squealed as it opened behind Sean.

A shuddering sense of anxiety flashed through the room. "No, fuck you," Sean told their prisoner.

Anna Corday came through the door, letting it close behind her. Twenty-one years old, she had long dirty blond hair that hung loose at the sides of her head, so similar in shade and texture to Sean's anybody who didn't know otherwise could be forgiven for mistaking them for siblings. She wore a black jacket, black pants, black boots, and black gloves that matched his exactly, as did the black switchblade clipped to her belt. A puff of yellowish-white air materialized in front of her face. Bringing a hand to her mouth, she yawned as she said, "Morning, how'd everybody sleep?" Her tone was casual, her expression calm, as if she was meeting them for breakfast rather than an interrogation.

Jason squirmed in his chair, squeaking and splashing the metal legs on the floor, as if hoping to somehow break free of his restraints. "Okay," Sean lied. "I can't stand the smell of this place though."

"You're telling me." Anna joined Sean in the room's center. "I don't know how those soldiers stay down here in six-month intervals."

"Maybe they get paid more than the average troops," Sean suggested.

Jason nearly tipped himself over, continuing his useless struggle with the wire. "Please." Anna and Sean turned to their prisoner as he begged.

"What's gotten into you?" Anna asked him, as if she didn't know.

Jason tilted his head away from Anna's voice. "Please, I can't."

"Huh," Anna said with composed surprise, placing her hands on her hips. Glancing at Sean, she said, "Here I was walking in thinking he'd give us the Cavaliers' base camp straight away, save us all the trouble."

"I can't give her up."

"But no, no. For some reason, he thinks he has to hold out." Sean stepped aside, giving Anna her place in front of Jason.

"Katherine's still there."

Anna shook her head, dissatisfied yet smiling. "Yes I know Katherine's still there, Jason. You've told me a hundred times. You and this girl, in your combined wisdom, decided it would be a good idea to join the rest of those Cavalier fucks. And then, you two helped the Cavaliers stick a couple IEDs in the ground, helped them take out twenty Marathon soldiers. Now you're here."

At once, Jason summoned the strength to shout, as if finally realizing his pleas would not lead to his freedom. "Murderers!"

Anna yawned a second time, deflecting Jason's attempt at insult. Smirking at Sean, she said, "Hold his head for me, please." Sean nodded without a word and stepped behind Jason.

"What," Jason started to ask. Sean seized his head, bending it to the right and forcing his left eye upwards. "Fuck!" Sean dug his fingers into the detainee's scalp as Jason tried to shake him off. Even with his gloves on, Sean's hands grew cold. "What're you doing?"

Anna pulled her switchblade from her belt and clicked it open. "Oh, you'll see." Jason yelped in pain as she pried his inflamed eyelid open with her free hand, exposing the white of his eyeball to light. Above the watering eye, she held the knife. The blade gleamed under the room's light, making him recognize it was there. "Just know Jason, once I start you're the only one who can make me stop."

Jason mumbled something. "The Lord is my strength and my defense. He has become my salvation."

Anna snickered as she and Sean looked at each other. Sean let his partner speak. "Okay, one: I'm not sure which Lord you're talking about. And two: there's no Lord down here, pal. It's just you, me, and Sean." Jason tried to blink, but Anna kept the lids apart, kept his eye on the switchblade. "You keep that in mind." Sean found himself cringing as Anna angled the knife down at Jason's face. The sharpened tip of the blade slipped under Jason's eyeball. Red seeped from the socket. Jason twisted about, as if misery was sucking away the air in his lungs. His cries filled the room, his agony unavoidable.

When the screams ceased fifteen minutes later, Sean and Anna exited the room together. Droplets of red sprinkled their faces, smeared their gloves. They walked side by side all the way down to the end of West Hall, where a single black door sat between the walls. Written on the door with dark blue letters was the word, "COMMAND." After straightening their postures, removing and tucking their gloves into their pants pockets, Anna knocked at the door. The response took a few seconds. "Enter," an older woman's voice mandated.

The command center of the base was of equal size to the interrogation room. Much of the room was taken up by a black table in the center of the floor. Hanging from the left, right, and back walls were three black monitors. The screen on the left was off, but the other two were on, lighting the room in bright blue. The monitor on the back wall displayed footage from the outpost's security cameras, alternating between images of East Hall, West Hall, the center hallway, and the area above the garrison. The monitor on the right wall showed a map of the region including the ruins of Serenity, a former city of the Previous Civilization, and the Serenity Hills that surrounded the city. A woman stood in front of this screen, focused on the map. A child of the Previous Civilization and survivor of the Reform, now in her late fifties, she was dressed in the same black uniform Sean and Anna wore. Her long brunette hair was tied back and neat behind her head. Sean and Anna knew her as Commander Darius; she'd never given her first name.

One of only three Marathon Commanders, Commander Darius served as leading officer of the Black Dragoons, the city's officially non-existent special operations unit. "Do we have it?" their superior officer asked without turning from the map, voice stern, hands behind her back. A cloud of blueish-white air floated between her and the screen.

"We have it, ma'am," Anna answered, her tone matching the Commander's seriousness. Sean stepped to Anna's left, standing beside her.

At that, Darius transferred her attention to her subordinates, much to Sean's unease. A glaring red scar ran down the left side of the Commander's face. Blue shined from her head as the light from the monitors reflected off her glass eye, giving her a presence that was more mechanical than human. And yet Anna held eye contact with Darius, externally unaffected by her rank. With a nod, the Commander said, "About time. I was starting to wonder if that prisoner would ever shut up." Her hands shifted to her sides as she moved from the monitor to the back end of the table. Sean and Anna took their place at the front.

Sean was quiet as Anna spoke for both of them. "It certainly took some effort, ma'am. Jason was a lot more dedicated than we'd first anticipated. Even cutting out his eyes took a while to have any benefit." Anna glanced at Sean, who gave a simple nod in agreement.

"They're always more dedicated than we think they are. Anyways, good work. Not just here, but with the capture as well." Darius's compliment was honest, impressed with their progress.

"Thank you, Commander," Anna said. "We got lucky though. If Jason hadn't been on a rendezvous mission with the Cavaliers' contact in Marathon, he would be long overdue back to his camp. The others would've known we grabbed him and evacuated."

"Looks like Marathon came through for us there." Darius turned to Sean, as did Anna. "So, where's Mr. Jason from?"

The Commander's question was straightforward, yet it shivered in Sean's spine. It wasn't Darius's rank, or her appearance, that delayed his answer for an awkward few seconds. Rather, it was his awareness of the critical difference in status between himself and the other two people in the room with him, the same sentience that kept him from speaking to Darius unless spoken to directly. Unlike Darius and Anna, he was not a native-born citizen of Marathon, because up until a year ago he had been a native-born citizen of the city of Carthage. And though he now had immigrated citizenship in Marathon, his was of a lesser kind. *I wonder if either of them sees me as any more of a person than Jason.*

With nervous rapidity, he said, "They're camped in the Serenity Hills, approximately ten miles west of here. There are enough trees still standing there to cover them from our patrols. From where they're located, they should have a clear view of the entire valley and the remains of the city itself. Whoever occupies that hill has instant knowledge of all activity in and around Serenity."

"Guess they got to it first," Anna quipped.

His partner's comment eased Sean's worry a bit as Darius mused, "That explains their success hitting our patrols and this station's resupply convoys." Sean and Anna nodded. "The other Commanders believe an air strike won't send the necessary message, and that terminating the Cavaliers in a ground assault is the best option." Darius simpered, her thoughts bringing her pleasure. "But then again, I like to trust my field agents more than glorified bureaucrats who rarely leave Marathon anymore." Sean thought he heard Anna giggle at this. Whether the laugh was genuine or manufactured, the Commander's statement was familiar to his partner. "So, what do you two think we should do?"

Anna spoke first. "Despite the other Commanders infrequent trips outside Marathon, they are correct this time, ma'am. We call in an air strike and there's nothing left of the Cavaliers for anyone to find. But, if you let Sean and I take them down ourselves, ma'am, we'll leave their bodies out for other terrorist groups to find later. That's the whole reason for the Dragoons, isn't it?"

Darius nodded, accepting Anna's answer. She and Anna looked at Sean again. This time, Sean made sure not to hesitate before responding. He knew Darius didn't care about his opinion, or Anna's. She wanted to hear them agree with her. "Anna's right, Commander. An air strike's too impersonal. I know my way through those hills well enough we can move on their camp without being spotted. There are only a dozen of them up there, according to Jason. I can provide cover from the trees while Anna advances on the camp, although if something goes wrong, she probably won't need my help."

"If anything, she'll be the one helping you," Darius retorted. Sean contrived a laugh.

Anna grinned at her partner. "I don't know Commander; he wouldn't be here with us if he wasn't somewhat competent," she joked.

Darius was satisfied. "In either case, your assessments are sound. From this moment on, all persons at or within the immediate vicinity of the Cavaliers' base camp are to be considered hostile. Anna Corday and Sean Halley, you have the blue light for your first assassination with the Black Dragoons. Everything there with a pulse dies tonight."

"Thank you, Commander," Anna replied.

Sean didn't dare speak, though he felt the impulse to. *Everything?*

From the command center, Sean and Anna walked back up West Hall to the center hallway. Halfway down the middle hall was a black door to the only room in the midsection of the station, labeled with dark blue letters that spelled the word, "ARMAMENTS." The largest room in the garrison, the armory was a tight yet elongated room lit with three lights on the ceiling. Contained within the armory were dark blue lockers, twelve lining each wall. Two black benches ran down the middle of the floor, separating the two sets of lockers. They sat on the first bench, Sean facing the lockers on the left, Anna sitting beside him and facing the lockers on the right, and began their arrangements.

Always three or four steps behind Anna, Sean dug out and readied his gear. His rifle was wiped down with a cloth from the locker, loaded, and slung over his shoulders by its strap. Just as the T-05 was the primary weapon of the regular military, its first cousin, the T-05 Sniper had become the signature weapon of the Black Dragoons. Though of course only the Dragoons and those who were permitted to know of the unit's unofficial existence were aware of this fact. Modified with a protracted barrel that improved the rifle's accuracy, as well as a scope that included normal, night vision, and thermal settings, and an exclusively semi-automatic function, the T-05 Sniper was advancement over the original T-05 rifle. However, Sean and Anna's T-05 Snipers held an extra adjustment, sound suppressors attached to the barrels, colored black as the rest of the weapon was.

Beyond his main weapon, the majority of Sean's gear was tucked into a black backpack, made with fake mended patches and dirt stains intended to give the pack an old and shabby look, so as to help disguise the Dragoon as a nomadic civilian. A black watch, with dark blue digital numbers reading 0830 was tied to his left wrist. A black earpiece, no bigger than a pencil eraser, was secured just inside his right ear canal. A black winter hat obscured his hair and his red soiled gloves were returned to his hands. Next to him, Anna performed the exact same preparations with much greater efficiency, so knowledge-able of her equipment she could probably complete the task with her eyes closed. No words were necessary, they both knew how to gear up, and they both knew full well what purpose their gear served.

Sean was still priming when Anna shut her locker and stood up from the bench, already set to move out. She waited as he fastened the loaded pack to his back and rose to his feet on the other side of the bench, the bag pressing against his shoulders. As he was sealing his own locker, however, Anna broke their silence with a curious question, bizarre in its modesty. "How do you know this area so well, Sean?"

Sean turned to his partner, who stood by the door, her hair bundled under her hat, rifle and pack dangling from their straps. "Why uh, why do you ask?"

"You were with the Carthage Scouts, right? Before you came to Marathon? Did the Scouts make a lot of contact with civilians in the area?"

Sean clenched his mutilated jaw until he relaxed, fighting off discomfort created by the mention of the Carthage Scouts. "Yeah, we spent a lot of time in the Serenity Hills. Most of it was hiking and mapping the area though, we didn't have much contact with other people on that trip."

His reply should've been insignificant, but he noticed Anna's interest becoming more apparent as confusion surfaced in her expression. "Hiking?"

"What?" he asked, not understanding why Anna was confused.

"Hiking. What is that?" Anna's confounded tone and mystified expression told Sean she truly had no idea what the word meant.

Taken aback and not quite sure how to answer, he said, "You know, walking trails and hills. Like going out for a walk."

"You mean, like a patrol?" she asked, still not grasping the concept.

"Sort of, except just for fun, not for Marathon or whoever else. Though with the Scouts, we did it to learn what we could about the places we went to."

"You mean you've walked around, for fun? They let you do that?"

Now Sean was lost. "Who are 'they'?"

"The government of Carthage, the people in charge before we." She paused, seeking a better way of completing her sentence. "Uh, before you came to Marathon. They allowed you to go...hiking? Wouldn't you've been arrested for trying to leave the city's supervision or walking around past curfew?"

"Uh, no. No, we were pretty much able to come and go as we pleased. As long as you were a registered citizen, the city legislature generally didn't stop you from going outside the walls. We didn't have a curfew either. Even when I was a student at the city's college, what we did in our free time wasn't regulated, as long as we didn't violate the law."

Despite his attempt at an explanation, Anna was left no less baffled than she'd been at the beginning of the exchange. "What's college?"

The station's exit was at the end of East Hall, past the room Sean spent the night in. The door brought them to the stairs, a black cemented stairwell, claustrophobic and narrow. The only light flowed from the top of the steps, thin and yellow, just adequate for Sean to find the metal railing. His boots tapped on the stairs and his gear rang against the railing as he followed Anna upwards, out of the bunker. At the top of the stairwell was a short hallway, slim as the stairwell. The hall led to the last of the base's doors. Two soldiers stood on the left and right sides of the hall, halfway to the door. Their mannerisms serious, T-05s held at the ready in their arms, loaded and safeties off, as if they'd shoot anyone who so much as spoke to them. Passing the safe house guards, the sign tacked to the exit door became legible, its dark blue letters saying, "WARNING! You are now leaving the Serenity Station. Stay Alert. Watch your surroundings."

The door swung outwards as Anna, and then Sean, marched into the gray. The fires that signaled the end of the Previous Civilization forty years ago had left their perpetual scars on the atmosphere, a memento from the day of the Reform. Gray dominated the sky, a monstrous expanse of overcast stretching for hundreds of miles in every direction. What light there was below the overcast glowed murky, as if a rainstorm was constantly moments away. Filled with microscopic pieces of frozen dirt, the air had a sandy texture to it, leaving a feeling of grime on one's skin that could not be washed off. Sean walked, talked, ate, drank, and slept with a sense that he had not bathed, even right after a shower. The smell was worse, a rotting stench of decay that arrived with the smallest gust of wind. The foul and freezing air bit at his face as he walked. His boots dug into deep ash gray snow. He shivered with each weighted step. Why the environment had yet to initiate its recovery process in this region, while in others the first signs of natural restoration had already appeared, was not abundantly clear to anyone. The leading theory, posed by children of the Previous Civilization, was that the area had been so heavily decimated during the Reform that the ecological comeback had been postponed several more decades, perhaps a century.

As the door locked back in place, separating them from the Serenity Station, Sean and Anna stepped towards the relics that used to make up the city of Serenity. Four decades of erosion and frequent snowfall had done away with the majority of the city's structures and every one of its roads. In its place was a vast field of gray, strikingly flat, as if the slopes had been stomped down by the Reform until they were even with the surrounding landscape. The only enduring signs of what had once been were the square-shaped building tops, dispersed throughout the field, none of them more than three or four stories tall, remnants of what was now buried underneath the surface of the planet. With their decomposing walls and their long since blasted away foundations, these legacies of Serenity were expected to disappear within another decade or two. Sean was convinced that were it not for the surviving children of the Previous Civilization, carrying the memory of this city like a torch, Serenity would've already faded into the permanent night of time.

Circling the field at all ends were the Serenity Hills. Tall and steep, not quite mountains but close, the Serenity Hills were as gray as the city, not a single patch of green. Though the trees remained, no branches held leaves. From the exterior of the Serenity Station, a black concrete wall designed to resemble the city's ruins, they turned left, facing the western sector of the hills. *Katherine's still there.* As he and Anna paced away from the outpost's entrance, their boots crackling in the sheets of icy snow, the words of their now visionless and soon to be executed prisoner recurred in his mind, as if demanding to be addressed. "He was only dedicated to her you know."

Anna turned to him as they walked, astonished he'd spoken first. "What's that?"

"Jason. You and the Commander were talking about how he was more dedicated than we predicted. It wasn't Jason's commitment to the Cavaliers that was making him hold out. It was his commitment to that girl, Katherine, the one he joined the Cavaliers with. Katherine's still in the camp. That's the only reason he resisted as long as he did."

"Right? So?" Anna retorted, as if annoyed he'd brought the topic to attention.

Sean was quick as he thought up a way to make his assessment relevant. "I just figure, we should make sure we know the difference. It'll be easier to work people like the Cavaliers if we know what they're fighting for."

Anna gave a brief nod that prevented him from determining if she agreed. Her hands brought her T-05 Sniper to the ready, as she asked, "Where to?" finishing the discussion if there ever was one.

Sean raised his rifle as well, relenting to their assignment. Gazing across the field of Serenity at a particular tree-covered hill in the distance, one that resembled Jason's description of the Cavaliers' hideout, he told her, "This way," and his partner followed him on the course to their objective.

2: ANNA

They crept through a labyrinth of trees strewn across the ice and snow-submerged hill, night encircling them in a stronghold of motionless black and vicious cold, their boots crunching in the snow, rifles clicking in their arms, packs tearing at their shoulders. Between the skeletal and frozen tree branches, snaking through the air above them, the overcast held its watchful position in the grayish-black sky. Though she hadn't lived in the time when the trees flourished with life, green plants she doubted she'd ever get to see and animals she couldn't remember the names of, she felt a glaring bareness to the woods around her, as if the world was missing pieces of itself. With decisive silent gestures, Sean led her to the base of a steep wooded embankment as they continued their trek west over the Serenity Hills. Back down behind them to the east, buried in the dark, was the valley that held the disintegrating city of Serenity. After following the city's cemetery fields to their end, a process that on its own had taken three hours to accomplish, they'd begun scaling and combing the hill Sean identified when they left the Serenity Station. Ten hours of slow climbing and searching later, they believed they were closing in on their objective. She kept pace behind Sean, checking their flanks as he watched the front. When the ground began to bend upwards beneath their boots, they stopped and lay flat in the snow behind a fallen trunk, Sean to her right. The scent was heavier now, more distinct than it'd been when they'd first caught whiff of it several minutes ago. Burning, though not the degraded aroma the breeze often smelled of. It was fresh. Turning to her partner's damaged face, she nodded and tapped her nose. *Campfire.*

A voice came to her right ear, composed yet intensive as it resonated from her earpiece. "Vanguard One," Commander Darius called over Marathon's military Network.

Anna raised her index finger to her ear, tapping the earpiece twice and holding her finger to it to connect. "Go ahead, Central," she whispered so only Sean would be able to hear her.

"Vanguard One, thermal imaging from the Aurora is reading two heat signatures fifty meters ahead of your current position at your ten o'clock." Though she knew she wouldn't be able to see anything, she found herself tilting her head up towards the grayish-blackness, trying to catch a glimpse of the Aurora plane that had been called in from Marathon to support their efforts. One of five Auroras operated by Marathon, and the last known aircraft model in existence, the Aurora was a sleek black V-shaped pilotless drone used to assist the military's ground forces through surveillance and missile strike operations. Though the Aurora was a troublesome craft in its old age, prone to frequent mechanical problems, narrow reconnaissance grids, and limited to a hundred thirty-five miles per hour in speed, the drones were capable of reaching and performing from heights above the overcast, out of sight and out of range of enemy ground fire. "The drone also drew a bead on a larger cluster of heat signatures a hundred meters past those first two. First contacts you've come across since you started up that hill. I'm thinking we've found Jason's friends."

"Roger that Central, I agree." She nodded at Sean as she muttered, "Location matches Jason's description and we've gotten wind of a campfire just over this ridge. First two signatures are probably guards, the rest are the Cavaliers' main force grouped at their base camp. We're moving on them now." Sean's hands tightened on his T-05 Sniper.

"Copy all Vanguard One, I'll be watching," Darius responded, with a hint of approval.

I'm sure you will be. Anna took her finger off her earpiece and set it at the trigger of her T-05. Her comfortableness with their task did not lessen as she said to her partner, "Aurora's got the camp on thermal. Two guards, fifty meters up at our ten." Sean said nothing as he brought his rifle to bear and mounted it on the log. He peered through his scope, scanning up the bank as white clouds rose from his face.

Anna did the same, the greenish-gray slope and its blackish-brown trees revealing themselves in the bright though shadowed green of her scope's night vision function. "Got em, two hostiles at the top of the incline," Sean mumbled to her. Glancing from her scope to her partner, she saw that his rifle was still, centered on their targets. "Pistol and bolt-action rifle, Previous Civilization." She returned to her scope and shifted her view uphill in the direction he was aiming his rifle, locating the guards on the greenish-gray embankment.

They were crouched between a few trees at the peak, less than ten feet apart, dressed in ragged and overused winter clothing. Greenish-white mist hung in front of their torn and depleted faces. As Sean stated, the guard's weapons were constructed during the Previous Civilization. Even through her night vision scope, Anna could see the firearms' rusted and diminished state; she questioned whether or not the guns would actually fire. Neither guard had the slightest notion of the danger surveilling them. It made Anna glad, she and Sean would kill them without them realizing. *After what happened with Jason, it'll be good to make it quick for the rest of the Cavaliers.*

"Glassed them," she whispered. "You take the one on the..." She stopped, as a thought bloomed in her mind. When her partner turned from his scope, she looked back at him and said, "Take them both. They're all yours." Sean didn't reply, but gave a surprised and knowing expression that told her he recognized she was testing him. Though he was a citizen of Marathon and the highest rated marksman among the recruits who'd come up from Carthage at the end of the Marathon-Carthage War, Sean had not been a citizen of Marathon for long, nor had he been Anna's partner long enough for her to judge his skill firsthand. By shooting both guards at her command, he would begin to prove his worth to their Dragoon team.

For a moment or two, she thought Sean was about to refuse. However, he refocused on his scope and the guards, his index finger making its way towards the trigger of his rifle. Anna did the same. Their mouths moved, what they were saying to each other Anna couldn't know, but she thought they must've been complaining about the cold as there wouldn't be much else for them to talk about as they sat in the dark. A hissing noise came from her right; she felt the air vibrating around her. In her night vision scope, she saw the guard with the pistol jerk backwards, his head erupting in a haze of black smog and chunks, as the other guard was soaked in black rain. A second hiss and the guard with the rifle disappeared as well. A splattering sound resonated downhill, ricocheting against the trees. "Targets down," she told her partner, impressed as she turned to him. Sean didn't retort, keeping his attention fixated on his scope, his index finger holding at the trigger of his rifle, as if he expected another guard to appear. A trail of smoke streamed from the front of his weapon's suppressor. "Sean," she said, not shouting but not whispering either. He looked to her then, as a white fog rolled past the webbed scars on his face, his eyes dense with what appeared to be exhaustion, though she wasn't sure. "You good to go?"

"You got it."

The bank was steeper than it first appeared in her night vision scope, but the extra effort required in ascending made little difference to her, even as her partner's movements became more and more sluggish. Operating on minimal sleep and having spent the last several hours mounting one slippery incline after another, Anna was only slightly more fatigued than she'd been at the start of the day, as if the time spent in interrogation with Jason and walking to the Serenity Hills energized rather than drained her. A few minutes of vigilant climbing later, they arrived at the peak of the slope and stepped onto one of many plateaus between the hill's embankments. Once there, they began the push through the final stretch of trees that would lead them to the hub of the Cavaliers' terrorist organization.

The camp came to them fast, in a small clearing between the trees, before the next ridge. Grabbing cover behind a pair of trees at the edge of the clearing, they knelt and glassed the camp with their rifle scopes. The site was in many ways underwhelming, so much so Anna doubted she'd have viewed it as the home of terrorists responsible for the murder of nearly two dozen Marathon soldiers, had she not forced that fact out of Jason. She would've believed them to be civilians, preserving their own community in the Serenity Hills. There were seven tents only, arranged together in two lines of three, running parallel to each other and horizontally facing Anna and Sean's position in the trees, with the seventh tent at the right side end of the formation. None of them were of considerable size and each tent was battered to a degree that Anna wondered how their owners got them to stand at all, their multiple tears patched with duct tape. The campfire she and Sean smelled a quarter mile back was going strong in the late night, a cocoon of bright orange at the left side end of the tents, broken by smoke that climbed through the trees into the grayish-black overcast. There were three people sitting around the fire together on a pair of logs. Two men sat to the right of the fire, a woman alone on the opposite side. With the flames illuminating the clearing to sufficient levels, Anna turned a knob at the top of her scope, setting the device back on its regular eyeglass function.

The group of three was conversing as orange-white air spread from their mouths, their voices drowned out by the pop of firewood and the orange sparks that rose between them, their clothes and expressions just as tattered and dwindled as the guards had been. It was the woman's appearance that stuck with Anna, however, her long disordered red hair, her concerned demeanor, and her age, which was about the same as Sean and Jason's. The idea didn't surprise Anna when it arrived, the notion that this person was up late and worried because Jason was still off on his assignment to meet with the Cavaliers' connections in Marathon, and two of her friends had stayed awake with her, hoping to calm Katherine's nerves.

Surveying the two men and the woman she'd started to believe was Katherine, Anna found them to be clear of any weapons outside their garments. From where she was, there was no way to tell whether or not the three Cavaliers had knives or firearms stashed beneath their layers of clothing, but she knew it didn't matter if they were armed or not. Replacing whatever feelings of compassion for Jason and Katherine she might've allowed herself to cultivate, a new sensation flooded into her chest, one that was familiar to her and yet somehow at the same time unfathomable. It was like a subject she would keep coming back to during her education in Marathon, but could never begin to understand no matter how many times she referred to it.

The unreadable feeling grew within her; a surge following the initial sensation that she wasn't prepared for, even as she called it out from inside. Under her skin, spreading from her head and torso to her arms and legs until it reached the tips of her fingers and toes, it consumed everything with a sense of calm, control, and focus. Rotating the knob at the top of her scope, she changed to the rifle's thermal setting. The camp morphed in her scope, becoming a field of cold blackish-purple, broken only by ten bright orange human silhouettes of heat, gathered in three separate groups, and the orange flare of warmth from the campfire. Except for the group around the fire, all of the Cavaliers were lying down inside their tents. Of the seven tents, five of them were empty. Given the cleanliness of the ground between the tents, it occurred to her that one or two of those vacant tents acted as storage for the Cavaliers' supplies. The two occupied tents were second and third, moving towards the right side of the camp, in the line closest to her and Sean. Three orange silhouettes filled the tent in the middle of the line, while four silhouettes crowded the tent to the right. "Thermal has everyone except those three asleep in their tents."

The knob on Sean's scope ticked as he switched his rifle's setting. "How do you want to do it?"

Energy washed over her body, this energy gave way to strength. Her alteration finalized, Anna looked from her scope to her partner. It was there in an instant, in Sean's scarred and impaired expression, his wordless reaction to the adjustment that had taken place in his partner. By now her irises were glowing. She'd observed this ghostlike signal of her change a couple times in a mirror, though never for long. Shock carried the brunt of Sean's response, as Anna's partner learned firsthand she was not human. She was a Second-Gen.

A member of a naturally evolved sub-species, she was one of a very few considered to be an evolutionary advancement over their parent species, humankind. Formally named Second Generation Humanoid, the abbreviated designation of this progressed species had been given by the Previous Civilization when the first Second-Gen was discovered, some years before the Reform. Anna personally would've preferred another title for her kind, but that was by far the least of her concerns when it came to the species she belonged to. Though the subdued yet noticeable fearful gestures she was receiving from Sean were in no way surprising or new to her, they bothered her all the same. Even as a native-born citizen of Marathon, with the same native-born citizenship as Marathon's human residents, she had never become accustomed to the terror some humans showed her upon learning what she was, or seeing her as she was now. In order to complete her and Sean's termination of the Cavaliers, she had entered the Second-Gen Stage, the alternative state of being where a Second-Gen's advantage over a human's was most obvious. If a human being could only drive a vehicle at a maximum speed of twenty-five miles per hour, then a Second-Gen, once in the Second-Gen Stage, was able to drive a vehicle at speeds closer to fifty miles per hour.

"I'll take the rest. Cover me from here," she told him, her strategy already planned ten steps in advance, her voice refusing to be affected by Sean's frightened gaze. He didn't seem able to muster a verbal reply, only a brief nod of his head before looking back through his scope indicated to her that he understood the order. With her partner set and his T-05 Sniper trained on the camp, Anna directed her own T-05 towards the campfire and reset the scope to eyeglass. Her index finger wrapped around the weapon's trigger, as the two men sitting to the right of the fire appeared in the crosshairs of her scope. Carried in the otherworld consciousness of her Second-Gen Stage, Anna felt her finger curl and pull at the trigger. The rifle kicked with a hiss, the butt of the weapon tapping her shoulder. Her T-05 Sniper swung to the left, her scope acquiring the woman that might've been Katherine. Her finger curled at the trigger once more, producing a second hiss and recoil from the rifle.

A cloud of orange-red seemed to explode from each person's skull at the same instant. Anna rose from her position as the men collapsed to the right on top of the log, both felled by one round. As she moved out from the protection of the trees, Anna saw the woman's neck and chest bend downwards. Even with half of her head separated into orange-red and orange-pink bits that floated in the air around the fire or scattered in the snow, her corpse somehow held to the log as it slumped towards the fire, the surviving strands of her increasingly bright red hair hanging just above the orange flickers. Anna didn't bother with a second look as she turned for the line of tents, smoke rising from the tip of her suppressor as she leveled her T-05 Sniper at the middle tent, hardly a sound made from the campfire.

The fire's orange radiance lit her way as she stepped between the first and second tents, rifle locked in both hands, knife secured at her belt in reserve. "Seven remaining, none of them stirred," Sean reported through her earpiece, covering her with his thermal scope as she'd instructed. Anna kept her weapon elevated as she approached and unzipped the tent with her left hand, finding the next group of three right where she expected. Like the campfire trio, they were two men and one woman. The two men lay together on a mattress on the right side of the tent, sharing a few blankets, another bolt-action rifle from the Previous Civilization at their bedside. The woman slept in a sleeping bag. Filthy and trapped in a deep sleep, with a mist of white air hovering over them, they didn't wake as Anna crouched inside and let her rifle hang from its strap, as if this was the first real night's sleep they'd had in weeks, maybe months. Anna's knife took to her hand, the dark red stained blade materializing with a snap. The act that followed was slower than what had occurred at the fire, yet no less effective. Starting with the men and moving to the woman, she used the same method with each of them. A single cut, as far down as the blade would sink, from one ear all the way across their throats to the other. With every slice, dark red spilled from the Cavaliers necks like a broken faucet, soaking their beds and collecting in a puddle at the floor of the tent. They woke when it happened, but it didn't help. Vocal cords severed, mouths clogged with blood, all each of them could do was choke and blink in horror, watch as Anna moved to her next victim. The gasps and trembling ceased as she exited the tent, stepping to the last tent in the line.

Dripping red from her knife and hands, ignoring the odor of burning hair, she opened the tent's flap, leaving smudges of red on the entrance. This final tent was larger than the middle tent, and split between two decent-sized mattresses. A man and a woman slept on the first mattress just inside the tent, wrapped together with only their heads unobscured by blankets. A pair of pistols from the Previous Civilization sat on the floor beside them. The second mattress had been placed to the left at the far side of the tent, hidden from the orange light that shined through the open flap. Anna could just make out a couple figures lying beneath the cover of several blankets, no weapons to be seen. Squatting inside the tent, she dealt with the man and woman on the first mattress, slashing their throats in the same manner. This time, neither target even opened their eyes. Anna got to thinking if they were aware of what was happening, they were holding out hope it was only a nightmare. As dark red swamped the front of the tent, Anna brought her attention, and her blade, to the back of the tent. That was when she got a good look at the only two Cavaliers left alive.

Both of them were children, a boy and a girl. The boy was eight at best, the girl no older than six. Their faces, no more sanitary or maintained than those of the adults Anna and Sean killed, were poking out from under the covers, their stretched and alerted eyes telling her they'd awakened to the black and red monster in their tent. Almost catatonic, the children weren't crying, weren't making the tiniest sound. Defenseless, their parents' throats slit a mere few feet away and their parents' assassin crouching over them, and still, Anna couldn't find the least amount of dread on their young tattered faces. Neither the boy nor the girl was afraid, not perceptibly. What Anna saw instead was acceptance, as if the possibility of this moment had been drilled into them from birth. Their parents weren't older than forty, too young to remember the Previous Civilization even if they had been born before the Reform. The life of nomads and terrorists was all the children knew, all their parents knew, and thus this boy and girl met Anna's invasion with a kind of tranquility, as though they looked forward to whatever they believed was to come after. The switchblade rose in her hand, but when she commanded her arm to bend the knife down at the children's necks, her body rebelled against the mandate.

Chloe!

After three seconds that passed more like minutes without any movement from Anna or the children, she issued the order again.

Chloe!

She felt her alternative state deleting itself, the physical and mental clarity diminishing as her Second-Gen Stage broke into rapid retreat. When the withdraw concluded, she demanded herself a third time to complete the task.

Chloe!

Anger took to her face, called for her body to explain why there was a delay.

Chloe!

The boy and girl held their places on the mattress, waiting in hollow anticipation, as if they didn't care when Anna got around to it, so long as it was done at some point. Anna was livid, enraged with herself for not giving more than a one-word answer. And yet, her arm didn't budge.

Darius was in her ear again, angrier than Anna was. "Vanguard One, you've got two active targets right in front of you! What the fuck are you doing?" Anna wanted to respond, knew she was obligated to, but the children had total control of her focus.

Sean's voice appeared from her earpiece after Darius's. "Anna, what's going on? I've got the Commander on the Network telling me she can't reach you." Her partner's concern was as prominent as her superior's frustration. "Are you okay? You're not moving on thermal."

Their parents were the terrorists, not them. I won't punish them for something they didn't do.

"Anna?"

Darius declared all persons at this camp to be hostile. You know what'll happen if she charges you with disobeying orders. She sends a message back to Missio.

"Anna!" Sean was much louder now, his voice coming from beyond her earpiece. There was splashing behind her, as boots connected with the red wetted floor of the tent. Anna swerved around and found Sean stepping through the flap, T-05 in hands, worry even more apparent on his face than in his tone. Surveying the scene before him, he started with the parents' dark red dressed bodies, moving to Anna and then the boy and girl. Anna's grip stiffened around her switchblade, as if clutching the weapon tighter would force it to put itself to use. However, the minute-long seconds continued to drain away. After ten more of these prolonged moments, far too many, Anna saw the sorrowing reluctance show in Sean's fractured expression as he realized she wasn't going to be able to finish the mission, meaning it fell to him. It wasn't another test, Anna wouldn't have dreamed of it, the assignment was now Sean's because despite all the abilities Anna possessed as a Second-Gen, even those advancements couldn't help her to murder children.

Sean took position at Anna's side, rifle rising with his hands, suppressor centering on the boy's forehead. The children denied them the luxury of turning away or closing their eyes, they glared straight at Anna and Sean both, as if mocking them, while Sean's index finger curled at the weapon's trigger. The report was hushed by the suppressor, yet not eliminated. Anna jolted when the hiss shook the tent, as if she hadn't been expecting it. Dark red shot from the boy's forehead, showered the bed and the girl. A sickening force struck Anna in the chest as Sean shifted the gun to the girl. Every ounce of her being blared for her to seize her partner's T-05, to interrupt the action, but she upheld her composure as an agent of the Black Dragoons. Another quieted boom, another fog of dark red that soiled the walls of the tent, and the Cavaliers were defeated. Anna and Sean gazed at the children's corpses in the bed of dark red, their faces clenched in disoriented shock.

"Vanguard One, what's your status?" the Commander asked over the Network a few seconds later.

Finally willing herself to speak, Anna tapped her earpiece twice, holding her finger to it the second time. Her eyes didn't leave the children. "All hostiles neutralized. Say again, all hostiles neutralized. Tell Marathon the Cavaliers have been sacked."

3: SEAN

On the seventh day since returning from their mission with the Black Dragoons, Sean woke with a fierce banging at his door. His skin was clean, though it didn't feel so. He lay in a dark blue long sleeve shirt and black shorts, the common underclothes for all citizens of Marathon, comfortable enough though made better by the soothing warmth of his bed and the heat of his barrack. The smell inside the building was hardly better than outside, but it was an improvement from the rusted odor of the Serenity Station. The pounding came again at the door to his quarters. Lifting his head to the yellow outline that poked through the sides of the black door, he became nervous. For a second, he believed he'd unknowingly committed a serious offense against the Commanders, who'd sent a party of soldiers to tie his hands with wire and black bag him. Then he heard his partner shout, "Sean get the fuck up, the game's in ten minutes!"

With an irritated sigh of relief, he buried his face in his pillow and rubbed his inflamed scars against the pillowcase. "Tell them I'm sitting this one out," he called back, having every intention of letting himself fall back asleep after she'd left.

"The fuck you are," Anna exclaimed. Harsh yellow light appeared at the edges of Sean's vision as the door screeched open and Anna's boots came stomping into his quarters. "You're the only one who can actually match me in pentagon. Without you there's no fun in it."

"When we played the other day you almost knocked my teeth out," he retorted, as he tried to sink his face deeper into the pillow.

"And you nearly broke my nose, that's what makes it interesting. Now come on."

Sean rolled his head around to Anna in disbelief. "You're a Second-Gen, there's no way I came anywhere close to breaking your nose. Second-Gens may bleed, but they don't break." His partner stood at the end of his bed, cleaned and rested as he was. The bedroom she'd joined him in was small and unsophisticated, the floor, wall, and ceiling all colored black.

"Fine, you came marginally closer than everyone else to creating a small fracture in my nasal bones. But unless the Commander suddenly finds another Second-Gen to put on our team, you're the closest thing to competition I have, so let's go." With excitement, she gestured for him to get out of bed.

Sean didn't budge. "What time is it?"

"0750, last I checked. I told you last night, we're supposed to meet up at 0800."

Sean turned his head back to the pillow. "We're supposed to be recuperating, until we're called out again. That means we can get as much sleep as we want, not run out at the crack of dawn so you can beat the shit out of soldiers."

"We've had all week to recuperate and dawn was over an hour ago. Are you really not coming?"

Glancing back at Anna, he saw that she looked concerned about the possibility he was backing out, as if she was a child whose friend was refusing to come play outside. With that, he conceded. "All right, I'm coming. I just need a minute to get ready."

An ecstatic grin stretched across Anna's face. Clapping her hands together with sarcastic joy, she asked, "Do you need me to help you get dressed?" Sean tensed his face in annoyance, wanting to swear at her but deciding against it. She appeared to receive the message anyway and stepped back to the doorway. No less sarcastic as she walked out, she said, "I'm just asking. As your partner its imperative I know you're capable of handling the tasks assigned to you."

A spurt of anger flickered in Sean's chest. *Last I checked, I'm the one who had to shoot those kids because you couldn't complete the fucking op!* However, he bit his tongue and let the spark die out instead of acting on it.

Grudgingly pulling himself out of bed, he stepped to his locker and retrieved his recreational uniform, a dark blue jacket, black pants, black socks, black boots, and black gloves, the typical casual dress for Marathon's military and an effective disguise for a Dragoon pretending to be an average soldier. Allowing his hair to hang from his head in a mess, he left his darkened quarters for the bright hallway outside his room. The change in illumination pinched his eyes, though his vision was quick to adjust. Narrow to the degree that two people standing side by side could block it off, the hallway was the epicenter of the rectangular barrack. The three sections of the building, including the lounge and dining room at the front of the barrack, two duplicate sleeping quarters halfway down the hall and across from each other, and the latrine, shower, kitchen and laundry at the back of the barrack were all connected by the hallway. The barrack itself was built specifically to house Black Dragoon agents, with the primary focus of its design being to accommodate as many of the Dragoons day to day needs as possible and limit their interactions with other citizens.

Anna was waiting in the hall, standing twitchily against the wall towards the lounge and dining room, hair loose like her matching rec uniform. He said nothing as he followed her to the front of the barrack. Though the room's lights were out, the yellow that spread from the hallway and the gray that poured in from the windows was plenty that Sean could read the dark blue digits of the clock attached to the wall above the door. 0755.

Departing into the bitter foggy gray of the morning, they stepped onto one of Marathon's many city roads. An oddly placed shack amongst several larger black buildings, their barrack was situated in Marathon's northeastern district, Terra. One of four city sub-districts, Terra functioned as the base for the military, with every one of the district's five thousand residents being sworn soldiers of Marathon. The majority of these soldiers, with the exception of ranking officers, were housed in vast fields of troop barracks. Black and rectangular as Sean and Anna's barrack was, these barracks were not divided into separate rooms, nor were they reserved for a mere two people. Rather, the interior of the common barrack consisted of a single room that was stuffed end to end with bunks, with as many as forty soldiers packed into one building and denied heating. As confined as his barrack was, Sean refused to allow himself to even think of complaining, not after a year in one of those soldiers barracks, set aside for him and other Carthage immigrants.

Sean and Anna walked down the road, their boots burrowing into the gray snow the pavement hid under, white exhaling from their mouths. The fog thickened and blurred the morning air, as if the overcast had spread from the atmosphere to the surface. The roadway behind and ahead of them was still visible, though reduced, so they hung to the far side. Anna pulled a black sheet of paper from her jacket pocket and gestured for Sean to take it. "I almost forgot, this came before I woke you up."

"What is it?" he asked, accepting the page.

"Notice from the Commanders," she answered, calm yet grim.

He knew in an instant what that meant. "About the Cavaliers?"

Anna seemed to hesitate to reply, as if pondering the news troubled her. "Who else would it be about?"

They continued alongside the street as Sean read the announcement's dark blue letters: "FROM THE COMMANDERS OF MARATHON

To all citizens of Marathon, it is with great pleasure and excitement that we inform you of our city's most recent victory against the forces of TERROR. Military units operating under Commander Darius located and defeated the TERRORIST organization known as the Cavaliers, approximately fifty miles north of Marathon in the Serenity Hills. The Cavaliers were responsible for a series of APPALLING and COWARDLY acts in and around the former city of Serenity, claiming the lives of twenty Marathon soldiers.

We could not be more proud of the COURAGE displayed by our soldiers and by Commander Darius, hero of the Marathon-Carthage War. Rest assured that all traitors of Marathon, who seek nothing less than TOTAL DESTRUCTION of this place we have created together, are being pursued with the utmost conviction. STABILITY AND PROSPERITY will soon be returned to the region.

Letter drafted by the Commanders, and presented to the citizens of Marathon on this day in the 31st Year of Marathon."

"The Commanders seem confident," Sean remarked, as he passed the notice to Anna.

Taking the paper, Anna replied, "The parts about stability and prosperity get me every time." Slipping the report back into her jacket pocket, she said, with unexpected pessimism, "I give it two months, before a new terrorist cell picks up the Cavaliers' slack and the Commanders have to find new words to assure people the colonies are still going to get built. They've run out of synonyms."

Sean nodded. "All this talk of Serenity, the Commanders never have anything to say about the Aegean Valley. Rate of terrorist attacks is three times higher there."

A light putrid breeze blew down the road into their faces as Anna asked, "How do you expect them to praise our triumphs in the Aegean Valley, when we don't have any? The Commanders aren't going to put that place in an announcement until something good comes out of it. Fuck, I thought Serenity was the only hostile territory. Then I joined the Dragoons." She hesitated, seeming to deliberate before continuing. "The war with Carthage was the only time the Commanders let everyone know about an outside threat, before the threat was gone. But that was because they had to explain why half the city's military forces were marching south."

Sean wanted to ask Anna if the full outcome of the Marathon-Carthage War had been detailed to Marathon's civilians, if people knew the scale of the death toll and the destruction that had been dealt to Carthage, if they even knew how many of their own soldiers died before breaching Carthage's walls. However, the question failed to surface. "Are the Commanders delaying the city's expansion plans, until Marathon gains more control over Serenity and the Aegean Valley?"

With a laugh, Anna said, "No, they're probably moving up the date."

"Why?"

"From what Darius told me, they're thinking the faster they get the settlements going, the easier they'll be to defend."

The street came to an enormous snow-laden field, nestled between more black military structures that lined the edges of the field on three sides. The center of the field was their game's arena: five black nets held up by black metal poles, spread out and positioned in the shape of a pentagon. Named for the shape of its playing field, this morning they would play in foot deep snow and icy air. Though pentagon was the most popular sport in Marathon, likely due to the fact it was the only sport citizens ever played, Sean had neglected to take part in a game until two days ago. Overall, it was not substantially different than the sports of the Previous Civilization Sean had come to know back in Carthage, except for one crucial element he had not become aware of until agreeing to partake the first time.

Their party was gathered on the pentagon, between the goals on the left side of the arena. Ten soldiers, dressed in the same rec uniforms Sean and Anna were wearing. The soldiers turned to the two late arrivals joining them, bringing the total number of players to twelve, or two teams of six. "Where the fuck you two been?" said Sergeant Aaron Rodriguez, who'd been infuriated by a delay of no more than a couple minutes. They had just met the Sergeant at the preceding pentagon match. The other nine soldiers stood silent around him, unwilling to try quelling his anger for obvious fear of having it targeted at them. For a person of his rank, Rodriguez was a surprisingly short man whose authority might've been compromised by his barely five-foot stature, were it not for the unabashed overconfidence of his demeanor.

"Sorry to inconvenience you," Anna said, with a smile she clearly intended to seem off-putting and false. "We were finishing up repairs on Aurora Five's left wing. That bird's been giving us shit all morning. I appreciate you waiting on us, Sergeant." Anna's lie moved about the group without the slightest objection from anyone, including Rodriguez. To them, Sean and Anna were Corporal Sean Halley and Corporal Anna Corday, mechanics assigned to maintenance on the Aurora squadron. These covers had been provided by Commander Darius when Sean and Anna were partnered, and used when they were back in Marathon between missions. Even knowledge that Sean was a Carthage-native and Anna was a Second-Gen was limited to as few people as possible.

Holding his boot over the black spherical ball that would be used for the game, Rodriguez responded with a quieter yet somehow angrier tone, as if Anna's tame reaction only aggravated him more. "I didn't want to tire my team out."

"You know that's good thinking Sergeant, but it's not going to make any difference." Holding her faux smile and relaxed posture, Anna stepped forward and planted her boot beside the ball. The resentment between her and Rodriguez glared, appearing as an unceasing necessity for both of them to prove themselves better to Sean and the others, despite no one asking them to.

Snickering, Rodriguez said, "All right, let's get on with it then." He pointed his finger at the ground. "My team's on this side. We get the ball first."

"Well all right then," Anna retorted, clapping her hands together. The soldiers split into two teams and began moving to their respective flanks of the pentagon, as if they were afraid to stand near the Sergeant and Anna any longer. Looking to Sean and tossing her animosity in favor of a friendlier competitive demeanor, Anna said, "Good luck. Try not to let him get in your way." Sean pulled off a grin as Anna chuckled and started towards the other side of the pentagon.

Sean joined the other five soldiers of his team in their huddle, just as Anna and her team did on the right side of the pentagon. Scanning three of the soldiers around Rodriguez, who had not been at the game two days ago, Sean at first thought he was seeing the same exhilaration for the oncoming competition Anna had when she'd woken him. After a closer look, he spotted the bemused and fatigued expressions, the healing gashes and scratches on their faces and necks, the marks of troops recently returned from duty. He found himself wondering where these soldiers had been deployed, Serenity or Troy, up in the Aegean Valley. Why any of them were out here in the snow and the cold to play pentagon, instead of recuperating, Sean couldn't guess.

Neither Sean nor anyone else contributed as Rodriguez moved his head back and forth among the group several times, outlining the team's strategy. His voice was assertive, as if he felt a need to intimidate with the simplest of commands. "Okay, you two are on the goals," he ordered, signaling to a couple soldiers, who nodded without disagreement. "Halley." Sean perked his head up as the Sergeant issued his position. "You've got the ball. Take it to the free goal." Sean nodded in acknowledgement. Rodriguez's tone elevated, as if he was leading troops in a combat operation or speaking to a much larger audience. "The rest of us, cover him with a triangle." With a level of seriousness Sean found too amusing not to smirk at, Rodriguez concluded by asking, "Everybody know what they're supposed to do?"

"Yes, Sergeant."

Rodriguez nodded back at them. "Okay." At that, the team split from their huddle.

Anna and her team were already set in a line between the goals on their end of the pentagon, ready to go, Anna in the middle of the group. Rodriguez's team formed up in their line between their goals, opposite to Anna's team. Sean retrieved the ball, moving it to his starting place with his boot. "You fuckers ready?" Anna called from the opposing end, continuing her effort to exacerbate the Sergeant's fury.

"We are," Rodriguez shouted back, his voice quivering as he pretended Anna wasn't getting to him.

"How'd you want to start this one?"

Rodriguez thought on it for a moment, and said, "All yours."

Sean could see Anna's bouncing smile as she said, "On three then!" The players on Rodriguez and Anna's teams tensed up, prepping themselves to run. "One, two, three!"

The crackle of boots hurled back and forth in the air above the field as the twelve soldiers sprinted from their starting points on the pentagon. Sean bolted for the goal at the pentagon's tip, the free goal. Gray sprang up around him, showered down on his uniform. His ankles were already throbbing as he stumbled and forced his way through the heavy snow. He punted the ball ahead of him, chasing it as his teammates ran with him. They broke into a protective triangle, Rodriguez in front of him and the ball, two other companions on his left and right. At the margin of his eye, he saw several dark blue and black shades closing from outside the triangle. "On the right, on the right," Rodriguez warned. Two players from Anna's team came in on an intersecting course. Sean's teammate stopped one of them, punching the player in the jaw and tackling him to the ground as the other player veered out of the way and charged at Sean.

Sean slowed and tapped the ball forward as the second player reached him. The attacking soldier curved to the ball, away from Sean long enough for him to stick his leg ahead of the soldier's feet. The player tripped on Sean's ankle and dropped before he could get to the ball. Leaping over the soldier, Sean landed in the snow and regained control of the ball. His teammate was at his side again, covering him. Up ahead, another one of Anna's team members arrived at the free goal, raising her hands in a defensive stance and waiting for Sean to shoot on the goal. Anna came into Sean's view, swinging in with another player, having run around the back of the triangle. Simultaneously, the soldier Sean tripped made for the triangle a second time, Sean's teammate on his heels. The soldier turned to face the woman, blocking her advance. She struck him in the neck at the same time he threw his boot into her gut. They both fell into the snow, the victor unclear to Sean.

"Halley, take your shot," Rodriguez demanded, as he and Sean's other teammate swerved at Anna and her companion. Sean fixed his attention back on the now occupied goal, increasing speed as the opposing players connected. Rodriguez's teammate went down first, felled by Anna's companion, who ducked the man's punch and dug his elbow into the side of the man's neck, before plowing his foot into the man's back and putting the man on his stomach in the snow. "Halley," the Sergeant called to Sean, as he engaged Anna. With formidable agility that trumped Rodriguez's strikes, Anna sidestepped one punch after another. Sean made eye contact with the goalie, each of them assessing the other's eventual move. Rodriguez shrieked in pain. At the edge of Sean's vision, he saw Rodriguez tumble onto his back, bright red erupting from his nose and mouth as Anna flew over him.

Knowing he was out of time, Sean took aim with the ball, about to release on the goal. The goalie saw this and tensed her lower body, ready to dive to whichever side of the goal Sean shot for. *It's like soccer.* Sean brought his boot back, and was swinging it forward when he felt a solid force slam into his side, bashing the air out of his chest. *But not.* He crashed on his right with a stunned groan, felt the icy snow digging under his jacket collar and freezing his spine as his attacker sprawled themselves over him, pinning him to the ground.

"Fucker," the Sergeant roared, enraged and dissatisfied.

"Almost had it," Anna said, lowering her face close to Sean's.

Lying on the ground, Sean watched as Anna's defender stepped out of the goal while another player from her team seized the ball and pounded it into the neutral goal, no one anywhere close to stopping her. "Almost," Sean mumbled. The anger he'd felt back at the barrack recurred. This time, however, it came not as a sudden spark but a slow surfacing sensation, a discomfort he didn't want yet couldn't ignore.

Anna pushed herself off of Sean and rose to her feet. "You're getting better at least," she said as she offered a hand, which he accepted.

Standing upright again as air refilled his torso, Sean began making his way to his team's end of the pentagon, only to halt when he detected Anna's gloved hand brushing against the back of his jacket, cleaning the gray snowflakes from his clothes. "I can do that myself," he told her, fighting to make himself sound more appreciative than annoyed.

Anna didn't stop as she jested, "You missed a few spots the other day, it made you look real unprofessional."

"Wait, when are you and I?" Sean jerked forward a bit as Anna smacked a batch of snow off the back of his pants. "At any time professional?"

Anna finished and stepped in front of Sean, grinning as she cleared the snow and ice from her own jacket and pants, then patted her hands together to dust off her gloves. "Call it impression management."

"Halley, move your ass!" Rodriguez shot Sean an incensed look as he held the ball under his arm and headed back to the staging area, bright red streaming down his neck from his face.

Sean nodded to the Sergeant. To further shield his irritation as he resumed the walk back with the rest of the team, he said to Anna, "Well, I'll try to work on making a good impression. I wouldn't want those years at the university to go to waste."

"What's a university?" his partner asked, with instant and obvious confusion.

He winced, the anger metastasizing inside him. "It's the same thing as a college."

His answer shaped Anna's next question. "Why did Carthage have two names for the same thing? That just seems redundant."

With a sigh of impatience that he meant for her to diagnose, Sean threw up his hands. "I don't know, there was a lot of stuff in Carthage that had more than one name for it."

"Why is that?"

Anna's questioning reminded Sean of a child's inquisition, always curious as to why something was the way it was. Comprehending that she had noticed his exasperation and was purposely trying to amplify it as she had with Rodriguez, Sean said, "I couldn't tell you."

Rodriguez and his team were grouped in their huddle as Sean rejoined them at the beginning point. "Why the fuck didn't you shoot when I told you too?" the Sergeant asked. Wiping a new surge of red from his nose with his glove, he added, "That was our chance to get ahead! Now what the fuck are we supposed to do?"

"He didn't have a good shot," one soldier yelled, the side of his neck blackened by a growing bruise, coming to Sean's defense.

"Corday knew we were trying for the free goal," one of the goalies' seconded. "That's the most predictable move a team can make."

Rodriguez was defensive. "Well if you had problems with my plan, why the fuck didn't you speak up?"

"Because whenever we do, you ignore us and just go with whatever the fuck you were thinking anyway," the other goalie explained.

As his embittered teammates engaged each other, Sean's own fractious mood caused his focus to drift from the game to the back-end of the field, away from the buildings and the pentagon. The morning had worn on, dragging the fog along with it. The mist had receded beyond the field and was retreating still, freeing the city of its haze. Oddly enough, it was through this natural and recurrent climate pattern that Sean finally came to understand the reasons for pentagon's existence. Why the Commanders had not placed intensive regulations on the practice, why exhausted soldiers were willing to take part just after returning from duty, why the people in attendance at this game continued to participate with personalities like Rodriguez and Anna, and why everyone who had ever played pentagon, including him, did so regardless of the dangerous conditions for play. The Commanders sanctioned game of pentagon was nothing more than a mass act of catharsis, a method for the soldiers and civilians of Marathon to purge themselves of the negative emotions that came with circumstance and occurrence before those sentiments built into large-scale unrest, like a community being released of fog by the change in weather. And with every spat that flared amidst the present match, Sean, Anna, Rodriguez, and the other nine soldiers were fulfilling the intended role of pentagon.

Looking over at the opposite end of the pentagon, where Anna huddled with her team, Sean chose in that moment not to reject the purpose of the game but rather to embrace it, for he had his own congested rage to expel. A strategy spawned in his head. "What if you take the ball this time, Sergeant?" Everybody was staring at him now, seeking an explanation. "We go for their goals, and use a pentagon formation to protect the ball until the Sergeant gets the chance he needs."

"That leaves our goals undefended," Rodriguez replied, with skepticism. "If Corday comes in and destroys us again, she'll get the ball and take her pick with our empty goals." The other soldiers nodded in agreement.

"Not if I put Corday in the snow first," Sean stated, crossing his arms.

"How would you do that?" Rodriguez asked. His interest in what another person on his team had to say was surprising.

When the two teams assembled in their lines a minute later, Sean's proposal had been described to and agreed upon by his teammates. Rodriguez set the ball beneath his foot; his players took a primed stance at his sides. Setting himself as the others were, Sean glared over the field, centering his gaze on his partner, his fury boiling towards an outbreak. *The people in that camp were her fucking responsibility! Those kids were her responsibility! Anna made them her concern when she ordered me to hang back and cover her!*

Anna made the call for the second round. "One, two, three!"

The teams launched from their starting points, barreling towards each other. Leaving their goals unguarded as all six of them crossed the field, Rodriguez's team took the shape of a pentagon, one soldier running at the front, two at the left and right in the middle, and two at the left and right on the end as well. Rodriguez was in the dead center of the formation, shielded by the pentagon and dribbling the ball at speed with the players around him. Sean had positioned himself in the middle on the right side of the pentagon, holding focus on Anna as she approached with three of her teammates, while the remaining two stayed behind as goalies. Anna and her players came on quick, closing on the pentagon before the Sergeant's team even passed the field's halfway mark. As Sean predicted, or at least hoped, Anna led the attack, sprinting at the front of the form, Rodriguez locked in her view. The soldier at the pentagon's point made an attempt at blocking Anna, but she brushed past him, knocking him to the snow as she went for the Sergeant and the ball. The trap was sprung. Veering to the left and breaking from his place in the pentagon, Sean curled his hand into a fist. Braced by wrath, his legs refused to give out on him as he dove into the air. *Anna drops eight Cavaliers like its nothing, but all of a fucking sudden she can't finish the mission? She kills all those people and I'm the one who has to kill the kids?* Anna was a yard from Rodriguez when Sean struck her on the left side of her face, his knuckles making a smacking sound against her cheek.

Sean landed on top of Anna as she fell into the snow. Rodriguez banked to the right as Sean continued his expulsion, punching Anna in the cheek a second time. Bright red emerged from her skin. *Kids! We killed two children!* Around them, the pentagon collapsed as the rest of Rodriguez's team broke from their positions and swarmed the other three players Anna had pounced with. As the separate fights occupied Anna and her team's attention, the Sergeant made his way to Anna's side of the field, covered by the soldier who'd been at the tip of their defensive shape.

Anna wrestled with Sean as he struggled to pin her to the ground, both of them snarling in frustration and rage. *I killed two children!* Sean hit Anna twice more, in the nose and on the right side of her face. His partner grunted at each blow, blinking as she absorbed the impacts. How much his punches actually hurt her, Sean didn't know and didn't care. *Those kids and those guards! Jason, Katherine, the children's parents, and the rest!* Again, and again, and again, until Anna's face was painted red with bleeding cuts, reminding Sean of how Jason looked in the first hour of his interrogation. Knowing his assault on his Dragoon partner was taking place in the legal context of pentagon, where not even a Second-Gen was valued any greater than anybody else, Sean carried on, not intending to stop until Anna surrendered. *And what the fuck did it accomplish? What did Marathon gain from the Cavaliers destruction?*

Sean was pulling his arm back to deliver another hit when Anna gained the upper hand. Flinging herself upwards, she rolled him off of her onto his back, restraining him as he'd done to her. Warm drops of red dripped from her face to his, the blood falling from an expression of blaring incensement, equal to his in ferocity. Though afraid at first glance, Sean calmed as he got to thinking he was not the source of his partner's anger, she was not fighting back purely for the sake of retribution. In her shattered eyes and underneath the streams of red, Sean saw, or believed he saw, that Anna's anger had been produced from the same raw materials as his. It was why she'd pushed him so hard that morning to come out and play pentagon with her: this game was just as much her catharsis as it was Marathon's and she wanted someone who'd witnessed the same events to release with. The annihilation of the Cavaliers and the murder of the boy and girl, whose names they would never know, after that all Anna could do was hit someone.

Her first two punches struck him in the left cheek, sending an unbearable stinging sensation up and down the lines of his scars. The third and fourth hits came at his nose and his right cheek, distributing the pain across his face. His face became wet with bright red, his human wounds bleeding at a faster rate than those of his Second-Gen partner. Three more times she beat him, in the same places he'd hit her, as if she wanted to even the damage dealt by their purge. Dizziness took to him after those last strikes, spun the field around him, and swapped the gray sky with the gray snow-covered ground, until he wasn't sure which was which. Responsiveness in decline, he caught only the concluding bits of his team's celebration. Rodriguez and the others were little more than dark blue and black dots dancing at the precipice of his distorting vision. The match was now 1-1, and yet the numbers didn't matter to him in the slightest. Pentagon wasn't a game for keeping score.

Sean never fully lost consciousness in those moments that followed the second round, as far as he was aware. Were it not for Anna telling him at a later time that his eyes had been open, blinking and scanning about, he would've thought they'd been closed because his eyesight had been disabled, leaving him in a place of darkened nothingness. Sight was the only sense to fail him, however, the freezing snow on his clothes and skin, the foul smell and taste of the air, and the voices on the field beyond his oblivion all stayed by his side, as if he were just below the surface of slumber, not far enough asleep to lose touch with the awake world. Anna's voice was the first thing he heard whilst in the dark, quiet and concerned, telling him, "Let's head back to the barrack. I think we both could use a break." There was a feeling of movement that came to him while he was absent from the field, the snow disappearing as his body rose and someone's gloved hand gripping his own, pulling him along.

The next voice wasn't his partner's. Instead, it was Rodriguez, yelling from somewhere, his tone blended at some indiscernible point between happiness and antagonism. "Hey, where the fuck are you going? The game's finally getting interesting!"

Anna came back then, soft though not in any way forgiving towards the Sergeant. "You disposable fucks can keep the match going without us."

"You should watch how you talk to your superiors, Anna."

"Do you actually still believe you outrank me, Aaron?"

Time passed where no one was speaking, conversation supplemented by the crackle of snow under boots. Sean could feel his legs wobbling in some unknown direction, guided by the hand that clung to him. Then, his boot slid out of place and his leg buckled as he lost his footing. "Whoa, I got you," someone told him, as their arms wrapped around his chest. The voice was one he remembered, yet he didn't recognize it as Anna's, or even Rodriguez's. His face began to burn, right in the spot where he knew his disfigurement to be.

Derek, is that you?

When his vision at last rematerialized, Sean found himself back on the road, heading away from the field, his face numb, his jacket stained with dark red. His arm was slung over the shoulders of his partner, who walked beside him, dried red casing her face, neck, and jacket, white air floating above her. Anger escaping her mood, she expanded her red coated lips in a smile. "That was your plan, I'm assuming. Not bad," she said, impressed.

Sean glanced between two buildings. The fog had lifted from the city in its entirety, revealing the line of black fence three hundred yards away. Forty feet high and laced at the top with barbed wire, the barrier known to the citizens of Marathon as the Outer Fence served as the outermost limits of the city. Patrolled regularly, the Outer Fence narrowed entry into Marathon down to two main gates, North Gate and South Gate. With his anger dissipating as Anna's was, Sean said to her, "Didn't work out so well for me though."

"Eh." Anna gave Sean his arm back, seeing that he could walk on his own. "You've got a punch, I'll say that."

They walked back along the street towards their barrack, as Sean replied, "Which is nothing compared to that battering ram you have. Was that Second-Gen, or are you just that good at pentagon?"

Anna giggled. "Eleven months of Dragoon training with the Commander. That and I used to play the game back home in Missio when I was a kid."

"They let little kids play?" Sean asked with astonishment, as a drop of red rolled down his neck onto his collar.

"Yeah all the time," she replied, as if the concept of young children beating each other down over a ball was no major issue to her. Reaching behind Sean, Anna started sweeping the snow off the top of his jacket. "I was three, I think, when I played in my first match." She moved her hand to the middle of his jacket. "Once when I was eight, there was this one asshole who kept picking on me during school, pulling my hair, telling everyone my mom was fucking our teacher so she didn't flunk me, that sort of thing. So at one of our pickup games, I broke his jaw."

Sean nodded, keeping his reaction tame. "I had someone like that when I was in school, except for the part about starting a rumor that my mom was sleeping with my teacher."

"Oh no that was true, but it was private information. He was lucky that was all I did." Sean jolted as Anna brushed off the back of his pants.

"Wow," he whispered to himself, wiping some of the red from his neck with his glove. "So snow on our backs is unprofessional, but punching ourselves to shit isn't?"

"Yep, the Commander sees pentagon as the Black Dragoons off-duty training regime." Stepping in front of Sean and beaming, she teased, "I could bite your ear off and Darius wouldn't bat an eye so long as I did it during a game."

Sean's eyes grew wide. "You haven't done that before have you?"

Anna laughed and turned her back to him, showing the snow that drenched her own clothes. "Can you get me?"

A Nightwalker vehicle was parked outside their barrack when they returned, engine purring. Black, box-shaped with an enclosed roof, and elevated above four snowmobile treads that allowed it to move through the snow with ease; Nightwalkers were the military's main source of transportation both in and outside of Marathon. Though not an unanticipated sight, the vehicle was an instant source of uneasiness for Sean. They approached the driver's side, both of them understanding that the Nightwalker had been sent to fetch them. The driver and passenger doors opened, as a pair of troops in full dark blue combat gear and armed with loaded and readied T-05s stepped out into the snow beside the vehicle. The Nightwalker's driver said to them, "ma'am, sir, Commander Darius sent us to..." He paused, noting their condition, the red gashes and the black bruises that were forming around their cuts. "Do you need me to call for a medic, ma'am?" the soldier asked Anna, with obvious worry.

"No, just pentagon," Anna explicated. "Does Commander Darius want us to report to her?"

"Yes, ma'am. She's ordered us to bring you both to the Detention Center; she'll be meeting you there."

With that, Sean's anxiety converted into genuine fear. The idea that he'd unwittingly broken one of Marathon's laws and was on the verge of arrest reoccurred in his mind, making him more afraid than he'd ever been during the Cavaliers mission. *Unless you're a guard, you don't leave the Detention Center.*

4: ANNA

They weren't fifteen minutes into their drive when the Nightwalker reached the Marathon Bridge. Anna and her partner sat in the metal backseats of the vehicle, Anna on the right and Sean on the left. Prior to departing, they'd gone inside their barrack and cleaned their wounds. By now the bleeding had ceased on Anna and Sean's marks, leaving faces crossed by gashes that were more black and purple than red. What aching Anna felt had subsided due to her enhanced pain tolerance, a welcome gift from her species. Her partner, however, had been trembling from the moment they took their seats in the Nightwalker and set off from the barrack. Up until this point in the commute, she'd assumed Sean's shaking was a result of lasting faintness from her hits. But as their shuttle came to the Marathon Bridge, she realized fear afflicted Sean, a dread she should've guessed was inevitable. After all, this was going to be his first time on the south side of Marathon.

Their escort vehicle was on Broad Street, the most extensive snow-packed road in the city. Designated as the central nervous system of Marathon, Broad Street began at North Gate, before moving south between the city's four sub-districts, all the way to South Gate, allowing swift access to the entire community. On the city's northern end, Broad Street divided Terra to the east and the district of New Terra to the west. Both sides of the street were sealed by the Inner Fence, a barricade identical to the Outer Fence in every way, except for being twenty feet shorter in height. Just as the Outer Fence blocked Marathon off from the rest of the world, and vice versa, the Inner Fence separated the sub-districts and their populations. Venturing outside a district without authorization led to a sentence in the Detention Center. On the other hand, individuals who went beyond the Outer Fence and attempted to leave Marathon were subject to shoot-on-sight orders or risked wandering into one of the military's numerous external minefields.

The Marathon Bridge spanned the so-called heart of Marathon, the Marathon River. Nature's wall between north and south Marathon, the Marathon River flowed into the area from the northwest, cut straight down the middle of the city, and continued on southeast. Polluted by the incapacitation of the Reform, its waters were as murky as the ground and sky, and strewn with rubble from the Previous Civilization, carried endlessly downriver. Like the woods of the Serenity Hills, it was reported that the Marathon River once swarmed with thriving ecosystems. However, any trace of those underwater habitats had been removed.

But despite plowing through the funnel of the city with flash-flood-like rapids and temperatures cold enough to kill a human being in minutes, the river had not claimed a significant death toll. This was thanks in large part to the positioning of the city's districts in comparison to the river. All four sub-districts bordered the Marathon River, but were elevated above the waterline on steep rocky bluffs. The different sections of the Inner Fence that ran straight up and down Broad Street each made a turn at the river, following the shoreline at the top of the cliffs, wrapping around the districts, and isolating the river from the population. The cliffs had protected the city from flooding for decades, while the Inner Fence made accidentally falling into the river almost impossible. Virtually everyone who died in the Marathon River intended to do so.

If the Marathon River was the heart of the city, then the structure they were using to cross the river was the arteries, pumping life into the rest of Marathon. Because the Marathon Bridge was not just a bridge, it was also a hydroelectric dam. Built in the first decade of the city, the Marathon Bridge served as the sole linkage between the north and south ends of the city, provided a consistent flow of electricity, and acted as a water purification and dispersal system.

Past the bridge, Broad Street cut between the southwestern district of Ignis on the right and the southeastern district of Missio to the left. Of the four city sub-districts, Ignis was the only one that didn't contain any kind of citizen housing. This district was made up of factories, gigantic black structures, the tallest buildings in Marathon. From objects as trivial as the bed in Anna's quarters to such critical tools as weapons for the military, the factories mass-produced all of Marathon's common everyday items, filling their role as the community's vital organs. As for nourishment, factories built with artificial ultraviolet lights to mimic sunlight and grow crops represented the frontline of the Commanders efforts to keep the people of Marathon from starvation, though they weren't always successful. A major percentage of every harvest was reserved for the city's supply of biodiesel.

While each factory was managed by governmental supervisors, the workers of Ignis were all residents of Missio. Home to ten thousand citizens, making the district the largest in population, Missio belonged to the civilians of Marathon. Aside from the Community Offices, Missio's grounds from the Inner Fence to the Outer Fence were laid with row upon row upon row of black single room barracks. Crowded together in those heatless metal containers, with as many as ten families living inches apart, civilians spent almost every conscious moment in the company of others, their bunks the closest thing to property they possessed. Even their clothing was regimented, as Marathon provided all civilians with garbs that were alike the recreational uniforms soldiers wore, loose dark blue jackets, black pants, black boots, black socks, and black gloves, ensuring no one looked too different from anyone else. After twenty years living inside the same fences, the same barrack, the same bunk, there was little else Anna despised more than Missio. And yet, as she rode past her former district for the first time since joining the military and relocating to Terra, she was plagued by an anxious longing to return home. *Chloe.*

Her desire for a homecoming was so intense and discomforting that for the majority of the drive down the final stretch of Broad Street, Anna kept herself twisted towards the west side of the Nightwalker, coercing her attention through her window and staring at the factories of Ignis. All the while she let Missio float by behind her back, unobserved. Even when the vehicle passed by the gateway to Missio, she didn't bother a glance. The barrack Anna lived in for two straight decades was just down the road from Missio's gate, no doubt visible from outside the fence, and still, she wouldn't indulge in a view of what had been. *Chloe hasn't lived there for practically a year now, you know this.*

The Detention Center appeared to Anna by surprise, revealing itself while she was still hiding from Missio. Black and built with the common rectangular shape of Marathon's buildings, the Detention Center sat on the east side of Broad Street, encircled by Missio's barracks. The Inner Fence diverted around the Detention Center, isolating the building from the barracks, before carrying on to South Gate. Windows were absent from the structure, forbidding even an ounce of natural light from the interior. Half a dozen troops stood watch atop the prison, geared and armed with T-05 Snipers. Like most citizens of Marathon, Anna had never set foot inside the Detention Center, much less its boundaries. Until that morning, the building had been more of a folktale to her than a reality. Only when the Nightwalker pulled off Broad Street and stopped at the entrance, and she saw the dark blue words above the front door, was she reluctantly sure they were in the correct location. "DETENTION CENTER. RESTRICTED ACCESS."

Exiting the vehicle with their escorts, they stepped up the building's snow-caked steps and waited at the door behind the soldiers. One of the soldiers pressed a black button to the right of the entryway, which Anna presumed was a bell to signal the guards inside. Staring down at them from the walls of the prison, the Detention Center's security cameras undoubtedly gave those on the other side of the door a clear assessment of the new arrivals. Glancing at Sean, Anna noticed her partner's unsteadiness had worsened, as if he'd become hypothermic. The expression between his lacerations and scars was held in unmistakable terror.

She reached over and tapped him on the shoulder, smiling as he looked at her. "It's not as bad as you think."

"Yeah?" he asked.

"Actually, I've never been here before either," she confessed, allowing her own uneasiness to show around her cuts. Holding her grin, she quipped, "I'm sure it's a lovely place though." And to her respite, her partner was able to laugh.

A high-pitched click unlocked the entrance, cracking the door open. One of their escorts gripped the handle, tugging the door outwards for the four of them to step through. Anna followed the troops inside, Sean trailing her, hesitant. The forward-most room of the Detention Center was a lobby of sorts. Black walls, flooring, and ceiling, the conditions of the foyer were scarcely better than the weather outside. White clouds materialized from the breath of the occupants. Decaying jagged air, perceptible in the yellow rays of the ceilings lights, rose from the grime and snow-crusted floor, filling the room in a fog of clay. Two black metallic desks were set in the center of the floor. A guard was posted at each counter, without the standard tactical helmets and T-05s, but strapped with pistols around their waists. Monitors were embedded in their desks, likely connected to the surveillance cameras. A door, labeled in dark blue with the words, "CELL BLOCK," was on the opposite end of the room, protected by a single guard, armed as the soldiers at the desks were.

Kicking the snow off their boots, the four visitors walked up to the left side desk, as the guard's eyes elevated to meet theirs. "I take it you're the ones the Commander's been waiting on?"

When their check-in was finished, the Dragoons left their escorts at the desks and stepped across the room to the "CELL BLOCK" door. Black surgical masks dangled from black strings in their hands. The guard turned and keyed a passcode on a dust-smeared pad attached to the top of the doorknob, black with dark blue numbered buttons. Opening the door, the guard pointed to his face, gesturing for them to put on their masks. Anna walked ahead of Sean as she raised her mask, slipped it on over her mouth and nose, and wrapped the thread around her ears and the back of her head. Nodding to the soldier, she stepped through the doorway, her masked partner behind her once again. And in an instant, she understood why the guards gave them face covers.

Doors branded with dark blue numbers sat along both sides of a black hallway. The ceiling held lights that brightened the space to the same degree as the lobby. These features seemed reasonable to Anna. It was the swamp of human feces and urine engulfing the cell block that she couldn't rationalize.

Saturating the floor from the front to the back of the hallway were pools of bright and dark yellow liquid. Assorted with these puddles were runny and crispy mountains of brown, black, dark green and, in some places, dark red muck. It was as if Anna and Sean had been mistakenly led to a sewage tunnel. The odor was worse than the sight. Even with her mask, the debilitation was instantaneous, a revulsion and vertigo that dragged Anna's senses away from the task that had called her and Sean to the Detention Center. Her eyes watered, her hand came over her mask and pressed it tighter against her mouth and nose. And still, she was able to taste the stench and the decaying excrement particles in the air. Swinging her head around to her partner, she saw his hand covering his own mask, his sickened and baffled reaction equivalent to hers.

"Quite the sight, isn't it?" Commander Darius's voice ricocheted down the hall, acting as a type of vocal siren for Anna and Sean to follow. Standing ahead of them, Commander Darius waited by one of the detention cell doors. Fitted in her own recreational uniform and wearing an amused grin across her face, Darius appeared unaffected by what surrounded her, as if she lacked the ability to see and smell. She and the guard that stood beside her were both without masks. Anna couldn't comprehend how many trips to the Detention Center one had to make before adjusting to the building's environment. When neither of Darius's subordinate Dragoons replied to her comment, the Commander continued. "I got the idea for it back in the 3rd Year of Marathon, when the building opened. The people we detain here are always expecting the interrogations and the lack of daylight, but they never come close to thinking they won't get a shitter in their cell. You couldn't count the number of prisoners we've broken just by telling them they had to shit and piss on the floor for everyone to see. We let them clean it up once every fourteen days. Two weeks with this stink and you can't get them to stop talking."

For the first few paces, Anna and her partner made an attempt to step around the prisoner's deposits, but they ran out of clean flooring to walk on. When they were close enough to Darius and the guard that Anna could see Commander Darius's tied back hair and the yellow glare of the ceiling lights sparkling off her glass eye, Darius said, "I take it you two were at pentagon when I called you down here?"

"Yes, ma'am," Anna responded, her speech muffled somewhat by her mask, but her tone automatically attuned to mimic Darius's relaxed manner, as if she lacked control over her own voice.

Darius snickered, her laugh seeming to vibrate against the cell block walls as she turned to the guard. "I'm telling you, Private, once you get a taste for life outside the Outer Fence, things in Marathon are just too tedious. Pentagon's the only thing keeping our soldiers sane between assignments."

"Yes, Commander," the soldier retorted, the Commander's conduct making him uncomfortable.

The Commander's right eye widened, shifting between Anna and Sean's faces as they reached Darius and the guard's place in the hall. "Fuck, he got you good," she commented with pleasant surprise, concentrating on Anna's black and purple expression.

Anna made herself laugh, and complemented it with a nod. "That he did." Glancing behind her, she saw a light grin below her partner's mask, though she doubted Sean's sense of accomplishment was genuine. "He's improving."

"Glad to hear it. I wish there was time for me to see you two go at it again, but we've got someone to attend to first." Darius motioned to the guard. Pulling a black iron key from his belt, the guard moved to the detention cell on Anna and Sean's left, his boots stamping in the filth. He stood at the door, waiting for Darius to issue the order. Still focusing on her Dragoon agents, Darius told them, "We've got a walk-in. A nomad by the name of Joseph Holloway surrendered to a patrol, all the way out on the southern outskirts of Troy. He claims to have information on Sword of God."

What caused her to turn towards Sean, Anna didn't know for sure. But upon hearing Darius's announcement that the Black Dragoons had a new potential source of human intelligence, Anna's gut reaction was to look to her partner. The restrained yet noticeable flicker of guilt around Sean's mask and between his contusions convinced Anna he was beginning to worry for the same reason as her. *Darius said this guy came in voluntarily, but she also said Jason would break in an hour, two at the most.*

Adding a layer of skepticism to her tone, Darius said, "We're here to debrief this Mr. Holloway, see if he's got something legit. Who knows, he might be the one who finally gives us the intel on Sword of God we need."

"And if he does have something legit?" Anna asked, finding herself anxious of what could happen if Holloway actually gave the Black Dragoons info on Sword of God that was worthwhile.

"If he does, we'll have options to explore," Darius responded, keeping her answer vague, as if she was well aware of Anna's unease and wished to aggravate it further.

"There's no light in there," the guard explained, as he stuck the key in the slot of the cell. "So I'll leave the door open." After glancing back to make sure they'd heard him, he turned the key and popped the lock out of place. Swinging the door outward, the guard pushed a pile of brownish-green feces out of the way of the doorframe and revealed the tiny blackened room on the other side of the door. Darius went in ahead of Anna and Sean, stepping through the doorway without hesitation. Anna and her partner followed their Commander into the cell, their boots squeaking as the hallway muck smeared on the black floor. From behind, the guard added, "I'll just wait out here, if you need me." His statement went unacknowledged by the Dragoons.

Anna took her place at the Commander's side. Sean stood behind them both, just barely inside the entryway. The reek from the hall was not depleted in the cell. The floor and its black windowless walls were encrusted with so much smut brown clouds appeared to form with every step Anna, Sean, and Darius planted. Frozen crumbs of dirt sprinkled on Anna's cheeks, burned in her cuts. It wasn't a stretch to assume the room hadn't been scrubbed down in over a decade. An empty black tray and a black cup lay in the corner. The object of Darius's interrogation had situated himself in the back corner, where he sat and held a hand up in front of his eyes, shielding them from the flash of the hallway.

When the prisoner's eyes began to adjust to the change in lighting, he lowered his hand and craned his head up at the three Dragoons, giving Anna a good look at the current state of Joseph Holloway. As best as Anna could tell, Holloway looked to be in his late forties, making him a child of the Previous Civilization between the age of eight and ten at the time of the Reform. The man's head was shaved yet not barren. Lacerations sliced through the top of his head with something of an X-pattern, as if they were carving his skull into separate chunks. A couple of those wounds had faded over several decades; Anna suspected they were scars from the Reform. The others were recent, red, undressed, and only just starting to heal. Holloway's face was ensnared from one cheekbone to the other in coarse burn marks, so devastating to his facial structure it took Anna a second to confirm everything was still there beneath the defacements. The burns extended halfway down his neck, where patches of skin seemed to be missing. His eyes were dazed with prolonged exhaustion, his frame skeletal with starvation and repeated illness. Since his arrival at the Detention Center, Holloway had been provided with a black winter jacket and black pants. His detention uniform did not include socks, boots, or gloves, which allowed Anna to view the identical burn wounds on his bare hands and excrement soiled feet. *How is this man still alive?*

Holloway's eyes moved from one visitor to the next, examining Anna and Darius with minimal reaction, as if they were the exact people he'd expected to walk into his cell. When he got to Sean, however, his observation became stagnant, shocked even. He stared right through Anna and Darius for several moments, as if they weren't present at all, apparently not knowing what to make of the third guest standing behind them. Anna glanced around at her partner, who had directed his vision to the floor out of fear of looking at Holloway. Holloway broke from Sean when the Commander spoke with that strict voice she always used when she wanted control of the room. "Mr. Holloway, my name is Commander Darius. I've been told you wish to share information with us on the Sword of God organization. Is that true?"

Holloway nodded, and choked as he tried to cough out a reply, as if part of him was still trying to resist the urge to talk with affiliates of Marathon. "Yes," he was able to drag out after a few seconds.

Darius nodded back, not dropping her distrust of Holloway but willing to listen to him. "Well all right then, let's hear it."

Holloway gazed at Sean once more, and this time both Anna and Darius looked to Sean in confusion. Sean's unhinged silence gave nothing close to an explanation as to why this prisoner had become fixated with him. Anna's partner was at as much of a loss as her and their Commander. Speaking came easier to Holloway, though his volume remained weak. "Before I do this, I'd like to discuss my terms."

Darius produced a chuckle, as if this wasn't the first time a prisoner had brought up the issue of terms in an interrogation. Anna felt Darius's hand tap against her shoulder as she too found enough absurdity in Holloway's appeal to smile. "Mr. Holloway," the Commander said, smirking with mockery and shaking her head. "You're not anywhere close to being able to list out terms. Your present situation is as follows: you are located in the city of Marathon, the largest and most heavily defended spec of civilization for three hundred miles in any direction. If I say no to your terms and you refuse to relay the intelligence you've promised us, you'll be driven to gates of the Outer Fence and left outside our perimeter. In your condition, I don't see you lasting another night out there. You certainly won't make it back to Troy. Quite simply Mr. Holloway, either you give us what you have or you die. And if what you have isn't worth shit, you still die. So really, all you can do now is talk and hope it's enough to save what's left of your pathetic existence. That is, if saving your life is something you want."

Holloway's reaction was not at all what Anna or perhaps any of them anticipated. He didn't break down in despair at the realization he'd been cornered, nor did he merely relinquish what information on Sword of God he possessed. Instead, the detainee placed his scalded hands on the walls of his cell and rose up onto his feet. When he was standing in his corner, frail and unbalanced yet persistent, he glanced at Sean again and then addressed his audience. Urgency seemed to strengthen his speech. "Commander, a week ago Sword of God sacked my community."

"Your community?" Darius asked, still unconvinced, though surprised Holloway was in fact not a nomad as had been previously reported, but a citizen of another settlement.

"Athens," Holloway retorted. And with that, a stunned quiet came over the detention cell. The name Athens referred to a town at the northernmost point of the Aegean Valley, one hundred fifty miles north of Marathon. Thriving, as far as the military's recurring Aurora surveillance operations had shown, Athens had grown into a settlement of major interest to Marathon. Rumor had been the Commanders intended to annex the town of Athens, once Marathon's colonies had been established in Serenity and throughout the Aegean Valley. The ground Athens and its people inhabited would be key in the defense of the Aegean Valley's northern entrance, whenever Marathon succeeded in bringing the territory under control. But now, according to Holloway, that critical piece in the war for the Aegean Valley had fallen to Sword of God.

The lull in the conversation was ended by Darius after several moments. "Athens?" she said, no longer held back by disbelief.

"Yes, ma'am. There were forty of us, up until last week. We had fortifications, weapons, and enough rations and supplies for two months; though I'm sure your people knew most of that." Pride entered Holloway's tone. "In Athens, we chose to stay out of the fighting. We had offers from the insurgencies."

Darius corrected him. "Terrorists."

"We had offers to join the war against your city, help halt your expansion into the valley, but we didn't want to get involved. We'd allowed ourselves to believe that in Athens, we could live free." Holloway's expression became somber. "And then Sword of God arrived at our barricades. We'd heard of them before of course, their name was brought up every time nomads came passing through Athens. But none of us saw them as anything more than another, terrorist, group trying to bite back at Marathon. They showed up a few hours before dark, outside the North Gate, requested a meeting with our council. We granted them that and allowed their leader to enter. He told us Sword of God is trying to expand their presence in the Aegean Valley. They're branching out from their base of operations."

"Which is where?" Darius interrupted to ask.

Holloway shook his head. "He didn't say. But wherever Sword of God comes from, they're growing their operation just as Marathon is doing. Their leader asked us to be a part of that effort, let his fighters use Athens as an outpost for their activities, supply them with food, medicine, weapons, and commit our people to their cause. In exchange, he promised Athens the protection of his forces. We considered his proposal. As you might've already gathered it didn't sit well with the council, so we turned him down. After that he left, didn't make a fuss about it or anything, just thanked us for agreeing to meet with him and rejoined his fighters outside the barricades." The prisoner's voice became uneven. His attention gravitated towards Sean, as if it was more important Sean hear this than Anna and Darius. "We all thought that was the end of it, but they came back. They hit our perimeter in the middle of the night, punched through and stormed Athens in minutes, killed all of our guards without losing a single fighter of their own. When that was done they went building by building, raping the people they liked, slaughtering the ones they didn't. Adults, children, it made no difference to them."

The first few tears came, gliding down Holloway's crumbled face as if his skin was made of rock. Standing before him and watching this occur; Anna noticed a light prick of guilt at her side. *Chloe.*

"They didn't get all of us though," Holloway continued. "I managed to lead a group out the South Gate before Sword of God reached them. There were ten of us, still are ten of us as far as I know. We followed the Highway south to Dresden and took refuge there. And after a couple days there I decided to carry on alone to Troy, see if I could get help from one of your patrols. I would've walked all the way to Serenity or even here to Marathon if I had to." Holloway was glaring at Sean, especially at him: he meant for Sean to hear this part. The prisoner's composure was collapsing now, the delay in his misery concluded. "They took my children."

Darius was unfazed by Holloway's disclosure but Anna was startled, the minute jab of guilt she'd hardly detected before was now stabbing at her hip, tearing into the side of her stomach, as if she was responsible for the man's despair. *Chloe!* When she glanced back at Sean, she saw him staring straight at Holloway; he looked nowhere else except at Holloway.

"Your children?" Darius asked with an annoyed and unsympathetic sigh, seeming to lose what little hope she'd gained that Holloway would have significant intelligence on Sword of God.

Holloway shouted as he sobbed. "Jacob and Mia, Sword of God kept them alive for themselves! I saw them with those monsters, but I couldn't get to them! I was too far away!" Holloway stepped forward, towards Anna and Darius, but really towards Sean. "Those scars on your face, I've seen plenty like them before," Holloway said, pointing at Sean's disfigured face. "You're a survivor!" Sean didn't reply; if he somehow had a response the words were certainly stumbling at his tongue. "You're too young to have been there for the Reform, but you've seen the things I've seen. Those wounds can't be more than a year old. What city are you from?" The detainee paused, appearing to ponder over his fellow survivor's community of origin. Sean was backing out of the cell, leaving a terrified and confronted gaze as his boots returned to the hallway compost. It was as if Holloway had unlocked a passageway to a place in Sean's mind he'd spent the last twelve months trying to seal off. And in doing so, Holloway had overturned the entire encounter: Sean Halley was now a prisoner of Marathon's Detention Center, and Joseph Holloway was his interrogator. "Carthage. You're from Carthage! What're you doing here? Why're you wearing that uniform? You're one of us!"

Anna looked on with a feeling of uselessness as Darius stepped in front of Holloway, blocking him from Sean and the exit from his cell. "You need to calm the fuck down," Darius told the detainee, seizing him at his shoulders.

"You're going after Sword of God! When you do, please, please save my children, my children and my people in Dresden and Athens! Those are my only terms!" Holloway struggled against the Commander, attempted to push past to Sean. His strength was marginal; Anna wondered how he was able to stand at all. "I'll give you Sword of God! Please just save them, save my people, save Jacob and Mia!"

"Move!" Darius's thundering order sent Sean jumping out the doorway and into the hall. Heaving Holloway by his jacket, Darius ripped the prisoner from his cell, threw him out into the hallway, and down face first into a pool of black and dark green feces. The squishing sound of his impact was followed by the thump of the Commander's boot pressing down against the back of Holloway's neck. Whatever patience Darius began her interrogation with was well past exhaustion.

"What the fuck?" the guard blared. Anna walked out of Holloway's cell and stood behind Darius, as dumbfounded by the spectacle as the guard appeared to be. Holloway began thrashing as his head and neck sank below the muck, under the weight of Darius's boot. "I'll call for assistance!"

"No need, Private," Darius interjected, all concern lacking from her voice as she went about drowning Holloway in feces.

"Ma'am, I..." the guard started to protest, baffled by the Commander's actions.

"Resume your post, Private. And don't bother us again." Darius turned away from the guard and glared down at the prisoner's writhing and squirming upper body, sunken in the black and dark green filth.

"Yes, Commander," the guard replied, before twisting himself around and facing down the hall towards the lobby, so he didn't have to bear further witness to this incident.

As Darius reduced her hold on Holloway, permitting him to lift his head out of the excrement, Anna turned to Sean. Her partner stood next to the doorway, trying and failing to catch his breath beneath his mask as he rested a hand against the wall, his distress obvious. What the prisoner had asked him, and then asked of him, him and no one else, had forced its way into his psyche and left him scrambling to make sense of the man's request. Anna wanted to approach him, console him in some way, but her better judgement won out. Besides risking disapproval from Darius for not being focused on the present task, Anna could've exacerbated her partner's momentary turmoil. *A native-born citizen of Marathon trying to help a native-born citizen of Carthage, not more than a minute after being asked why he now serves the very same city that destroyed his, what the fuck can I do that Sean can't work out by himself?*

When Holloway finished puking the chunks of feces from his mouth and throat, and was resting his black and green face on the mound of manure in front of him, Darius resumed her interrogation. "Mr. Holloway, tell me about Sword of God." And at last, the Dragoons prisoner became their informant, calming himself out of his temporary state of madness.

Desperation and filth stuck to Holloway's voice as he answered. "There are thirteen of them, Sword of God fighters."

"Only thirteen?" Anna asked before Darius.

"Yes. From what I heard about them in Athens, they have additional operatives stationed throughout the Aegean Valley, but their principal fighting force is always those thirteen. Find them and you'll bring down the organization."

Darius nodded, accepting what Holloway was saying for the time being. "What do you know about these thirteen?"

"Each of the thirteen uses codenames for themselves. Nobody knows their real names."

From the pocket of her jacket, the Commander removed a black notebook and a dark blue pen. "What do the thirteen call themselves?"

"Phillip, Peter, Andrew. Peter and Andrew are brothers." Darius wrote the names on her notepad as Holloway listed them out. "James and John, those two are brothers also. Bartholomew, Thomas, Matthew, James."

"You already said James."

"There are two James's."

"Who are the others?"

"Thaddeus, Simon, and Judas. Those twelve refer to themselves as the Disciples. They're led by a man who likes to call himself."

Darius beat him to the punch. "Jesus Christ?"

Anna observed with confusion. *Jesus who?*

"Yes," Holloway confirmed.

"How original," the Commander remarked with sarcasm Anna didn't understand. "How do we find this Jesus and his Disciples?"

"Considering they wanted to use Athens as an outpost, they should all still be there. You'll be able to track them with your aircraft."

"What else?" Darius demanded, as if somehow able to sense Holloway had more to give.

"They have blue crosses painted on their foreheads, all thirteen of them."

Anna didn't know what to make of this response either. "Crosses?" she inquired, her question directed at Darius and Holloway both.

The Commander explained, without taking her eyes off Holloway. "Symbol of Christianity, two lines crossing like two roads at a four-way intersection."

The clarification did little to help Anna. "Christianity?"

That time Darius looked at her with noticeable irritation. "One of the major religions of the Previous Civilization, lost a lot of followers after the Reform, but some still hold onto it. Apparently this Jesus Christ fellow was executed on a cross configuration of some sort, but rose from the dead three days later. There's also a thing about a tree, a snake, and an apple." Darius snickered and shook her head. "I don't know; don't ask me how it all works. Frankly, I don't give a fuck."

Glancing back at Sean, Anna saw her partner had managed to relax himself much like Holloway and was now standing without the aid of the wall, though his troubled demeanor remained in the clear parts of his expression.

Turning her attention back to Holloway, somewhat yet not totally satisfied, Darius asked him, "What do our thirteen friends look like?"

Holloway shook his head from side to side in the muck. "I can't match a name to every face." His speech was diminishing, as if he was beginning to lose consciousness. "I didn't get a good look at all of them anyway."

"You've seen Jesus, or did you not get a good look at him either?" the Commander barked, ready to dunk Holloway in feces and urine a second time.

Holloway conceded without additional resistance. "Late thirties to early forties, between five-ten and six feet, short blond hair and glasses."

Darius copied the description down in her notepad as she had with all the information their prisoner supplied them with. "Is that all you have for us, Mr. Holloway?"

"Yes," the detainee admitted, his head shifting around for a glimpse at his interrogator and her agents.

"Well all right then," Darius said, raising her boot off Holloway's neck. "Your service to Marathon is appreciated." The Dragoons cleared out of the detention block, leaving their detainee curled on the floor of his cell in unshakeable excrement-filled dejection, his children nowhere close to him.

That evening, just after nightfall, Anna, Sean, and Darius gathered at the Command Building, Marathon's military headquarters. The office was located in the center of New Terra, the northwestern sub-district of Marathon. Just as Terra's five thousand residents were soldiers in the military, all five thousand of New Terra's inhabitants were government officers. And whereas the vast majority of Terra and Missio's populace were stuffed wall to wall in one room barracks, the people of New Terra lived in black multi-room houses. At most four government workers were housed together, though it was sometimes less. The exact living conditions of the Commanders were unknown to most of Marathon's citizens, though rumor often suggested each of them lived in a mansion of their own personal design. Whether or not this was true made little difference to Anna.

In addition to housing units of greater comfort, Marathon Hospital was in New Terra, which offered medical treatments and medicines similar to those available before the Reform. Of course, to be admitted to the hospital as a patient, a citizen had to be registered as a military or government employee.

With the Detention Center's feces cleansed from their boots, Anna and Sean met with Darius in a small auditorium. Built with nine descending rows of black metal chairs that started at the elevated back wall of the room and ended at the speaking floor, the auditorium was one of the more spacious rooms Anna's association with the Black Dragoons brought her to. A black metal stairwell ran down along the left side of the seats, from the exit in the back to the front. The front wall of the room was taken up by a black twenty-foot long monitor, used for visual aids. A black projector was attached to the rear wall, behind the seats, and displayed images on the screen.

During their post-interrogation briefing, Darius stood to the side of the screen, using a remote to work the projector. Her underlings sat in the second row from the bottom, in the middle seats in front of the monitor, Anna closer to Darius and Sean closer to the stairs. The space was empty save for the three of them. The lights were out, leaving the blue illumination of the screen to fill the auditorium. From where the Commander had positioned herself to lead the meeting, the shadowed mixture of black and blue not only bounced off her glass eye, but enhanced the red complexion of her scar, making the facial mark a difficult distraction to avoid as Darius spoke. "After securing an Aurora for the reconnaissance operation, I sent the plane on several passes over Athens. The pictures you're seeing now were taken this afternoon."

The screen was divided down the middle between two images of Athens. The picture on the left was a standard aerial surveillance photo, taken from twenty-five thousand feet above ground level. The image showed fields of gray snow laid over an alpine landscape, which encircled the tiny hilltop town of Athens. The community the Commanders apparently sought to govern was little more than a single gray roadway. Lining both sides of the street were numerous brick buildings from the Previous Civilization, varying from two to four stories tall, their walls conjoined. Despite the fortification, the walls were not without gaps. Openings at both ends of the road separated the buildings into two rows. Metal gates, estimated at fifteen to twenty feet high, had been erected at each opening. North Gate and South Gate, like Marathon's own. However, the gates had not been sufficient to hold back Sword of God. There was nobody on the road as far as Anna could see, no one standing watch on the rooftops or at the gates. Even the grounds outside Athens were barren, as if everyone in the Aegean Valley had the good sense to stay far from the settlement. Were it not for the second image on the right side of the screen, Anna would've insisted Athens had been abandoned.

The second photo was another aerial reconnaissance image of Athens captured from the same altitude. The town in this photograph, however, was veiled in the blackish-purple sheet of thermal imaging. Orange dots were strewn about the buildings. "We estimate at most, fifteen to twenty people within Athens's walls," Darius told them, adding to what the picture was already saying. "What movement there was for the Aurora to see was limited to the buildings. There wasn't one person outside during the entire time the plane was overhead."

"And when we compare what we're seeing here to one of our routine recon ops from three weeks ago." There was a click from Darius's remote as the images changed on the monitor. Again the screen was split between two aerial photographs of Athens, the picture on the left taken in normal optics and the picture on the right taken in thermal. The image on the left showed a bustling Athens, at least two dozen human silhouettes out and moving along the road or standing atop the buildings. The same could be said for the thermal image. "We projected thirty-five to forty people in Athens when we took these pictures, the same number Mr. Holloway gave us. And as you can see, these people don't have any issues being outside. A population drop of this rate does support Mr. Holloway's claim that Sword of God has annexed Athens. I spoke with the other Commanders an hour ago; they've already given the go-ahead for an incursion into the Aegean Valley. But then again, they've been waiting for the Black Dragoons to move on Sword of God for a year now, ever since they saw these." Darius clicked her remote once more.

The half and half two picture screen converted into a four square display, showing four photographs at once. Unlike the first two sets, these slides were not images from an Aurora but security camera footage. The photo on the top left was washed in the luminous dark green of night vision, showing an exterior shot from a building. Greenish-gray snow lay across the image, surrounded by barriers of pitch black night. Six people were marching across the snow in a group, towards the camera's position. The night vision made their clothing appear dark greenish-blue, but Anna still recognized the tactical gear worn by Marathon soldiers, the dark blue suits, body armor, boots, and gloves. The only pieces of the ensemble Sword of God hadn't stolen were the dark blue tactical helmets. In place of the helmets, the group wore black wool masks that shielded every part of their heads, save for their eyes and mouths. Their arms held black T-05 rifles, raised and ready. "Welcome to the Troy Station, or the last day of it, I should say."

The remaining three photos in the collection had a pronounced orange glare to them, which Anna determined to be the result of several fires. The top right photograph presented a hallway, identical in design to West Hall at the Serenity Station. Orange flames raged along the black floors and walls, eating away at the structure as they raced up and down the hall. Three corpses made their final resting places within view of the camera's lens, their mangled bodies lying in pools of dark orange-red. The bottom left picture was of the Troy Station's center hallway, engulfed by the blaze as West Hall was. The last image on the bottom right of the screen was likely of East Hall, but she couldn't confirm because the photo was blocked. The obstruction to the camera's lens was a face, no doubt belonging to one of Sword of God's attackers. The face was concealed by the same masks the assailants were wearing in the top left picture. Only the individual's eyes and mouth revealed themselves for the camera. Even with the low lighting and the orange shimmer from the flames, she was able to spot the terrorist's bright lime green eyes. At the bottom of the mask, the fighter was showing his teeth with an elated smile, as if he were goading the Marathon affiliates who observed the station's footage, daring them to come after Sword of God.

"Based on all the footage we've collected from the garrison's cameras, we've determined that this man led the assault on the Troy Station one year ago, destroying our foothold into the Aegean Valley." Darius allowed a touch of cynicism into her report. "Assuming the intel Mr. Holloway gave us is accurate, this our first and only close up of Jesus Christ himself." Their Commander kept the images of the Troy Station up as she detailed their assignment, as if she wanted the pictures to intensify their hatred of Sword of God. "This operation's going to be problematic, to say the least. We have a possible location on Sword of God that we'll continue to monitor with the Auroras, but the coverage won't be constant. And if Jesus and his Disciples are in fact in Athens, the other Commanders want them done in as the Cavaliers were. Face to face confirmation. The Aegean Valley is far too hot for us to send you two up to Athens by Nightwalker. You'll be hit before you get past Troy. If we're going to eliminate Sword of God's thirteen, you'll have to be inserted just inside the valley and then head for Athens on foot, without immediate support. Which means you'll both be spending a few days, maybe even a week, in the field chasing these people down." Darius paused and narrowed her focus on Anna and Sean's places in the auditorium, as if she was about to ask a question she expected to hear them answer. Anna looked to her Commander, demoting the images on the screen to the periphery of her vision as she braced herself for Darius's query. "I've said this before and I'll say it again. The other Commanders can beg for this mission as much as they like, but before I blue light this I want to know how the agents taking the assignment feel about it. So Anna: what do you think?"

"Well ma'am," Anna said, trying to concentrate on and give an adequate reply to her Commander. "Holloway's desperate. While that doesn't guarantee what he gave us is legitimate, I believe it justifies a mission. I saw a lot of people get to where Holloway is back in Missio. Sick, starving, people so hysterical they'll give themselves over to the people they hate. As you know, that's how the drug gangs recruit many of their dealers. I think Holloway turned himself in to us so we can do what he can't."

"Rescue his children?" Darius said for her.

Anna felt a stitch in her side. *Chloe.* "Yes, ma'am. And for us to rescue Jacob and Mia, he had to give us something that could actually be used to find Sword of God. Even if it's not much, I think his intel his genuine."

Darius nodded, pleased her underlings had once again agreed to an assignment without objection. "All right, looks like we have the break we've been searching for. Head back to your barrack and get your gear ready; you two step off at 0100."

"Thank you, Commander," Anna replied, restricting any uncertainty from her voice. With their briefing concluded, she and Sean rose from their chairs and walked down the aisle to the stairs, both of them giving a last look to the man with lime green eyes. But Darius wasn't finished.

Anna and her partner were halfway up the staircase, the exit in their sights, when their superior called from across the auditorium. "Sean, why don't you go on ahead and tell your escorts to warm up the Nightwalker. I need to speak with Anna for a minute."

Standing on the step in front of her, Sean hesitated and turned to Anna. His expression to her was one of confusion and moderate fright, as if he wanted to ask his partner if he'd made some mistake, done something that warranted his expulsion from a secondary meeting. Anna said nothing to him, but nodded and gave a small wave, signaling him to leave her there, alone with Commander Darius. "Yes, ma'am," Sean said, and scampered to the door. When he was out of the room, Anna turned to face whatever the Commander had in store for her.

She waited at her place on the stairway as Darius walked across the speaking floor towards her. The Commander's face and frame were obscured by darkness on the other side of the screen as she asked, "Do you think he's up for this?"

"What do you mean, ma'am?"

"Sean," Darius said, as she stepped in front of the monitor, the light of the screen immersing her in a blueish-orange glow, her blackened silhouette crossing over the four images from the Troy Station. "Do you think he's prepared for what this mission demands of him?"

Anna allowed herself the false hope that she could get by with quick answers. "Yes, ma'am, I do." But her Commander was too observant to miss that.

"Are you sure, Anna? You two haven't been paired for long; you only met five minutes before the drive up to Serenity." Anna's dread fortified with every tap of the Commander's boots on the floor. "I'd say Sean has proven himself to be a skilled and loyal agent, so far. Be that as it may, he's still a native of Carthage. A year ago he lived against the will of Marathon. To him and his people, defiance was daily life. Now, twelve months later, he's a sworn protector of the very same city that brought Carthage to its necessary end? All sorts of unknowns come into play in these circumstances. You could be out there in the middle of the Aegean Valley when Sean starts questioning the mission, refuses to watch your back, or hesitates to terminate visible and active targets. Are you comfortable being partnered with someone who has so much to work out in his head, who might hesitate to neutralize the targets in his sights?"

Darius left the glare of the monitor and rounded the front aisle to the bottom of the stairs, while Anna answered, as honest as she could. "I'll admit I don't know much of anything about Sean, ma'am, but I trust him as my partner. The military wouldn't have kept him alive after the fall of Carthage, given him the choice to come to Marathon, assigned him to the Black Dragoons, and spent all those months training him if he didn't have the endurance for a mission like this, or the knowledge of the region from his time with the Carthage Scouts." Darius was climbing the steps now, her expression masked by the darkness of the stairwell. "The op will run a lot smoother with his experience," Anna added, as if it was going help her in any way.

"Anna, just how fucking stupid do you think I am?" Panic boiled in Anna's chest, dried her throat. This petrified condition did not come as a result of the Commander's enraged voice, but rather what Anna saw in the Commander's right eye as she stepped out of the dark and joined her place on the stairs. Darius's iris glowed bright violet, a sign of that rare process Anna knew all too well, the alteration to one's Second-Gen Stage. The lack of response from Anna seemed to infuriate Darius further. "Do you see me as some officer who's so incompetent she can't tell what's happening on a fucking thermal imaging screen?"

The auditorium appeared to wobble in front of Anna, the stairwell slanting from one side to the other. "I? No of course not, Commander. You're."

Before Anna could react, Darius's hand gripped and tightened around the front of her neck. In shock, her hands latched onto Darius's wrist, but came nowhere close to prying the Commander's hand from her throat. With ferocious strength, Darius lifted her arm upwards, raising Anna into the air. She felt dazed as her feet left the floor and her eyesight hung above Darius. Her body swung, her back slamming against the staircase wall as Darius held her in total suspension. Air was cut off from her lungs. It was as if the Commander's hand was a rock implanted in her windpipe that halted every frantic attempt she made at oxygen.

"Never hesitate like that again," Darius roared, scorching Anna's face. "I don't care how fucking young the Cavaliers' kids are! I don't care if they're fucking ten-minute old infants! If I declare all persons at a target location to be hostile then you fucking take them all out, the exact fucking moment you get eyes on! That's what I brought you to the Black Dragoons to do! You're not here to sit around like some fucking halfwit and wait for your partner to run over and finish things off! Sean, we can replace him and everyone will forget he was ever a part of this unit! But you Anna, you have been the subject of far too much time and resources to start malfunctioning on us now! There are twenty-one other Dragoon teams I could be sending after Sword of God, all of them with more experience than yours, but I chose you because I believe you represent the future of this city! Pull something like that again and I'll go to the Commanders, tell them those eleven months I spent training you were all for naught, you aren't the agent I want to replace me when I retire! And then I'll send a message back to Missio, tell Chloe's guardians the entire arrangement is null and void! I don't have to tell you what'll happen to your daughter after that's done!"

Anna's insides were screaming, more from Darius's threats than loss of oxygen. Once word of Anna's nature had reached the northern side of the Marathon River, Commander Darius had come to her and made the offer. She would join the military as an agent with the Black Dragoons, commit every day of the rest of her life to the assassination of Marathon's enemies. And in return for her unwavering service, her child, Chloe, would be compensated consistently and considerably, cared for by government custodians until reaching an age where she could care for herself. However, just as the Commander had warned too many times before today, the whole agreement could be struck down with a single message to Missio.

The simple thought of Darius actually carrying out her threat spurred a memory Anna feared, yet clung to as if losing it would be fatal to her daughter. The recollection was of Chloe, five years old with long and loose blond hair, as bright as Anna's had been at that age, fast asleep in her bunk. Chloe was six now, but Anna hadn't seen the girl in nearly a year, not since she got in that Nightwalker with Darius for the first time, so the outdated image was kept in stock. Anna had watched Chloe for some time, pulled the bunk's blanket up over her daughter's nose, like her mother used to do for her. Already smarter than Anna ever hoped to be, Chloe was the kind of child all the other parents in their barrack privately thanked Marathon for not sending them, the one who was always asking questions. Every waking moment, Anna's daughter piled them on in that soft, almost reluctant, voice of hers. And yet, her daughter's pathological habit did not drive her mad day in and day out. Instead, Chloe's boundless curiosity was how Anna relaxed at the end of another day in Marathon. Nights, before they went to sleep, were spent unwinding with Chloe's questions, about her, about Marathon, about the places outside Marathon, about the world that was, about the world that would be, about every conceivable thing in existence. But Anna didn't live in that barrack anymore, she couldn't watch Chloe sleep or listen to her questions, and her daughter's higher intellect was not enough to protect her from the reality of Missio.

Chloe was the child of a Second-Gen, and as a Second-Gen's offspring she was guaranteed to be a Second-Gen herself, but none of that did her any good currently, because she had yet to experience her Awakening. Until Chloe grew mature enough for an Awakening to be possible, seven years from now at least, her abilities would hide within her, unusable, a dormant volcano not yet able to erupt. It was not unusual for a First Generation Second-Gen to go through their childhood and even early adulthood with complete obliviousness to their true nature, only to then experience their Awakening and have to contend with the loss of their membership in the human race. That was how it happened for Anna, and that's how she imagined it happened for Darius. Chloe had been informed of her standing not long after Anna's own Awakening, but at the meager age of five, now six, she could not call out the capabilities that waited somewhere beneath her skin for defense. If she was cast out of the Community Office her guardians housed her in, Chloe would be out in Missio's snowy streets alone, no living grandparents or father to take her in, and no salary to support herself on.

Darius released Anna from her grip; she crumbled to the floor, sat on her knees at the feet of her Commander, and did not retaliate. She inhaled gasp after painful gasp till she could breathe again, the muscles in her neck swollen and throbbing. Anna said nothing as she waited for Darius to issue a command. She would not endanger Chloe's life with so much as one more word.

"Look at me, Anna," her superior ordered.

Anna lifted her head up towards the Commander without delay, every fiber of her existence belonging to the woman that stood over her. Darius's expression was concealed in pitch black, Anna noticed now the monitor had been switched off, but she could still see her Commander's incensed violet eye, glaring at her through the dark.

Solemn, as if she also wished the circumstances were different, Darius said, "As Second-Gens, you and I belong to something bigger than us both. You keep that in mind the next time you have to kill a child."

PHASE 2: THE AEGEAN VALLEY

1st Day of Mission Deployment
Operational Participant #1: Anna Corday
Operational Participant #2: Sean Halley
Operational Call Signs: Vanguard One, Vanguard Two
Mission Objective: N/A
Mission Location: N/A
Mission Timeframe: Indefinite

5: ANNA

The Highway was invisible, blocked by the immense pre-dawn blackness. It was as if the world beyond her window had ceased existing. No headlights, not a single source of illumination inside the Nightwalker's cabin, their transport crept up on the insertion point in total darkness. They had been lights out since driving through the North Gate of Marathon, as per Commander Darius's order. As always, Anna and Sean rode in the backseats of the Nightwalker, Anna on the right and her partner on the left, packs strapped to their backs, listening to the crunch of the vehicle's tracks pushing through the snow-clogged Highway, abiding with the turbulence the eroded street created. Gear cleaned and prepped, they sat with their T-05 Snipers in hand, loaded and equipped as the mission required. The dark was successful in hiding the marks and bruises they'd dealt to each other in pentagon, as well as the more recent discoloration on Anna's neck. The contusions from her Commander had swelled over the last several hours into the distinctive shape of a hand, growing as prominent as the scarring on Sean's face. Sean noticed, but hadn't asked. She imagined he was afraid of what her explanation would be.

By the blue light of Anna's wristwatch, which she checked once per hour to limit even the smallest presence of light; it was 0500 in the morning, two hours of nighttime protection left until gray dawn. They'd been on the Highway for four hours. One of the last surviving major roadways built by the Previous Civilization, the Highway extended from Marathon, circumnavigated Serenity by way of the Serenity Hills, and continued into the Aegean Valley through Troy, Dresden, all the way to Athens. It was the primary access route utilized by soldiers on missions to the northern territories that Marathon planned to eventually colonize. The Highway also carried on south of the city. At the outset of the Marathon-Carthage War, it served as the main method of travel for Marathon's assault force. Though still in use, the Highway had been so diminished during the last forty years that any vehicle using the road was restricted to a maximum speed of twenty-five miles per hour. Vehicles driving over that speed limit ran the risk of losing a track in one of the potholes or flying off the collapsed sections of the street. With four hours spent doing twenty-five on the Highway, their Nightwalker had reached the southernmost tip of the Aegean Valley, one hundred miles north of Marathon.

Though the assignment itself was clear to Anna, she had little knowledge of the mission's environment. She knew the Aegean Valley was enfolded by two mountain ranges, the Troy Mountains to the west and the Aegean Mountains to the east, which converged at the valley's northern and southern points. She was also aware the valley was ten miles wide at the broadest and fifty miles in length. But outside the most basic navigational information, Anna would have to depend on Sean's experience in the Aegean Valley from his time with the Carthage Scouts to get them to Athens.

Using the night vision setting on her rifle scope, Anna scanned the landscape that crawled past her vehicle. Through the clouds of greenish-gray, produced by the vehicle's tracks, she saw the lifeless greenish-gray motorway and the tattered metal guardrail at the road's edge. Down a steep ridge on the other side of the railing, she eyed the disintegrating collection of trees and the climbing greenish-gray slopes of the Aegean Mountains they would follow to Athens. Then, the night vision clad soldier at the wheel of their vehicle uttered the first and only sentence he would say to Anna and Sean. "Two minutes to jump." He spoke without taking his eyes off the road, as if he was trying to pretend he was talking to the soldier in the passenger seat, and that she and Sean weren't there in his backseats at all. Anna felt the Nightwalker shifting to the right. An exit ramp appeared out her window as the vehicle turned towards the opening in the guardrail. They followed the ramp off the Highway, the descending road delivering them into the black of the forest below. As the Nightwalker swerved, avoiding a large rusted and disabled vehicle of the Previous Civilization that had met its end at the bottom of the ramp, Anna performed a final check of her weapons and gear. Turning to Sean, she noticed he was still looking out his window.

She leaned over and tapped him on his shoulder. When he didn't respond, she whispered, "Sean, ready up." He didn't even glance. Seeing that his rifle had slipped out of his hands, she realized her partner had fallen asleep. Quick, so as not to catch the attention of the troops, she punched him in the side. "Sean, wake up."

Sean stirred, his hands constricting at his rifle and his head rising from the window. His face was still turned away from her when he mumbled something. "Derek?"

Anna was confused. *Who's Derek?*

He brushed his hand against the scarred side of his face several times, before looking over at her. She saw the bewildered sleepiness that populated his eyes, sharing space with a deepened anguish that expanded as he regained consciousness and became aware of where he was. "We jump in less than two minutes. Make sure you're ready," she told him, knowing she couldn't ask about Derek now. Sean nodded, and began double checking his own equipment.

From the Highway the Nightwalker made several hard turns around the woods decaying trees, crushing limbs that had already fallen with heavy bumps and sharp cracks, no longer on any kind of road or pathway. Veering right, the vehicle descended once more. Through her night vision scope, she saw that they were dropping down another embankment, deeper into the tree-spotted ravine that sloped down from the Highway. Below them, the greenish-gray ground flattened out again, but to the right the snow appeared to fall away, a cliff face, how steep and how far to the bottom unclear. *That's not where we're jumping out, is it?* The soldier in the passenger seat elevated her hand, holding her palm out towards the front windshield. *Great.* Recognizing the signal, Anna planted her hand on the door lever, primed herself to leap from her seat. Behind her, Sean wasn't sitting down any longer, but hovering between his seat and hers, wide awake, anxious to move, as if fleeing whatever he'd dreamt of. She watched the soldier's hand, waiting as the Nightwalker continued down the hill. Even on a descent, the vehicle's speed was declining, dropping below twenty, fifteen, and then ten. Anna felt the vehicle bounce as they hit the bottom of the embankment. At that precise moment, the soldier's hand balled into a fist.

The door opened. Bitter night came at Anna like a vacuum, sucking her from the Nightwalker's cabin. She landed on her pack in the snow, arms spread across her chest, clutching her rifle. The cliffside she'd thrown herself onto was iced over, and she started sliding through the dark, picking up speed. "Fuck," she muttered. From above, she heard the crackling of Sean hitting the cliff in the same manner, the rustling of ice rolling downhill with them both. There was a thump that she knew to be the Nightwalker's door automatically closing. The grayish-brown trunk of a tree shot up in front of her, joining her in the blackness. "Fuck," she said again, as she swerved to the left. Her right flank made contact with the stalk. Though the pain was slight, the impact knocked her on her stomach. Her rifle skidded across the ice. She twisted back onto her pack, slid several more feet—how many she couldn't tell in the dark—before her boots touched soft and even snow. Sean landed at the base of the hill, a couple seconds after she did. At a distance overhead, beyond the black curtain that hung between the bottom and the top of the cliff, the Nightwalker's engines revved, its tracks burrowing through the snow in an upward climb. The vehicle drove off into the early morning, seeking out a path up to the Highway, the soldiers beginning their trek back to Marathon. The Black Dragoons were on the ground in the Aegean Valley.

Kneeling, Anna and Sean scanned their immediate surroundings with their night vision scopes, and then again with their thermal scopes. When she'd completed her sweep and found no indication of life beyond the two of them, Anna reached over and patted Sean on the shoulder. He glanced over at her and she gave him thumbs-up, wordlessly reporting she was ready to move, asking him if he were as well. Sean nodded and returned the thumbs-up. At that, Anna tapped the Network earpiece in her right ear, once and then a second time, holding her index finger to the miniature communications tool. Quiet, so even the last fleeting shouts from the Nightwalker were enough to drown her out, she said, "Central this is Vanguard One, deployment complete. Repeat deployment complete, we're moving out. Do you roger?"

"Copy all, Vanguard One," Commander Darius replied. "How copy?"

"Copy all Central, Vanguard One out." Anna took her finger off her earpiece and turned back to Sean, who awaited her order. With her hand, she waved herself and her partner forward into the trees, wisps of breath fogging the air in front of them, their rifles clanging as their boots crunched in the snow. And then, there was something in her night vision scope.

Her subconscious picked up on the oddity, informing her that something wasn't quite right, but her active mind refused to comprehend what was out of place until she was right on top of it. The snow had grown darker in her night vision scope, altering from the customary greenish-gray to a greenish-black color around a stand of trees, as if a shadow had been cast over that particular patch of snow. She came to a halt, angling her T-05 Sniper downwards, waiting for the glitch in her night vision to correct itself. When the cracking from Sean's boots stopped as well, she thought to tell him about her scope's malfunction, but then she eyed a few drops of black liquid falling to the snow with a gentle tap, adding to the black snow. A horrifying notion came to her, and she elevated her rifle, finding three pairs of boots floating in midair. Attached to these boots were three pairs of legs and above those legs, three torsos, arms bound at the back, and three soldiers necks, strung up with thick rope and tied to a branch above.

Sean gasped with revolted surprise, his T-05 Sniper clicking as it rose to the same level as hers. They were Marathon soldiers, or had been. Their tactical helmets were missing, but they were fitted in the rest of their combat gear. No visible wounds, except something was wrong with their expressions. They'd been disfigured somehow, torn by shrapnel from an explosion, Anna assumed at first. It took her a few more seconds to realize these troops didn't have faces at all. The skin had been cut in a circular pattern on the outer edge of the face, and then peeled off, leaving a mess of exposed flesh, muscle, and bone. The eyeballs had been left in their sockets, open and glaring out into the dark from their vantage point. On the trunk of the tree to her and Sean's right, three faces hung, the skin nailed into the bark. The green and gray-brown stalk peeked through the holes where the eyes and mouths should've been, as if the faces were nothing but masks. A message was written in black blood below the masks. "MURDERERS!"

The memory came to her with swift and repulsive force, she and Sean dragging the corpses of the fallen Cavaliers through the snow; lining the bodies up between the tents one by one, even the woman that Anna thought to be Katherine, whose hair, flesh, and clothing had burned away in the fire, even the boy and the girl; demolishing the Cavaliers' supplies and tents; and carving the word on one of the trees, all of it by the command of Darius: "TERRORISTS!" And through her recollection, Anna questioned which side had written the first message and initiated the tradition, Marathon or the terrorists they battled.

Leaving the faceless soldiers hanging, Anna and Sean marched through the snowy woods, over the rolling hills of the Aegean Valley, rifles raised to the ready, communication regulated to noiseless hand gestures and signals. Though she commanded their team, Anna was not the one guiding them towards their objective. That role fell to Sean, who took point and led her north. They stayed parallel to the Highway and the Aegean Mountains, her partner's mannerisms tense and focused like they'd been when he was taking her to the Serenity Hills, as if he feared the slightest turn in the wrong direction would be reported to Commander Darius and deprive him of his immigrated citizenship. Anna might've tried to reassure him, had their surroundings been less dangerous and had she herself not worried that a minor mishap from Sean was all it would take for the Commander to replace him.

By the gray of daybreak, they were negotiating a series of open empty fields and distorted tree lines that lay on the eastern flank of the former city of Troy, sidestepping the city without taking the risk of walking within sight of it. The remainder of that first day in the Aegean Valley they spent moving north towards Dresden, through gray woods, fields, and hills that didn't vary much from what they'd trekked so far. It was as if they weren't making any progress at all but were instead caught in some outlandish wheel that had them going around and around, dooming them to march through the same forsaken and decomposing landscape again and again. The only spectators to their journey were the high walls of rock and snow of the Aegean Mountains to the east and the Troy Mountains to the west. Not once did they make contact with any hostile forces, nor any other people for that matter. For a few hours, it seemed apparent to Anna that terrorists and civilians alike had disappeared from the valley, but then she started to take note of lasting signs of human activity. Boot tracks less than a day old, sometimes one pair, sometimes many, heading east for the Aegean Mountains or west for the Troy Mountains, but never south to Troy and Marathon's claim on the valley, and never north to Athens and Sword of God's newly obtained territory.

They found trees riddled with human-made holes, branches ripped from their trunks by the exchange of rounds.

At 2000 hours they were outside the former town of Dresden, halfway to Athens and hopefully halfway to their targets. Heeding Darius's orders, they detoured around the town's eastern border as they had with Troy, intent on passing Dresden without a single look at the ruins of the Previous Civilization. Though nighttime's return had given them cover, it'd been accompanied by brutal gusts of wind from the northwest that decreased the temperature to below what their clothing could handle. Thus, the pair sought shelter from the squall where they could rest for several hours and then move out again before dawn. They came across a vehicle, made by the Previous Civilization, buried up to its roof in snow at the center of a small field, just off the Highway. Not even the front and rear windshields were viewable, only by accidentally stepping on the vehicle's roof did they realize what was there below ground.

Prying open the glass top window, they dropped down into the artificial snow cave. Inside the vehicle, the outside odor of scum lessened, yet the graininess appeared to be concentrated in the interior air, leaving layers of clay and dirt on every inch of the vehicle's cabin, and frozen particles that pecked at their eyes. Flakes of snow descended with them through the top window, but not an unbearable amount. The overhead window was sealed behind them, preventing the night's wind from pursing them.

Anna volunteered to take the first watch. Divided into two sections, the vehicle's cabin provided a tight though comfortable setting. She sat upfront in the passenger seat, T-05 Sniper in her lap and her head directed at the rooftop window. In the back of the cabin, at most two feet away from Anna, Sean lay on the vehicle's conjoined backseat, his pack on the floor behind the driver's seat, his rifle snuggled up with him as if it were a romantic partner. As for Anna, there was little to do except sit and make routine scans of the overhead window, a task that became monotonous within the first ten minutes.

"Stars are out tonight." Sean's voice came from close behind her, awake and humorous. Anna turned around in her seat, startled, thinking he'd fallen asleep. Her partner sat up in the space between the two front seats, resting his side against the back of the driver's seat, his rifle loose in his arms as he looked to the front of the vehicle. Behind the white clouds that flowed from his mouth, the barely healed cuts and bruises, and the webbing scars, his expression was sarcastic, unusual.

"What was that?" Anna asked with confusion, exhaling. White frosted air tingled against her own marks from the pentagon game, which thanks to the Second-Gens superior curative capabilities were well ahead of Sean's in their recovery process, as if her wounds had been healing for three days instead of one.

Sean pointed at something past her head. "On the mirror."

She glanced around to the rearview mirror. Dangling from the mirror on slim chains were two pendants. The necklace hanging to the left looked something like a couple of triangles, one overtop of the other, the front triangle upside down, the back triangle right side up. Together, the triangles made a six-pointed star. The second pendant on the right was a crescent moon with a single star held within its curve. Neither design was familiar. Anna had seen, but not understood them when she first entered the vehicle. "What're those supposed to be?" she said without immediate interest.

"That big star is called the Star of David. The other one is the Star and Crescent. I think they're significant with some old religions, Previous Civilization stuff."

Turning back to Sean, she asked him, "Why'd you say the stars are out?"

The sarcasm bolted from her partner's face. He spoke with quiet importance, as if he'd been hoping she would ask. "I haven't been able to see real stars since I came to Marathon, not with all those clouds floating up there. I don't know, I just thought I'd pretend with those pendants for a second. I'll admit it wasn't my best joke."

He began to withdraw, pulling back from his place between the seats to lie down again, as if he didn't expect her to say anything more. But there was something Sean said that stayed with Anna, demanded an inquiry, as if she'd wanted to ask a Carthage-native this question from the moment Sean and his party arrived in Marathon last year. "You could see stars before you came to Marathon?"

Her query took him in the same way many of her questions seemed to, with unanimous amazement and confusion, as if she were the only person he knew who ever asked him anything about anything. "Uh, yeah," he said, still seeking out a full reply as he rose back up to his spot between the front seats.

Anna jumped at her next questions, aware but not caring that her curiosity had become obvious. "How many? What'd they look like?"

"Dozens or, I don't know, probably more than that." Sean reacted to her questions as if he was under interrogation, carefully selecting his answers, never appearing sure if they were the correct ones. "And there's not a whole lot to see with the naked eye, little dots of yellow mostly. Sometimes they blink."

She felt a smile form and stretch to the corners of her face with playful disbelief and excitement, like the kind she used to feel when her mother told her that school had been cancelled for the day because the drug gangs were having a shootout outside her Community Office or there had been an outbreak of typhus or influenza. "No fucking way. You could see that many from the surface?"

A flicker of amusement reflected in Sean's expression, joining his visible puzzlement. "Not every night. Down south we weren't under this overcast, but there's still a ton of flak in the atmosphere from the Reform, so what we had was always pretty spotty. But on nights it was clear, yeah I could see that many."

Though her smile held, Anna was stunned. "You didn't need any special optics or anything?"

Shaking his head, Sean said, "No, not really. Well." He paused, as if hesitant to tell her what he was thinking.

Anna leaned in, wrapping herself around the side of her seat, close enough that they exhaled puffs of cold white air in each other's faces. "Well what?" she heard herself say, eager.

With a sudden chuckle, there was a full-grade joyous grin on Sean's face, bigger than hers. Whatever he was thinking about, the thought delighted him. "I liked to go stargazing."

"Stargazing?" Anna asked with a laugh of her own.

Her question was genuine and unforced, yet it procured the same shocked, almost offended, look from Sean. "You never...you don't know what stargazing is?"

"No," she said with a shake of her head, beckoning him to continue.

Sean let his enjoyment return as he explained. "Stargazing is where you use a telescope. And it wasn't only stars. You could look at the moon, other planets, and shooting stars if it was the right night for it."

Anna listened as if she was sitting at a briefing in the Command Building, taking in every word. "This was something your, uh, city did?"

Her partner glanced away for a second and laughed. "Yeah, it was pretty common." His smile grew somehow. "When I was a kid, we used to hike up to this field north of the city. Me, my dad, and my brother, Derek."

That's who Derek is.

"We'd wait till it got dark and set up a telescope, sit on a blanket and take turns looking at whatever we pointed the scope at. Derek and my dad liked looking at the moon. Some nights you could see these craters on the surface of it."

She tried to picture the scene he was describing, but couldn't. "You'd sit outside the city walls, in the dark?"

"Yep." Sean appeared surprised she was still asking questions.

"And your city government, they let you do this?"

"Yep." He rolled his eyes.

"What about the weather? Weren't you worried about freezing to death?"

"No, we always did stargazing in the summer."

"Yeah, but weren't the temperatures still life-threatening at night?"

"Nope, the weather was temperate enough."

"What about gangs and bandits? Didn't you have to worry about them?"

Sean shook his head. "No, the Scouts kept the area reasonably safe."

"What's a shooting star?"

"It's what you'd see during a meteor shower. When a meteoroid enters the atmosphere, the light of it burns up and shoots across the sky like a moving star. We only got to see them if we were lucky, they were a rare catch."

Anna's eyes widened with astonishment, the idea of witnessing a meteor as it entered the planet's atmosphere too fantastic to totally consider. Her wonder convinced her to continue enquiring, even as she sensed Sean was becoming weary of her numerous questions. "What'd you like about stargazing?"

"What?" he asked, submitting to her latest question.

"You said your brother and dad liked looking at the moon when you went stargazing. What'd you like looking at?"

"It wasn't really what I could see. I liked thinking about how old the light of the stars was."

"What do you mean?"

"The light from all those stars, it's been traveling millions of years across the universe to get here, long before any of us. And that light will still be moving through space, even when there's no one left to look up." She saw Sean's focus shift to the top window. "They're still there. We can't see them now, but the stars are up there, while we're down here, doing this." Anna took notice of a hissing noise above them, which she recognized to be the wind brushing across the overhead window. "So in the end, what does it really matter?" Though she didn't understand much of what her partner was saying, she nodded. Sean beat her to the next question. "Have you never seen any stars?"

An abrupt and frightened disinterest overwhelmed Anna's investment in their conversation. Her smile retreated at the sound of Sean's question and she sat back in her seat, beginning to turn away from him. "No." Facing the front dashboard, as if not wanting to see how Sean reacted to this part, she said, "But even if I did, it was always too cold and too dangerous to go out stargazing." She hoped the discussion would collapse there.

"Oh," he mumbled. His shock was more of horror than confusion.

Bitterness grew in her tone. "You need to get some shut-eye, while you can. We've..."

Sean interrupted her, as if he was desperate to keep the talk going. "You know, I've never been to Missio and Ignis. Fuck, I hadn't been to the south end of Marathon until yesterday. What's it like in those districts?"

She knew he was just trying to revive her enthusiasm, making an attempt to keep her talking by showing that each of them had not experienced everything the other person had, but her enjoyment had drained for the night. Swinging back around to her partner with an angered expression and a forceful tone, she said, "We've got a lot more walking to do tomorrow and I can't have you slipping up, so take your sleep while you can get it."

The gentler demeanor that had complemented Sean's tone evaporated and the neutral face he wore as an agent of the Black Dragoons returned. "You got it."

Anna resumed her night guard position, listening as Sean lay down again in the backseat and faced away from her. When she was confident he was asleep, she tilted her head up at the overtop window, hoping somehow there would be something, anything, to see. But there was nothing, except the glass and the howl of the breeze on the black air. No moon and absolutely no stars. She let her gaze freeze itself to the night sky, let the envy and the yearning flare under her skin, until the agony was all that was required to keep her awake and warm. *I'll never see a star in my lifetime.* A tear dropped from her eye, glided down her icy cheek to her jacket. *And neither will Chloe.* A second tear began its descent, but she brushed it away.

6: SEAN

"Sean, get the fuck up. How many times do I have to tell you?"

The scarred half of his face sweltered as Sean forced his eyelids apart. He raised his head to the vehicle's ceiling to find Anna standing between the driver and passenger seats, lifting her head through the windowless space at the top of the vehicle. Her rifle was firm in her hands, her pack already strapped. "What is it?" he whispered to her, white fog filling the cabin.

"Listen," was all she needed to tell him. Sean heard it seconds later, the distant yet thundering booms he associated with automatic weapons.

In moments Sean was up, putting on his pack, trailing Anna through the roof of the vehicle and out onto the snow-covered field. "What do we got?"

The reports were constant. He suspected there were multiple sources to the bangs. Anna had dropped to one knee, her T-05 Sniper staring out at the blackened tree line on the western side of the field, her fatigue obvious yet ignored. "Heavy small arms fire across the Highway, semi and full auto both. It started less than a minute ago."

"Dresden?" he asked in reply, positioning himself as she was, rubbing his scars with his hand to relieve the burning. The thunder ceased as Sean peered through the night vision scope of his weapon, leaving an elevated grayish-green field and tree line that were washed in silence, no cries of wounds or terrified defeat, and no final pops to cap off a battle that had come and gone in fifty seconds max. "You think Sword of God followed Holloway's people to Dresden?"

Anna nodded, seeming to decide they would stick around to investigate. "I swept the field, it's clear. You ready?" He nodded back at her, and they set out into the field.

The snow grew thicker as they climbed the field towards the trees and the Highway. Their advance on Dresden was a slow one; every step joined with a scan of the ground ahead of them and the field at all other flanks, their T-05 Snipers shifting from zone to zone. The only sounds were the clink of their rifles and the crack of their boots in the snow. As they arrived at the tree line, Sean detected a slight change in the field's illumination. Glancing around to the east, he saw dawn's initial flecks of gray just starting to emerge from behind the Aegean Mountains. In the sky above the valley, the sweeping grayish-black of the night was being pushed to the west, the streak of marginally brighter gray making its entrance onto the landscape. "It's almost dawn," he told Anna.

She didn't look back at him, didn't show her expression. "We'll have to be careful about crossing the Highway, then."

He entered the trees as she did, his night vision scope searching through the skeletal thickets. The forest was thin with decay; many of the trees were already dead across the floor. "You let me sleep the whole night? You were supposed to wake me for my half of the watch."

"One of us isn't a Second-Gen," she snapped back, as if to warn him to not even start with her. So he didn't.

The brief wooded incline opened on the Highway's eastern guardrail, a line of metal bar broken and debilitated from forty years without repair, which parted the roadway and the trees. They crouched for cover at the railing and observed the road from south to north, as well as the tree line on the western edge. Divided into two lanes by a central median, both sides of the Highway were clear of people and vehicles to the south. To the north the Highway was equally barren, its grounds devoid of tracks or footprints. When a thermal scan indicated the same, they pulled themselves over the guardrail and trotted across. Anna raised a finger to her right ear and tapped twice at her earpiece.

"Central this is Vanguard One, how copy?" she whispered. The woods on the western side of the Highway had been similarly corroded by the conditions of the environment, but extended for a good hundred yards at a gradual downward slant. Thirty seconds of traversing the timbered hill passed before Anna spoke again, her finger holding to her earpiece. "We're just outside Dresden; there's been significant weapons fire from the direction of the town. Want to confirm, are there any other Marathon units currently operating in the vicinity of Dresden?" They reached the end of the trees, and shielded themselves behind the tree line as Anna heard back from the Network. "Copy that, I'm requesting Aurora surveillance of Dresden."

Kneeling, Sean commenced his own recon of the Previous Civilization town that lay below them. Through his night vision scope, he glassed the snow-laden treeless lands that pushed out for a quarter mile in the form of greenish-gray fields and small rolling greenish-gray hills. Dresden, or more accurately the minimal details of human society that had somehow subsisted, began where this expanse of greenish-gray nihility finished.

"We're the northernmost Marathon force, and the only one operating north of Troy," Anna muttered to him as she crouched at a tree to make her observations of the town. "Whoever was shooting down there, it wasn't us."

Sean nodded at the new information. "Copy." *The northernmost agents of Marathon, the farthest away from help.*

The town was bordered by the Trojan River. The river poured into the valley just west of Athens, flowed down the valley to the west of the Highway, past Dresden. Except the Trojan River didn't just pass Dresden anymore, now it inundated the former community. No one knew for sure if Dresden had taken a direct hit on the day of the Reform and the subsequent detonation had blown away the riverbanks, or if the water had overwhelmed the unattended floodwalls and never been drained from the town's streets, but in either case Dresden's memory was sunk beneath an icy greenish-gray plain of frozen water. The entire river, or at least the section that flooded through Dresden within sight of his optics, was iced over at the surface. An assortment of sporadic rooftops sticking out of the ice on the community's eastern edge indicated the municipality's submerged location. The only other marker of the town didn't even belong to the community itself, yet it was by far the most striking.

"Ship," Sean had learned the word as a child in Carthage's school system, from the stories of the Previous Civilization. A gigantic vehicle made to drive on large bodies of water by floating at the surface and using a device called a propeller for forward motion, ships had allegedly been a popular method of travel in the time before the Reform. And in the intermediate years of the Reform and the 31st Year of Marathon, one of these ships had become lodged in Dresden. The ship hung over the town with its front, or what Sean deduced to be the front, facing downriver. Standing at the back was a T-shaped tower-like structure, likely some sort of command post for the craft. The water vehicle was listing to the east, one side enveloped by the river, its exterior deck slanted towards Sean and Anna like an icy artificial hill, its tower tipping with the deck, and the other side forever hanging in midair. If the Athenian refugees had actually taken shelter on this ship, then their living conditions would be unceasingly lopsided.

"Fuck me," Anna mumbled with soft amazement. "I heard about that thing back in Terra, but it's different seeing it for yourself."

Sean nodded with agreement. "There used to be thousands of them, or so I've been told."

"Where'd they find the time to build that many?" Sean turned and saw her focus on something with her night vision scope. "Look there," she said with immense interest. "Side of the ship's tower."

He did as instructed and glassed what she discovered, huge letters painted towards the top of the tower that spelled out the ship's name. "DRESDEN."

"So the ship's named after the town?" Anna inquired with confusion.

"No," he told her. "Nobody knows where the ship came from. But as it turns out, nobody knows what this town used to be called either. So when the Dresden floated into the town, people just took to calling the whole place Dresden." Glancing at his partner, he offered up some consideration. "I can see how that might be confusing."

"Fucking ye." Sean couldn't keep from chuckling at Anna's puzzlement, as she pressed her earpiece twice. "Roger that, Central," she said with noticeable frustration and disappointment filling her expression. "Be advised, we're going to investigate closer. I'll report back when we've cleared the area." Wincing and lowering her finger from her ear, she told him, "No Auroras are up and ready for a sweep. We're on our own."

He shook his head, but didn't voice his disproval of moving on such an exposed target without air support. "Right, so what do you think then?"

Anna took a second to consider their situation. "If Holloway's people were taking refuge here, the only place would be on that ship."

"So we're tunnel rats now?"

"That's affirm," she responded, half-sarcastic.

"Rules of engagement?"

His partner answered with a swift decision. "All armed persons in Dresden are hostile. Anyone who's unarmed will be given a chance to surrender." She turned to him. "Understood?"

Is that the Commander's order, or yours? Sean grinned, supportive. "Got it."

They moved forward from the tree line, trudging straight into the wind. By the time they'd crossed over the fields and hills, and descended on the Trojan River, the gale was generating mists of gray that glided across the river's ice from west to east. Stepping from the snow onto the ice, the ground stiffened and yet somehow became uneven at the same time. It was as if the current beneath the ice was nudging them downriver. The ice possessed a harsh sulfuric smell, as though the Trojan River had been flooded with acid instead of water. Every step was met with an unsettling crack, and a white breath of anxiety, built on the fear that the ceiling would give way at any moment. Worse still was their present target, the mammoth ancient craft that appeared to grow in size with every meter of gray ice they passed. The ship hadn't moved an inch, yet it evolved into a daunting structure, enshrouded in the ghostlike presence of the gray snow clouds.

They took up a new surveillance position out over the river, this one atop the decaying roof of an otherwise sunken building. Constructed with angled sides facing east to west, the rooftop was twenty-meters downstream from a roof of duplicate design. After scaling the steep albeit brief slope, they lay flat on the eastern section of the roof, set their T-05 Snipers on the edifice's rotting snowy plaster, and converted their scopes to thermal, having no use for night vision in the gray though illuminating light of the morning.

"I've got nothing but purple on the lower decks," Sean reported as he stared through his scope at the tipped main body of the ship, which lacked any speck of orange life.

"Same, but our optics aren't as strong as the Auroras," Anna retorted, glued to her own lens. "With that much steel in the way, we can't be certain."

He shifted his weapon up, centering his vision on the ship's tower. A single dot of orange emerged in the window frames along the side of the tower. "Hold on," he whispered, as if speaking to himself instead of Anna. He switched the knob at the top of his scope from thermal to standard optics. In the crosshairs of his scope appeared the glassless windows, bent towards the ice due to the tilting ship. Located at the second window from the left was a human figure, a dark blue Marathon uniform with a black wool mask. Instantly Sean recalled the ensemble, for it was identical to those shown to him from the images of the assault on the Troy Station. *There's not much wool clothing left in the world, not since the last of those animals, sheep, died out. If a piece of clothing is not synthetic then there are not many people wearing it.* A scope-less T-05 rifle, customary with Marathon troops, was raised in the individual's arms and pointed out the window at the river. "Sword of God's here," he had time to announce, at once frightened and excited, before witnessing the front of the T-05's barrel come alive with a yellow flash.

The rooftop quaked as the western side of the roof exploded in front of Sean and Anna, raining chunks of plaster, snow, and ice down on them as they leapt from their positions. The bang of the T-05 reverberated over the Trojan River, as they slid down the roof on their sides, feet planting back on the ice. "Fuck," Anna exclaimed with self-frustration. "Why didn't we think they'd have someone on lookout?"

"Maybe we didn't expect them to be so smart," Sean suggested, as he turned his head in the direction of the ship. His voice and body trembled, not from panic but adrenaline. This was hardly the first time he'd been shot at. "Maybe the Cavaliers spoiled us."

"If anything spoiled us, it was those fucking Auroras," Anna retorted, also without fear. "You said it's Sword of God?"

Sean kept his attention on the roof, the ship, and the long stretch of foggy but no less unprotected ice between them. "Yeah."

"How do you figure that?"

"Same stolen Marathon gear, same wool masks they were wearing at the Troy Station." He glanced upriver at the other roof, sixty feet away from them.

"Right. Where's he at?"

A strategy came to Sean as he unscrewed his suppressor from the barrel of his T-05 Sniper, knowing his weapon's accuracy at this range was improved without the extension. He slipped the suppressor into the side pocket of his pack as he told his partner, "Second window from the left. Regular T-05, that close of a shot at this distance, he knows what he's doing."

"Terrific. So Mr. Crackshot, how do you see us handling this?"

"He's got this location zeroed so I can't take a shot from here, unless of course, we had something to distract him with." He twisted around to his partner and noticed it, the glowing blue irises of Anna's Second-Gen Stage. A chill iced over his shoulder blades. He wasn't afraid of her or scared of what she was becoming—-he'd never been—-but he made sure she thought he was. What he felt towards the Second-Gens, what he'd felt from his first time learning about the Second-Gens in Carthage's history and science classes, what he'd felt from the moment he became aware of Anna Corday's true nature, was envy. The advancement of one's physical capabilities past that of any human, to block off illness and infection, and to recover from wounds at an accelerated rate, all abilities Sean yearned for. He wanted to be like Anna. *If I was like her then I wouldn't be here, Marathon wouldn't have me for the rest of my life.* However, this desire to be a member of her species was something he had resolved to prevent her from seeing. Therefore whenever his partner changed to the Second-Gen Stage, he masked his jealousy with the fear she was likely used to receiving from humans. And based on her angered and offended expression, he assumed his ruse had been maintained.

"What do you need me to do?" she asked.

Sean glanced to the nearby roof, then back to her. "Give him something else to shoot at. How fast can you run?"

"Faster than you."

"Good."

They moved to the corner of their roof, the last bit of cover obscured from the sniper's view, Anna taking place in front of him at a hunched standing position, Sean doing the same as he stood behind her. Twenty-meters in front of them, the other roof waited for Anna. He was about to ask her if she was ready when he heard her mumbling something to herself. "Chloe." The manner in which she said it reminded him of her demeanor the previous night, when she clearly thought he was asleep but he wasn't. He was certain he'd seen her crying. What that was about he didn't know, but imagined the bruises on her neck had something to do with it.

"You good?" he asked, wondering who Chloe was.

"What?" she replied, sounding preoccupied.

"Ready?"

"Yeah. Don't miss."

"I'll do my best," he said, trying to reassure Anna, and himself.

For a few seconds, he thought she might be hesitating. She held her place at the edge of the roof, seemingly unwilling to run out into the shooter's field of fire, even as a Second-Gen. But then the breeze intensified as a burst of wind passed over their place on the river, like the waves of current below the ice, and Sean came to understand what Anna was waiting on. With that whistling gust came a haze of gray that encased the roof and surrounding ice, one of several natural smokescreens crossing the river with the squall. It didn't shield any more than the first five feet of Anna's path to the next roof, but it would be enough to surprise the sniper with her sudden appearance on the open ice.

Boots smacking on the ice, rifle rattling, pack bouncing, even with all the Black Dragoons gear weighing her down, Anna sprinted at a miraculous speed, leaving the fog's curtain behind and making for the second roof, no sign of wavering. As she ran and made herself a target, Sean jumped out from the roof's corner as well. But instead of running, he dropped to one knee and elevated his T-05 Sniper into the gray, adjusting the weapon as mist carried on around him. When the cloud was gone, and the frozen river and the lopsided ship were back in their places, Sean curled his index finger, setting the ball of his finger at the trigger of his rifle, so as not to jerk the weapon to the side when he fired. His scope found the line of windows once again. He'd worried Sword of God's lookout would change position to a different window, as snipers were often instructed to do with each shot, but the black-masked sniper was in the exact same window, apparently overconfident in his superior location.

The shooter's T-05 shifted from south to north, the barrel of his rifle swinging to follow Anna, his senses failing to detect the second Dragoon on the ice. Yellow flashed from the weapon and the river vibrated, a puff of ice and snow rocketed up less than a foot behind Anna's stride, sprinkling her with the river's winter floor. The sniper was resetting his rifle to compensate for the recoil and Anna's continued dash along the ice, when he was encircled in the crosshairs of Sean's scope. He took in a large breath of white air, and his finger pulled at the trigger. The flash and boom from the front of the T-05 Sniper launched the rifle back into his shoulder, the rebound flinching through his body as bright red vapor shrouded his scope's sight of the window. Tumbling through the red, out the unbalanced window, and down to the icy ground below the tower, was the headless

corpse of Sword of God's sniper. The rumble from their exchange
rang through the hills beyond the Trojan River, enduring long after
the marksman's body landed on the river's surface.

Sean set the scope's knob back on thermal and made a sweep of
the entire ship, end to end, taking his eye off the hostile vessel when
purple was the only replying color. Sixty feet upriver, Anna had set
herself on the side of the second roof, kneeling and scanning the ship
with her T-05 Sniper as he was. Her hand rose to the side of her
head, and her voice sounded through Sean's earpiece a moment later.
"Dead?" she said, not at all winded by her race with the sniper.

He lifted his index finger to his right ear and tapped his Network
earpiece once, holding it to connect him with her. "Affirmative. No
heat signatures on thermal."

"Copy, my scope's reading the same. There'll be more of them
though."

"What's next?"

"Up and down."

"Roger."

They pushed for the ship, keeping the twenty-meter spread between them that their engagement with Sword of God's shooter created. Whoever fired upon them next would have to manage two targets instead of one. They kept their thermal scopes on the ship, seeking out the tiniest bit of orange. They reconvened where the vessel
angled into the river. Separating the blankets of ice from the partly
submerged top deck of the ship were mounds of iced-over snow, between eight and ten feet tall, extending the full length of the craft.
Anna went up first, launching up the embankment in as little as two
quick steps, undeterred by the equipment she carried or the slipperi-
ness of the bank. At the top, she made a customary screening of the
ship with her thermal scope, before turning to Sean and lowering her
hand for him to take. He made the same rushing attempt with the
knoll, but what traction his boots were able to find on the smoothed

freezing ground was only enough to get him halfway up the mount. However, as his legs began to give out under the pressure of his rifle and pack, his hand caught Anna's and she yanked him up the rest of the way to the peak of the mound. A nod of thanks and a nod of acknowledgement circulated between them, and they slid down the other side of the embankment, landing on the sloping deck of frozen metal with a conjoined thump.

The angle of the deck was too sheer and slick for either of them, even a Second-Gen like Anna, to climb without any kind of support. To compensate, Anna pulled herself up a railing at the base of the tower. One hand over the other, her rifle slung over her shoulder, her Second-Gen Stage mixing with her own upper body strength, she carried herself three-quarters of the way to the top side of the tower in less than two minutes. Watching from the bottom of the deck, away from the tower to avoid putting her in his line of fire, Sean alternated his thermal scope between lower sweeps of the ship's deck and higher checks of the tower. He was making a scan of the tower's windows when Anna shouted down to him, "Movement up top!"

Sean raised the unsuppressed barrel of his T-05 Sniper to the top side of the tower, just as an orange human silhouette materialized around the corner of the tower, a purple T-05 fastened to his arms. The second shooter's weapon was gravitating towards Anna's defenseless spot on the railing, but Sean's index finger tugged at the trigger of his own rifle before the man could engage Anna. The bang and echo of his first shot passed with minimal recognition from Sean, and he pulled the trigger twice more, keeping his rifle elevated until the orange figure buckled and collapsed, falling head first off the tower. Three cracks of thunder crashed into the surrounding hillsides, as Sean dropped his thermal scope from his eyes and got a real look at the second person he'd killed that day.

This one was dressed in the unofficial uniform of Sword of God, looted Marathon combat clothing and a rare wool mask, the same attire that'd been worn by the tower's sniper. The shooter rode the deck down, sliding on his face and stomach, barely missing Anna and leaving a trail of dark red liquid to stain the floor. The corpse careened into the mounds of snow that overtook the deck, colliding to a stop with a crunching sound. The body's T-05 followed a second later, skidding and settling in the snow beside its owner. After twice skimming the deck and tower for further hostiles, Sean moved on the stiff, readying his weapon in the event the man somehow clung to life and was about to make a try for his rifle or dig into his body armor for a sidearm or grenade. But upon reaching the body and turning it onto its back, Sean assessed the shooter was well beyond rescue.

"Check his forehead for a cross," Anna ordered from above. She stood on the top side of the tower, where the attacker had attempted to fire on them, surveying the ship with her unslung T-05 Sniper. Sean squatted down next to the corpse, grabbing and putting the safety on the man's T-05 before tossing it behind him. A bright red hole ripped through the mask, just below the opening for the left eye, and soaked the black wool. Upon removing the mask he found the man's face in worse condition than the covering.

The round had buried itself in the left side of the attacker's face, beneath the left eye, and devastated the exterior facial structure. The skin that wasn't obscured by red crumpled inwards, toward the hole that swallowed half of the man's eye socket and eyeball and half of his nose. What this person had looked like before he'd been shot, Sean couldn't tell. Viewing the results of his shooting up close created noticeable discomfort for him, like a nudge in the back of his mind and in his chest that hadn't been there before. It was the same jolt he felt when walking past the two guards he'd slain outside the Cavaliers' base camp. However, this uneasiness was minor compared to his memory of the Cavaliers' children. So he pressed on. Visible on the man's forehead, above and between his eyebrows, was a light blue cross. The Christian symbol had been painted to his skin, just as Holloway claimed. Two of Sword of God's thirteen had been terminated, their names and rank within their organization presently unknown.

"He has a cross," Sean shouted up to Anna, standing, leaving the terrorist where he lay, his defacement exposed to the world.

"Copy that," Anna responded, excitement distinguishable in her voice. "There's an access hatch up here we can use."

"On the way."

His ascent of the tower took twice as long as Anna's. When he'd pulled himself up to and was standing on the top side of the askew tower, he saw the entryway Anna found. What had been a doorway was now a rectangle-shaped hole in the tower that one had to climb through in order to enter the tower. The door hung to the side, likely opened by Sword of God during their pre-dawn assault on Dresden. They crept up to the hatch, Anna taking the lead, their rifle barrels centered on the entranceway. The morning's gray light was deflected by the hull, leaving a darkened space between the sides of the door. Anna circled around the hatch, pointing her weapon at the doorway as she positioned herself on the door. Sean changed his scope to night vision, setting himself on the front side of the hatch. His partner converted her scope to night vision as well and together they made a sweep of the vessel's insides.

The night vision scope's shadowed green revealed a tiny room that felt more like an anteroom than the actual internal decks of the craft. The floor had become an uneven wall, the wall a slanted floor. The first casualties from Sword of God's ambush of the Athenian refugees lay on this tilting floor. A man and a woman, both their chests stitched with black bullet holes, a pool of black liquid encasing them and the floor. Their eyelids were locked open, their expressions eternally surprised and terrified.

"Poor fuckers," Anna mumbled, with some genuine sympathy. She stepped off the door and dropped down into the room, her boots landing behind the refugees' heads and splashing in the black. Duck-

ing down to fit under the room's low ceiling, she swung her rifle side
to side. With a thumbs-up, she gestured to Sean that the room was
clear.

Loosening his gaze from his night vision scope, Sean jumped
through the hatch, boots stamping in the dark red next to Anna.
Bringing his scope back to eye level, he scanned the room and found
it was indeed a sort of anteroom rather than a main deck of the ship,
a dividing space between two stairwells. The staircase to the left led
up the tower, while the stairs to the right went down to the vessel's internal decks. Both stairways were narrow, of equal width to the room.
However, the stairs were on the wall, and what were once stairwells
had morphed into upward and downward sloping tunnels, caves in
an artificial hillside.

Knowing from their thermals the tower was empty of activity,
they turned and aimed their weapons down the descending tunnel. A
third Athenian refugee lay a quarter of the way down the shaft, pep-
pered with rifle fire as the first two refugees were, except in the back
instead of the chest. A stream, colored black in Sean's night vision,
flowed down the tunnel from the first two Athenian corpses, grew
in volume at the third body, continued to the end of the tunnel, and
rounded the corner, pouring down the uneven deck just outside the
tunnel.

"Fuck," Anna whispered, anxious.

"I told you," Sean retorted, "We're tunnel rats."

A voice that belonged to neither of them shouted up from the
skewed lower deck, originating from around the corner of the tunnel's exit. "Who's there?" The voice was male, too young to be an
adult and yet too old to be a child.

They focused on the corner. "Who wants to know?" Anna called
back. Her tone reminded Sean of her performance during Jason's interrogation in the Serenity Station, a casual almost sociable manner
meant to confuse those subjected to it.

"Fuck you, I asked first," the voice snapped, with the snarky attitude of someone in their late teens.

"Anna." She added a feeling of naiveté to her conduct. "What's yours?"

Ignoring Anna's question, he asked, "Where're James and John?"

"You mean the guys that attacked us? Well seeing as it's me talking and not them, I think you can figure out where they are."

They heard the teenager talking again, but not to them. He was speaking to someone else, away from the tunnel, but his voice had bounced back and echoed up the shaft. "Andrew, she says she killed them. What the fuck do we do?" He sounded worried now, not so much that he feared he and his associate were doomed, but that their situation had become more complicated.

He's wondering how they're going to explain to Jesus that they lost two of his Disciples.

"We just came to Dresden looking for supplies," Anna fibbed. "We didn't mean to get caught up in your drama or anything. How about you point us in the direction of some food and medicine and we'll be on our way. We'll forget you ever took a shot at us."

The teenager was incensed now. "Fucking shit, everybody knows Dresden's been cleaned out for over a decade."

"Really? My party's new to this valley; we just came down from the north a couple weeks ago."

"You're not as good a liar as you think you are, Anna," the teen said. Sean found himself agreeing with the teen, he didn't understand why Anna was still keeping to her story. "Jesus keeps tabs on everyone coming down from the north. That crossing is his territory. If you'd passed through there we would've already met."

"Look why don't we just talk this over?" Anna replied. "Sort out what happened up top. I don't have much use in killing again and I'm guessing you don't want to lose any more of your people. Diplomacy's still a thing out here, isn't it?"

"Listen here," the teen said. "I don't know what you think you're pulling off." A figure Sean suspected to be the teenager appeared around the corner. Same wardrobe, same weapon, the eyeholes of his mask covered with the same night vision goggles employed by Marathon troops, like two black tubed extensions of his eyeballs. He seemed to be going for a quick peek at the visitors rather than trying to engage them. "But if you've got any sense you'll."

The suppressor on the barrel of Anna's T-05 Sniper hissed twice, the rifle lurching as two shell casings clanged against the wall and floor. The teenager got quiet and fell onto the slanted deck, body, goggles, and T-05 dinging against the floor, black mist filling the air and expelling from his mask and skull. He rolled out of sight, not by will but by the command of gravity, adding to the tunnel's black stream.

"Shit, Peter," an older man yelled. Sean assumed this man was Andrew, the other person Peter had been talking to, his brother. Boots stomped away from the shaft at an accelerated pace, as Peter's corpse and gear rang out against the deck for several seconds, before growing faint and becoming lost in the ship.

"All right, good talk," Anna said, and began a crouched walk down the tunnel, Sean at her heels.

Amidst the splash of their boots in the tunnel's creek, Sean said, "I wonder why he wasn't waiting in the tunnel when we came through the hatch. He would've had the drop on us." They stepped around the Athenian's body.

"Guess they aren't all smarter than we expected."

"Social variation."

"What?"

"Don't ask."

"Then don't say anything." They reached the end of the tunnel and stacked up at the corner, along the wall. "If it's something you know I won't understand then don't mention it, so I don't have to ask so many questions."

"They teach social variation in college if that helps."

"Fuck you," Anna replied, as she pulled a flash grenade off her belt.

"Yep, that's what I thought."

Anna yanked the pin off the black bottle-shaped grenade and tossed it around the corner, sending it bouncing down the deck with a clank. Sean shut his eyes and put his fingers in his ears. Even with his eyes and ears sealed, a hint of white light penetrated his eyelids and a deplorable drumming plucked his eardrums. Realizing he'd just have to deal with the effects, he returned his hands to his T-05 Sniper and readied the weapon. His partner went first, turning the corner onto the deck with her rifle up. Sean followed.

A startling sensation of unbalance struck Sean, his footing skated out from under him, his side slammed on the floor, he didn't stop but began sliding, fast, rifle and gear skidding with him. Nothing to grab onto except cave-induced blackness, twirling around and shouting in panic, though the ring in his ears subdued his voice, Sean lashed out with his arms in desperation, his fingers failing to grasp anything that might've been there. Down he dropped.

What he landed on was rigid, rough enough that his frame blared in pain and throbbed long after touchdown. Lying on his stomach, the surface grew in smoothness, as if a softer foundation lay beneath a stiffer top coat. Damp cold snaked through his clothes and an acidic odor raced into his nostrils, allowing him to gather that he was resting on a floor of iced over snow.

The buzzing hushed in his ears as a noise rose to his right, the slush and crack of people struggling to stand on the snow flooring, not one person but two. *Anna and Andrew.*

Alarmed, Sean forced his hands through the black into the snow, and tried to push off with gloves and boots, only for his feet to catch on a spot of ice and slide out from under him. Back on his chest, his rifle burrowing into his ribcage, he heard a call from his right, less than a foot away, he guessed. "Flash?" It was Anna he knew for sure, thanks to her use of a military challenge and the blue shimmer of her irises in the dark.

"Thunder," he answered.

There was a short yet sharp click, followed by the scuffle of what sounded like one body driving itself on top of the other. "Christ," Andrew bellowed, angry rather than scared, his breath obstructed, as if something were pressing on his chest.

Sean's hands tracked the strap of his T-05 Sniper to the rifle, retrieving it out of the darkness and feeling for the night vision scope. A mound of greenish-gray appeared in his sole source of vision, bounded by the slanted walls and ceiling of the deck. An agonized gurgling pulled his attention to the right, where he discovered Andrew, immobilized on his back, his rifle and night vision goggles behind his head, out of reach. Anna was above him, her knee planted in his stomach, her left hand gripping his right hand, twisting his wrist well past the breaking point. In her right hand her switchblade hung, drenched in black. Below the blade was Andrew's neck, sliced open and discharging black into the snow and across his captured Marathon uniform. Black spurted from the mouth-hole of his wool mask, his eyes twitched, as if he believed blinking would help him escape. Anna had completed the act in silence, without as much as a grunt of exertion. The darkened green manifestation on the face of his partner was indifferent, well acquainted with the actions her service in the Black Dragoons demanded, and yet somehow dispirited, as if she wished to be someplace else.

When Anna had finished with Andrew and they found the greenish-blue cross painted to his forehead, they searched the remainder of the deck's snow-filled bottom with their night vision scopes. There was the body of Peter, a cross under his mask as well.

Also joining them in this pit, two more departed refugees from Athens, encircled by blotches of black snow. After clearing the bottom of the hole, they raised their weapons up in the direction they'd fallen. The deck was a hallway. Halfway up the hall was a junction to another hallway, which moved towards the ship's front. Sean assessed that after Peter was shot, Andrew tried to reposition himself at the intersection of the two hallways, so when they came out of the tunnel and slipped on the uneven floor, he could shoot them both mid-fall. But, Anna's flash grenade tripped him up and sent him down into the pit with them.

Railings ascended both walls of the hallway, the same type used on the stairs and the top deck. Sean understood now these railings had been installed throughout the ship for the Previous Civilization's passengers to clutch when the vessel rocked back and forth in poor weather. Four decades later, the rails continued to have a purpose, just as Dresden did.

Anna climbed first, while Sean covered her from below in the event a fifth Sword of God soldier arrived. Sean doubted it though. The quiet throughout the ship had become chronic and it made sense to him that Jesus Christ would only send four of his Disciples from his newly obtained town in pursuit of the refugees, instead of a larger part of his main force. Anna reached the juncture and swept it without anyone popping out to meet her. She covered him as he mounted the railing, again taking twice as long as she did. There was something about climbing in the pitch black that drew out the time he spent on the rail, turning ten minutes into half an hour, worsening the environment of the false cavern around him. The temperature was only somewhat improved by the absence of the outside airstream, and the air decayed so acutely by rust Sean wondered how spending more than a week in this place had not incapacitated all of Athens's migrants with illness. *Maybe the Serenity Station wasn't so bad after all.*

Scaling the hallway corner, Sean regrouped with Anna on the floor of the frontward moving hallway. A hatch straight ahead of them was open, its door dangling inside the entryway. They looked through the trapdoor, finding sights comparable to what they'd seen in Dresden so far, but not precisely the same. The lowest side of the room was waterlogged with greenish-gray snow. The rows of metal circular tables and benches nailed to the floor, plus the cabinets and counters extending from the right wall of the room, indicated this was the ship's chow hall. What Sean presumed to be the kitchen door hung open on the right wall, in front of the cupboards and counter. A refugee from Athens lay on the floor, suspended above the bottom of the room by a table. A man with black emitting from his gut and partially disintegrated skull. Black drizzled down the deck, staining the lower tables and benches.

Four backpacks lay on the floor near the hatch. As Anna rummaged through them for any possible intelligence on Sword of God, Sean jumped down into the chow hall, catching himself on the tables and benches and using them to traverse the room. He vaulted from table-set to table-set over to the kitchen door. Wanting to clear the kitchen, he hopped from the last table in the front row to the top of the counter and cabinet, pulling himself up onto what was now more of a ledge. Stepping through the slanting kitchen doorway, he set his boots on what his night vision scope showed to be the side of an oven. He scanned the kitchen from top to bottom. Twenty feet deep, the galley was loaded with several Previous Civilization appliances. What kitchen supplies hadn't been lifted from the ship were strewn about the room. That didn't catch him off guard, in the vessel's position it wouldn't have made sense if everything was as it was supposed to be. Yet still, there was something out of place in this blackened, ransacked kitchen.

Scraps of clothing, like the winter gear the refugees were outfitted in but torn apart, as if ripped right from a person's body, lay on the floor, too much to have come from one set of clothes, but more likely two or three people. The implication of discovering this in what was essentially the backroom of the Athenians hideout was just peeking out over the horizon of his mind when his scope found the first body. Lying on a floor of black at the bottom of the kitchen was a woman. The overwhelming presence of exposed skin told him she was naked, and had been murdered that way. Then his eye made the distinction between the woman and the other two corpses in the room with her, both of which were too small to be adults, or even teenagers.

He threw his head away from his scope, driving in multiple deep breaths as his chest caught fire. Every ounce of his being begged him to vomit, to have some sort of physical reaction to demonstrate his disgust. And he would've, had he not seen plenty of this already, one year earlier on the day Marathon's soldiers overran the walls of Carthage. He thought to tell his partner what he'd seen, but it was his memory of Anna's refusal to kill the Cavaliers' children that convinced him she could never know what was in here. "It's clear," he reported. Climbing out of the kitchen and back atop the cabinets and counter, he shut the hatch. When it was sealed, he flipped his rifle over and pounded the doorknob off with the butt of his weapon, and then tossed the knob to the bottom of the chow hall, hoping it was buried by the snow.

7: ANNA

Their exit from Dresden was a hastened one. When nothing of importance came from the Sword of God fighters' possessions, Anna suggested they be on their way. Their detour to Dresden had set them back a good amount and there was no time to write Marathon's message to those who would later discover the bodies. Her partner, having finished clearing the ship's kitchen, was eager to get going. Something had changed in his demeanor. The controlled manner of a Dragoon had been erased. Filling the void was a distressed yet unrevealing expression and speech, as if he wanted her to know something was wrong but wouldn't admit it.

Her alternative state of being withdrew as they turned their backs to Dresden and left the former community in its watery resting place. As they climbed back up the barren hills and fields, away from the frozen river and towards the Highway, Anna brought her index finger to her earpiece and tapped the device twice, holding the second time. "Central this is Vanguard One, checking in."

"Roger that Vanguard One, send traffic."

To her right, Anna's partner twisted his suppressor back onto the barrel of his T-05 Sniper as he walked. "Central be advised, terrorists by the names of James, John, Andrew, and Peter were located in Dresden and removed from Sword of God's rotation. I repeat, James, John, Andrew, and Peter have been eradicated. We are en route to Athens to terminate the remaining nine and should arrive before dawn tomorrow morning."

An impressed Darius answered. "Copy all Vanguard One, good work. I'll have an Aurora available for over watch before you move on the town."

Anna was relieved by the Commander's brief approval, as well as the assurance that air support would be present during their pending assault on Athens. It was as if for some time she'd been stranded at the lowest point of a massive pit, and with this victory she'd begun to lift herself towards the surface, sanctuary not yet in reach but visible. "Roger that Central, Vanguard One out." *Maybe she's starting to forgive me for Serenity. Nine more till we go home, nine more till I can sleep.*

They crossed the Highway a second time and resumed their march north. However, the walk from Dresden to Athens proved itself to be much more challenging than yesterday's trek. The squall that originated from the west the previous night and returned that morning seemed to be waging its own personal war against the region, dumping gust after gust of frozen soot on the landscape, and on top of them. It was as if the wind that sailed over the Troy Mountains were the commencing ceremony for a much more potent winter storm, barreling through the outside lands towards the Aegean Valley. Only the marginal warmth of the day's gray light stopped the temperature from falling below what their winter gear could defend against. As for the numbness in their faces and extremities, some things they had no choice but to suffer through.

Before long though, an enemy of greater formidability than Sword of God and the elements combined showed itself, one that as a Second-Gen Anna had not expected to be so impeded by. Both she and Sean had managed a meal of precooked tofu blocks and water, yesterday before nightfall, but that hadn't been enough to stop hunger and dehydration from taking their toll. Their black minibags of rations and black filtered water bottles were meant to keep them adequately fueled and alert until their mission's conclusion, and nothing more. Even with her evolved endurance guaranteeing she could last twice as long without food and water as any human, the effects were intolerable. The dryness on her tongue and gums and the rock in her gut allied with the airstream in pressing her down. The tiredness from their mission so far, plus their detour on the Dresden, was no friend of Anna's either, but after a while exhaustion became indistinguishable from all the rest, the least among many, many concerns.

Five miles north of Dresden, the terrain at both ends of the Highway collapsed into a series of vertical cliffs, too abrupt to traverse. This left them with the choice of persisting straight along the Highway itself, exposed to whomever they might be sharing the valley with, or diverging around the cliffs by descending east away from the road and further postponing arrival at their objective. Knowing if they were attacked on the Highway there would be no place to retreat to, and with little chance for support from Marathon, Anna reluctantly selected the latter option. Thus, at 1400 hours they had progressed ten miles north of Dresden, still fifteen miles south of Athens with dark and life-threatening cold a mere few hours away.

They were traveling along the Aegean River, close to the water's edge, using an assemblage of trees that lined the river for cover. Slim and gray, their bark breaking apart and disintegrating at the smallest touch, the trees were like the decaying hair fibers of an elderly child of the Previous Civilization whose life was long past its peak and whose death was taking far too long to arrive. The creaking racket the trees made with each wind gust seemed to speak to the travelers who passed them by, pleading with their momentary visitors to listen to their tales of youth and green, back in a time less than half a century old. Yet to Anna, those stories of days lost felt much older, hundreds, a thousand years at least, out of sight, out of grasp, and unrecoverable.

In the brush ahead of Anna and Sean several trees looked to have been decapitated, the top sections of their trunks smacked off in equal manner, as if felled at once by the same striking force. To their west, the trees became a gray field. Lying on the field, parallel to the beheaded limbs, was another relic of the Previous Civilization. Unlike the Highway and Dresden, Anna was unable to identify this artifact. Gray with snow and wrapped in white metal skin, the object was diseased with numerous brown spots of rust. Shaped like a pill capsule, the object's design was odd to say the least, forty feet long yet only five feet or so wide. To the east, the river tiptoed south at a leisure pace, not even a quarter width of the Trojan River. Shrouded in murky gray, its aquatic life vacated from its depths, the channel had been reduced to nothing more than a freezing creek bog. Resting in a field on the other side of the river was a second capsule. Aside from Sean, there was not another living thing in sight.

"I still don't get it," she told him as they trudged under the headless trees. Their boots cracked in the snow, clicked against the rocks stuck beneath the pages of gray. She was bemused, neither able to picture nor grip the concept of what her partner had been describing.

"Which part don't you get?" he asked with a low tone. The sluggishness that tormented her was minute compared to whatever he must've been feeling. At times, he appeared to be struggling to keep speed with her, even as he tried to direct them towards Athens.

A pesky smile arrived on her expression. She hoped her grin would transfer to him. "All of it." And to her pleasure, she and Sean shared a chuckle. A fatigued cough interrupted Sean's laugh, but it was still a laugh. "So those capsules used to float up in space?"

What could've been the day's ten thousandth draft of wind shrieked over the field to the west and crackled into the tree line. "Yep," Sean answered with a nod, shivering as the swaying branches popped against one another overhead.

"Attached to a bunch of other capsules like them?" she said, with a glance to the capsules, scanning the land as she did so.

"Yep," he replied, watching as the squall coerced the river into flowing away from its own western bank and dragged the water in gray micro-sprays towards the eastern bank.

"And together these capsules formed a space station?" The bafflement in her voice was embarrassing, but the flapping sound of the ripples on the water seemed to have more control over his attention.

"Yes, like the Serenity Station or the Troy Station, but in space," he said. A cloud of white appeared in front of his face, only to be instantly seized and forced out over the river by the wind.

She respired, and observed her own mist of white being enslaved by the breeze and driven around her partner's head, out of the trees. "And this space station was called, Anubis?"

"Yeah that's right." He turned from the river and smiled at her, as if proud of her for comprehending this notion of a space station. That, or he was glad to have something to distract him from thirst, hunger, fatigue, and what had troubled him in Dresden.

But she didn't have a sense she was grasping the idea any better. "Wait, so what's a space station again?"

He was silent a good several moments, another blast of air blew over the field, crashed through the trees, and dumped their breaths into the river as he worked out his answer. It was as if the thought of a space station had always been clarified to him and this was the first time he tried to define it for someone else. "It's like, you know the Dresden, how the ship would float and travel on water?"

"Yeah," she said, her side skimming against a tree trunk, the tree cringing in reaction as a haze of grayish-brown bark engulfed the air.

The fog of bark was compelled over and under the water by the all-powerful airstream. "And how people in the Previous Civilization would live and work on the ship?"

A tree root snapped beneath her boot. "Yeah."

Glimpsing the capsule to their left, he said, "Well, now imagine if the Dresden didn't float on water but floated above the planet, in space." His voice shook, as if dwelling on the details of the so-called Anubis Space Station made him anxious.

She was more amazed than confused, a surge of questions overwhelming her ability to vocalize them as she glanced the capsule across the river. "How the fuck does a ship hover in space? No, how the fuck does a ship get to space?"

Her partner snickered, and had to think on this for a few seconds as well. "You know, I'm not really sure how the Anubis worked. I do know it was built up there though."

Realizing that asking her partner to solve one question at a time was the best they could hope for, as this topic was likely well beyond what either of them were taught in school, she said, "Who built it?"

He seemed to light up with energy, as if this part of the conversation interested him enough that it fueled him for the rest of the day's walk. "That's the cool thing about it. The Anubis was a multinational effort. The station was constructed, maintained, and owned by every nation of the Previous Civilization. For fifty years it proved the world could live and learn as one."

A sarcastic smile took to her. "That's the cool thing? Not the fact that this station allowed people to live in outer space, but that?"

Her partner giggled. "Yeah I suppose that's cooler." His laugh stopped as he commented, "Especially considering the whole union fell apart."

"What happened?" she asked without rationalizing if it were best to ask such a question.

His tone grim, he told her, "Well, after the first Second-Gen was discovered and the nations broke their alliances in search of others, the Treaty of Anubis as they called it was basically voided. My parents used to tell me, it was like five decades of progress were tossed out the window overnight. Before long the competing nations were threatening to shoot down any transport that went up to the Anubis from an enemy nation, so eventually the station was just abandoned and left to rot in space. Then there was the Reform."

A new glacial discharge flared between the trees, prickling her face with icy grime and bits of bark. The environment's degeneration became more potent in the air, as the water rippled from the river's western edge. A piercing snap interrupted this noise, and she placed her index finger on her rifle's trigger, the weapon rising in her arms. But as the pop reverberated against the cliffs below the Highway, she lowered her T-05 Sniper and loosened her grip on the trigger, the report converting to the sound of a tree crumbling. "Is that how these two capsules ended up all the way down here?" She too was now without a laugh.

"Yeah as incredible as the Anubis was, it couldn't stay up there on its own without constant upkeep. From what I've heard it was two years after the Reform when that thing finally dropped out of orbit. Most of the station was burned away in the atmosphere, but a good chunk of the parts that weren't came down and slammed into the other side of the mountains over there." They both turned towards the intruding face of the Aegean Mountains. "These two capsules landed here." A fleeting look was given to the capsules on both sides of the river, and to the guillotined trees, the cause of which she now understood. "The rest touched down fuck knows where."

She nodded. "At least now, you and I can see one of the Previous Civilization's greatest achievements. If it was still up there we'd never be able look at it."

"Yeah, but it would've been nice to go up to the Anubis while it was still in space."

"Yeah."

At 1700 hours they were back on the eastern bank of the Highway, eighteen miles north of Dresden and seven miles south of Athens. They walked through a quarter mile long and across field, flat as a table top, gray snow ironed over the ground. The Highway was cloaked in a sparse tree line, the guardrail poking through the brush, stone tips of the Troy Mountains peaking over the gray treetops. Their route to the objective was taking them to another dense forest where the terrain ascended again, continuing the valley's cycle of hills, fields, and woods, and refusing to let them bask in the respite of even ground for more than a few minutes. In the sky above, bands of gray and black were fusing together, like black paint mingling on a gray canvas, the midpoint of the day where dusk and night overlapped before darkness claimed total domain over the atmosphere. On the surface, gray light had begun its evacuation from the surrounding lands, leaving them with, at best, a blurry grayish-black line of sight in all directions. And with every grade of illumination that fled the valley, the temperature followed close behind. Powered by the ongoing windstorm from the west, the frosted and grime rotted air had already delivered to them the shaky beginnings of hypothermia. *We're going to have to shelter overnight again. So much for reaching Athens before dawn.*

"So Carthage had three sports?" she asked him, ducking her head in a feeble effort to avoid the latest breeze, her boots slushing through the thick darkened snow.

"No, we had more than that," he told her, voice trembling against the cold. He dipped his head as she did, his winter cap failing in its defense of his skull, same as her hat. "I just named those three because they were the most popular." His white breath appeared yet didn't shine in the gray air. Instead, the puff made its departing gesture and disappeared into the black.

"Those three weren't enough?" she said with surprise. She fought to visualize the people of Carthage inheriting any more than one solitary sport from the Previous Civilization, not to mention three or more.

Her partner chuckled, as if hoping a laugh would warm him up. "Not even a little bit. We had so many. Everyone just wanted something different I guess." He forced a grin.

"How many did you have?" She smiled back, even as a draft of dirt coated her face, the frozen particles hitting at such a speed they managed to burrow into the last holdouts from her pentagon made cuts, singeing below her skin.

He shook his head. "Fuck if I know." Another laugh came from him, not a shield this time but honest. "We used to have this one sport where players would slide around on a lake when it iced over, like the Trojan River, and try to whack a little ball or something into goals with a bunch of sticks."

She laughed at the absurdity of his description, ignoring the aching pain her giggle along with the wind created on the mostly healed yet still present bruises on her neck. "You're fucking with me. What was it called?"

"I swear I'm not, it was real. We called it..." He hesitated, straining his soot clouded face as he appeared to try and recall the name. "You know, I can't remember what we called it? But it was an actual thing. It was always too rough for me though. Players would beat the living shit out of each other and only have to sit out five minutes as penalty."

"You had penalties in this sport?"

"All of our sports did. Punishments for breaking the rules, you know like in pentagon where you can't score a point on your own goals."

"I meant penalties for attacking other players? You got in trouble for that?"

They passed the halfway mark of the field, the oncoming trees and snow becoming less visible. "Yeah most of our sports weren't like pentagon. You couldn't punch another player's lights out and expect to stay in the game, at least not a sport with a ball."

Flabbergasted, and letting that shock show on her face, she replied, "How do you play like that? What's the point of even playing if you can't take the ball away or protect yourself when you're going for a shot?"

He pondered over this. "You were still allowed to do those things, just in a lot of sports you had to do it without making too much physical contact."

She couldn't picture what her partner was suggesting. "How does that work?"

"Well take that one sport I mentioned earlier."

"You mean the one you made up?"

"Ha, no the one before that." He laughed and she reciprocated. "And hitting things with sticks while sliding on ice was a real fucking thing."

"Sure! And what was it called?"

"Fuck you."

She laughed and he reciprocated. "Yep, that's what I thought. Soccer was the other one right?"

"Yeah, with that one, say you have a player dribbling the ball downfield, trying to get open for a shot."

"The only goal they're allowed to go for?"

"Yeah that's right."

"I still don't get why soccer only has two goals."

Ignoring her comment, he explained, "So while this player is making an attempt at the goal, a player from the other team can come up and try to take the ball. But, this player can only take the ball by stealing it with their feet or kicking it away. At the same time though, the other player can only protect themselves from the player who wants the ball by holding their arms out and trying to maneuver the ball away from them, or passing it to another player on their team."

He spoke but none of it reached her, everything was taken by the breeze. "What the fuck are you talking about?" she asked with a wide smile and a wider-eyed look of confusion.

Another gust of laughter blew through them both, persisting until they were less than three hundred feet from the forests first line of trees. "Trust me; it makes more sense when you play it."

"All right then, show me." Letting her rifle hang from its strap, she stopped walking and turned away from her flank to face him. The wind punched at her back, as if under orders from Darius to keep her moving.

"What?" he said, also coming to a stop and turning to her.

When her partner let go of his own rifle, she told him, "Pretend that you're the player with the ball and I'm the player trying to take it from you. What am I allowed to do and not allowed to do?" She raised her arms out and approached him, glancing at his feet and pretending the ball from their pentagon games was between them, her rifle clicking as the weapon dangled from the strap.

Taken aback yet following along, her partner brought his arms up to equal measure and shifted his side towards her, facing the woods again, his weapon clacking from its strap. "Right, so if I've got the ball then you can come up to me and try to kick it out of my feet or dribble it away."

She came alongside him and kicked in front of his boots. "Like this?"

Swaying from their straps, their T-05 Snipers clanged into each other. "Yeah, and to protect myself I can either pass to a teammate or try and dribble away from you." He twisted around to the east, turning his backside and pack to her.

Turning as he did, she resumed her simulated attack from her partner's side. "If that doesn't work out for you, and I keep coming?"

"I can also try to put space between you and me as we move down the field." He pushed against her with his arm, and started forward with the imaginary ball at a half-run half-walk.

His partner came after him, pushing back with her arm and continuing her effort to steal the non-existent orb. "How is this any fun?" she asked, skeptical.

Swerving to the direction of the woods, he said, "It's the closest thing to pentagon we had." She turned with him, refusing to drop back even as the airstream returned to her face. "If Carthage had to pick a single sport, soccer would probably be the one, considering how many people used to play it."

With a thought, she seized his wrist, yanking him to a stop before plowing her foot in front of him, pretending to punt the invisible ball out of his feet. "Got it," she declared in a high-pitched tone of excitement, not caring for the moment that she might be talking too loud for the mission's sake.

She was about to dart after their mutual fantasy when he stopped her with a tap at her arm. "That's a penalty," he said, his chapped lips stretched in a heavy smile of mockery.

"What is?" she retorted, with a giggle fueled tone of joking exasperation.

Trying to hold in a laugh, he told her, "Holding, you're not allowed to grab the player's wrist and hold them back."

"You've got to be fucking kidding me."

He chuckled. "I didn't make the rules when they invented this game."

Relenting, she said, "All right, all right, do over." They recommenced their game, moving down the field like before but at a faster pace, their boots munching on the snow and ice. Snowflakes sprinkled their pants and jackets, but they disregarded the warnings from their already hypothermic bodies. Both were caught in the fictional realm of their dance, a realm where they didn't have another seven miles to trek, another nine targets to kill, and another night of cold to hide from. In that moment, if she'd had her way, she could stay in that field forever, provided Chloe was there with her. "Fuck," she yelled, after a few seconds of attempting and failing to break through her partner's self-defense.

"You know if this were a real game, I'd be fucked for hanging onto the ball this long without passing it," he remarked, as if hoping to make her feel better about him besting her at this pretend game. "Because your teammates would be swarming me right now."

She had another idea. Rather than continue her series of repetitive strikes at the fictitious ball, she stuck her boot out in front of his feet. He tripped over her ankle as she'd intended, managing to catch himself before he fell down but no doubt losing control of the ball. Regaining his balance, he halted instead of chasing the ball and looked at her with minor annoyance. Amidst a reluctant sigh, she asked, "Is tripping also a penalty?"

"Yep."

"Fuck."

Her partner glanced towards the hazed lines of bark the trees had been condensed to. "You want to get back to it?" he asked, disincli-

nation in his voice, as if he'd only suggested resuming the mission because he felt like he had to, not because he wanted to.

"No not yet, I want to get this first." She repositioned her boots
in the snow to start jogging again. Her partner did the same, relieved.

Their game had them running to the brink of the forest, sprinting
through the lightless field, compressed by the same night that by now
had all but consumed the valley, clouds of blackish-gray shooting up
around them, the commotion of their activity skipping across the
landscape. The Dragoons shoved each other with a ferocity that was
second only to a game of pentagon, again and again, as she tried to
overpower his blocks, only to be deterred by his higher knowledge of
the sport. Then, she felt her feet glide out from underneath as they
met a covering of iced over snow. Down on the side of her pack she
landed, the snow submerging her clothes, weapon, and gear, the pu-
trefied cold reminding her of its presence with something that resembled an electric shock. Shifting onto her pack and looking upwards,
she saw him standing over her, his glaring smile penetrating the blanket of dark that encased him. "Guess you can't beat me at everything,"
he proposed, celebrating his win. Offering up a fabricated expression
of defeated agreement, she raised a hand to him. Falling for her ruse,
her partner bent over and lowered his hand. And when he did, she
swung her leg out of the snow like an opening door, swiping his legs
away.

He tumbled into the snow beside her, hitting as she had with
a startled grunt. She gave her partner no time to register what happened before she rolled over on top of him and pinned him to the
ground. She held her face inches above his, close enough they blew
freezing breaths of white exertion in each other's eyes. "No fucking
chance."

A grin of amusement and something she couldn't decipher
formed in the expression that surrounded the permanent scarring
and healing pentagon gashes that misshaped his face. "This is also a

penalty by the way." Their latest round of conjoined laughter, in that spot on that field with the air screaming in bitter rage, was when she first acknowledged it. The impression had been there from the start of their first operation together in Serenity, less than two weeks ago, but was so well stifled by the demands of Marathon and the Black Dragoons the awareness didn't become conscious till now. She was reminded of her daughter then, how Chloe could ask a million and one questions in a single day. And yet despite Chloe's penchant for curiosity, hardly anyone in Marathon had been on the receiving end of her inquiries, not the families in the neighboring bunks of their barrack, not the teachers at their Community Office, not even the citizens and soldiers they passed on Missio's streets. The only person Chloe trusted and cared for enough to ask so many questions so often, the one whom she depended on for everything, was her mother. Thinking on this now, Chloe's mother realized that, like her daughter, there was but one single person she'd come to trust and care for to the point that she felt comfortable articulating her own barrage of questions about this world in the time of the 31st Year of Marathon: Sean, her partner in the Black Dragoons.

They held their place together in the field, neither of them making a motion to stand up out of the snow. "Sorry I fucked up your face," she told him. She wanted to sound more sincere, to reflect her understanding she'd caused her own partner pain.

"That's all right," he told her. "If I'm remembering things correctly, I hit you first."

How he wanted her to respond to his apparent forgiveness she didn't know, and what he was saying behind those words she couldn't tell. She began to speak, not yet knowing what she was going to say but starting to anyway, only to be redirected by a flash of yellow at the periphery of her eyesight and an earsplitting snap.

The echo of the report rumbled over the valley as they returned to their feet, raised their T-05 Snipers, and aimed the rifles towards the eastern end of the field, where both of them assessed the discharge had come from. A second flash and boom occurred before they could peer through their night vision scopes, which they needed to observe the far edges of the field, and with that report, she comprehended the light they saw was not a muzzle flash, nor was the boom they heard a firearm. The flash did not originate in the field; rather it brightened the valley from several miles off. Appearing not from the ground up as the flares of a firefight would do, but instead from the overcast of the night, the flash shot towards the surface in the shape of three yellow zigzagging streaks, like the prongs of a distorted fork. It was lightning, she realized. The noise that reminded them of their place in the Aegean Valley, as field agents of the Black Dragoons in the midst of a high priority operation, was actually thunder. For the second the veins of lightning lit the valley, she saw the serrated crests of the Aegean Mountains, yellow sparkling to life off the listless gray that covered the summits. The sight was but a small rebellion of light against the overwhelming darkness, a transient period between two separate yet identical eras of night.

Their fantasy lost to them, she said to her partner, "We should move."

Hesitant though not disagreeing, he responded with a modest, "Copy that."

As they shifted focus from the thunderstorm to the woods, she noticed the snow that draped her partner's backside. "You need me to get your back for you?" she asked, pleasure surviving in her voice.

She heard him laugh despite the dark. "Don't push it."

Six miles from Athens and deep into the woods that had taken more time to reach than expected, they sought cover underneath a Highway bridge, planning to wait till daybreak when the cold would lessen and they could make the final push to their objective. The bridge stood above a ravine, its body held by concrete pillars and metal beams laced with ice. They sat atop a slope of concrete that rose up from the dirt, the bottom of the bridge less than a foot from their heads, the wind shrieking through the gorge below them. Between them, a small fire made of dry twigs and branches, all recovered from the snowless sanctuary of the underpass. The fire was encircled by stones, the size of the blaze just large enough to stall the effects of hypothermia, dry their gear, and keep them warm. They didn't dare raise the fire any more than that, in the event someone else was traveling through the woods. Her partner had turned himself to the east, facing outwards from the fire. She sat on the opposite side of the fire and looked west. Rifles hanging from straps, they held their dinners in their hands. Another cold night in the Aegean Valley, another meal of tofu blocks from their ration bags and water from their filtered bottles. *Still better than the shit people are eating out here.*

When their meal was finished, they returned their rations to their packs, and took their T-05 Snipers in their arms. With their breaths glowing and twinkling in the orange glare of the fire, mixing with the pale smoke that bumped against the bridge's underbelly, they began the night's watch. Though she'd spent the entirety of the previous night sitting in a freezing vehicle, doing nothing except stare through her night vision scope, no more than an hour passed before she was no longer able to sit still, as if she'd gotten so used to moving that being off her feet was too much to bear. Glancing around to Sean, who had just finished adding a few more twigs on the shrinking fire and was back at his post, she said, "Hey, I've got a question."

A flurry of orange and yellow sparks divided them as he looked back at her with a startled jolt, as if he'd been dozing and her voice had slapped him back to full awareness. "Really, that's unusual," he responded with obvious sarcasm.

Both of them turned towards their respective areas of surveillance as she retorted. "Funny. Did you want to hear it?" She found herself afraid of what would happen if he said no.

"Why not?" he answered from behind.

An orange breath of relief puffed and she remembered she didn't even have a question. A silence of awkwardness floated over them as her numbed cognizance grasped for something, anything to talk about, before he could change his mind. Plucked from a thought that couldn't have been more random was the question. "Is it true that kids in Carthage used to color with more than just dark blue and black colored pencils?" Even she was mystified by her words. She could practically feel the befuddlement in her partner's restricted re-action. *What the fuck has gotten into her?*

"Yeah that's true." Apparently he also wanted to escape the ago-nizing quiet.

"How many colors?" she asked, making sure to sound curious.

His voice replied from the other side of the fire. "I don't remem-ber. It was definitely more than two, I can tell you that much."

This question she asked with true interest. "Why did you need more than two colors to draw with?"

In return, she received a question from him. "Why does Marathon only use dark blue and black colored pencils?"

The question was serious, as if the subject had been bothering him for some time, but her answer was unrewarding. "Those are the two colors the Commanders permit. You've seen our buildings."

He wasn't done. "Why're dark blue and black the only approved colors?"

She was. "Because those colors were declared sacred when the city was founded."

"Right," he said with clear disappointment, as if he'd already heard that explanation from many citizens and hoped to hear some-thing different from her. Except there was no other reason, at least none that she'd learned from her teachers in childhood.

At that their short-lived exchange crumbled, returning her to the unendurable noiselessness of the night, so frightening to her she rif-fled through her mind, desperate for another topic. Surveying the forested hills outside the bridge with her night vision, something came to her. "You know, as dangerous as it is, this valley has a lot going for it."

"You think so?" he asked her. If his interest was fake, she couldn't tell.

"Yeah it's strange. I felt the same way about the Serenity Hills. Terra might be more secure, and our barrack has heating but there's...It's just...Sometimes Marathon, it's all just..."

Sean said what she was having trouble putting to words. "Suffocating?"

She turned around to face him, but he'd already turned to her, intrigued by her musing. "Yeah, that's what I mean." She smiled at him. "Sometimes while we're there, I worry that the place is going to smother me in my sleep or something." He smiled back at her and they shared their first laugh since the field. "But out here there's a, a kind of..." Again she was stumped.

And again, her partner filled the gap in her speech. "A kind of freedom?"

At once, with that sentence, that word, it was as if her fears reversed themselves. No longer did she fear the silence; now she feared what discourse would come next. *We keep this up and we'll be saying things that'll get us sent to the Detention Center for treason, but only after Darius sends a message to Missio and kills all of Chloe's benefits.* She threw a wedge in the conversation, deliberately sabotaging it. "Get some sleep, Sean. I'll take over the watch and wake you before dawn."

An expression of stunned anger built over her partner's face. "How about I take full watch this time? You..."

"No," she cut him off, commanding him to sleep.

Yet he pressed. "I slept last night. You haven't slept in two days Anna, going on three. You may be a Second-Gen but you're not invincible."

"No," she said, her voice straining. "Get some fucking shut-eye, and I'll wake you before dawn." When he seemed to hesitate, she told him, "That's an order."

With a moan of discouragement, he yielded. "Yes, ma'am." Without another word to her, he unstrapped his pack and set it behind him to use as a pillow, then unhooked his rifle and placed it at his side. He lay on the concrete hill, face hidden by the orange of the fire, head resting on his pack.

She didn't know if he would truly sleep, or stay awake as an act of defiance. In either case, she knew she was going to be awake all through the night and all through the next night if their mission was not finished. She turned back to her side of the ravine, planning to scan her section for a minute and then switch to survey her partner's sector, alternating between the two ends until it was time to step off. As she lifted her T-05 Sniper and placed her eye at the night vision scope, she noticed it standing at the borders of her awareness, the massive steel building of exhaustion constructed on sixty plus hours with no sleep. And yet that weariness was unable to take full enervating effect, as if her deactivated Second-Gen Stage was calling out and denying the fatigue access to her system. *You don't sleep; you don't sleep until all thirteen of them are dead. When they're dead, you can sleep. You'll show the Commander that you're committed to Marathon. Chloe.*

8: SEAN

Through the night and into the morning, the windstorm stomped down on the valley with biting drafts of glacial grime, the savagery of the blasts reaching a degree where every new breeze seemed to herald the snap and thump of a falling tree. The winter storm that trailed these preliminary squalls couldn't have been more than a day away by Sean's estimation, though he knew quite well this might just be wishful thinking. Into this hail they marched the last six miles to Athens, the wind forcing them back two paces for each forward pace they took, as if the airstream was in league with Sword of God and working to keep them away from the organization's new stronghold.

Against the weather, however, at 0800 hours that morning, they arrived at the territories that surrounded Athens, a rugged land of gradual yet high rising stony hills at the northernmost point of the valley where the Troy and Aegean Mountains converged and tapered off. Aside from the town at the summit of one of these hills, the numerous embankments and mini-valleys amid the slopes were not only emptied of trees and other decaying plant life, but were barren of any suggestion of contact with human society. No rubble of a former town from the Previous Civilization, no rusting vehicles and ships. It was as if Athens had sprung from the sole pocket of ground that tolerated life. At 0900 hours, they were positioned at the crest of a hill on the southern flank of Athens, surveilling the hostile town from behind a cluster of icy boulders. Sapped of vigor by fatigue, thirst, hunger, cold, pervasive soreness from his neck to his feet, and clay that coated every bit of his skin and nipped at his facial gashes, Sean struggled to keep himself awake as he looked through his scope.

Athens was situated on the adjacent hill, four hundred meters to their north at a lower elevation, allowing them to scan over the town's South Gate onto the interior road. As the Aurora's reconnaissance photos showed, the community's brick buildings were divided into two rows by the street, and the gates that sealed off the exits. Sean and Anna dubbed the rows the Western Block and the Eastern Block. Inside the town walls, Athens appeared as deserted as the surrounding hillsides. The snow-covered road was as abandoned as it'd been in the aerial photographs. None of the window curtains moved. No doors were open, not even cracked. Nevertheless, the presence of fifteen warm and breathing bodies was confirmed on thermal by the Aurora that soared high above them on Darius's order, well out of sight.

Only eight buildings were presently inhabited, the fifteen living persons sprinkled about them. With four of Sword of God's thirteen dead in Dresden, nine of these fifteen were assumed to be Sword of God, the other six Athenian hostages, their signatures impossible to decipher from Sword of God's. This left Sean and Anna to sit in the cold and wait for the terrorists blue crossed, blond-haired, glasses wearing commander to show himself on the street for even the briefest moment, so his precise location could be known before their assault. Jesus Christ's place of residence had to be the first building Sean and Anna visited after breaching the town walls. Otherwise, their operation ran the risk of letting him flee while they were engaged with his Disciples. After three hours of observation, Anna spoke. "There, center of town, heading our way," she said with an unrestricted tone of exhilaration that told him she'd acquired at least one of Sword of God's elite.

And indeed, when Sean centered his scope on the roadway, he spotted two men, no wool masks covering their heads but two discernable blue crosses on their foreheads. Like the terrorists who fell at Dresden, they were fitted in the captured dark blue clothing of Marathon and carried T-05 rifles, slung over their backs. They walked through the snow and the wind, onto the street from a building in the Eastern Block, stopping to face South Gate and, unknowingly, Sean and Anna. Conversing with each other, their mouths moving inaudibly in Sean's scope, they appeared to be inspecting something on the gate, gesturing towards the side of the twenty-foot metal entranceway. One of the fighters, a man in his early thirties at the oldest, stood with long unkempt red hair that blew in front of his face during the gusts and fell below his shoulders between them. Measuring six and a half feet in height at Sean's approximation, the red-haired fighter's appearance was far more intimidating than the man to his left, yet it was the man to his left that had Sean and Anna's attention.

The second Sword of God fighter that had shown himself was a little older than his companion, late thirties to early forties, and shorter than the other man by several inches. His glossy blond hair was strangely, almost professionally, cut and arranged, as if he always had a barber and stylist at arm's length, the same kind the legislators of Carthage hired to obsess over what hair setup made them the most presentable to the public, a practice that ate up more of the city government's time than any of them were willing to admit. Over his eyes he wore glasses, the lenses so thin Sean wasn't sure if they were meant to improve his eyesight or were for show. What show he might be trying to put on, Sean had not one guess. Nonetheless, the man's look matched the account supplied to the Black Dragoons by Joseph Holloway. This man was Jesus Christ, commander of Sword of God.

"There he is," Anna said, the excitement of finding their prime target undiminished in her voice. "Can you take a shot at him from here?"

Sean wished he could take both Jesus and his confidant down at this exact moment, bring him and his partner that much closer to the end of their mission, and the Aegean Valley that much closer to a life without Sword of God. But to his infuriating reluctance, he assessed he would not be able to. "At this range, with the wind like it is, I wouldn't put a lot of faith in it."

His own irritation seemed to transfer to Anna. "In Dresden you got a kill with a shot into the wind," she challenged.

He refuted her objection. "The wind wasn't as strong yesterday. Plus the hostile I shot was already firing at us, so we didn't have much of a choice. Now we have alternatives and if I shoot and miss, those options will start to dwindle before we can even move off this hill." *Not to mention when Darius finds out I took a shot at Jesus and missed, letting him slip away when we could've gone in to take him down at close range, that'll be the literal death of me.*

With a nod of hesitance but otherwise understanding, his partner said, "Okay. Looks like we're going in then."

Down in Athens, Jesus and his red-haired Disciple had turned up the street to stare at North Gate, their backs rotated towards the Dragoons location. "What're they looking at?" Sean asked Anna, not expecting her to know.

"The gates are booby-trapped." Her response was blunt, as if this was something she thought he already knew. "Jesus's friend is showing him where the tripwires are set."

"Where do you see that?" he replied, unhinged by embarrassment.

"Look at the handle on North Gate."

He adjusted his scope to zoom past Jesus and the red-haired Disciple and concentrated on the gate's metal grip. Hanging from the handle was a black sphere, a frag grenade of Marathon's design, no doubt stolen from one of the many Marathon soldiers ambushed and slaughtered by Sword of God. Suspended on a string that ran from the wall, through the handle, and finally, through the pin of the grenade, the trap was simple yet deadly in creation. Anyone who opened the gate, both from the outside or the inside, would yank the string and release the pin. "Fuck," he muttered, recognizing if one gate was booby-trapped than it was likely they both were.

"So much for the let's just stroll through the gates and shoot all the terrorists option," Anna stated in a mocking tone, more critical than comical.

"I never endorsed that," he retorted, defensive.

"Yeah, but I'll bet it was one of your alternatives."

Retreating from the pummeling drafts of icy dirt, Jesus and his Disciple turned to the centermost structure of the Western Block, a three-story brick building. Stepping through the front door, they disappeared inside and did not reemerge over the forty-five minutes Sean and Anna spent staking out the edifice. Like the rest of the town, the building that now housed Jesus and at least one other Sword of God fighter was locked down tight, windows shut and curtained, door sealed. And after Darius radioed Anna at 1300 hours to inform her that the building Jesus and the red-haired Disciple first appeared from was now entirely purple—-empty, according to the Aurora—-Anna told Sean, "That's it."

Sean kept his eye at his scope, scanning the community south to north in case any other fighters were making themselves known. "What?"

"That's his building," she said with stern confidence. "We go in and that's where Jesus will be."

He wasn't as sure. "Assuming that's true, we've still only glassed the two of them. There are seven other hostiles in that town we haven't seen, mixed in with six prisoners." His T-05 Sniper moved back down Athens's only road, north to south, but failed to spot a single blue cross, or any Athenians for that matter.

Anna's conviction didn't falter. "Two's plenty for now. We just have to get in there and keep one of them alive long enough to get the others."

"Is that all?" he asked, not hiding his skepticism.

"Their defenses are too focused on the perimeter. They don't have anyone walking patrol. Once we're over the wall, moving through the town won't be difficult, as long as one of us is up top providing over watch."

"By one of us you mean me, right?"

"Unless you want to lead the interrogation."

"Point taken."

"The Commander also assured me during our last exchange that the Aurora will be with us until it has to return and refuel, and that another plane will already be on the way up in replacement." There was determination in Anna's demeanor now, a notice to Sean that she'd become steadfast in her intent to assault Athens this afternoon.

Still not convinced, he said, "These people, Sword of God, they're extremists, in action and ideology. When we interrogated Jason, it took us twelve hours to get the Cavaliers out of him, and he wasn't even fully committed. What makes you think you can get one of them to give up the others in the time available, which won't be that long when we're in there."

There was a silence from Anna, a big enough gap between words that Sean hoped she was reconsidering. But then, she countered. "It's like you said, Jason was only committed to Katherine, the person he joined the Cavaliers with." She paused again. "Love." The term seemed to recoil through them both, as if such a word had no place on that hill. "That's what made him hold out so long. These people though, they're not committed, not to each other. As long as they get to rape and pillage everyone they come across, they don't care who they're with. It'll only take but so much fear and pain to get one of them to cough up the rest." Another sweep of Athens, another forsaken street. Giving up his search, Sean turned to find Anna looking back at him, her face darkened by grime and exhaustion, demanding this be the last day of their mission. "An hour ago, you said terminating Sword of God from a distance was more problematic than storming the place. Now what, you're saying the infiltration option's no good either? I don't know what other choices you think we have Sean, but beyond those the only one left is having an Aurora drop a bomb on the whole fucking town. And taking those six Athenian hostages into account, I'd much rather an option that doesn't blast the village into extinction."

Sean said nothing in return. He was at a loss. *We have the chance to avoid what happened in the Serenity Hills. Darius hasn't declared everyone in that settlement hostile, so it falls to Anna. The only hostiles to her are the ones with blue crosses. And it isn't going to be like Dresden either. Some of the Athenians are still alive.* He turned away from the community below, dismounting his rifle from the boulders as he sat in the snow with his pack against the rocks, relishing in the enormous relief of being out of the wind.

His partner dropped down beside him, weapon in hands yet pacified. Together, they stared out at the frozen gray hilltops that rolled up and down, west to east, until meeting the far taller, and more menacing, Aegean Mountain range. "I'll make them tell me where Jacob and Mia are," she told him.

More confused than surprised, he twisted his head to her. "What're you talking about?"

She turned to him in response; her expression now layered with sympathy. "Holloway's kids. If Jacob and Mia are down there, if they're among those six, we should get them out along with the rest. And if they're already gone, we can at least fulfill one of his terms and rescue the last of his people. We were too late in Dresden, but not here."

An approving grin spread through the numbness of his face. The satisfaction of hearing the idea that he and Anna liberate these besieged people was too great to ignore. It didn't last, because Sean had another uncertain thought. "What happens after we get them out?"

Anna was confused as he'd been a second ago. "What do you mean?"

His smile left him. "After we've freed these people from Sword of God, assuming they live through our assault, what'll become of them? Will Marathon give them immigrated citizenship and relocate them to Missio? Will they even want to be relocated? Holloway did say he and his people were trying to live free of the fighting. Migrating to one of the main contestants for the valley, right after being liberated from another, may not appeal to them. If Holloway's kids are alive, how do we tell him either they can't or they won't come to Marathon to be with him?"

Sean saw from the change in Anna's expression that she hadn't considered this. "Let's just focus on what the Commander's instructed us to do right now. If the time comes that we have rescued hostages on our hands, we'll figure something out."

There wasn't a shred of assurance left in her tone, as if she didn't truly anticipate them being able to save any of the Athenians and had just said so to raise his morale. He noticed a spike of cold air at the back of his neck, the weather somehow finding them behind the rocks. Knowing the lives of Jacob, Mia, and the other Athenians were at best of secondary importance in the eyes of Commander Darius, Sean asked his partner, "How are we getting in?" The hazed limit of his vision was where he first perceived the dots of gray that began to drift down from above. "We can't go through the gates and they're too slick to climb over." Stopping and craning his head upwards at the same time Anna did, he acknowledged the army of gray flakes that were raining from the overcast, shavings scraped off the skin of the clouds. Falling in an unremitting charge, no visible gaps to be seen, the flecks flooded the air and stuck to the surface as they met the rocks around Sean and Anna. And with this snowfall, he knew the storm, whose pending arrival had been publicized for nearly two full days by the wind, was making its way across the Troy Mountains and into the Aegean Valley. "Shit," he said, already processing the sinking temperature.

They moved out under the snowstorm's umbrella, descending into the gorge between their observation post and their objective. The snow and wind partnered and escalated, forming a roaring blizzard, its gusts manufacturing a fog that was in motion and yet at the same time immoveable, a blinding gray-out that swallowed the valley and everything in it. Even with their night vision scopes illuminating the rocky grounds in front of them, it took close to a half-hour for them to reach the eastern side of Athens's boundary. By that point, Sean could feel his body heat descending towards hypothermia, as the polar wind and rocklike snowflakes smacked him and his partner over and over again, turning their gear gray. Anna entered the Second-

Gen Stage, her alternate place in the universe letting her operate as if there'd been no change in the weather at all. Her transformation was noticed by him when he scanned his night vision scope in her general direction, giving him a look at her glistening greenish-blue irises. His response was minuscule, he hoped, a simple shift of his focus, the spark of envy hidden by the storm.

When they paused and knelt in the snow, the eastern wall of the community was directly ahead, as indicated by their scopes. The section of external wall they would scale, chosen by Anna before they left the recon site, belonged to the centermost building of the Eastern Block. Four stories tall, the building had a flat square-shaped roof upon which one could walk or take up an overhead position. Most crucial, the structure was straight across the street from their target building, where Jesus hopefully remained. "Let's go to thermal." Anna's voice invaded Sean's right ear through his Network earpiece, the only way they'd been able to verbally communicate in the howling squall. He glanced to the side, where he knew Anna to be, the jagged snow piercing his eyes, compelling him to blink repeatedly. Through the gray, he saw Anna's hand grip the knob at the top of her scope.

Tapping his earpiece once and holding his finger to it, he answered, "Roger that," before turning the knob and changing the view on his own scope. Surveying the building with his thermal, he found the floors swamped by purple, no orange signatures occupying the structure. Tapping and holding his finger to his earpiece again, he said, "No one inside."

"Copy," Anna was quick to reply. "Adjacent buildings are empty too, no hostiles in this part of town."

"Who goes up first?" he asked, despite knowing what she would say.

"When I get to the top, I'll call you up," she answered without the smallest hint of apprehension, her plan set. "You good?"

"You got it."

His partner's bright orange signature appeared in Sean's scope, her silhouette materializing out of the purple, her arms in front of her as she raised her rifle. Her hand rose to her right ear. "Moving up, cover our flanks." She trotted towards the wall of the Eastern Block, the cracks of her boots muffled by the wind.

"Roger," he replied, and swept the grounds below the walls. Anna stayed orange in his scope as she moved to the corner of the four-story building. To the naked eye she was already long gone, her tactful movements a shadow. Unlike Sean, who knew she was there, anybody else who somehow managed to catch sight of her would dismiss what they'd seen as a trick of the blizzard, her presence not lasting in their mind. To the soldiers of Sword of God they had become phantoms, inhabitants of the storm carried into Athens by the wind. Bringing his finger back to his earpiece, he said, "Area's clear."

"Good to know, keep me updated." There was a slight coarseness in her voice that Sean recognized as exertion. Glassing the corner of the building where his partner should've been, he saw nothing but blackish-purple. Angling his weapon up he found her, already ten feet above the ground, hanging from the building. Her orange arms were wrapped around something in front of her, her orange feet snug together on some sort of narrow foothold, T-05 Sniper suspended over her shoulder. It was a pipe she was climbing. Her silhouette ascended the wall with remarkable speed, never mind the blizzard or the forty-plus-year old pipe surely coated with frost. Less than two minutes later, she was up and swinging herself over the side of the roof. Dropping to one knee, she retrieved her rifle and made a semicircle scan of the sectors around her. Then, her orange arm rose to her head. "I'm up top, your turn."

Fuck, the Serenity Hills, Dresden, now this wall, how many more times are we going to have to climb up shit? He tapped his earpiece, speaking with true amazement but false calm. "Got it, on the way." He trailed Anna's path to the corner of the building where the makeshift ladder would be. The pipe came to him a lot sooner than he anticipated, so much so he almost banged the tip of his rifle's suppressor against it. He wasn't sure if it was because of the optical illusion created by the storm or his fatigue, but he comprehended his sense of depth perception had been hindered. Lowering his weapon and gazing at the pipe, he saw the piping was coupled to the wall with a set of metal rods, one for every foot of pipe. The space between the pipe and the wall was minimal, barely enough room for him to put his hands and feet. Looking up, he found the second story of the building, a blur of bricks that appeared to be hovering in midair rather than attached to the ground. The wall and pipe evaporated beyond that level, soaked up by the gray. The roof, he knew, was somewhere within that mist, forty feet above his current position. But standing at the bottom of the pipe, it seemed as if there was no end to the pipeline, no top of the wall. He would scale the pipe for hours, climb hundreds of feet into the blizzard, and then succumb to hypothermia without ever reaching the roof. *I never liked the whole climbing thing, at least on the Dresden we didn't have a fucking snowstorm to make it worse.*

"Sean, what're you doing just standing there? Move your ass." Anna's annoyed command in his ear provided him with a large enough surge of focus that he shouldered his rifle and forced himself to step up and place his hands on the rods of the pipe. And there was ice, as he'd predicted. The rods were so cold that the touch of the frost burned through his gloves. The pipe and the bars that linked it to the wall weren't just cased in ice; the ice appeared to be growing, thickening over the metal. At least an inch of frozen water separated his hands from the rods. It wasn't forty feet of pipe Anna ascended in less than two minutes; she'd climbed forty feet of pure ice in less than two minutes.

He threw his hands off the pipe, his resolve depleted. *No way, no fucking way!* Staring up into the clouds, where he was certain Anna watched from the roof with her thermal scope, he tapped and held his earpiece. "I can't, there's too much ice."

His partner's reply was more angry than surprised. "Fuck you, I got up here just fine. Now move it Sean, that's a fucking order."

Desperate panic was freezing the veins in his chest, shortening his breath, watering his eyes with cold tears. "Fuck you Anna, I'm not like you, all right!"

She was furious now; he could almost feel the heat of her rage descending from the rooftop. "You fuck! If you aren't up here in the next three minutes, I'll report this to the Commander; tell her how you interfered with the operation! You'll have nothing to look forward to except a cell in the Detention Center!"

It was a bluff, a scare tactic used to pressure unwilling soldiers of Marathon to follow even the most unreasonable of instructions, Sean was positive of it. Had he thought Anna was so heartless that she'd be willing to banish him to a life in a feces flooded hallway and a tiny pitch dark detention cell, the threat still would've bounced off him all the same. For at this moment, it was the pipe that he feared more than the Detention Center. "Why the fuck do you think humans are so afraid of your kind, Anna? When we see what you are, what you can do, you remind us of everything we're not! You can do this, but I can't!"

He had the urge to cringe as he waited on her response, half-expecting his earpiece to explode and blowout his eardrum. When Anna did reply, however, a good twenty seconds later, her voice was perhaps the calmest he'd ever heard, not livid, not offended, not even that fake composure she'd used on Jason and Peter, just unadulterated compassion. "Sean, I know. I know you're scared of me. Everyone is. I'm scared of me. And I know there's a lot I can do that you can't, but I know you can do this." There was begging in her tone now, again not contrived, honest vulnerability. "It's not just that I know you can, I know you have to. You have to because I need you up here with me.

As good as I am, I can't do this without a partner. And Sean, you're the only person I have, not just out here but back in Terra. So please Sean, you have to climb."

For several seconds Sean was left stunned by what Anna had allowed him to hear. *No native-born citizen of Marathon tells a native of Carthage they need them.* When his shock passed, he decided he would have to ascend the pipe, for both their sakes. "Okay, I'm coming up," he told her, and grabbed the rods, letting the temperature of the ice slice through his gloves.

He was curling his arms around the rods above him, trying to get as good of a grip as the ice would permit, when Anna responded, her relief obvious. "Okay, okay. I'm going to talk you through it. Our boots were made with ice and snow in mind, so concentrate on pushing yourself up with your feet, that's the best way to do it." Sean lifted his feet to the rods and stepped out of the snow, his boots pressed together between the wall and the pipe. His boots slipped as he projected, yet not as much as his gloves. After he'd stabilized himself as best he could, by squeezing his body against the icy bars, he noticed his boots were indeed gripping to the ice somewhat, enough he trusted himself to begin moving upwards. He raised his right foot up first, finding the rod above, as Anna said, "Okay, now step up with your feet, like you're on a ladder." When his right foot was as steady as he could make it, he lifted his left, bringing himself up as his left foot crammed into position next to his right. His hands held their place, performing the task required of them. "Yeah that's it," Anna told him with encouragement. "Just keep doing what you're doing. Sword of God can wait; just take it one rod at a time."

And that's what Sean did. One rod at a time, one foot after the other, over and over, until he'd lost track of how many bars he'd passed. He didn't look up, nor did he look down. The roof would show itself when he got there, he didn't have to look for it. The wind was insistent, the storm making a valiant effort to fling him off the pipe, which screeched with vibration more often than not. All the while Anna's reassurance persisted, as if the completion of their present mission was no longer her chief concern, regardless of the Aurora that continued to observe them. What she was saying to Darius over the Network to explain why the Aurora's thermal imaging showed they were taking such a long time to surmount the village walls, Sean could only guess. *Right, left, right, left, right, left, right, left.* He raised one foot up to the next rod, where his other foot waited in place. Then, his foot slid from the bar and fell into open air. His other foot, still midway into its ascent, dropped. "Fuck!" Gravity pulled his legs, and then his torso, down into the gray void beneath him. His hand let go of the rod above his head, his arm falling to his side. But his other arm, wrapped around the same bar, clung to the frosted metal. He swung to the side, generating a loud thump and a clank as his pack and weapon crashed into the wall.

"Ah fuck," was Anna's first terrified reaction, as if his fall from the pipe appeared inevitable from where she was.

Hanging by one arm, his boots dangling under him, Sean's head titled downwards. There was gray, that's all there was below him: no ground, no snow, just the fog of the blizzard that encircled him, transported him to another universe entirely. He wasn't hanging but floating, levitating above a dimension of oblivion. This place of non-existence seemed to call to him with each howl of the storm, pleading with him to join the people who were already there. *Derek's waiting for me there, mom and dad too.* The thought of tumbling down there, into that place of gray nothing, was so frightening to Sean that in one motion, he had swung himself back against the pipe and replanted his feet and hand on the rods, his eyes turned away from what he'd both seen and not seen.

"Fucking shit, that was close," Anna was saying into his ear, her voice caught between panic and respite. "You all right?" she asked, as if forgetting he couldn't answer her over the Network, unable to risk using his hand to tap and hold his earpiece. He nodded his head, knowing she would see it on her scope. "Okay, well fuck. You're almost there Sean, twenty feet or less. Just keep doing what you were doing."

Twenty feet! Another twenty feet of this! I'm not almost there, Anna! Fuck, I'm only halfway! Sean didn't move, up or down, and didn't think he could again. He'd stay still on the pipe, until his body heat diminished and the ice finished him off.

When his partner spoke again, her tone was so casual he wondered if she'd forgotten where she and he were right now. "You know, I was thinking about those sports you told me about yesterday. Soccer was one of them, and I think the others were football and..." It took her a few moments to remember the last one. "Bucketball, I might be saying that wrong but work with me here. And no, I'm not counting that one ice-lake sport you made up."

Sean's chest ached as he laughed with uncontrollable amusement, his hands and feet still holding to the rods.

"Honestly, if you're going to make up a sport to make your city sound better, at least think up a name for it. As for bucketball, it seems like that's pretty much the same thing as soccer, except with bucketball you dribble and pass with your hands and the goals hang above you instead of sitting on the ground. Having both soccer and bucketball makes some sense to me now. But what I cannot and never will understand is how and why Carthage willingly inherited a game like football from the Previous Civilization."

His laughter was chronic, warming.

"From what you told me, and based on what you told me I'm betting you barely understand the game at all, football makes absolutely zero fucking sense. It sounds like a game a bunch of five-year-olds came up with while they were high. Not even the name makes sense. Football, you said the players almost always use their hands, so why the fuck is it called football?"

Making it his goal to sort out Anna's confusion, Sean's resolve resurged and he scaled the pipe at a much greater speed than he had before.

"And while we're on the subject, what the fuck kind of name is soccer?"

Right foot, left foot, right foot, left foot, one bar after the other, a few slip ups here and there but none as bad as his near fall.

"Why isn't soccer called football, everyone uses their feet in that game."

Sean was still climbing, reaching up for the next rod, when he felt a hand on the back of his shoulder. Glancing around, he found Anna's face right behind his. There was no rod that Sean was grabbing for; he'd reached the roof. His partner sat in a squat, her weapon hanging from its strap, hand extended out to him. "Oh," he said, accepting his partner's hand. He pushed off the rods with his boots; she pulled. In a gray blurred instant, he was up over the side of the roof.

They sat crouched in the snow that buried the roof, giving Sean a minute to catch his breath before moving on to the next phase of the operation. Beaming at her partner, Anna tapped her ear and said, "So what's the story?"

He chuckled in return, tapping and holding his earpiece to reply over the Network as the icy soiled air replenished his lungs. "Soccer was called football by most people in the Previous Civilization. Only a handful called it soccer. What you called it really depended on where you lived."

Anna started laughing, stumped. Sean joined her, not sure what to make of his clarification either.

9: ANNA

The good fortune that kept Sean from falling off the pipe stayed with them as they moved to the frontend of the roof, and stood above the one and only street of Athens, their principal target on the other side. Despite the gray blizzard, they found a ladder secured to the side of the building. Iced with equal severity to the pipe and rusted to such a grade she wasn't confident its fasteners would hold to the wall, the ladder nevertheless ran from the roof to the snowy ground below as her scope revealed. While Anna hung her weapon over her shoulder and stepped on the top rung of the ladder, Sean took a kneeling position at the centermost point of the roof's edge and mounted his T-05 Sniper on the two and a half foot brick wall that crenelated the rooftop.

With Sean procuring his observation and sniper post, Anna descended the ladder. Her hands and feet clung to the sidebars of the ladder as she slid from the top, down four stories of gray air to the gray floor of the town. At touch down, the impact of her boots on the ground only faintly meeting with her cognizance, she readied her rifle in her arms and swept the road in both directions with her thermal scope. Not a single orange silhouette from North Gate to South Gate, the roadway as desolate as it'd been during their four hours of surveillance. Clear on all flanks, she surveyed the target building across the street. Out of the building's three floors, the first and second were blackish-purple. On the third floor, however, there were four definitive heat signatures, bunched together on the left side of the building, in the same room it appeared. The proximity of the four silhouettes was peculiarly close, as if they stood face to face with each other against the back wall of the room. Tapping and holding her Network earpiece with her index finger, she said, "At ground level, moving on targets now. How copy?"

Her partner sounded in her ear, reinvigoration in his voice, as if the incident on the pipe happened ten days ago and he'd had ample time to recuperate. "Copy all. I've got four heat signatures reading from the target structure, third floor. How copy?"

"Roger that, my sights are showing the same. Hold current position and report all movement as you acquire it." Concentrating her weapon on the building, Anna trotted across the street, towards the front door Jesus and his associate entered. The rancid airstream barreled through the community, the rows of buildings converting the village into a wind tunnel that sent the snowstorm roaring into Anna from what seemed like all directions at once. Her Second-Gen Stage lessened the force of the gusts, but the numbing of the cold and the bite of frozen clay was not diminished.

She was still crossing the road when another voice penetrated her ear, one that made the snow feel warm by comparison. "Vanguard One, what's your status?" Darius demanded, already well beyond irritated by the interruption to their mission the pipe created.

Stacking against the frosted brick of the target building, Anna tapped her earpiece twice and held the second time. "Copy that, Central. I'm moving on Jesus and Disciple at this time." She passed a window frame, sealed by curtains, setting herself to the left of the door. "Vanguard Two is up top providing over watch. Will report back upon securing structure, how copy?"

"Copy all. And Anna?"

Pushing past her unnerving surprise that Darius had called her by name over the Network, she said, "Yes, Central?"

"You would stand to benefit from not being held up by Vanguard Two's fear of heights from here on. Understood?"

"Yes, ma'am."

But apparently that response wasn't satisfactory. "Anna, do you remember what I said about Sean, back at the Command Building?"

"Yes, ma'am, of course."

"Good, you keep that in mind. Otherwise, Missio may get a message from me." There was a snickering in Darius's voice; Anna imagined she was speaking now with a massive smile on her face.

Chloe! A spike of worry prodded her as she replied. "Copy all Central, loud and clear. Vanguard One out." Gripping her T-05 Sniper with one hand, she stretched her arm out and wrapped her other hand around the doorknob. When the knob didn't turn, she conjured up a fallback plan and pounded on the locked door a good four or five times, making sure to knock hard enough the people on the third floor could hear over the bursts of the blizzard. Tapping her earpiece once with her index finger and holding, she asked, "Sean, are any of them coming down?"

"Affirm," Sean responded after a few seconds. "I got one moving downstairs, the other three staying put."

"Roger."

A minute later, Anna was able to hear boots thumping on the opposite side of the door. She took one step back from the doorway. There was a pop in the door, just above the knob, and then the handle itself popped as it was unlocked from the inside. A thin ray of indistinct orange shined through the entryway, and was overtaken by gray as the door cracked open. Anna stood far enough to the left of the doorway that whoever'd come to answer the door couldn't see her through the cautious fissure they'd made in the entrance. As she'd calculated, the individual forced the door open against the snow until it was halfway ajar and they could slip through while maintaining partial cover from the storm. A man appeared in the dim orange glow that escaped the building's interior. Six and a half feet tall, long red hair, and a blue cross painted to his forehead, the Disciple Anna and Sean spotted with Jesus. A T-05 dangled from his back, the strap wrapped around his chest. His vision found her in the gray, the cross expression on his face measuring the black-hatted and black-clothed figure who waited by the door. The man's eyes were starting to enlarge with alarm, when Anna's rifle rocketed up, the suppressor centering on his cross. Her index finger pulled at the trigger, one hiss and one kick from the weapon's barrel. Sentience vanished from the man's expression. Orange-red mist clouded the front of his skull as he dropped into the snow, the cries of the blizzard canceling out any last declarations he might've made. *Eight to go.*

"Sean, are any of them moving upstairs?"

"Negative, they're all in the same place."

"Copy that."

She hauled the corpse through the door by his ankles, his weight miniscule, orange-red draining onto the wooden floor of the doorway. When the body of their fifth Sword of God kill was settled on the floor, she closed, bolted, and locked the front door, and turned around to face the inside of the building. A long hallway led away from the entrance, constructed of brown wooden floors and walls. Lining the left side wall of the hallway were three doors to other rooms, all shut. On the right side wall, two lit candlesticks and a single kerosene lantern had been set on a short wooden table, lighting the hall in shadowed orange. Anna had learned a little of candles and kerosene lanterns in school and more so during training with Darius, their mass production in the Previous Civilization, their scarcity yet continued existence in today's world, and their reliability as a light source in circumstances where electricity was not available. The building was strikingly free of grime, even the few feet ahead of the doorway where Anna conformed to the custom of kicking snow from her boots upon entry. It was as if every surface of the structure's interior was cleaned on a daily basis, never mind the town's presence at the heart of a war zone.

Raising her weapon with both hands, Anna moved down to the end of the hall, her boots squeaking on the floor. The inside air was warmer than what the blizzard offered, but still cold enough that puffs of orange-white breath glowed with each exhale. Turning the corner, she came across a narrow stairwell, dark and lacking any candle or lantern lights. After ascending the stairs, she aimed the T-05 down the second floor of the building. Almost identical to the first, this hallway consisted of the same setup and features, except it was nearly pitch dark, its two candles and one kerosene lantern unlit. Only trickles of orange spreading from both ends of the passageway made it possible to see. There was a curtained window frame to the side of the staircase corner, where the front door had been on the first floor. Anna moved towards the next stairway at the end of the hall. Five feet from the turn to the stairs, she heard a man shout down from the top floor, voice just reaching over the shrill of the wind against the building's walls. "Who was that, Thaddeus?" His tone was calm despite the high volume, anticipating an immediate reply. She took to the second stairwell. The man spoke again, vigilant yet not frightened. "Thaddeus?"

She neared the top of the stairs, weapon ready in her hands, when Sean returned to her ear. "Anna, you've got one moving your way. Arms are up like he's holding a rifle."

Passing the last stair, she heard the stomping around the corner, a single pair of boots. They entered the hallway, Anna from the staircase, the man stepping out from the first room on the hall's left side. He faced her from the open doorway, blond hair, glasses, a blue cross, and a T-05 beginning to raise itself in his arms, the barrel directed at her. "Fuck," Jesus Christ had time to blare, before Anna's index finger yanked at the trigger to her T-05 Sniper, the rifle expelling its muffled hiss and shudder, once, twice, thrice, four times in less than a second. Orange-red exploded from Jesus's shoulders and knees, the four slugs finding not-instantly fatal locations on the terrorist commander's body. His legs failed him, his kneecaps blown apart, a flash erupted at the front of his T-05, trailed by three rapid booms that shook the walls and tore a set of holes in the ceiling, dumping plaster down on Jesus and the floor in front of Anna.

He collapsed between the doorway and the table, wailing in pain before he'd even hit the floor, glasses flying from his face, rifle leaving his hands.

Anna advanced down the third-floor hall to the door, boots crunching on the crumbs of ceiling, the smoking suppressor of her T-05 shifting from him to the passage. An exact copy of the first two, the hallway's lighting was likewise to the first floor, achieved by two candles and one lantern set on the table. The doors to the second and third rooms on the left side of the hall were closed like the others, but the entrance to the first room was wide open, revealing the last two inhabitants of the building. Across a contented looking room of cushioned lounge furniture and two small circular wood tables, on which stood lit candles and lanterns, were two of Athens's surviving citizens.

A man and a woman, older than Jesus and Thaddeus both, somewhere in their early to mid-fifties, Anna assessed. They were situated against the back wall of the room, their chests facing the door and curved downward as their bodies held a sort of half-stand half-crouch that appeared excruciating from the first glimpse of it. Anna knew this to be a stress-position, a method of interrogation.

Placed at both sides of a small brick fireplace embedded in the wall, filled with bright orange wood-burning flame, the man and woman's arms were stretched around their backs, their hands tied and locked to the wall with chains that rattled with the slightest movement. Their ankles were seized in the same fashion, bound tight together so even standing upright would bring eventual strain on their leg muscles. They were stripped of any and all clothing, their naked skin discolored by so many bright orange-red and orange-purple gashes Anna wondered how either of them hadn't fallen unconscious from blood loss. Tape sealed their mouths, yet the subdued shrieks of exhausted and agonized terror were still audible between the rages of the storm. At their bare feet, puddles of brown and orange-yellow covered the floor. These Athenians had been chained to the fireplace for several hours at least, no timeouts for the latrine included. *Like Jason. No, not like Jason. Jason was about gathering intelligence. These people have nothing Sword of God doesn't already know. Jesus was probably bored and needed some amusement. That's all this is to him, stimulation.*

She was about to step into the room, release the man and woman from their restraints, when her partner called over the Network, his worry obvious. "Anna, what the fuck was that sound?"

Tapping her earpiece once and holding with her index finger, she answered. "Jesus's weapon went off. You heard it?"

"Loud and fucking clear, the thing echoed all the way to North and South Gate. I guarantee the rest of them heard it too."

"Fuck," she yelled into the room, adding to the Athenians hypothermic and wound-induced trembling, as if wanting them to recognize the self-intended frustration and anger she felt. *Fuck, any minute now we're going to have every last Disciple bearing down on us, plus any Athenians they decide to bring along at the whip, all because I wasn't quick enough.*

"Whatever you're going to do, Anna, it'll have to be fast."

With a last look to the bloodied man and woman, regretfully accepting she did not have the time to rescue them, not even to cut their chains from the wall, Anna turned away from the room, knowing the Athenian prisoners would not see her remorse. To them, she would be the one who stared right at them, saw their suffering, and left them as they were. "Copy that, Sean. Maintain position and report all contacts as they appear."

Anna brought her attention back to the Sword of God commander. Crouching down in the pool of dark orange-red that spread over the floor, she lodged her boot on his demolished kneecap, crushing what little bright orange-red flesh and bone endured with a piercing crunch. The building's foundation seemed to deteriorate under the punishment of Jesus's screams. "Fuck! Fuck you! Fuck that hurts!"

Anna shouldered her T-05 Sniper, knowing it wasn't necessary for this part of the operation. "I know it hurts, all right. I just need some information from you and then, then I'll make the pain stop. Okay?" Jesus twisted his head away from her, saturating his face and hair in the bright orange-red, but she gripped the sides of his head with her hands and pulled him back into focus. "Hey!" Lowering the volume of her voice, she said to him, "I promise you, once you tell me everything, the pain will stop. Understand?"

The man began pleading then as he writhed in pain, but not to her. "Fuck, fuck, Jesus help me!" Tears flooded his blue eyes, the same shade of light blue as his cross, not bright lime green as the footage from Sword of God's raid on the Troy Station showed. And with that, Anna discovered the catastrophic miscalculation she, Sean, Darius, and everyone involved with the mission had made. This man was not Jesus Christ, but another Disciple.

"Understand?" Anna asked again, as if nothing had changed, as if Sword of God hadn't lied to Joseph Holloway, who then unknowingly gave the Dragoons incorrect information.

"Yes," the Disciple yelped with a nod, submitting to her control.

"Good, now we're both up to speed. Your friend down there, you called him Thaddeus. What do you call yourself?"

The blond-haired Disciple was quick with his answer, voice sharp with continued agony. "Judas."

Sean reported to her. "I've got contacts on the move at ground level. Two by the North Gate heading this way, three more from the South Gate. They look like they're in a hurry."

Anna nodded. "Judas. Okay Judas, tell me, where are Jesus and the other Disciples? What buildings are they staying in?"

Judas hesitated for a few moments, almost too long for Anna's patience, but then he answered. "Matthew, James, and Bartholomew, they're in the two buildings linked to North Gate."

Her partner was afraid now. "Shit, they're going straight towards your building, Anna."

"Philip and Thomas are in a building next to South Gate."

"Which side of the road, east or west?" Anna asked, not turning away from her prisoner.

"West, this side."

Almost there. "Okay Judas, I still need two more. Where are Jesus and Simon?"

Judas shook his head. "They're not here." His speech was hesitant; Anna could see he was stalling.

Her boot pressed deeper into his knee. Drops of water streaked from his eyes, down his cheeks, as she said to him, "Where are they, Judas?"

"Jesus left Athens before dawn this morning," Judas admitted after too many seconds. "He took Simon with him."

A burst of scorching rage, with dread packed in somewhere, came over Anna at the thought that she and Sean had gotten to Athens a mere couple hours too late to terminate Jesus and the Disciple, Simon. But before she could demand an explanation from Judas, her partner interjected, his message coming into her ear with the haste of someone who was terrified. "Anna, they're gunning for you. You better wrap things up with that fucker. They're going to be at your door in sixty seconds or less."

With this account from outside, she tapped and held her earpiece. She wasn't sure if she was scared, but if she was she didn't let Judas see. "I'm not done yet."

"Do you want me to engage?" Anxious as he was, Sean didn't stop mid-sentence or try to take back what was being said, he spoke with the anticipation of an answer.

And yet for some reason she differed her response. "Are they armed?"

"Four are for sure. One I can't tell, but I think so."

There are only five of them. Sean's a Dragoon. "They're armed, light them the fuck up."

"Copy that."

Anna resumed her interrogation, confident her partner could hold off, if not eliminate every hostile he'd spotted. "Where'd they go?" she ordered Judas to tell her.

The wounded and captured Disciple rocked his head back and forth again, as if starting to believe he had a choice over which questions he could and could not reply to. "I can't I. I don't know."

Aware that Judas was baiting her to repeat the same question a dozen times, Anna pulled her boot off his kneecap. As he squealed from the ache, she found the shards of glass that broke from the lenses of Judas's twisted glasses, lying in the pond of dark orange-red that had flowed into the lounge room. Taking a small yet sharp fragment of glass in her hand, she picked one of the candlesticks up off the hallway table, lit and burning dim orange. The orange-red spread under the table as well. The rate of the man's loss of blood seemed equal in severity to his agony, enough that he didn't notice the glass until Anna drew the shard over his left eye, slicing a line of bright orange-red across his light blue eyeball. Judas's screams were monstrous, his thrashing so violent Anna had to thrust her boots to knee and chest to clamp him down.

The building shuddered with the rumbling of multiple discharges from an automatic rifle, out on the street, which complemented the whines of the storm. Yellow flashed into the hall, through the window beside the stairs, the light shining between the cracks in the curtain. *They're firing at Sean. He's been fired on before, plus those shots could be his. He might've taken the suppressor off his weapon again, like he did in Dresden.* Pressuring herself to not be distracted by the firefight her partner was engaged in, she tossed the orange-red soaked shard of glass from her glove and gripped Judas's ear with one hand, keeping his head in place. With her other hand, she lowered the burning end of the candlestick towards the man's slashed and bleeding left eyeball. Outside, the simulated thunder and lightning created by the automatic rifle stopped, as if the shooter had been interrupted mid-burst. Anna felt relieved. *Sean brought that one down.*

Judas saw the orange flame approaching with his good eye, and when he realized shifting his head wouldn't save him, he begged. "No fuck, I don't know, please!" His interrogator jabbed the candle into Judas's left eye, forcing the flame and the hot wax that surrounded the flame against the gash on his eyeball. "Fuck! Help, help me!" A trickle of smoke rose from his head as his eyeball singed.

Sean came back, his voice soft, so quiet Anna almost didn't hear him over Judas's pleas, even on the Network. "Anna, I'm hit." His already weakened speech tapered with a pain and alarm driven groan. "Fuck." The automatic rifle surged back to life, the swift bangs flashing through the window curtain, and she couldn't hear Sean on the Network anymore.

Letting go of Judas's ear, Anna pressed and held her earpiece with her index finger, hard enough she nearly dislodged the earpiece and sent it plummeting down her ear canal. "Say again, Sean?" She felt as though her chest was condensing around her lungs, she could hear the panic in her voice and knew Judas could too, but right then she didn't care. "Sean, repeat your last," she said over the Network when she didn't hear back from her partner after five seconds. Another three seconds of silence in her earpiece. "Vanguard Two this is Vanguard One, what's your status?" No response.

Hammering echoed up to Anna from the front door of the building. A man called, shouting at such an intense volume he was overheard through the window, despite the blizzard. "Judas! Thaddeus! One of you sound off!"

She trembled, fearing not for herself but for the voice that was no longer in her ear. Knowing if Sword of God was at the door, then Sean must've been defeated, Anna halfheartedly decided the intelligence Judas possessed would remain her priority. Like the liberation of the man and woman chained to the fireplace, the determination of Sean's present status would have to wait. When the candle went out on Judas's eye, she chucked the stick, leaving a brown and cauterized blotch at the center of the eyeball, hints of blue and white restricted to the edges of the blinded eyeball. "Where the fuck did Jesus go?"

she growled into Judas's ears, whether the people outside heard her or not wasn't important. But Judas didn't give in, and she curled her hand into a fist and struck him in his ruined eye. "Tell me!"

There was a crash from below as the locks and hinges of the front entrance were blown off by the pops of a rifle. The door slammed onto the first floor, the shriek of the wind joining a moment later. "Shit, they got Thaddeus too," a man exclaimed.

A stampede of stomping squeaking boots and clattering weapons moved down the hall towards the first staircase. "Up the stairs, up the stairs!"

Anna punched Judas's eye again. "Tell me!"

"Where the fuck's Matthew?" the man who'd spoken of Thaddeus asked. "I thought he was following us inside."

The pack of boots and clanging weapons was on the stairs now, heading for the second floor. "He's probably checking the gates."

She punched Judas in the eye a third time. "Tell me!"

"Fort Valley," Judas bellowed. "Jesus and Simon went back to Fort Valley!"

Fort Valley? She didn't know what the name signified, but there was no time for that. "Why did they go back to Fort Valley?"

"Our camp's there!" Judas was weeping from his right eye now. The tramping and screeching boots reached the second floor, directly beneath Anna and her prisoner, immediately starting for the second staircase.

Her demeanor pacified again, her voice relaxed, as if she wasn't about to be overrun but rather she and Judas were the only two people in the building. "Why'd they go back to the camp?"

Judas had no resistance left to deny Anna the answers she pursued, yet he talked fast, as if hoping she wouldn't catch everything. "Supply cache there." The boots were at the bottom of the second stairwell now. "Jesus wants to move it here."

The boots and their weapons were dashing up the stairs, but Anna wasn't finished. "What's in this supply cache?"

"Food, medicine, weapons. Previous Civilization made."

"That's how Jesus got his start," Anna concluded aloud.

"Yes," Judas wept in confirmation.

She nodded. "Thank you, Judas." Anna rose from the orange-red mess on the hallway floor, redrawing her rifle as she stood over the Disciple. And with a single suppressed shot delivered to the cross on Judas's forehead, the interrogator kept her promise to her prisoner. She swung around as the leading boots of the oncoming party arrived at the top of the steps and rounded the corner into the hallway. Another man, another blue cross, another thieved Marathon uniform, and another T-05. A pair of night vision goggles was wrapped around his head, the black tubed lenses raised above his eyes, unneeded in the orange light of the building. Anna couldn't gauge anymore about him than that, because the Disciple took one step forward before her T-05 hissed and jolted at the yank of the trigger. The man's head detonated in a burst of orange-red and white skull fragments that showered the corner of the hallway, shredded the curtains to rags, and shattered the window into bits of twinkling orange glass. The first Disciple fell on his stomach as the second Disciple arose from the stairwell. A second hiss and kick from her T-05 Sniper and the Disciple's head jerked to the side through a smaller mist of orange-red, the rest of his body following along. As he spun around and tumbled, however, a lone flash boomed from his T-05. Anna felt a numbing sensation at the side of her right arm, just below her shoulder, as the second Disciple collapsed beside the first, T-05 clanging on the wooden floor. She turned the suppressor of her rifle on the group's third attacker. This Disciple never had the chance to take a shot at her, not even get a look at her. He was coming off the steps, his head and chest just beginning to peek around the curve of the hall, when Anna's weapon whistled for the fourth time in the last three seconds.

The haze of orange-red was supplemented by the crash of the Disciple's frame on the stairs, a banging almost as loud as the T-05, which continued as the man's body rolled all the way down the stairwell, making a wall quaking collision with the second floor. No fourth Disciple came.

Though she was certain the third Disciple had been quelled along with the first two, Anna moved to the stairwell. The building became silent, save for the ongoing blizzard and the anguished mumblings of the Athenians in their chains. *I'll come back for them when I know the terrorist at the bottom of the steps is dead.* The space in front of the staircase was drenched so greatly in streaming orange-red that dripped down and collected in orange-red slicks on each step, the glare stung Anna's eyes as her boots splashed downward through the aftermath. Facing the second floor, her T-05 still in hand as smoke exited through the tip of the suppressor, she laid eyes on the carcass of the third Disciple, recognizing then that the fifth person she'd killed since coming to Athens was not a Disciple at all.

Anna didn't recall walking down the stairs. It was as if at one instant she was at the top, looking down at the departed Athenian, and at the next she was at the bottom, on her knees staring over the sprawled out body. Wearing a black and purple winter jacket, dark purple pants, black boots, and purple gloves, this citizen of Athens was a girl. With the girl's clothing torn in more than a few places, her face and neck discolored by days old purple cuts and bruises, her eyes encased by black circles, Anna speculated she had spent the last week and a half as a prisoner of Sword of God, held in relentless close proximity to the two Disciples lying dead on the third floor. The Marathon-issued switchblade hooked to her belt told Anna that when the girl's imprisoning Disciples had rushed from their building at the sound of Judas's T-05, they'd dragged the girl into the blizzard with them, cannon fodder. Brutalized into complete unquestioning obedience, the girl had followed without an escape attempt.

Head swathed with glistening and untamed blond hair, her face older though enduringly innocent, the girl appeared exactly as Anna imagined Chloe would look at age eleven or twelve. She knew this child was not her daughter, there was no conceivable way it could be, and yet Anna felt the girl laid to rest before her was indeed Chloe. It was as if six-year-old Chloe was residing under the city's care in the Missio sub-district of Marathon, during the same period of time twelve-year-old Chloe was living in Athens. This adolescent Chloe had been captured by Sword of God on the night the town was occupied, her mother a hundred-fifty miles away, unable to help her. Then, ten days later, Chloe was ordered to join Jesus's Disciples in thwarting an attack on Athens, doing so out of pure desperation and the fear of what might happen if she declined. It was in the midst of this engagement that Chloe was felled by a bullet wound to the side of her head, which now wetted her hair and jacket with orange-red. Her murderer, her own mother, her own mother who'd violated the oath she'd unconsciously made at the beginning of her service with the Black Dragoons, the pledge to never murder a child. It was the vow that prohibited Anna from terminating the two Cavaliers' children and forced Sean to conclude the mission, a promise she swore to because of what Chloe had made her, a parent. As a parent, Anna understood that in war children had about as little control over their environment as they did in deciding who their parents would be. On the scale of blame that graded everyone involved in every conflict that had ever transpired, from the Previous Civilization to the 31st Year of Marathon, children stood on the absolute lowest pedestal, a place where there were no perpetrators, no combatants, and no victors, only victims.

10: SEAN

Anna's partner witnessed it through his thermal scope, the heat signature he knew to be hers meeting a heat signature he suspected to be Sword of God on the third purple floor of Jesus's building, that

Sword of God soldier's orange silhouette collapsing, most likely shot down by Anna, and yet not dying. What Sean did not see but heard, were as many as three shots from what he judged to be an automatic rifle, the bangs shouting out through the shrilling gray sprays of the blizzard in one group, and ringing up and down the community's walls to the gates at each end. The source was an inadvertent discharge, he guessed, the Sword of God fighter's finger squeezing the trigger as he dropped with Anna's quieted rounds, a relatively small incident, whose titanic ripple effects were recognized by Sean. *We're blown.*

The other seven Disciples and their Athenian prisoners would've heard those reports. It wouldn't take long for them to flock to the town center in search of the origin of the gunfire. A warming blanket of apprehension was placed over Sean's body, except not at the thought of a pending Sword of God counterassault; he had the superior firing position and the gray cover of the blizzard. He dreaded how Commander Darius would punish a Carthage-born immigrant for failing to take down Sword of God, should any of the Disciples survive and escape. The threat was well clear to him. However, as he peered through his thermal scope at the third floor of Jesus's darkish purple building, he gathered that the danger was not so apparent to his partner.

Anna's orange silhouette was turned towards the other two heat signatures in the building, while the silhouette she'd just wounded squirmed on the purple floor, as if trying to get back on his feet. The affiliation of the last two building occupants was unknown to Sean, though considering Anna hadn't killed or wounded them yet, he hypothesized they were Athenian prisoners, which now distracted her from the situation outside the structure. Tapping his earpiece once and holding it with his index finger, he said, "Anna, what the fuck was that sound?" as if hoping the storm implanted the illusion of rifle shots in his head, and Anna would tell him there was no sound.

That wasn't her reply. "Jesus's weapon went off. You heard it?"

At least she's got Jesus in there. Maybe I'm not completely fucked after all. "Loud and fucking clear, the thing echoed all the way to North and South Gate. I guarantee the rest of them heard it too."

"Fuck," she yelled back in frustration.

Sean cringed with a sting in his ear. "Whatever you're going to do, Anna, it'll have to be fast."

Through his scope, he saw her silhouette twist around to Jesus's silhouette, apparently disregarding the other people on the third floor. "Copy that, Sean. Maintain position and report all contacts as they appear."

Without wasting even a second to confirm Anna's instruction, Sean adjusted the positioning of his T-05 Sniper on the roof wall he held over watch from, shifting his scope to observe the north ends of the purple roadway. Then, he twisted his weapon around to scan the southern end. The street was as empty as it'd been when they scaled the eastern wall. He only had to wait about a minute.

They appeared from the north first, two orange human silhouettes exiting the northernmost building of the Western Block, next to North Gate. Checking the south, he spotted three more silhouettes leaving the southernmost building of the Western Block beside South Gate. Switching between the two groups every couple seconds, he watched the two northern-based silhouettes begin trekking south along the western side of the street, while the three southern silhouettes headed north on the same flank of the road. All five silhouettes moved at a hurried pace, about as close to a run as the wind and snow would allow. One silhouette in each group seemed to be angling their head upwards, as if scouring the rooftops as they traveled. How they expected to see anything through the storm, Sean didn't understand. Clicking and holding his earpiece, he said, "I've got contacts on the move at ground level. Two by the North Gate heading this way, three more from the South Gate. They look like they're in a hurry."

His partner didn't answer as he continued to track the silhouettes. He hoped the approaching persons were not sure where the bangs had come from and would take a few extra minutes to search the rest of the town center before turning attention to Jesus's building. However, as the seconds wore on that possibility was debunked in Sean's mind and his unease escalated to registerable fear, though not of how Darius would penalize the botched operation. The two groups held a straightforward path towards Jesus's location, towards Sean's partner, towards Anna. Second-Gen she was, a more proficient close quarter's fighter she was, and yet he was scared for her, much more than he'd been when he offered her up as a target for the sniper in Dresden. "Shit, they're going straight towards your building, Anna."

No response from his partner still, and the silhouettes kept coming down and up the street until he estimated they were a minute away from the front door of Jesus's building. With every meter of gust and snow the silhouettes conquered, Sean's fright adapted to terror for Anna and the growing chance of her being overrun. And when he contacted her again he talked fast and nervous, hoping his waning composure would better convey the situation and draw a reply from her. "Anna, they're gunning for you. You better wrap things up with that fucker. They're going to be at your door in sixty seconds or less."

Finally she retorted, and quick. "I'm not done yet."

Fuck that, you got the fucker now clear out before you become the first Second-Gen to die for Marathon. With a deep breath, he commanded his thoughts to ease. *She needs this, you both do. Dresden, Athens, these people have to fall.* "Do you want me to engage?"

He expected immediate approval but didn't get it. Instead, she hesitated; as if afraid to put him up against five potential Disciples. "Are they armed?"

Making another inspection of both onrushing groups, he focused on how their arms swayed with their strides. The arms on four of the five silhouettes maintained a stagnant outspread position, even as their legs swung through the snow. *Rifles.* Only the third individual in the party from the south ran with free arms. *Not a rifle but maybe a pistol, maybe.* "Four are for sure. One I can't tell, but I think so."

Anna's reaction was firm, as if she wanted to seem more aggressive than she did a moment ago. "They're armed, light them the fuck up."

"Copy that," was all he could think to say before taking his finger off his earpiece.

There was a practical reason for why he chose the group to the north. If the breeze or a dirt-snowflake in his eye caused him to miss, there would only be two silhouettes to track the shot rather than three. He centered his thermal scope on the silhouette closest to the walls of the Western Block. Index finger wrapped at the trigger, arms, body, and T-05 Sniper unmoving despite the cold. With a grimy snow-filled breath, the trigger pulled back, the suppressor hissed, and the weapon kicked him in the shoulder, and scraped the top of the brick wall.

The first silhouette buckled, his orange head vanishing from his orange frame into the purple, as Sean moved to the second silhouette, fixing on their head. Another breath, hiss, kick, and scrape, and both silhouettes toppled at what looked to be the same instant, dropping to the snow and not getting back up. The threat from the north was cancelled in a single two-second volley. Sean found himself chuckling at the relief of his success. "White Death," he said, and lifted his rifle, training the T-05 Sniper on the party to the south. His scope marked the leading silhouette, his index finger holding on the trigger. He took in a third rotten breath but a noise yanked him away from his weapon, a long series of cries from directly across the road. His head turned to the gray, never mind the fact there was little for his eyes to look at. The shrieks were a man's, sheer, with colossal agony glued to them. *What's she doing to...?* There was a flash of yellow at the fringes of Sean's right eye.

He lay on his side in the snow, facing the wall, his rifle lying between him and the brick, the top of the barrier disintegrating in a thunderous flash of automatic weapons fire that brought a downpour of brick chunks upon the roof. His position was compromised and under fire, that was obvious; how was less clear. There was a third silhouette from the north, Sean theorized, one that had moved south out of his line of sight by hugging the walls on the eastern side of the street. The shooter must've been wearing night vision goggles, or using some other type of special optics equipment, that was the only way he could've seen his two companions fall on the western end of the road, found Sean on the rooftops, and returned fire. *The Disciples in Dresden had night vision.*

What held the majority of his attention, however, was the excruciating pain on the right side of his head, at once both boiling and numbing his skin, as if a fire was spreading on his face, dwindling, and then growing again. The piercing burns began at his right eye and extended to the right side of his skull, just short of his ear. All of the physical pain he'd encountered on the mission thus far was diminutive by comparison, an inconvenience he was able to push back against by turning his mind to something else. This was inescapable. The firing from the street ended, as Sean placed his hand over the right side of his head, and sensed the heat of slush and blood warming his hand through his glove, and saturating his hat. He was hit, though it dawned on him that he hadn't taken a direct hit from the shooter's automatic rifle. If he had he wouldn't have been able to feel the pain in his head; he wouldn't be feeling anything anymore. More likely, he'd been struck by shrapnel and fragments of the brick wall that were blown apart beside his head. Nevertheless, the delirium that caused the roof to vibrate below him and the blood on his head indicated his wounds were severe, a stop the operation kind of severe.

Tapping his earpiece once and holding, he struggled to bring his speech out above the pain. "Anna, I'm hit." His wounds fought back with an interruptive and voice diminishing moan. "Fuck." The shooter's automatic rifle flashed and boomed again before Anna could acknowledge or reply. Sean rolled onto his stomach, burying his face in the snow and shielding the back of his head with his hands, but only after his right ear was smacked by what he guessed was a portion of flying brick, adding to his injury. This second barrage lasted a few seconds, and then concluded as swift as the salvo that wounded him. However, when he put his finger back to his throbbing right ear and said, "Anna," there was no earpiece for him to connect with. Prodding his finger around the outer rim of his ear and even a little ways into his ear canal only further certified his access to the Network was gone, lost in the gray of the blizzard. Shifting back onto his side and staring at the brick wall, decreased to a one-foot high hole-laden defense, Sean realized he would have to go to Anna for medical assistance. He couldn't ask her to come to him.

Then, he noticed the change in his eyesight.

It was as if the storm had worsened, the gray pressing down on his vision and compressing what he was capable of seeing. The right side of his field of vision was absent, not fuzzed or shortened, but simply gone. To look at his right shoulder, he had to rotate his head to the right until his left eye could capture what his right eye no longer could. At the bottom right of his left eye's perspective, was the left nostril of his frosted gray nose, his vision no longer centered but left side dominant. Sean knew his right eye was still there, he felt the eyeball searing in sharp pain, as if tiny bits of metal were entrenched in his eye socket. But when he poked around for the eye with his fingers, he discovered a mushy substance had overtaken his eyelid. Holding his fingers in front of his left eye, he saw dark red sticking to the black covering of his gloved digits. Sean was blind in his right eye.

Flight was Sean's initial reaction to his partial blindness. The last message his partner received from him was he was wounded, followed by the weapons fire that disconnected them. It wasn't much of a stretch that Anna may think him dead for the time being. With the blizzard there would be no verification of his status, unless he rendezvoused with her himself. He had the opportunity to flee Athens, escape the machine of Marathon, treat his wounds, and strike out wherever he pleased, free to determine his own course of survival. Then, a set of flashes and bangs from a rifle down on the road snuffed those thoughts, because he knew those shots weren't targeted at him but at his partner. Anna, an agent of the Black Dragoons assassination unit, a torturer, a murderer, just as he was. Anna, the lone person in the world he cared for, who he thought might care for him too, his one and only commitment. And like Jason's commitment to Katherine, Sean's commitment to Anna wouldn't break with the loss of one eye.

He couldn't go down the ladder. As far as he knew, the Disciple that had already blinded his right eye was standing on the street, rifle aimed at the roof and waiting for Sean to stand up above the wall. Without his right eye to look through his scope, Sean couldn't use his T-05 Sniper on his right side, and there was little chance he'd be able to bring the weapon to bear on his left with the speed needed to return fire successfully. As hindered as he was, however, Sean had another means of getting to his partner. Revolving onto his stomach again, he crawled from the damaged portion of the brick wall to the side of the roof, where the wall was intact. Beyond this wall was the next building down in the Eastern Block, a three-story structure. A ten-foot gap fell between the two rooftops. Another snapping rifle shot from across the walkway ensured the fear of heights he experienced on the pipe would not reappear here. Out of sight of the road now, he rose to his feet and stepped over the bricks, letting his boots, legs, and chest slide off, until he was hanging from the wall by his hands. Looking down, he let go of the bricks.

The landing was softened by snow, but the lower half of his frame still cried out as his boots impacted and he fell on his pack. When he recovered, he stood back up and moved across the roof. The next structure in the line was two stories, he knew, another ten-foot drop. He took it all the same. On this roof he returned to the edge overlooking the street, crouching, and then crawling again. There was no brick barricade, just the end of the roof and the gray that swirled past and obscured the road. At this new observation post, Sean lay prone and tried to ready his rifle, setting his right hand on the barrel of the weapon, his left hand at the trigger, and his left eye at the scope, all in a sluggish and awkward manner that would bring any weapons instructor to tears with scornful laughter. It was as if he was back in the opening days of training with the Dragoons, wielding the T-05 Sniper for the first time. No, it was as if he'd never held anything close to a rifle in his entire life. The voices of his muscle memory were raging from the right side of his body, insisting he was carrying his rifle in the wrong place, a commotion that delayed his attempt further, forced him to approach every step with the utmost attentiveness. And while he eventually set himself in a position of moderate comfort, his arrangement was far below perfect. With the collar of his jacket growing wet with what he assumed to be blood from his head, Sean made a clumsy scan of the street.

At last the day seemed to be working for him rather than against. The roadway was purple from Jesus's building to North Gate and South Gate. Of course, the shooter who'd bested him could've been hiding along the eastern walls, but at this point in the battle, Sean didn't think so. The Disciple had probably joined the effort to rescue Jesus, believing Sean to be suppressed. *In his mind, if I haven't shown myself by now that means I'm down for good.* Shifting his scope to the building that took center stage in this mess their assault had become, he swept each floor of the now inactive structure. Overcoming the obnoxious chore that readjusting his scope had mutated into, he found the first floor exclusively purple and the third floor purple save for the two silhouettes he'd previously thought to be Athenian prisoners, who strangely retained the exact same position on the floor they'd been in before the Disciples clustered at the building. But it was the second floor that concerned him the most. Towards the back of the floor was one orange silhouette, sitting on their knees, immobile. The prospect that this silhouette belonged to a wounded and fading Anna convinced Sean he had to somehow endure the twenty-foot drop that separated him from the road.

Although this building lacked a ladder, there was a gutter pipe, dense with thick ice. Distracting himself with the sustained burning pain that ailed his head and eye, Sean strapped his T-05 Sniper over his shoulder, enfolded his boots around the gutter, and lowered himself below the roof. Denying his better judgment the chance to intervene, Sean moved one hand from the rooftop to the gutter, followed straightaway by his other hand. With both hands and feet on the drain, he began to slide on the ice, fast. Down the gutter he skated, keeping his left eye shut and not bothering with his right. The ground seemed to raise itself up to greet him, the iced snow connecting to his boots with a brief yet noticeable crunch. His legs pulsated in fury once more, but he disregarded the relatively minor aching and unstrapped his rifle to face the hostile street.

Suffering through the concerted blasts of wind that blew between the blocks and gouged his eye and head with showers of spiked dirt that packed his wounds and certainly quadrupled his chances of infection, Sean moved on the open doorway of Jesus's building. Finding the door shot from its locks and hinges and lying on the floor of the building's interior, Sean stepped inside and out of the blistering cold, though that did little for his wounds. The body of the red-haired Disciple was sprawled in a disarray of orange-red and disseminated door fragments, just in front of the collapsed door. He walked around the corpse without a second look, his focus caught by the pairs of orange-red boot prints that stained the floor, two or three as best as Sean could tell, and continued to the end of the hall. Clearing the faint-orange lit floor, he advanced to the staircase at the end of the hallway. Up the steps and onto the darkened second floor, he made the same scan of the hall and moved towards the bottom of the next stairwell. Closing on the corner to the stairs, he spotted a slick of dark red seeping into the hall. *Anna!* He sprinted the last several feet, thinking more about retrieving his med gear from his pack than sweeping the staircase for Disciples. Rounding the corner, he found that the silhouette he'd seen through his thermal scope was Anna, wounded as he'd feared. But, the blood that leaked onto the floor of the hallway wasn't hers.

There was a rip on the right sleeve of Anna's jacket, just beneath the shoulder, that revealed a large bright orange-red gash on the side of her arm. Sean saw bright orange-red oozing out the bottom of Anna's sleeve, dyeing her glove. Despite this, his partner didn't seem to notice or care about the wound that was sending blood down her arm. She didn't even appear to grasp that he was there, standing over her. Her Second-Gen Stage was disengaged, her expression frozen in a place of emotional stillness more human than anything Sean thought her species was capable of. It was as if she'd had an experience so upending that her Awakening had been reversed and she was relapsing back to an inactive Second-Gen, no more evolved than any other human being. Every piece of her actuality was centered on the body that clogged the foot of the stairway, and served as the base of the orange-red blood that dampened the floor. It was a girl, not a young child but not a teenager either, somewhere between ten and twelve years old, an Athenian no doubt. Deducing how Anna and this girl came to be, Sean lowered his T-05.

PHASE 3: DRAGOONED

3rd Day of Mission Deployment
Status of Vanguard One: WIA (Minor)
Status of Vanguard Two: WIA (Severe)
Operation Status: 77% Complete

11: ANNA

On a winter's night in the 30th Year of Marathon, twenty-year-old Anna Corday and her five-year-old daughter Chloe Corday sat cross-legged on their bed in the cramped confines of their Missio bunk. Their mattress was swaddled in black sheets and blankets, the black frame of the bunk squeaking less than half a foot above Anna's head, the world beyond the bunk made invisible by everlasting blackness. Dressed in dark blue long sleeve shirts and black shorts, mother and daughter faced one another with reliance, each trusting they could say anything to the person who sat before her.

Chloe, her glittering blond hair damp and straightened from a trip to the showers, spoke first. "Are we in trouble, mommy?" Young and innocent as she was, Anna's daughter talked with the serious expression of someone several years older.

"Why would you think that, Chloe?" Anna had some notion of what caused the girl's concern, but she wanted to hear her reasoning.

The girl's eyes danced around the bunk. "I don't know. Everybody's been acting funny today, no one at school would talk to me. Why did the soldiers walk me to school and back? Did we do something wrong?"

Anna was quick to try and counter her daughter's fears, knowing the damage they could wreak if allowed to persist for another day. Placing a hand on Chloe's shoulder, she said, "No, no, dear, we didn't do anything wrong. You're just going to have to get used to people treating us a little differently now."

Chloe used her favorite word. "Why?"

"Because they know what we are and that scares them." Anna paused. "So they think they have to be mean to us."

"Because we're Second-Gens?" Chloe's ability to infer what her mother was saying never ceased to astound Anna.

Nodding, Anna told Chloe, "Yep. Second-Gens and humans don't get along so well. Just remember, you're still the same person you've always been, still Chloe."

"Are we dangerous?"

Leaning in closer, as if to emphasize the importance of her next question, Anna said, "Chloe, who told you we're dangerous?"

Chloe dipped her head down towards the blankets, like she would do when she knew she'd done something wrong. "I heard kids in my class saying how their daddies and mommies told them Second-Gens are dangerous."

Anna put her hand under Chloe's chin, propping her daughter's head back up. She'd done nothing wrong.

"They said Second-Gens can rip your head off with their bare hands."

"Chloe, I want you to listen to me. You listening?"

"Yes, mommy."

"You and I are not dangerous," Anna said, stern. "Those kids don't know what they're talking about, neither do their parents." It wasn't hard for her to believe such prejudices had been born before the 1st Year of Marathon, even before the Reform, exaggerated perceptions of Second-Gens superior strength, fueled by distrust and spite. She herself had bought into several of them before she and her daughter's true nature became known. "They're all being tricked by stories that aren't real."

To Anna's respite, a look of surprised relief overtook her daughter. "They're being tricked?" she asked, the curve of a grin beginning to surface on her face.

The girl's mother started to smile as well. "Yes, all of them. Chloe, you've never hurt anyone in your life, you are the least dangerous person I know. I don't think you could hurt anyone if you wanted to."

Chloe's grin became the glowing smile Anna often thought of during the days when work was more exhausting than usual. "You can't hurt anyone either, mommy. A lot of adults like to fight, but not you."

"You think so?" Anna asked, her grin growing with her daughter's. Chloe was wrong of course; her mother was only three years old when she threw her first punch in a kid's game of pentagon. Anna could still hear Chloe's grandmother cheering for her as she bloodied another girl's nose.

The girl jumped on the bed a little as she answered her mother. "Yes, yes, I swear it." She resettled herself as she asked her next question. "When will people stop being scared of us?"

Anna knew the correct reply was never, but she didn't say that. "I'm not sure; it might take a long time."

Chloe abandoned this subject as swift as she'd reached it, delving into another, one that troubled Anna more than the topic of human-Second-Gen relations, frightened her even. "When do you start your new job?"

A sorrowful terror built itself up inside her, yet Anna maintained her outward calm. "Soon."

To her slight though unsubstantial relief, her daughter's retort wasn't something like, how soon. Rather, Chloe said, "And you won't have to work at the factories anymore?" Her voice and expression were occupied by cheery hope, as if the recent news her mother would no longer be employed at the factories of Ignis was something she'd been waiting for from the day she was born.

"Nope," Anna replied, holding her smile as she thought over the proposal Commander Darius had presented her with, which she'd so far neglected to tell Chloe of.

Chloe was exhilarated, as if she was thinking her mother's new job would somehow keep her in Missio, not take her away. "Are you happy?"

"The valley's just over this last hill," Sean was saying, but Anna didn't want to hear him. "The weather's picking up again so we'll have to take cover in one of the caves. There're several of them before the valley floor."

Anna wasn't happy, not even enough to lie. The truth was out of the question, however, so she dodged it altogether. Motioning towards the two black pillows at the end of the bed, she said, "It's late, Chloe. Let's get you tucked in."

Her daughter was disappointed, though not any more than she was at end of every other nighttime conversation they had. "I want to keep playing question and answer." Anna decided a year ago that Chloe's perpetual inquiry should have a name. She'd regretted her decision almost immediately.

"That's what you say every night, now go on, get under the blanket before it gets too cold in here." Anna pressed Chloe to the pillows, and watched as the girl slipped beneath the covers without further disagreement. As if right on time, Anna noticed a puff of white air emerge in front of her face, the barrack's temperature nearing its typical nighttime lows.

With the blankets at her chest, Chloe told Anna, "I can't wait to grow up so I can stay up all night."

Anna was able to chuckle at this, despite the dread that encroached upon her. "Trust me dear, when you get to my age, sleep will be your best friend."

Her daughter found this funny for some reason, and giggled. Clouds of white appeared between them as she responded. "You're tricking me, mommy."

"You got that?" Sean asked when Anna didn't reply to his report.

"Are you going to bed, too?" Chloe asked, resting her head on one of the pillows.

Anna lied; this was a fib she could get away with. "Eventually. I need to make sure you fall asleep first."

"Okay, goodnight mommy," her daughter said as always, before shutting her eyes and turning to one side.

"Goodnight dear, sleep well." The girl's mother could've ended the talk there, but she realized she was nowhere close to finished. Even when the Nightwalker that Commander Darius was sending for her arrived in the morning she wouldn't be ready, she never would be. "And Chloe?"

"Anna?" Sean said.

Chloe rolled back over to face her mother, opening her eyes. "Yes, mommy?"

"You know I love you."

With a smile, Chloe said, "Yes, you loved me from the second I was born."

Anna leaned in and kissed her child on the forehead. "From the second you were born to the second I die."

"Anna!" Chloe's mother returned reluctantly to the northern areas of the Aegean Valley in the winter of the 31st Year of Marathon, and to her life as a Black Dragoon. The steep and rocky upward climb she stood on was shielded by a forest of gray and skeletal trees that slanted downhill from a hefty blend of gravity and snow, the overcast peering through the interlocking nets of branches. Her partner stood a few feet in front of her, flustered with ire and frustration. "That's the third time you've shut down in the last hour, we don't have enough daylight left for you to keep doing that!" Sean's condemnation didn't upset her. For one, he had every reason to be angry with the delays her periodic daydreams had caused. Two, she knew his foul mood was mostly reactionary. The lacerations across the right side of his head and over his right eye caused him constant pain. She was certain he didn't mean to be so harsh, but couldn't help it. Black gauze and bandages from their supplies were wrapped around his cranium and covered his wounded eye like a makeshift eyepatch. This was a temporary fix at best, treatment at Marathon Hospital was essential to cure Sean's wounds of infection and save his right eye from permanent blindness, if they could ever get back to Marathon. The dried blood that clung to the side of his head and neck in dark red stripes and tainted the collar of his jacket gave sufficient warning that her partner's health had taken a dangerous turn. If it was up to Anna they would be marching south, back to Troy and towards extraction by a medically equipped Nightwalker that could begin addressing Sean's wounds on the drive back to Marathon. As made quite clear by Commander Darius though, the operation was still active. She and her impaired partner would continue the hunt until Sword of God was ended.

"Sorry," Anna replied, taking notice of the darkening landscape. The light of the late afternoon dimmed away, retracting from the woods by the minute. They had at best a half-hour to get out of the open air before nightfall. Hypothermia had a head start on them, thanks to the afternoon's blizzard, and Sean's injuries only made him more susceptible. But as in-sync as she was with her partner's condition, Anna had become disconnected from her own stance in the universe. She wasn't in the Second-Gen Stage: her alternative state had disabled itself when she saw the Athenian she'd killed. Gray flecks of snow dropped through the trees, the branches swayed with the wind, though she received no gusts of freezing prickled air, nor did she hear the fluttering woods. She couldn't hear the ice and snow under her boots or her T-05 Sniper clicking in her arms, couldn't smell the decay in the breeze, couldn't even taste the dirt that trickled into her mouth from her face. It was as if she no longer physically existed on this gray and disfigured planet, but rather viewed its affairs through a monitor from someplace other, allowing her to see but preventing her from feeling. What was happening to her she had no clue, all she was positive of was that this suspension had begun with that child in Athens, the girl who looked like her daughter.

After Sean found her crouched over the girl's body, it took him at least five minutes though probably more to get her to stand up. From there he led her downstairs, away from the carnage of the second and third floors. Only then did Anna comprehend that her partner was wounded so severely. A slurry of bright orange-red washed over his head and masked his right eyeball, yet he'd made no attempt to dress the wounds himself, as if there was something of greater importance he had to attend to. Sitting at the bottom of the first-floor staircase, Anna sealed off the openings in her partner's skull with the gauze and bandages from her pack. Neither of their packs had anything to lessen the pain. As she treated Sean, she told him of Thaddeus, of the Athenian prisoners chained to the wall on the third floor, of Judas and Jesus's deception, of the other two Disciples shot down on the third floor whose names were not known to her, and that Jesus and Simon were not in Athens. The disorientation produced by her partner's wounds meant he absorbed these news updates with minimal response, though she still sensed his disappointment, his understanding that their mission was unfinished. "What's Fort Valley?" she asked him, once she'd transmitted everything Judas told her.

Flinching as his partner set the bandages over his disabled eye, Sean said, "Fort Valley is a second valley inside the Aegean Valley itself. Not a whole lot of people know about it, but Marathon has to be aware of it, with all the Aurora surveillance they've done of this region there's no way they couldn't. Guess the Commander never thought to tell you."

"Fucking ye. Where is it?"

"In the Aegean Mountains. We passed it on the way up here. The mountain range splits in two and creates this gap between them. Makes a valley within a valley."

His wounds dressed, Sean repaid the favor by binding the wound on her arm. Anna wasn't even slightly aware the wound was there until Sean grabbed his own stock of gauze and bandages from his pack and told her so. It was a grazing wound from a T-05 round that ripped a bright orange-red line in her jacket and skin, beneath her right shoulder, and spilled blood down her right arm through the sleeve. The gash didn't hurt in the least. Her arm moved as if there was no wound at all. As her partner bandaged the noiseless injury, he detailed to her the battle waged on the street outside, how he'd dropped two more Disciples but failed to find the one who'd wounded him. He'd assumed the shooter had joined in the effort to rescue Judas, but now it was clear the Disciple was still active.

Just as Sean finished bandaging Anna's arm, and they were about to head back upstairs and free the first two of what they now knew to be seven total Athenian captives in the town, Darius hailed Anna's earpiece. "Vanguard One, what the fuck is going on? Why the fuck is Vanguard Two's earpiece offline? Give me a fucking situation report!"

Anna's body was numb as she divulged everything to her Commander. The whole briefing took close to ten minutes, yet at its conclusion there was only one detail Darius saw as important, and it wasn't the horrific captivity the surviving Athenians lived in, nor was it Sean's wounding, nor was it the girl whose body continued to lie on the second floor. "So what you're telling me, Vanguard One, is you still have three active members of Sword of God's elite in the wind?"

"Yes, Central."

"Then, what the fuck are you two still doing in Athens? Get your fucking asses on the move to Fort Valley! I want Jesus and his last two Disciples removed from the Aegean Valley by tomorrow, no later! Is that understood?"

The thought of her and Sean trying to navigate their way through the Aegean Mountains to Fort Valley with the snowstorm as it was came across as ludicrous to Anna. With visibility as poor as it was, they would be lost from the instant they stepped outside Athens's walls. And if by some miracle they found the right course, they would freeze to death long before they arrived at the valley.

These factors mattered little to Darius, Anna knew.

"Yes, Central." Anna almost left it at that, but the outstanding circumstances she and her partner inhabited convinced her to object, if only so marginal. "Central, I request that Vanguard Two and I remain in Athens one additional hour to wait out the storm. There are several Athenian prisoners around the community we could free during that time, and it would give a better window for our bandaged wounds to settle." *I never got the chance to ask Judas about Jacob and Mia. They have to be here somewhere, if they're still alive.*

The Commander's response was about as ferocious as Anna anticipated, yet she still winced as it came through her earpiece. "Anna, why the fuck should I let you waste time on those people? Athens will belong to Marathon in good time; the people living there now aren't relevant to the city's expansion! And what the fuck is this you're telling me about waiting on the weather? Civilians have made do in that fucking valley for forty years! Are you saying that as a Dragoon and a Second-Gen, you can't handle snow? Do I need to put the word out to Missio, give the Community Office the go-ahead to toss your daughter out in the streets? Don't think for a second that I won't!"

Anna shut her eyes and gritted her teeth. "Copy all ma'am, Vanguard Two and I are inbound for Fort Valley."

Darius didn't reply. She didn't have to say anything further.

"You got to be fucking kidding me," Sean said. "She won't even give us a minute to unhook the hostages upstairs?"

"How long will it take us to reach Fort Valley?" Anna replied.

Her partner's resentment persisted, even as he mandated himself to focus on the newest phase of their mission. "The northern edge of the valley's got to be five miles southeast of here at least, probably closer to eight. It would take a couple hours to get there with good weather. And that's not including the ascent through the Aegean Mountains. No fucking chance in a blizzard."

Denied the time to help the Athenian prisoners, Anna and Sean readied themselves to move out. Cautious of the Disciple who'd wounded Sean and then disappeared, and seeing that Sean now had to gracelessly brandish his T-05 Sniper on his left side, Anna elected to exit the building first. When she'd scanned the street and rooftops, finding them purple going both north and south, Sean joined her in the still thrashing blizzard. No longer able to talk to her with his ear-piece, the Dragoons had to converse through hand signals and gestures as they walked against the wind to South Gate. Expecting they would have to dismantle a grenade based booby trap like the type seen on North Gate, Anna was surprised when they came across an open gate with the undetonated grenade lying in the snow. It occurred to her, and probably to Sean as well, that the only surviving Disciple in Athens had fled the battle to Fort Valley to alert Jesus. Through South Gate and back down the hill the settlement stood on, the artic blasts hounded them the whole way. At the bottom of the slope, however, the storm seemed to hit a wall, as if it'd started out too strong and exhausted itself. The ends of the blizzard passed over the valley, the gray fog released the terrain from its hold, and the breeze calmed. Though a light snowfall trailed the storm, the weather was far more manageable.

But as the miles that parted them from Fort Valley wore away over the next couple hours, another force took the place of the storm and proceeded to obstruct her every motion. Whether this irregularity was physical or psychological in nature, Anna couldn't determine. Either way, this post-Athens illness deprived her of sensation and left her a sluggish residue of the person she'd been earlier that day. Before long, it was as if Sean had become the commander of their partnership. Numerous times, he had to urge her along or draw her out of the daydreams that plagued her. Some were of her and her daughter, others of the girl who resembled her daughter at an older age. As they'd crossed the waters of the Aegean River, using an assortment of collapsed tree trunks as a bridge, Anna wished she could send the girl downriver as Marathon did for its citizens. *Any gravesite would be better than the foot of that stairwell.*

Now, on a wooded hill nestled between two towering mountain peaks at the cusp of Fort Valley, Sean said, "Let's just get over this ridge and find a cave while we can still see."

"Right," Anna agreed, but Sean had already turned away and started up the slope, as if he had no more tolerance to wait for her. She pursued, a meter behind him.

A hundred meters of uneven snow, ice, and rock later, they came to the top of the hill, the trees halting with the incline to unveil the land that lay ahead of them. They were standing at the northwestern end of Fort Valley. In front of them, the ground bent downwards and dropped in a decline as steep and as jagged as the mound they'd just climbed. Clusters of drooping gray trees spotted the descent as the hill continued all the way down to the valley floor. The bottommost point of the valley drew an instant recollection of the field in Serenity. Even with the dwindling light restraining her view of Fort Valley to a few miles at best, Anna recognized the plate-like flat gray ground which could only have come from the Reform. Why the floor of Fort Valley was targeted on the last day of the Previous Civilization interested her enough to ask Sean, "Why is it called Fort Valley?"

Gazing out at the sights before them as she was, her partner took a moment to reply. "This whole valley was a military base, that's what I've been told anyway." Raising a finger to the valley floor, he said, "The main facilities were constructed down there and ran all the way to the southern end. Whoever built it thought the mountainsides would keep the place safe from enemy incendiary weapons. You could say the design didn't live up to expectations. There's bound to be a couple bunkers on the hillsides that survived, though. Like I said, these mountains are full of caverns. Civilians have been making homes out of them for decades."

Gawking at the serrated ramparts of gray rock and trees that cordoned off and isolated the valley to the east and west, Anna said, "So that's where Sword of God's base of operations will be? In a bunker from the Previous Civilization?"

Sean had twisted away from the valley floor and was looking towards the peaks of the western Aegean Mountains, as if he'd perceived something that hadn't been there before. "It makes sense, doesn't it?" he said without turning back to her. "Jesus comes to Fort Valley or maybe he was here from the very beginning. He finds a bunker, loaded with all the supplies Judas told you about. So now he has the material, he just needs his soldiers, say twelve of them. And when he has them they go out to raise shit in the rest of the Aegean Valley, then retreat back here before Marathon or anyone else can get a trace on them. The problem for us will be finding the right cave."

In the air above the valley floor and between the two sides of the divided Aegean Mountain range, a mist of gray snowflakes fell from the blackening gray sky into the massive ditch at the bowels of the universe that was Fort Valley. "I'll get on the Network with the Commander and ask for Aurora surveillance of the..." Anna was met with a single elevated hand from Sean that signaled her to be quiet.

Her partner had centered his one good eye on the pointed tops of the western mountains, ignoring the rest of the valley. "Listen," he whispered. "You hear that?"

A low distant rumbling, what seemed at first like the reports of some miles away firefight, which resonated over the western line of the mountains and collided with the eastern line on the opposite side of the valley. She heard what had already netted Sean's attention and understood that whatever the root of this noise was, its power was so enormous even her numbed senses did not deaden the sound. Each reverberation yielded to a louder and more proximate explosion of thunder until she associated the uproar with the detonation of a thousand T-05 rifles, as if an armada of Marathon soldiers was doing battle just west of Fort Valley. The booms didn't stop there, but lengthened as the hillside trembled under Anna and Sean's boots, an earthquake to broadcast the onset of the event. And finally, the true wrath of winter made its entrance between the knifepoints of the mountain range, striking Anna with a greater terror of weather than the coldest nights of her childhood.

A titanic sea of gray fell over the mountain tops in the shape of monstrous fingers, snatching trees from their roots and boulders from their highlands. The howling seemed to be trying to deafen the planet in its entirety. A shadow eclipsed the valley floor as the storm barreled towards Fort Valley and its occupants.

"Go!" Sean pushed her down the initial steps of the hill in front of them, and then she was running at a dead sprint beside him, through the snow, ice, and rock. Between the trees towards the valley floor, for a few strides Anna questioned why they were fleeing deeper into the target area of the storm. But she evaluated that going back down the way they'd just come wouldn't have done any good either. Her partner was leading them to the caves, where they were exactly he didn't know, but with a minute at most till they were consumed and added to the surge it was the sole chance for survival they had.

A momentous crashing noise shouted up from the bottom of the valley. Anna saw a plume of gray rising from the valley floor as the storm smashed into the foot of the mountains. In an instant, the cloud was a hundred feet high and spreading across the valley, over the floor and up the sloping hills, including the knoll she and Sean now dashed down. Then, it was as if gravity itself had been sapped from the planet. Her boots broke traction with the hillside as she hurdled into the air, and was flung to the side. She came down hard on her stomach, striking rock with a startled grunt, bounced, turned over in mid-air, and landed on her pack, her left hip meeting the side of a tree.

Snarling thunder rumbled through the snow, bending the stalks of the trees to the east as Anna recovered her bearings and lifted her head off the ground. Her jacket and pants were torn in a dozen places from her chest down to her lower legs, displaying the bright cuts she'd obtained in her momentary flight. Though they bled, her injuries were miniature, not even worthy of a round of pentagon. And as a Second-Gen, her hip wasn't shattered as a human's would've been. At worst it was sprained. She couldn't run, yet she could stand. When she stood with the support of the tree, however, she realized what the shockwave had cost her. Her switchblade and flash grenade were gone. The glass frame of her wristwatch was broken, her Network earpiece gone. Worse still, catastrophic actually, her T-05 Sniper was nowhere in immediate sight, the rifle and its strap had been ripped from her body. Bands of her disheveled hair dangled and swayed in front of her eyes, as not even her hat had endured the storm's blast. But turning west, the unarmed and battered Dragoon knew the loss of her gear did not matter in the least. What approached her now from the valley floor could not be survived by anyone, human or Second-Gen. "Chloe, I'm so sorry I never said goodbye."

The cloud curled over the embankment on her right, swallowing limbs and rocks as it sucked away the land. She waited her turn, as if it was a reprieve. One hundred feet, fifty feet, Sean was at her side, seizing her with his hand. Like Anna, the shock of the onrushing storm had deprived him of his gear, and assaulted his already wounded body. His hat was gone, his hair waving in the squall. Rifle, knife, grenades, even his pack was absent. Identical bright red gashes on his frame exhibited through the tears in his clothing, twice as many as hers. Most significant, his left arm sagged from his shoulder in a warped manner that told her the arm was dislocated. Anna was relieved. *He chose to stay with me. At least I won't die alone.* She stretched her hand out to Sean, so they could hold tight to each other as everything went gray. But her partner had a different idea.

"You're going to hate me for this," he said, before tugging and throwing her around the tree, down the hill. Anna caught a look at what Sean had heaved her towards a millisecond prior to dropping through it, a tiny black hole in the surface of the slope. Into the pitch dark, below the storm's battleground, she rolled over and over on a sharp bank of icy snow. Stopping when she struck some object she couldn't see or judge the nature of, she lay on her chest and was hit from above by another object, knowing this to be her partner tumbling into the cave behind her. She heard him grumble in pain, exhaling with a panicked shortness of breath. Overhead, the front of the storm pounded up the side of the hill, thrashing the cave until it seemed as though she and Sean were bouncing up and down as they lay in the darkness. Anna heard a quick pop, followed by Sean's agonized cries. He had forced his arm back into socket.

They spent a half-hour lying on the floor of that cave, awaiting the storm's decision. When the storm had grown distant, the brunt of its strength having moved out of Fort Valley, Anna and Sean rose wearily in the lightless room. Without night vision or thermal scopes to illuminate the cavern, and with neither of them daring to venture back outside, Anna feared they would stumble around in the dark until they succumbed to hypothermia. Using the blue light of his wristwatch, which was apparently the last piece of equipment her partner had left, Sean found his way to a number of sticks, twigs, and even a few of the bigger tree branches blown into the cave with them. Assisting him, Anna grouped the wooden debris together on the ground of the cavern. And after they had a sufficient pile, she scraped two of the driest sticks together for forty-five minutes straight, until she produced an orange spark, and from that, their campfire. Bunched up next to the fire as the air slowly warmed over them, breathing out puffs of orange-white air, Anna watched as the orange light unveiled the cavern. It occurred to her then that this desperate shelter of theirs was not a naturally formed cave.

Positioned in front of the fire, the hole she and Sean entered the cave through and the mount of ice and snow that led up to the entryway were the only real cavern-like features of this chamber beneath the hillside. The ceiling above them and the walls on either side were built of metal, browned by a few decades worth of rust. Lining the walls towards the bottom of the cave floor were a number of small square-shaped holes, flooded with snow, that Anna recognized as windows. Much of the overall floor of the cavern, save for the front section where they'd set the fire, was carpeted, the material black with the same mold particles that floated about in the air. Whatever this cave actually was, it had existed in a state of advanced and undisturbed decay for many years.

Crowding the cave behind them were rows of cushioned seats. Anna rationalized that one of these seats had been the object she'd struck upon landing in the cave. The rows were divided by a narrow aisle. Attached to the walls just above the seats and windows were cupboards, only a few of which still possessed doors. There were ten rows between the campfire and the back of the cave, where a wall of frozen black dirt blocked the aisle. Two metal walls, one on each side of the aisle, stood between the clay and the rows. Written in faded paint on these partitions were words. On the left, "REGIONAL," on the right, "AIRWAYS."

"We're in a plane, or part of one," Sean told Anna. Her partner got up from the fire and walked down the aisle, through the rows, exploring the buried remnants of an aircraft from the Previous Civilization. "Must've crashed here on the day of the Reform, probably brought down by the bombs that hit the valley." His tone pitched and dropped from obvious discomfort in his left arm.

Taking off her pack and limping from the ache in her hip, Anna followed Sean down the aisle of the fuselage. "If this is just one piece of a plane, where do you think the rest of it is?" she asked him.

Glimpsing her with the scarred left side of his face, he said, "I don't know. I'd imagine the pulse from the surface detonations sent the plane into such rapid descent the aircraft ripped apart and scattered."

Anna had a thought. "Like the Anubis when it fell through the atmosphere."

"Yeah a little bit. This whole region's really nothing but one huge boneyard for the..." Sean paused, glancing down the last row on the left, where something stole his attention. Anna didn't take the time to gauge his expression before joining him at the back of the cave.

The skeletons sat in the seats nearest to the window, their skulls crushed at the forehead, their breastbones and ribs annihilated in a manner that indicated death had come at the moment of impact. Oxygen masks held to their skinless mouths, their clothes withered into frayed slices of cloth. But despite the distorted state of the long departed passengers, Anna saw the difference in their sizes. The skeleton that decomposed in the middle seat was adult; the skeleton sitting beside the window was a child. Their arms were wrapped around each other, the adult and child had been embracing, cowering together as the plane made its plunge. Though Anna didn't know the sex of the adult and the child, she imagined a mother and daughter traveling together by plane, their appearances identical to those of Anna and her own daughter. She saw herself and Chloe sitting in their seats as the plane flew towards its terminus, joyfully playing question and answer, much to the chagrin of the passengers who sat near them. And when the plane arrived at its fatal descent, she saw herself take one of the oxygen masks that dropped from the ceiling and tie it to Chloe's mouth, before securing her own. Anna and Chloe held tight to one another as the various segments of the plane disconnected and everyone else was yanked out to their deaths. Somehow their seatbelts endured while all others snapped, and they rode the displaced fuselage the whole way down. *They died as parent and child, bonded and together. Chloe and I won't have that. Because of me.*

"There's a latrine through here," Sean announced, interrupting though not quelling her panicking mudslide of thoughts. Her partner had moved on from the adult and child skeletons. He stood in the aisle a few feet ahead of her, holding a door that opened the right side wall. "So we have that at least." Worry combined with the pain on his face as Sean became mindful of her distress. Shutting the door to the plane's latrine, he stepped back over to her, calming his tone to say, "Let's see what we have left to eat, all right?" He raised his right arm then lowered it again, as if he wanted to give her a supportive tap on the shoulder but lost the nerve at the last second. Anna nodded, restricting her eyes from as much as a fleeting glimpse of the two passengers.

With Sean's stock of tofu blocks and water no longer available to them, they shared the remainders of Anna's rations, finishing off their supply of food and water.

When dinner was done and Sean had found more scraps of wood to keep the campfire at a suitable size, they settled themselves on opposite sides of the fire to try and sleep off the trials of the day, though of course Anna wouldn't actually be sleeping. However, unlike the other nights spent in the Aegean Valley, she wasn't planning to stay awake because of the mission, it was over, failed. Anna wouldn't sleep because she was physically unable to do so. Almost eighty-four hours without a lick of sleep, even more exhausted than she'd been at the end of her first week with a newborn Chloe, and yet it felt as if she was being propelled at hundreds of miles an hour. Taking her spot on the side of the fire closest to the hole, so as to give her partner the space farther away from the deadly night air, she lay on her back and made herself as stationary as possible. But even when she might've passed for dead, she was imprisoned by a sensation of being zipped over the planet at a speed likely similar to that of the plane she took shelter in. All of her regular sensory functions had been incapacitated by the girl in Athens, and then the skeletons in Fort Valley had trapped in her a bizarre feeling of perpetual motion. So severe was this state that when Sean said, "I guess I shouldn't offer to take watch tonight," it seemed as if he was speaking from the other side of the Aegean Valley.

Anna shook her head, incapable of glancing over at her partner.

"What'd the Commander say to you, at the Command Building? After the briefing, she told me to go on ahead while she spoke to you alone. What'd you talk about?"

The desire was there to call back to Sean from across the Aegean Valley, to tell him everything. But she could only shake her head again.

"Okay, you don't have to tell me. But is that why you haven't slept this whole time, because of what Darius said to you in there?"

Anna nodded. The gesture said something, but it was miniscule. She wanted to say so much more.

"Ma'am, the Nightwalker's waiting outside." The soldier stood over Anna, pressing the uncertain new recruit to leave, no doubt afraid of testing Commander Darius's patience. Anna sat on her knees next to the bunk, and her sleeping daughter. Her arms were crossed, her chin on the bed, her attention scarcely acknowledging the intruding soldier. Her concentration belonged to Chloe. The girl's head lay on the pillows of the bed, everything under her chin covered by the blankets. The time was still quite early morning, early enough deep sleep still protected Chloe from the slightest clue her mother was about to leave her. As much as Anna tried, even now in the last seconds of her involvement in Chloe's life, she couldn't summon the fortitude to wake her daughter and attempt something of a goodbye. There were no words that would help her sudden exit make sense to Chloe. Plus if the girl knew Anna was going away, she would beg her mother to stay, and Anna knew if Chloe did that she would never leave.

The thought was there, of course, that she could change her mind. Anna retained the option to reject Darius's proposition and remain a civilian in Missio, she wasn't sitting in that Nightwalker yet. The idea was a dream, however, a non-existent reality where she didn't have to leave and Chloe was still entitled to all the benefits doing so would yield. The opportunity to ensure her daughter's future was impossible to pass on. The Second-Gen Stage remained dormant within Chloe, and Anna had no means of safeguarding her until her Awakening. By accepting Darius's offer, Chloe's security would be assured by the guardians assigned to her care. The only viable choice available to Anna was to leave, and in order to leave, she had to walk out of this barrack.

"Ma'am, the Commander's given me specific instructions to..." the soldier started to say, her own patience reaching its end.

"Okay," Anna choked in submission. The tears were coming, one or two at a time, as she kept her eyes on the snoozing child. "You'll stay with her?"

"Yes, ma'am." The soldier brought some sincerity to her answer. "Per your request, I'll be standing watch over your daughter until her caretakers arrive."

The tears flowed faster than Anna could blink them away, her composure crumbling. "And when will they get here?" she asked.

"Sixty minutes at most," the soldier claimed, motioning towards the door with her arm. "Please, ma'am."

Nodding and forcing several heavy breaths of white air, Anna rose from her knees. Her daughter's breathing was softer, slow and calm puffs of white above the bed. Calm, that was what Anna hoped she was giving Chloe now, a world of safety, quiet, and calm. The girl would live a life her mother had never thought possible. With her left hand, Anna pulled one of the blankets up over Chloe's nose. The blanket vibrated with the girl's breaths as Anna kissed her on the forehead, then turned and walked off with the soldier.

Her heart dislodged from her arteries and beat relentlessly without regulation, like a Nightwalker hurtling downhill with defective brakes. Clouds of orange-white air carried up towards the ceiling of the plane, one after the other in unremitting exasperation as her lungs and brain panicked from an apparent deficiency of oxygen. Coughing and coughing to no end, she clasped her quivering chest with her hand, her fingers ready to dig into her chest and manually slow her erratic heartbeat. Anna's frame dampened and shivered, her gut knotting with nausea, a weight of sickness so intolerable she believed her stomach might buckle and rip apart.

The burning in her hip was now minor compared to the ache throughout the rest of her system. Pushing to her feet, she looked to the back of the human-made cave, where the latrine Sean found was located. The campfire between Anna and her partner had withered, but continued to flare and light the plane's cabin. Sean was asleep behind the fire. Though he tried to stay awake with her out of solidarity, his exhaustion had been too devastating, his wounds too demoralizing, and death-like sleep had crushed him in less than ten minutes.

Hobbling around the fire and Sean, neither of which was stirred by her movement, Anna stumbled down the alleyway. She gripped the aisle seats for balance as the plane tilted, inverted, and then returned to its proper positioning, before lifting off the hillside. It was as if the aircraft had been restored to working order and was taking to the air once again. Averting her eyes from the skeletons, she clutched the door handle to the latrine. The slim entrance creaked open with a single tug.

She'd luckily wiped her eyes dry before ducking into the back of the Nightwalker, because she found Darius waiting there for her. To her genuine shock, Anna realized the Commander had come to Missio personally to see that she joined the military. She'd come to Missio to make her original offer, but Anna was certain the Commander wouldn't dare come back here so soon, especially for something as routine as driving a new recruit over the Marathon Bridge. "Good morning, Ms. Corday."

Letting the door shut behind her, Anna was careful in her response. "Good morning, ma'am. I didn't know you were coming back down."

The Commander's smile was large, yet seemed contrived. Her glass eye and the red scar on the left side of her face beamed at Anna as if sentient. "No one knew until this morning actually. You're the first recruit I'm seeing over the bridge in all my years as Commander. Normally this is a task I'd detail to a Lieutenant, or a Sergeant, but your enlistment is not part of the norm. Wouldn't you say so, Ms. Corday?"

Anna's mouth dried as she spoke. "Yes, ma'am."

The engine of the Nightwalker screeched awake as Darius remarked, "I imagine you're wondering what happens next."

Through the hazy orange of the fire, Anna saw the latrine was at most three feet in length and width. A toilet stuck out from the back corner of the room, degraded by splinters and forty years without use. A sink and mirror were attached to the wall between the door and the toilet. Broken from its fasteners, the sink slanted towards the floor. Though the glass somehow held to the edges, the mirror itself was so mutilated by fractures and so filthy Anna almost missed it. Decades of grime, rot, and rust caked the floor, walls, and utilities, all dusting the air as her boots entered the latrine. Turning around, she shut the door and reduced the room to near pitch black. Orange leaked underneath and through the sides of the doorway as she twisted the door lock from, "VACANT," to, "OCCUPIED," sealing herself off from her partner.

Alone in the latrine, Anna collapsed to her knees in front of the unusable and waterless toilet, gloved hands grasping the rim of the bowl. When she could no longer stand the revulsion in her stomach, she heaved. Sludge erupted through her throat and vomited out her mouth, splashing against the insides of the bowl. Her gut seared in pain as she upchucked until there was nothing left to give the plane. Still, she dry-heaved several times, before pushing up and rising to the sink. Leaning on the metal of the sink, Anna gazed at the ruined mirror. Among the crevices and the dirt and the dark, she found her, the person Anna had come to despise more than any other. The disgrace of knowing this individual and seeing her in the mirror became too difficult to bear, and Anna had to close her eyes.

Chloe was always going to be in danger, whether I accepted Darius's proposition or not. If I'd stayed I could've cared for Chloe, like a parent is supposed to do. But no, I got in that Nightwalker with Darius and joined the Dragoons. I didn't even wake my daughter to say goodbye. Darius has to believe I'm dead by now. Chloe will have no one to help her when the Commander sends word to Missio. She won't last a night on Missio's streets.

Her eyes shot open, and when Anna caught sight of herself in the ruptured mirror, she clenched her teeth in self-hatred, leaped over the sink, and slammed her forehead against the glass. A loud shattering noise resulted, supplemented by the ring of glass shards sprinkling on the floor of the latrine. As Anna withdrew, a sharp blistering pierced the skin on her forehead. Without delay she launched forward again, smashing her head into the mirror a second time. The crackling came as her skull extracted the glass that remained in the frame. Shards tangled and pricked at her hair and at the sides of her jacket collar. The wet and boiling presence of blood spread down the middle of her face, in-between and around her eyes, dripping from nose and chin. The pain and faintness showed themselves, but it still wasn't sufficient. Anna threw herself at the mirror a third time. Her brow smacked the metal wall behind the mirror, the force of the blow driving her backwards into the wall opposite the sink.

Glass shards crunched underneath her boots and pants as she plopped herself down on the floor, her back bracing against the wall. Tears mixed with the blood that fell from her head. The agony worsened, but she greeted it. The damage she'd dealt herself was not yet fatal. She could slam her head against the wall another ten or fifteen times and not produce a single dent in her skull. *Second-Gens don't break, but they do bleed.*

The orange that shined below the door reflected off the slivers of glass strewn about the floor, illuminating a shard beside her leg. With her hand she rolled the left sleeve of her jacket up to her elbow, exposing the bare skin of her arm to the latrine. Then, she took the shard in her right hand and held out her left arm, knuckles facing down. The glass lowered to her arm, the jagged edge of the splinter hovering over the skin.

The door shuddered with an alarmed knock from outside the latrine. Her partner called to her. "Anna?" When she didn't respond, he added, "Talk to me, Anna." The fright in Sean's voice intensified with every word.

Chloe, the daughter I abandoned. She punctured her skin with the tip of the glass, slicing a horizontal incision across her arm, through which dark orange-red appeared.

"Anna!" Four or five times Sean struck the door, the thumps bounced back and forth against the walls of the latrine.

The children in the Cavaliers' camp. From left to right, Anna made another orange-red gash in her arm.

The entrance bellowed and quaked from what Anna guessed to be Sean's boot colliding with the door. "Fuck," he said with a painful half-shout.

The Athenian girl who looked like my daughter.

Again and again, Sean jolted the door with his boot.

Jacob and Mia.

The door lock popped and orange light overtook the doorframe.

Dark orange-red doused her arm. *Sean, who I dragged along through all of this. Sean, the only person besides Chloe I was able to talk to. Sean, the only person in this world besides Chloe who I cared for, who I loved.*

Her partner's shadowed silhouette stood in the doorway, his left arm sagging in disuse, his left eye needing a moment to acclimate to what it was seeing. And when his view of the latrine was realized, Sean's eye seemed to double in size. "Jesus Christ in fuck!"

12: SEAN

He dashed into the latrine and dove upon his partner, interrupting her suicide. They fell as one on the serrated floor, thrashing and rolling about. She fought him with the ferociousness of the storm they'd barely escaped a few hours before. A voice neither human nor Second-Gen shrieked in unnerving despondency, her body lurching and squirming in such desperation that Sean had to use both of his arms to hang onto her. He screamed with her, not from sorrow but of shooting pain as he commanded his frayed left arm to seize Anna's right wrist, while his right arm took hold of her blood-moistened left wrist. Tortured groans came from both of them as Sean separated Anna's arms, putting space between the orange-red shard of glass and the wounds she wreaked.

Anna lay on her back, Sean sprawled over top of her, pinning her as if this was a game of pentagon. She should've been able to subdue him, call on the Second-Gen Stage and throw him off before resuming her cutting, but the glowing blue irises and the superior strength never arrived. In the chaotic and raging superstorm of Anna's despair, the mental transmission meant to rouse the Second-Gen Stage must've been distorted. What the Second-Gen Stage was receiving from up top wasn't precise enough to warrant a reply. Though Anna normally had the physical stamina to hold her own without her evolved state, more than eighty sleepless hours had gridlocked her endurance. For the first time in the two weeks since he'd met her, Sean was stronger than Anna.

His left hand grasped at the shard of glass she continued to hold to. He tried prying the fragment from her grip but her fingers held firm, as if she had transferred all of the lingering energy from her body to her right hand. Sean's left shoulder screeched. "Let go of it! Let go of it!"

Anna's face and hair were discolored with orange-red from the glass filled lacerations on her forehead, her eyes flooded to the brim, and her expression overflowed with hopelessness. "Let go of me! Just let me go," she whimpered, banging her head on the floor in resistance.

"Let me help you! Tell me what's happening to you!"

Anna shook her head. "Why the fuck should I listen to you? How the fuck can you help me?" she snarled, incensed by the offer alone.

At that, Sean acknowledged what he'd known for some time. "Because I've been where you are right now!"

Her rage persisted, and yet confusion made an appearance amidst the frenzy. "The fuck are you talking about?"

Sean hesitated for a second, his chest clogging in terror. The only thing that scared him more than what he was about to say, was knowing that once he'd told her everything it would be impossible to rewind. "Carthage."

"Carthage?"

His spider-web scars of the Marathon-Carthage War began to singe as Sean spoke. "We didn't know Marathon was coming until the night before. My brother Derek and I were assigned sniper posts at the walls with the rest of the Carthage Scouts. Wasn't till dawn when Marathon threw the first waves of troops at us. They came straight at the wall, as if we weren't there. Darius must've ordered them to charge the wall or face the Detention Center, their advance was absolutely fucking mad. None of them made it. A lot of us on the wall thought it was over after that."

Anna wasn't about to release the shard, but she stared at her partner through blood and anguish. Orange-red continued to leak from her arm and forehead, though at a measured rate, as if Sean's account sedated the flow of blood from Anna's veins.

"Of course, we didn't know Darius was just feeding us those soldiers to expose our firing positions. The Aurora strikes did away with most of the Scouts, brought down the walls. Somehow Derek and I came out of that and pulled back to our parents' home."

The searing in Sean's face converted to a sadness that extended down his body. "Derek, my mom and dad, and I, we tried to make a run for the south gates. Turns out half of Carthage had a similar idea. We couldn't have gotten more than ten minutes down the road before Marathon started firing on the crowd. Then..." His voice croaked as his left eye began to wet. "Then, they started tossing grenades." A handful of tears dropped from his left eyeball, onto his partner's bleeding forehead. "A grenade landed right at Derek and my parents' feet. Fuck, we had just enough time to look at it before the fucking thing went off."

He loosened his grip on Anna's left wrist and used his glove to mop up the spill from his left eye. Anna kept her gaze on Sean, as if doing him the courtesy of waiting before trying to kill herself again. "First thing I can remember was waking up to a Marathon soldier sticking a T-05 in my face, or what was left of my face." Sean brushed his scars with his free hand. "While he's restraining me, I look over and see my family lying on the road." The tears reappeared in his left eye. "I couldn't tell where one of them stopped and the next one started, there was too much. That was the last I saw of them. The troops brought me and the other prisoners to this field outside Carthage, so we could watch them set fire to the parts of the city that weren't already ablaze. When that was done, the Commander came over to decide who got to come back to Marathon."

Sean paused. He tried to clean his left eye with his glove again, but his eye socket was drowning now. For a second he considered stopping there. A gentle tap on the elbow from Anna urged him on. "The Commanders agreement on survivors was simple. Nine thousand people in Carthage before the war, Darius spares one percent of us, the ninety most capable. I ended up being one of those ninety. The other thousand prisoners or so were grouped together in the center of the field, that way the soldiers could finish up in one volley. Everything else is a blur at best."

He saw her fingers uncurl from the glass, the craving for death relieving itself from her expression. "You know, a lot of the time I wish I was a Second-Gen, like you. As scared as I appear to be whenever you go into the Second-Gen Stage, really I just despise myself for not being able to do that. If I could do what you can, my family would be alive, they'd have made it out of Carthage. Then again, I suppose if I was a Second-Gen, I never would've met you." The orange-red shard of glass fell from his partner's hand, clattering on the floor.

She let him lead her back to the campfire. He set her down in her spot beside the fire and looked to her pack for medical aid. Her supply of gauze and bandages were wrapped around his head, and his own medical gear had vanished with his pack and weapons. Fortunately, Anna's black packets of clotting-agent remained. Sean tore open the packets and spent the next several minutes pressing the substances against her self-incurred arm and head wounds. When her bleeding had been capped, he dumped the ammunition and empty water bottle from Anna's pack, and pulled at the bag's stitching with his uninjured right arm, ripping the pack into several pieces. Swathing her head and arm in the pack's black fabric, synthetic like their clothing, he thought of his own black colored dressings and said, "At least we match now." Anna grinned for half a second or so.

Having tended to her wounds, Sean made another search of the plane's cabin for woodland shavings to revive the declining fire. Finding none, he resorted to tearing portions of cushion from the seats. His partner returned to lying on the floor as she'd done before he'd fallen asleep. Doubting he would ever get back to sleep that night, no matter his aching fatigue, Sean sat down against the back of the seats on Anna's side of the fire. He hoped Anna would sleep. However, when she raised her head off the floor and beckoned to him, Sean understood their night wasn't over yet.

By some, almost telepathic-like, means he gathered what she was asking. Nodding, he moved from the seats and lay down between her and the fire. Anna turned on her side, facing away from him. Reaching back, she grasped and tugged at his right arm, motioning him closer. Sean wasn't sure if Anna was comforted by their connection, but as he shifted his chest into her back, drew his arm around her trembling body, and rested his face behind her hair:

A pure and imposing sensation of calm enveloped him.

It was as if none of their current quandaries existed. In the relaxing corners of his mind, he began to contemplate the impossible yet attractive notion that he and Anna could stay in that plane for years, let the military list them as deceased and never return to Marathon. To do that though, he still had to know. Thinking of the name he'd heard Anna mutter the day before on the Trojan River and speak to just as he was about to throw her into the artificial cave, Sean whispered to his partner, "Who's Chloe?"

Anna shuddered, as if the mere mention of the name could lead to regression and another attempt with the glass. But when she answered, she did so with relief. "Chloe's my daughter."

A surge of empathy shocked through Sean, as the purpose of Anna's service with the military and her refusal to harm children emerged in his cognizance. "How old is she?"

She answered without looking back. "Six. She was five when I left Missio. I haven't seen her in a year."

"That's why you're out here." He was angry with himself for not reckoning this on his own, and at an earlier time.

"She's the only reason," Anna retorted. "That and I couldn't handle everyone knowing I'm a Second-Gen, that Chloe and I are Second-Gens," she added. "My Awakening came a few weeks after Marathon slaughtered Carthage. Finishing work at the factories in Ignis, this fucker Elias tried to rob me in one of the backrooms. The guy couldn't make enough to feed his kids doing honest labor, so he would hold people at knifepoint till they paid up. No one turned him in, we didn't want the Commanders learning about his method in case any of us decided to copy it. Needless to say, we were both fairly surprised when he put the blade to my throat and my eyes shined for the first time. I'd been in plenty of fights before then, but I'd never put someone on the deck that quickly before. The commotion was enough the guards came running and sent Elias to the Detention Center, then called up the Commanders and told them there was an Awakened Second-Gen south of the river. The news was all over Missio by the next morning. I think you can guess how that went."

Sean shook his head. "Shit, a lot of people with their sights on you. I can't imagine how challenging that made things."

"Impossible or at least I thought it was, until we got here. You asked me a couple nights ago, what it's like in Missio and Ignis. Let's just say that housing the Commander gave us in Terra is better than anything I ever believed possible for someone like me. Darius was the one who made me the offer to join the Dragoons. At the time, what she was proposing for my daughter was the kind of benefits you spend the rest of your life detesting yourself for not agreeing to. Of course, I didn't know the Commander was going to hold Chloe's life over me whenever I began to disagree with her."

His recollection of Anna's unquestionable obedience to Commander Darius during their mission to Serenity was overturned by the recognition his partner's loyalty was an act. Those interactions with Darius were no more sincere than the performance she utilized with Jason in the Serenity Station and Peter in Dresden. However, something didn't quite settle with Sean. "Was it just you and Chloe? What about her dad or grandparents?"

"Just Chloe and me for five years, yeah. I had her when I was fifteen. Her father was an orphan from my year, living in the next barrack over, Chloe never met him." A degree of mourning turned in Anna's voice. "Owen, he found out he'd gotten me pregnant and made the brilliant decision to try selling drugs for extra pay." Sean heard her sniffling. "Got himself dropped by another dealer six months before his daughter was born, something about selling on the wrong corner. Chloe's grandparents were long gone by then. I didn't know my dad either; some scaffolding at the factories flattened him when I was two or three. My mom brought me up till I was thirteen. Flu took her in the winter of the 23rd Year of Marathon. After that I had some help from the neighbors in my barrack, but mostly Chloe and I were on our own. Marathon's raising her now."

He tightened his arm around her body. "I'm so sorry, Anna."

She sighed, exhaling a cloud of orange-white air that rose to the ceiling. "I don't think I'll ever see her again. Even if we make it back to Marathon and the Commander allows Chloe to stay with her guardians, I'll be in the field until this job kills me or Darius retires, and that won't be for another thirty years at least. Darius will certainly outlive us both."

Sean respired, inadvertently blowing a puff of orange-white through Anna's hair. "Why does it matter when Darius retires?"

"She wants me to replace her, or so she says. That's why she gave this mission to us instead of a more seasoned team; she's grooming me to command the Dragoons. I figure she believes only a Second-Gen is suitable for the position, humans are too inept for her taste."

"Darius is a Second-Gen," Sean stated rather than asked. He'd seen and heard too much that day to be any more shocked than he already was. "That's why she spent all those months training you personally."

"That's why she spent all those months teaching me how to kill. Last day of training, Darius called me to the firing range. When I get there, I see she's brought the poor fuck that tried to rob me up from the Detention Center. He's tied to a chair in the middle of the room, shitting himself as I walk in. I ask the Commander why he's here, and she just hands me a knife and tells me to cut his throat. I ask why. She says those are my orders. I tell her no. Try to give the knife back. She grabs me by the ear and screams in my face that Chloe's benefits are gone if Elias isn't dead in the next thirty seconds. So I slashed his neck open, and watched him stare at me while he choked and bled out." Anna stopped for a second, seeming to ponder something as she wiped her eyes. "I'm not sure I could bring myself to see Chloe again, even if Darius gave me the chance."

"What makes you say that?"

"After all this, I don't think she'd recognize me. I'm still just the apprentice, but eventually you won't be able to tell Darius and me apart."

He elected to be firm, fearing the shards of glass in the latrine were becoming desirable to Anna again. "None of that's true, Anna."

"How would you know?" Her stubbornness had survived the evening's psychotic incident.

"You're still yourself. You're out here on a mission for Darius and Chloe's who you're thinking about most. You're the same as you always were."

Quiet followed for a few moments, as Anna digested what her partner had said. Then, to Sean's respite, her chest vibrated with a laugh. "If Darius heard that, she'd put you in the Detention Center."

Chuckling, he said, "Oh definitely, but at least I'd have the scent of this place to get me ready for the shit halls."

"Truly, I just got my sense of smell back, now I'm wishing it was gone."

"Wait, when did you lose your sense of smell?"

"Right, I didn't tell you about that. Busy day. I never told you about Chloe's question and answer game either."

"Question and answer?"

"Imagine being asked a shitload of questions, half of which you barely know the answers to. And no matter how many questions she gives you one day, the next day she has even more."

Sean snickered. "So it runs in the family then?"

Anna poked him with her elbow. "Fuck you," she giggled.

They lay together and conversed as they were for another hour or so until finally, for the first time in days; Anna Corday fell asleep and stayed asleep. Sean joined not long after. Slumber's black partition remained for a considerable amount of time, far longer than either of Sean's previous nights in the Aegean Valley. When the shield lifted, Sean was met by a much-unexpected feeling of revitalization. His throat and stomach roared in a petition for water and food, but the heft of his exhaustion had been moderated. Checking the dark blue numbers on his wristwatch, Sean saw the hour was 1500, three hours past noon. He and Anna had spent almost the entire day sleeping in the plane.

With his waking came the predictable searing in his scars, but the lasting pain throughout the rest of his body and especially in his head and left arm depowered the ache of his disfigurements. The campfire was out, the plane's cabin dark and biting cold, yet Sean had been kept warm by the person curled in his arms beside him.

Sean was hesitant to get up out of fear of disturbing her recovery. He wouldn't mind if Anna slept all the way through the upcoming night and didn't wake till the next morning. For a half-hour he lay at her side, listening to her low breaths of white. Becoming convinced she would stay asleep for the time being, Sean rose from the floor.

His initial thought was to restart the fire, but he realized there were much more essential tasks to be addressed first. Without water, food, and firearms, they would not survive the walk back to Marathon, or at least back to Troy where they might come across a patrol. Sean made water his main goal for the abbreviated day. Using the blue light from his watch and the slight illumination from the late afternoon gray that slipped through the hole, he found Anna's empty water bottle. Before making the short climb up the snowbank, however, Sean glanced back to his partner.

She was smeared from the top of her head to the bottom of her boots in dark red, some of it hers some of it not, her hair frazzled by weather and glass, the wounds on her head and arms bound with bandage and scraps of backpack, her clothing tattered with dark red scratches, and her skin encrusted with soot. Yet beneath this, Sean could still see the person he had come to know. His family notwithstanding, he couldn't remember knowing anybody else so intimately, in Carthage and Marathon both. Last night a bridge had risen between the two of them, across the span of human and Second-Gen, between Carthage-born and Marathon-born, between Sean Halley and Anna Corday. The first of its kind and invisible to all others, their secret conduit was Sean's motivation to live, and it was by far the most inspiring reason for life he'd ever felt. Sean smiled at Anna with silent gratitude, and then turned to the mound of snow and ice.

The grayish-brown log of a collapsed tree stretched across the edge of the hole, obstructing his exit. With his left arm sagging at his side and his right hand wrapped around Anna's water bottle, too big to tuck in his pocket, Sean had no free hand to grab onto the trunk.

As his boots began to lose traction on the slope, he chucked the bottle out beyond the fallen tree. The bottle clanged somewhere down the hill ahead of him as he gripped the log with his right hand. Pushing off with his boots and pulling himself up over the trunk with his right arm, he dropped onto the slanted surface of snow, ice, and rock behind the tree. Facing the valley floor, he was about to search the hill for the water bottle, but his focus was distracted by the devastation of yesterday's storm.

From his elevated vantage point and with the afternoon's gray light providing a better look of the valley than what he'd seen before, Sean saw a landscape outspreading for miles and skinned to the bone. Every last tree of the valley had been torn from its roots and shattered against the ridges and the floor of the valley, forming a series of chaotic mazes of splintered wood and branches that more closely resembled the ruins of a former city than the remnants of a forested region. The icy gray rocks of the Aegean Mountains withstood, of course, but appeared somewhat transformed, as if the fury of the passing storm had chipped away at the outer layers of rock and forced the mountains to adopt new darker coatings. The overcast retained its grayed place in the afternoon sky, though between the clouds and land the air was stagnant, possibly the calmest weather he'd ever seen. It was as if the storm had sucked away every last filthy draft of wind when it departed Fort Valley. *That's one less thing we have to worry about.* He walked forward a few meters, scanning the sliding hillside for the water bottle. Something cracked behind him.

A stick breaking under a boot, too many feet away and too far to his right to be Anna following him out of the plane. Sean knew it was a visitor. He began to turn to his right, his muscles once again failing to remember he had no vision on that side of his face. Before he could rotate his left eye into view, someone spoke to him. "Keep staring forward, if you please." The voice was male, older than the others Sean and Anna had come across in the last four days, casual, comfortable.

That was what alarmed Sean the most: the speaker was so assured of his control over him he felt no need to sound threatening.

Gazing out over the valley floor, fighting the maddened impulse to check the periphery of his left eye as his breath evacuated in frequent white puffs, Sean wondered if the speaker planned to kill him or interrogate him first. He got his answer when he heard the snapping of a pair of boots, descending the hill towards him. Above these noises that accompanied the speaker's movements, or the person Sean guessed was the speaker but couldn't be certain, came the clicking that Sean knew well. The man that advanced on him from behind was carrying a rifle. "Could you put your hands on your head for me, please? Sorry for the inconvenience."

Sean's arms rose at a sluggish pace, his right arm allowing his left to determine their speed. He hadn't even gotten his hands over his neck before his left arm was begging to be put down again, the agony flooding his eye and tempting his vocal cords to cry out. The trembling started throughout his frame as his gloved hands interlocked on the back of his skull. Whether it was fear or pain or both that incurred his quivering, he couldn't tell.

"That's good, thank you," the speaker told him. Sean's shaking worsened to seizure-like degrees as the man stopped and stood behind him, less than a foot away it seemed. His nerves sensed the physical presence of a man equal in height to him, if not taller. "Can you stand still for me?" the speaker said into his left ear. He tried, but almost jumped from his boots at the feeling of the speaker's gloved fingers patting at the back of his pants. From his legs, the speaker frisked Sean's torso, and then his arms. He groaned, soft but not mute, as the man's hand tapped and jolted his left arm. A light creak came from the man's clothing as the speaker leaned in closer on the prisoner's left side, yet still concealed himself outside Sean's eyesight. The man was breathing beside his ear, exhalations Sean felt on his neck, the air first warm then icing. Clouds of white flowed in front of his eye, mingling with his own breaths before dissipating over the hillside.

"You look like you're in a lot of pain." The prisoner heard a click and the edge of a Marathon-issued switchblade, the exact same type he and Anna used, came hovering inches away from his left eye. Even as the speaker brandished his knife in front of Sean's eye, his demeanor did not change in the slightest, as if he was trapped in that one tone. "Stop me when I find the spot that hurts." The knife fell from Sean's eye level and skimmed his legs, the blade producing a sweeping sound as it brushed against his pants. The speaker glided the switchblade over Sean's gut and chest, halting for a few seconds to lightly prod at Sean's heart with the tip of the knife, as if to say he could end his prisoner at any moment he saw fit. From Sean's chest, the edge of the blade slithered across his neck, a centimeter from severing his throat. When the speaker had drawn the knife off of his neck, Sean capitulated to the grinding in his arm.

With a jagged shriek and a single tear from his eye, Sean's left arm unwound and plummeted back to his side, his right arm lingering on his head. "It's your arm, I take it." The switchblade clicked again, Sean hoped the speaker was putting the weapon away. His hopes were answered, only to then be laughed at when he felt the man's knife-less hand palpating his arm, the speaker's gloved fingers stabbing at his jacketed limb. The speaker started at the prisoner's elbow and moved up to his bicep and triceps, bringing about a wince of pain from Sean. "Feels like you dislocated it, popped it back in, but not perfectly. I wouldn't suggest lifting your arm like that in this condition." Releasing Sean's arm from his clasp, the man caressed the spider-web scars that deformed his prisoner's cheek. "Huh, these are pretty recent. This isn't your first time, I presume." The man stroked the bandages that covered Sean's head and right eye. "And these are very interesting. Matthew, I think we found one of your friends from Athens.

Guess that shot to the head wasn't as close as you thought it was. So, who did Matthew not kill?"

As he kept his right hand at the back of his head, afraid lowering it without the speaker's permission would invite some hidden wrath from the man, Sean recalled Marathon's protocols for agents captured by the enemy. His voice pitched and squeaked with fright as he said, "Halley-Corporal-four-nine-one-two-one-zero."

Sean heard the man snicker. "You're Marathon then. I suspected that already, but Marathon's the only operating force that uses that response, so thank you for confirming. Of course, the esteemed Commanders of Marathon wouldn't send a soldier as low as Corporal after me and my people. I figure you're a Black Dragoon, who's been unlucky enough to get shot in the head and then caught up in the biggest storm this valley has ever seen, since the Reform that is." The shock of the speaker's admission that Sword of God was aware of the Dragoons dragged Sean's head to the left. Resting his hand back on Sean's scars, the man stopped Sean's tilting and prevented the prisoner from getting a look at his captor. "Don't be so surprised. Your military isn't nearly as inconspicuous as they think they are. What's more amazing to me is the fact I found you walking out here without any means of protecting yourself. Maybe you left them in that old plane. You know I saw that thing crash, if you can believe it. Looked more like a meteor than an airplane when it came down, it's a miracle any of that jet survived to be used as a hideout."

Anna! Sean tried to jerk his head to the left again, but the speaker pressed his eye back towards the valley floor.

"Anyhow now that you're here you ought to know that this hill, this valley, everything you can see right now, this is my house. You might be visiting and some migrants may be renting space up in the mountains, but this is my house. This has been my home for forty years, so you can trust me when I say I know every last hole and cavern in this place, including where Marathon agents are most likely to take shelter if they're following Matthew from Athens."

Sean closed his eye for a moment, as the veracity set in as to just how badly Sword of God had outmaneuvered him and Anna. *What's that old Previous Civilization expression? Fish in a barrel?*

"You'll be pleased to know Halley-Corporal-four-nine-one-two-one-zero, you and your clan won't be departing without a tour of the valley. I'll be honest the sights aren't as good as they've been in the past, but don't fret, that's the least of your problems."

Something smacked him in the back of his left shoulder, blasting his arm with pain. Sean dropped to his knees with his hands in the snow. "Fuck."

"Watch your language, please," the speaker told Sean, before talking to the other members of Sword of God positioned someplace behind Sean's back. "Matthew, you're with me, Simon, this fella's yours. Walk him back to camp, we'll meet you there."

There were now a few pairs of boots snapping along the terrain, moving up and down the hill yet not speaking to each other, as if Matthew and Simon were under orders not to say a word. On his knees, Sean heard a new set of boots walk down behind him. Simon's, he presumed. Breaching the silence, Simon spoke with a tone of clear menace and attempted intimidation. "Stand the fuck up. Don't turn around. Keep your eyes on the valley floor." A rifle clicked in the man's arms, as if he were shivering.

Though Sean did as Simon commanded without defiance, he judged this man did not possess the confidence of his predecessor. "You mean my eye? Your pal Matthew got the other one, remember?" he replied, pecking at the patience of his guard like a child deliberately trying to infuriate their parents.

"Fuck yourself. Start moving down to the right. Stay two meters ahead of me at all times, keep your eyes, eye, on the ground. You run and I'll shoot you in the back." Simon's weapon tapped with a sway to the right. "Move."

He walked to the right, between the woodland debris in a sideways descent of the hill. His stride was slow, the sort of pace that would irritate anyone stuck trailing behind him. Above the racket of his and Simon's boots cracking in the snow, Sean asked, "How am I supposed to know if I'm two meters ahead of you, if I can't see where you are?"

"Stop talking, and fucking pick it up," Simon barked back, annoyed.

Sean stepped over a log in his path. To the left, he noticed the angle of the slope was beginning to steepen. "Okay what should I do first, stop talking or fucking pick it up?"

"How about I cut your tongue out?"

"That would hurt." It was a cliff face Sean and Simon were passing, a twenty-foot near-vertical drop onto a collection of sharp iced rocks and snow-coated lumber. "But it would also make it difficult for me to answer your questions."

Sean heard the rifle butt coming before it hit him in the back of the shoulder, giving him a microsecond or so to brace for the blow. Again he was on his knees, not because of the hammering sensation in his arm but rather by his own power. His lone good eye shifted towards the brim of the cliff, a meter away, as Simon's boots dug into the snow behind him. Jabbing Sean in the spine with the barrel of his weapon, Simon said, "You done?"

"Yeah, I'm done," Sean mumbled, losing the sarcasm he'd employed against Simon.

"Then move," Simon retorted, nudging Sean to stand with the tip of the barrel.

But Sean didn't move, he had to say something he wouldn't let himself say in the presence of his partner. He was quiet, so Simon

would only partially hear him. Yet Sean could still hear his own dec-
laration. "Anna, I love you."

"What?" Sean heard Simon leaning in, felt the man's weapon
drop away from his back. Simon's gloved hand clutched Sean's left
shoulder.

Sean swung around and soared to his feet, his boot punting Simon's strapless T-05 rifle from the equation, his right hand gripping
the Disciple by his dark blue Marathon uniform, his eye centering on
the man's face, masked in black wool like the other late Disciples. Simon's hands seized him in self-defense and Sean hurled them both to
the right. The hillside inverted before disappearing from view. Someone was shouting as they clung to each other through the plunge. The
bluff's icy rock wall appeared and rammed into Sean's back. Grunting
from a pain that disseminated itself across his backbone, they rolled
over and the wall took a turn with Simon's back. The Disciple delivered a similar groan as Sean bounced against him. They flipped over
again and the wall whacked at the back of his head. A third tumble
and something cracked in Simon's neck. Sean was struck in the lower back by a fiery stabbing sensation. Simon slammed on the ground
beneath the cliff, absorbing the brunt of their fall with a crushing
thump. Sean rebounded off Simon.

Sprawled on his back amidst the ice, rock, and timber, grumbling
in sheer agony, Sean knew he was conscious, and with that, he knew
he was still alive. Most of the throbbing came from his ribs and conse-
quently from his breathing. Sean was sure he'd fractured at least two
of the bones in his ribcage. The right side of his lower back burned
in continuous concerted pain. Reaching under his back, his hand
grasped a splinter of wood that impaled his torso. About as thick as
the barrel of a T-05, the stick had penetrated too far for him to risk
pulling it out without assistance and available bandaging. Tilting his
head far enough to the right for his left eye, he saw the log at the
base of the cliff, where the branch came from. And lying between him

and the tree was Simon, the snow turning dark red around his dented skull, his eyes immobile in the holes of his mask. "That went better than I expected," Sean muttered to himself. A scampering noise echoed down from the peak of the bluff. Straining his eye to see the top of the cliff, he spotted a dark blue silhouette standing at the edge, training a rifle on him.

13: ANNA

"Simon!"

The shout that stirred her was a dream, that's what Anna thought until she stretched her arm back in search of her partner. Anxiety carried her to full awareness when her hand bumped against the floor. She found his spot vacant, their campfire long since dead. *I was asleep! How long was I asleep?* Anna faced the cold, darkened space of the plane as she rose, her frame stiff and dazed by what must've been eight hours of sleep at the least. Her Second-Gen advantage had already quelled her sprained hip. "Sean?" she said, waiting for him to pop out from behind one of the seat rows and explain he'd gotten up to gather more cushion for the fire. When no such reply came, her eyes gravitated to the floor where her water bottle should've been. It was occurring to her that Sean had gone out to find water, when a crunching resounded from the snowbank behind her. Anna turned to the plane's exit, about to ask Sean if he'd found anything, and was consumed by a booming flash of yellow light.

Anna crashed on the floor, between the fireplace and the seats. The volcanic agony in her right shoulder told her everything she needed to know before she saw the wound. Curving her head, she watched the dark red erupt out of her jacket from the hole in her shoulder, quite close to where she'd been shot the first time. Her arm was dead, all sensation and mobility forever snuffed by the bullet. Already she could feel the blood wetting her clothing, a pool of dark red growing on the floor beside her.

Her Second-Gen Stage activated, racing through her insides. It breached the surface at an exceptional speed, in reaction to the danger of her condition, but the Second-Gen Stage wouldn't be enough to save her life. Her alternate state could only stall her blood loss, it couldn't stop the current. Unarmed and one armed, even if she somehow defeated the assailant who shot her, she had no medical gear left to treat her wound.

The boots materialized first, twisting as they advanced from the snowbank, as if their owner was sweeping the plane for other residents. The limited exposure from the gray external light diminished even further as a dark blue shadow stood over Anna. A T-05 shifted downwards in the figure's arms, smoke rising from the barrel as the weapon tilted towards her. "Good afternoon. Sorry to disturb you, but are you the only person in this plane?"

The man's tone and choice of speech were so out of place Anna wondered if he genuinely knew where he was and what he was doing. It was as if the assaulter had borrowed the false casual behavior tactic she'd used in Serenity and Dresden, but overreached and embraced that performance as authentic. Whoever this person was, his sanity had abandoned him years ago. "Corday-Corporal-one-two-one-one-four-one," Anna scratched out of her throat.

The attacker laughed in reply. "Wow, again. Marathon really should reconsider what their soldiers are allowed to say. It's gotten old over the years." The assailant bent down, as if trying to get a more precise look at her. He stayed that way for an upwards of a minute and a half, whilst Anna lay below him, bleeding and confused. With a chuckle that seemed more thunderstruck than humored, he said, "My word, you're a Second-Gen. I can see it in your eyes; you're in the Second-Gen Stage right now. I mean obviously, why wouldn't you be? I just shot you in the shoulder." The man took his hand off his weapon and held it out, waving to her as if she was someone he knew. "Truly though, I'm thrilled to make your acquaintance. I'll tell you, I've lived in this valley for forty years and not once have I met another Second-Gen."

Another Second-Gen?

"I think you and I are going to have a lot to talk about, Corday-Corporal-one-two-one-one-four-one. I'm looking forward to it." His rifle turned upside down in his hands, the butt of the weapon dropping and striking Anna in her bandaged forehead.

She regained consciousness with impaired eyesight, the world black and unfilled in front of her, even as she widened her eyes without blinking. Several moments of alarm passed in which Anna thought her attacker had blinded her while she was out, but then her eyes began to adjust to their new location. The soft feeling of synthetic fabric surrounding her head and the haze of dim orange light that slipped through a multitude of tiny holes in the darkness indicated her head was covered by a black bag. Her lips were stuck together and immoveable, her breathing restricted to her nostrils. *Duct tape.* The sensory gauges from the rest of her body reported in a few seconds later as widespread responsiveness was reestablished, and with that, a different sense of panic etched at Anna's nerves. She was sitting upright in a chair, her back sore from hours propped against the metal furniture. Her hands were tied behind her back at the wrists with what felt like wire, her ankles fastened the same way. The wound on her right shoulder continued to burn, yet her shoulder wasn't moist from seeping blood. Instead, the exterior of the wound was layered with an adhesive substance she assessed to be residue from a bandage.

Where she was being held, Anna couldn't know for sure. The rusted and acidic aroma in the air, added to the lack of even the smallest breeze, suggested she was in a human-made structure of some sort, decades old, unmaintained. The temperature was freezing, but Anna had come to trust there wasn't a single warm place in the Aegean Valley. *Sean talked about bunkers from the Previous Civilization, built into caves on the hillsides. Fuck, where the fuck is Sean?* Her fear for her partner triggered Anna's wrestling with her bindings, causing the legs of the chair to screech across the hardtop floor. The wires held, and even the Second-Gen Stage proved futile as well. The restraints were too tight, and she was too wounded, too thirsty, too hungry, and too tired. A door squeaked open somewhere in front of her.

Anna dipped her head forward and forced her breathing to a slow, brittle crawl. The door banged to a close and her visitor's boots tapped along a few steps of floor space towards her. His boots halted a foot or two ahead of her and pulled the bag away. Grime-laden concrete flooring and four windowless walls enclosed her. A line of electric bulbs hung from the ceiling, cracked and dirtied, as if they hadn't been touched in half a century. The room was lit to a shadowed orange by six kerosene lanterns that followed the walls at Anna's sides. These Previous Civilization devices and Anna's chair were the only objects in the otherwise barren room. The single entrance and exit was a wide metal door, five feet from where she sat. And, standing between Anna and her sole means of escape was a child.

The visitor was a boy, around ten years old as best as Anna could guess. His black hair was bushy and ruffled. He wore the unstated uniform of the nomadic civilians and others who dwelled in the Aegean Valley, winter coat, pants, boots, and gloves, all grayed by filth and ravaged by overuse. The boy's skin bore dark red gashes and bruises that were far too familiar to those of the girl Anna killed in Athens. Some of his injuries looked fresh, less than a day old and still lumped by swelling. The expression these wounds encircled was drained and listless. Like the Cavaliers' children who numbed themselves to the contingency of death, this boy numbed himself to the will of the individual in power. He and Anna were prisoners of the same man, yet the boy had lost the ability to care.

Not speaking a word, the boy raised a hand to Anna's face and peeled the duct tape from her mouth. Holding the tape and bag, he pried at the strips of bandaging on Anna's shoulder. Cringing from the sting of having her wound reopened, Anna watched as the stream of blood resumed its course onto her reddened shoulder and jacket. Turning away from her, the boy dropped the bag, tape, and bandages on the floor and walked to the corner of the room on the right side of the door. "Hey," Anna said to him at a hushed volume, as he stood in the corner and rotated to face the room. "Hey, can you help me?" The boy's reaction was none. No response. No sign he was even listening. The door shrieked open a second time.

"Morning. How'd you sleep?" the man asked her as he entered the room. Bringing a hand to his mouth, he yawned as the door sealed behind him. In the corner, the boy tightened his stance and stared towards the back of the room, as if trying to appear so unsubstantial his abductor forgot he was there. The man stood in front of Anna, close enough he blocked her view of the door. His attire classified him as Sword of God, shredded and dark red stained Marathon uniform, a Marathon switchblade clipped to his belt, a T-05 clicking from its shoulder-hung strap, and a light blue cross painted on his forehead. "I do apologize for the smell. Normally I try to clean the place up a bit when I'm having guests. Lately though I've been in the process of relocating to Athens, so I just haven't had the time. But the Black Dragoons know all about that, don't they?"

Anna's Second-Gen Stage remained active in speechless response to the man's knowledge of Marathon's death squad. To her horror, as she studied the terrorist's face, she concluded that the Second-Gen Stage would be of little help to her. Because this man, a child of the Previous Civilization in his early sixties, with balding grayish-black hair and an abnormally tame facial structure that omitted any marks or scars the Reform and the four decades since should've supplied, did not belong to the human race. His irises revealed that much.

What Anna saw in his eyes, a bright lime green color that elicited the Troy Station security footage from her memory, was worse: she had found the true commander of Sword of God; or, rather, he had found her, one of the agents liable for killing ten of his elite soldiers. Jesus Christ himself was a Second-Gen.

"You're Jesus," Anna said. Her tone was constrained more by terror than satisfaction, regardless of her best attempts to obtain some form of fulfillment. She had come face to face with an individual who'd eluded Marathon for a year as commander of Sword of God and probably several years before that as a lone hunter. Not even Darius had been able to locate this man. Anna knew this and still, the relative success of the operation meant little to her. Now a prisoner, Anna acknowledged she held no true commitment to the mission of the Black Dragoons, to the orders of Commander Darius, to the service of Marathon. Her only commitment was to Chloe Corday and Sean Halley.

Jesus raised his hand, as if answering a question. "Guilty. And you've done away with seven of my Disciples. Unless of course, you caught the group I sent to Dresden as well, in which case it would be eleven."

Sean must've killed one of them. "James, John, Peter, and Andrew, we killed all four in Dresden," Anna retorted with a manufactured sense of bragging.

Jesus had no reaction to hearing he was one of the last two fighters of Sword of God's inner circle. It was as if Anna told him the sky was gray and the air was cold, facts so rudimentary no response was warranted. "Splendid. As I was saying, you've made these great strides against my forces after doing circles in the dark for so long. And while I already know you're a Dragoon, I do not know how many of you there are. The scope of your unit has proven a better-kept secret than the unit itself. So, how many agents does Commander Darius keep on her payroll?"

There it was, the first question, and it couldn't have been easier. All Anna had to do was give him the number, forty-four, including her and Sean. Nevertheless, she held back. "Corday-Corporal-one-two-one-one-four-one."

Snickering, Jesus glanced at Anna's wounded shoulder. "Let's get that round out of your shoulder, I'm sure it's quite uncomfortable."

The comment was so abrupt, so lacking in relevance to what Jesus had asked her the only word Anna could summon in reply was, "What?" Then, he moved. In a second he was crouched against her chest, his hands attaching themselves to her shoulder in an aggressive unsympathetic manner, as if she was a piece of lifeless machinery he had total domain over. "Fuck!" The chair was squeaking on the floor again, Anna noticed she was squirming, as if that would liberate her from the wires at her wrists and ankles, a feat the Second-Gen Stage could not achieve.

"Watch your language, please."

"What're you doing?"

"Oh, you'll see. This may hurt a bit."

Something was slithering about where it shouldn't be. Though discomforting, these preliminary moments were painless. That was before Jesus's gloved fingers started scratching at the ruined muscles, veins, and nerves, defiling the interior of Anna's shoulder with what seemed like the same brute force as the bullet that generated the hole. It was as if he was trying to split her shoulder blade open by tunneling in and pushing outwards. Of all the ways Jesus could've removed the bullet, to do so by hand was surely the most agonizing and the most damaging.

Her cries overtook the slushing of his fingers clawing the round out of her arm, but the walls of her cell contained her suffering to the room. The chair bounced on the floor as she thrashed, struggling to shift her unworkable right arm out of his hands. But Jesus's grasp was as secure as the wires.

She glimpsed the right side corner of the room, where the boy stood as an unwilling spectator. Why she looked at him she had no

reasoning for; she knew he couldn't help her and she no longer wanted him to make the attempt. Anna saw him standing with his eyes
shut and his hands over his ears, his lips moving as if he was talking
to himself. *It's not real, it's not real, it's not real!*

At the end of the surgery, when Anna felt Jesus's hands leaving
her shoulder, she tilted her head down and heaved, not minding if
she vomited all over herself. Her throat was dry, with no offerings to
gratify her pain-induced nausea. The toilet in the plane had received
her last supper.

"You certainly are a Second-Gen," Jesus was saying to her as she
sat, clamped in her misery. "Can you imagine if I'd done that to your
partner? He'd be dead before I could even get my fingers on the bullet. Anyhow, here it is." He stuck his dark red sodden glove below
her dipping eye line, showing her the mangled slug of iron he'd sal-
vaged from her body. With its pointed tip obliterated and its frame
painted dark orange-red and orange-pink, the bullet had been denied
of its shape and now looked more like a sliver of intestine sliced off
her entrails. She dry-heaved again, hoping to puke in Jesus's hand. After nothing resulted from the effort, Jesus put the bullet in his pants
pocket and asked, "How many Dragoons are there?"

"Corday-Corporal-one-two-one-one-four-one," Anna countered
without lifting her head up, her voice inflaming to a defiant snarl.

Jesus grumbled. Anna's resistance was amusing to him the first
time, but her refusal to cooperate had regressed into annoyance.
"Why don't we get that bleeding stopped?"

She elevated her eyes to him then, confused. Jesus turned and
walked to the door. Hauling the exit open a crack, he spoke to the
darkened void. "Enter." The gateway shut again as he resumed his
post in front of the Dragoon prisoner. A silent hiatus on the interrogation befell, Jesus strangely having nothing to say, Anna too afraid
to ask, and the boy glaring at the back of the room again. The pause

broke when the door opened from the outside, then immediately re-closed behind the third visitor to Anna's cell.

The boy's younger sister, that was clear from the moment she showed herself. Seven or eight years old and the same black bushy hair, scruffy civilian wardrobe, and stark physical welts of her bondage to Jesus. She carried two objects, heavy enough the girl pant-ed several orange-white puffs of exertion. A hammer and a blow-torch. A fleeting exchange transpired in which the girl handed the items to Jesus without eye contact, whereas he accepted them as if they hadn't come from her but rather out of thin air. The girl stepped to the left side corner and faced the back of the room, as her brother was doing.

Hammer and blowtorch in hand, he made Anna the center of his attention once more. She stiffened in her chair, priming for Jesus's next operation. The hammer was set on the floor beside the bag, tape, and bandage. Jesus told her, "You might've gathered from the ban-dage that I have more conventional medical equipment here."

Anna glanced at the boy and girl. Both of them had shut their eyes and shielded their ears. *It's not real, it's not real, it's not real!*

"But you've lost a lot of blood as it is, so we should get that wound closed as fast as we can." A click from the blowtorch's switch, then a shrill hiss and a small orange-blue flame was lit at the tip of the torch. "This will definitely hurt."

The blowtorch was shoved into her shoulder before Anna had an opportunity to look away. Black dyed liquid flooded into the room through the walls and the door, smothering the lanterns, enveloping the boy and girl, then Jesus and Anna in pitch darkness. A blitzkrieg of arctic water soaked through her bloodied clothes and skin, seem-ing to drench her bones. Her head dripped as she scanned the room and its occupants. Brother and sister in their corners, ears unplugged and open eyes pinpointed on the room's rear. Jesus stood in his place between her and the door, the blowtorch on the floor with the hammer, a bucket in his hands. "Welcome back," he said, tossing the bucket with a clang.

Understanding that the shock of pain from the blowtorch had knocked her unconscious, Anna rotated her head to her scorching right shoulder. A sheet of blackened and browned flesh crusted over the hole, the wound cauterized. That time she did vomit, but only stomach fluid and off to the side on the dampened floor. Jesus didn't give her a chance to recuperate, asking for the third time, "How many agents does Commander Darius employ? What is the unit size of the Black Dragoons?"

She heard herself laughing. Spitting the taste of bile from her mouth, she responded, "Corday-Corporal-one-two-one-one-four-one."

He was on her again, pressing her body down in the chair, as though he believed she was going to launch out of it, his red-tainted switchblade snapping to life in his hand. No words on this go around, just the promise of continual agony. The knife cut down the burnt patch of skin on her shoulder, dividing the crust in two. Dark red revived from the wound, as the blood had done when the boy removed her bandage. With her wound reopened for the second time since she'd been restrained to that chair, Jesus returned his switchblade to his belt and gripped the hammer. Taking the mashed bullet from his pocket, he wedged the front end of the round in the bleeding hole of Anna's shoulder, until the slug was hanging in her arm on its own yet sticking out of her skin. Holding the hammer sideways, Jesus looked to her, mute as he gave her one last chance to submit the intelligence he desired. She grinned at him with disdain, bobbing her head up and down in a nod of approval and mockery. His enraged eyes stayed on her as the hammer curled backwards, then swung forward, crashing against her shoulder and driving the bullet back through the hole Jesus had tugged it from.

Anna lowered her head back down to her chest with a high elongated groan, her teeth gritting to fight off another shriek. The hammer rejoined the blowtorch on the floor as Jesus walked towards the door, as if about exit the room. Turning back to her with his red-gloved hands on his hips, he asked her a different question. "What is it with you two?" he said, befuddled.

You two? She dragged her head up, staring at her mystified captor.

"I worked your partner for hours last night and all I got from him was, Halley-Corporal-four-nine-one-two-one-zero."

Her legs and left arm tensed at the wires, anger soothing the pain and queasiness, though only somewhat.

"Why're you holding out for the city that threw you and your friend into the meat grinder? I seriously doubt either of you have been in the service for long. Marathon should've sent agents with several years' experience after a terrorist like me, but instead they send a Second-Gen who I'm assuming is barely past her Awakening, and her human partner."

Anna didn't retort, not because she was deterring, rather because she didn't know what to say to Jesus's frustrated question.

His curiosity wouldn't waver. "Come on," Jesus pried. "It can't be a sense of duty to Marathon. That's like when I tell my Disciples we're claiming this valley for the glory of God and his heavens." He smiled, amusing himself.

She was confused. "That's not why you're doing this, that old Previous Civilization religion, Chrisa, Chrisi?"

He chuckled. "Do I look like a real Christian to you?"

"Wouldn't know. Never met one."

"Just like you've never met a Jew or a Muslim either?"

"Huh?"

"It's all one faith in Marathon. That religion wasn't born till after the Reform, but apparently the thousands of attempts to decode the universe in the Previous Civilization all pale in comparison to the

Commanders and their holy city of Marathon. None of this has ever been about Marathon though, not at its core. Religious strife is the easy explanation, when you need it to make sense to your underlings without upsetting them. Same way the Reform was just a squabble over Second-Gens, and not a global explosion of pressure built up through centuries of international struggle. Marathon's war for the Aegean Valley, for Serenity, why they went ahead and trampled Carthage, those undertakings weren't made to spread Marathon's will to the world, they were made by the Commanders to capture the world. Your superiors want to rule the first post-Reform super nation and they're perfectly willing to rape and murder their fair share to achieve that."

Anna was dumbstruck: never before in her life had she come to agree with a person she so vehemently loathed. This man, who called himself Jesus Christ, was barbaric and homicidal, a rapist, and yet she felt he had a clearer picture of the world in the 31st Year of Marathon than anyone she'd ever met. Because now when she thought of her homeland, beyond the section of her mind the memory of her daughter was confined to, she saw only the atrocities committed in the name of the Commanders and their holy city. The butchery at Carthage, witnessed and communicated by Sean, she and her partner's extermination of the Cavaliers, the Detention Center, and even pentagon. But of course, Anna didn't let herself overlook the fact she was in the presence of someone completely mad. "Is that what this war of ours is about for you? Control?"

"Oh absolutely, this world is the new land of opportunity. I'm not the only person who's figured this out. The drug gangs in Marathon, the Cavaliers in Serenity, the Face Cutters in Troy, they're all scrapping for control the same as me and your people. Marathon's the largest player in this conquest, that's why the rest of us allow ourselves to take time out of fighting each other to mitigate your advance. The enemy of my enemy is still my enemy, but at times is also my friend. That's why Marathon's war with the entire world will go on forever, every time your city kills an insurgent cell, you birth two more. You and your partner have been dragooned by a collective much greater than yourselves. Second-Gen you are Corday-Corporal-one-two-one-one-four-one, but even a Second-Gen is a replaceable cog in their engine. There will be more like you who end up in the chair of someone like me before this war is done."

The reality was there now. Though she wished it hadn't come to her with the aid of Jesus, the cruel actuality of Marathon revealed itself behind the sub-districts of Terra, New Terra, Missio, and Ignis, behind the Marathon River and the Marathon Bridge, behind the Outer Fence and the Inner Fence, and behind the Commanders. And the final impetus that brought about this truth to Anna was a fact of life she'd never questioned, never heard anyone question, not even Chloe, until Sean asked her that night under the bridge, just south of Athens. The citizens of Marathon had been staring right at it since the 1st Year of Marathon, the true reason for dark blue and black being the only colors permitted. Marathon's sacred colors, the city had taught Anna and the other children in school, the colors of night, when Marathon's spirit was felt the most. It was a cover story that seemed to ridicule Anna as she unknotted it, teasing her for taking twenty-one years to do so.

Universe forbid Marathon's kids start drawing with anything more than dark blue and black pencils. Who knows what dangerous ideas they might conjure up with that kind of freedom? "Sword of God's just another engine, like Marathon, only smaller."

"Spot on," Jesus responded, pointing his index finger at her, like a teacher complimenting a student's correct answer to a question. "And my Disciples are components in that mechanism, as disposable as a Marathon soldier or a Dragoon. I wish you could've seen the baptisms I gave each of them when they joined. Humans really are the more gullible species. Don't feel too bad about the Disciples you and your partner killed, I've swapped out a few of them before. Shouldn't take me more than six months to refill the bracket, there're plenty of people in this valley looking to be saved. But, you still haven't told me why you've let yourself get jammed up between me and Marathon."

Anna's reply came fast. "I haven't answered your questions, because I've experienced a pain worse than anything you could imagine."

"And just what might that be?" Jesus countered, skeptical.

She smiled at him. "Giving birth."

With a pause, Jesus said, "You got a kid?"

"Yes."

"In Marathon?"

"Yes."

"That's why you joined the military?"

"Yes."

"And that's why you won't yield?"

"Never."

He nodded, appearing to accept his failure to break Anna and Sean. "Well then." The T-05 unslung from his shoulder and rose to position in his arms. "Let's take a walk outside. I'm sure Matthew and Halley-Corporal-four-nine-one-two-one-zero are growing impatient."

The boy untied the wires at his captor's direction, Jesus training his rifle on both the boy and Anna as she was released from her restraints. Such precautions proved unnecessary, because when Jesus gave Anna the order to stand, she rose and immediately collapsed onto the water and blood-sodden floor. She thought, slightly hoped, Jesus would just shoot her in the back of the head as she lay at his feet, sparing her the pain of a last walk. However, he instructed the boy and girl to carry her, which brother and sister moved to do, the girl taking Anna's left arm over her shoulders and the boy supporting Anna's right arm. The tap of the children's boots was counteracted by the skid of Anna's boots on the concrete as they exited the room, Jesus aiming his weapon at the three of them as he followed a few feet behind.

The structure beyond the room was of duplicate scent and temperature, yet concealed by a blackness of such totality Anna was reminded of the Dresden's interior tunnels. Veering to the right from the room, they stumbled forward for a distance Anna had no means of estimating. Jesus and the children walked this lightless space without caution, all of them having inhabited the place long enough to memorize the unseen passageway. When Anna felt her boots bang against the edge of a step, they began to ascend, brother and sister's boots thumping on the invisible stairwell, Jesus's T-05 clicking in constant pursuit. Their climb didn't last more than half a minute, and as it concluded they were received by a glare of natural light, dim and gray yet also blinding.

Her vision attuned after a few seconds, her nostrils rejoicing at the smell of marginally better air, her body shivering with the feeling of a glacial breeze, and her boots crunching as they toed in the snowy ground. Behind Anna and the children, Jesus stepped out from the square-shaped hatch. Two metal doors hung open at the sides of the hatch, dented and splintered from years of service to Jesus. *Sean got it right. Sword of God uses a bunker from the Previous Civilization.*

A veil of dense morning fog held over Fort Valley, the grime-misted air obscuring the valley floor in front of Anna and the towering mountainsides behind her. Nevertheless, the repercussions of the storm were visible on the hillside ridge the bunker had been constructed on. A strew of ruptured trees and shattered rocks blanketed the flat ground, crackling beneath the children's boots as they carried Anna towards the edge of the hillcrest at Jesus's order. Standing ten feet back from this boundary, the last stretch of tangible ground before a descent into the valley's haze, was Jesus's lone surviving Disciple. Black-masked and wielding a T-05, Matthew hid his face as he gestured his rifle in Anna and the children's direction, as if challenging them to try and race his bullets to the cover of the fog. "Any progress with that one?" he asked his commander as the group approached.

"I'm afraid she's ten times as stubborn as her partner," Jesus said from behind. "We're not going to get anything we can use from either of them. Go ahead and line her up too."

Matthew seemed to disagree. "Are you sure, my Lord?"

Anna would've laughed if she weren't so weak. *My Lord?*

"Maybe we should let them rot another day," Matthew continued. "See if they're willing to speak up then."

"Other Dragoons will be delivered to us in good time, Matthew, ones who won't be so resilient. God will see to it."

Matthew's misgivings were suppressed. Even in the direst moment of Sword of God's brief history, with all but two of its members slain, the promise that a higher power had aligned itself with them and was actively working to serve their interests had not diminished in the mind of Jesus's sole follower. *Marathon makes the same guarantees to its soldiers, just trade the name "Lord" for "Commander." Was faith abused like this during the Previous Civilization, or did we not figure out until after the Reform that you can get people to do basically anything by hijacking their deepest beliefs?*

"How's your chum doing, Matthew?" Jesus asked.

"A little better actually, I think the fresh air's been good for him. Doesn't matter now of course." The children walked Anna over a log that lay before the final twenty feet of the ridge, giving her a view of Jesus's second Dragoon prisoner.

Sean sat on his knees, five feet from the edge and three feet to Matthew's right, head angled down in the same heavy-eye weariness that prohibited Anna from moving on her own. The sight of him ignited a newfound sense of rage and guilt in Anna at the realization of just how much Sean had suffered during the night. His left arm suspended akimbo from his shoulder, the limb twisted backwards out of socket. No doubt, Jesus had dislocated and reset Sean's arm several times before choosing to leave the arm in its current incorrect position. That wasn't even the worst of Sean's wounds. Bright red shrouded the right side of his face, spilling down his neck and jacket in a quantity greater than that of his head wounds. The blood oozed from a series of gashes that mutilated the once intact side of his face. When she got within ten feet of the cliff edge, Sean lifted his head to her with a beaten stare. It was then Anna assessed that the new marks on the right side of Sean's face were identical to the Carthage scars on the left side of his face.

"Those old scars were such an eyesore by themselves. Drove me crazy all night," Jesus quipped. "Now his face matches."

With that remark, Anna's anger compelled her to swing her left arm off the girl's shoulder in a useless attempt to punch Jesus with the back of her left fist. Jesus did not react, and didn't need to; the burning in Anna's right shoulder pushed her knees to the snow and rocks after a step backwards. Facing the cliff-side and the subsequent gorge of gray fog, she looked to Sean as she groaned in pain. Any response she could gauge from Sean was subdued at best, as if he was ready to get on with their execution. *No point in fighting them anymore. At least we won't have to see Darius again.*

The brother and sister pulled Anna off the ground and resumed carrying her, while Jesus continued talking as if Anna hadn't tried to fight back at all. "As I said before Corday-Corporal-one-two-one-one-four-one, your partner was quite unhelpful as well." They reached the ends of the crest and the children lowered Anna back onto her knees, just to the right of Sean's spot at the edge. Anna and Sean were close enough to hold hands, if they chose to do so. "There was a tree branch stuck in his back when we first brought you two here. Halley-Corporal-four-nine-one-two-one-zero had himself a pretty nasty fall in a scuffle with my friend Simon." Anna glimpsed the bottom right of Sean's back, where a bright red hole pierced his skin and jacket. "So, I took the stick out, zapped the cut with the blowtorch, and started asking him how many Dragoons Darius has. Familiar question I'm sure. But even after I did all that for him, he wouldn't oblige." The boy and girl stepped around Anna and stood a few feet in front of Sean, regarding the departing prisoners with what almost appeared to be jealousy. "I opened the wound up again, and then played with his arm for a few hours, still nothing." Matthew strolled over, joining the children and standing in front of Anna. "But, in the end I can't say I really blame him for being so difficult." The ridge cracked under his boots as Jesus moved towards the Dragoon prisoners from Anna's right, his rifle elevated yet not centered on them. "After all." At Anna's side, he kneeled down and spoke into her ear. "People don't give up easy when they believe they're protecting someone they love."

Anna swerved her head around to Sean. He'd already turned away, shutting his one good eye in observable fear of how she would react. An array of emotions sped through her at nearly too fast a stride for her to interpret, surprise in the first couple seconds, joy in the next few, and then finally confusion. She couldn't understand why Sean was afraid of her knowing what he felt as neither of them had more than a minute to live.

Returning to his feet, Jesus said, "I apologize for the fog this morning. I like to give my guests a nice view of the valley before they leave, but the weather just isn't playing along today."

You mean you like to shoot your prisoners outside, and toss their bodies over the cliff to avoid the hassle of a large cleanup.

Jesus's boots crunched behind Anna and Sean as he situated himself between them and the drop-off, unhindered by his proximity to the edge. "Wish we could wait for things to clear up, although I'm sure you two are anxious to get on your way. Matthew, me, and the kids have a lot of work to do once you're gone." Anna heard the click of Jesus's T-05 shifting in his arms, the barrel gravitating towards the back of her and Sean's skulls. Glancing at the onlookers to their demise, Anna saw the children trembling where they stood, their eyes soaring throughout the mist. Matthew kept half his guard on the siblings, watchfully confident of their obedience to Sword of God.

"What're your names?" All eyes were on Sean now, Anna not knowing what to make of Sean's question any more than Jesus or Matthew. His eye was open and wide, his head arched upwards, gaze compressed to the boy and girl. The children looked back at him, their numb expressions revitalizing with fright. "What're your names?" he asked a second time, his tone insistent, as if the question netted his interest hours ago, jabbing at him until he absolutely had to find out before he died.

The brother glanced at Jesus and Matthew, seeming to survey his captors for permission to answer. Momentarily distracted by the abruptness and apparent randomness of Sean's query, the self-proclaimed prophet and his Disciple did not refute the boy's request. The child turned back to Sean, his voice coughing up a name. "Jacob, Jacob Holloway."

The girl spoke a second later, after no immediate penalty was dealt to her brother for talking without Jesus's authorization. "Mia Holloway."

To Jacob and Mia, nothing more had passed than a brief exchange between adult and child, a handful of words that didn't even amount to a conversation and were likely to be dismissed within a week or two, assuming Jesus allowed Jacob and Mia to live that long. For Anna, and no doubt Sean as well, it was as if the cliff face had given way underneath them. They turned to each other at the same instant, secluded by their nonverbal conversation.

A tick came from behind as Jesus tightened his grip around the trigger of his weapon, refocusing from Sean's brief disruption of the execution. Sean turned from Anna and looked to Jacob and Mia once again. "Okay," he said, his tone calmed and level. Then, escorted by a quick rasping yell, Sean rose to his feet.

In that moment it seemed as if her partner wasn't wounded at all. Sean flung forward, off the ground and through the few feet of space that separated him from Jacob and Mia, his grated shriek disorienting Jesus and Matthew for the millisecond he needed to reach the children. Sean collided with Jacob and Mia both, his arms sprawling to wrap around and shield them as the trio fell with his tackle. The conjoined jumble of Sean, Jacob, and Mia was midway through its fall when Anna saw, in the upper periphery of her eye, the barrel of Jesus's T-05 aiming at her partner and the children, his index finger already pulling at the trigger. Powered by the same temporary inspiration that recharged Sean and aided by her Second-Gen Stage, Anna leapt upwards from her knees, extending her bandaged yet still functioning left arm and seizing the rifle barrel. With a yank, she curved Jesus's T-05 to the right, the rifle losing sight of Sean, Jacob, and Mia just before a yellow flash detonated at the tip of the weapon.

The T-05 was set to automatic. The first half of Jesus's six flash burst exploded against the rubble in front of the bunker doors, the reports thundering into the fog. The latter half of the volley impaled Matthew's skull, at the precise moment Sean, Jacob, and Mia landed in the snow, the children vanishing as Sean protected them with his own body. Jesus's rifle continued to reverberate through the clouded hillside as a rush of bright red spray shot from Matthew's disintegrating head, the blowback hitting Anna in the face. Her boots lost traction on the uneven terrain of the ridge and she dropped back, ramming into the side of Jesus's chest. The footing of the now Disciple-less leader failed as well and the pair fell in one bundle like Sean, Jacob, and Mia. No hard surface caught their descent. They tumbled together, over the edge of the cliff.

The hillcrest appeared above Anna, and then disappeared in the mist she and Jesus plummeted through. Anna first struck ground with her defunct right arm. The gray sky was beneath her, the gray snow and ice-laden ground floating over her head. Her back was speared by crackling rocks, the Second-Gen Stage saving her spine from fracture though not from the titanic pain that sheathed her back muscles and nerves. With a short screech, she flipped and the land and sky returned to their rightful places. Chest and gut danced on a floor of pointed ice and jagged wood, slicing at her frame with a chorus of ringing and snapping sounds as she cried out. The slope twisted her to the side, her right arm slamming into a tree trunk. She rolled over the log, banging the back of her skull on the frosted wood, while her stomach met the rocks just beyond the tree. The landscape inverted again and she plowed into another tree, splitting the thin trunk with a crack as she crashed through it. Past the trees the hill ended, and Anna felt the breath-stealing weightlessness that told her she was in freefall over a second cliff face. From below, she saw a flat gray surface take shape in the fog, enlarging in her vision. The ground arrived less than a second later.

The snow popped, the ground displacing underneath her. In her stunned and agonized state, Anna recognized she'd fallen all the way to the bottom floor of Fort Valley. Respiring in small yet neverthe-less painful gasps of white, she shifted onto her side and took a look at her mauled self. The rips in her clothing and the cuts on her body wrought by the shockwave of the storm seemed to have been exacer-bated, minor gashes becoming extensive bright red lacerations.

Where's Jesus? Anna rotated her head about in every direction, sweeping the valley floor. The poor visibility up in the hills hadn't im-proved now that she was in the valley's core. The mounds of gray fog abridged her view to some fifty feet at most, and Jesus hadn't land-ed inside that radius. She shared these grounds with little else than a few uprooted and smashed tree stalks and split boulder fragments. Her legs were too frail, too beaten by the drop to stand, not to men-tion walk. The end for her was to come where she lay. How long Anna would have to lie in that spot depended on how long it would take for the multiple leaks along her body to drain a fatal amount of blood from her arteries and veins. Anna imagined she was to die when a pool of dark red snow had materialized around her, as had been the case for many of the people she and Sean killed. However, with the crack of ice being crushed under boots, some distance away yet coming closer, Anna realized she would die while the snow was still mostly gray.

An indistinct silhouette appeared thirty or forty feet in front of Anna. Lying parallel to the cliff she fell from, her legs pointed towards the shadow as it grew in clarity, each shattering footstep announcing its approach. "Not bad Corday-Corporal-one-two-one-one-four-one, not bad." Jesus stepped out of the mist. His rifle was missing, lost in the fall. His switchblade was in his hand. "You and your partner make quite the duo. Sad you two won't be working together again."

Anna turned onto her back, facing Jesus straight on. She wasn't about to give him the satisfaction of chasing her down by trying to crawl away; her resistant stare would be with him until he slit her throat or perforated her heart. His crackling boots advanced towards her, saying, "Once I'm done with you two, that'll just leave the kids." Jesus stopped at her boots and stood over her, waving the blade in his hand and sprinkling her with drops of dark red. "I suppose since they didn't actually play a hand in this rebellion of yours, I shouldn't punish them the same as you and Halley-Corporal-four-nine-one-two-one-zero. I'll just have." He paused. "What were their names again, I forgot."

Wrath was all there was now, all her Second-Gen Stage would supply and all Anna demanded of her alternative state. For this person, who occupied the children's home, massacred their friends and neighbors, separated them from their father, beat, and enslaved them, this person committed those atrocities and had not the slimmest decency necessary to remember the children's names. "Jacob and Mia Holloway."

"Right, I'll just have a nice heartfelt talk with Jacob and Mia. I'm sure they've been missing my..."

She swung her leg to the side, swiping Jesus's legs from the snow. Anna's fury wasn't enough to help her stand or walk, but it had been plenty to do that. And when Jesus hit the ground, on his side with a surprised though unafraid thud, as if he expected to regain control of the situation, Anna was there. Her body stretched over his, pinning him to the snow, her left hand clutching the knife. None of that was to last, she knew; she had seconds at best before his strength pushed hers aside. A growl of shrill viciousness roared from her throat, unlike anything she'd heard herself utter before, as she lifted her mouth to the left side of his neck, her teeth clamping down on his skin. The taste was bland at first, like the tofu blocks she'd carried in her pack throughout the mission, and then there was flavor. Sweet and boiling, maybe the most nourishing sustenance she'd tasted. Her teeth tore apart flesh with minimal difficulty, as if she'd grown fangs. Blood clogged her mouth; she drank and kept digging. Her throat burned, slimy chunks of skin and muscle squeezed in her teeth, and yet she didn't stop until she found Jesus's jugular vein. The terrorist snarled, not of fear or pain, but an angered denial of what was happening to him. His body thrashed beneath hers. Anna felt her Second-Gen Stage beginning to buckle as the mass of Jesus's superior alternate state became too heavy. Her teeth bit at his jugular vein, cutting through the meat until the two rows met in the middle. And when Jesus threw her off of him, her teeth clung to the vein, ripping the jugular from Jesus's neck by the force of his own throw.

Red, bright and sweltering, a decent source of warmth in the morning cold, that was what Anna saw as she lay in the snow, what she felt soaking her body. It blocked her eyes, overwhelmed her nostrils, and choked her lungs. A gurgling noise interspersed throughout this torrent, from where Anna couldn't see. But eventually the sound left her as she drowned in a river of bright red.

"Anna? Anna!"

She came back with Sean's face levitating under her, her head hanging from the ground, the gray overcast of sky below them both, the world upside down. Through his bandaged right eye, defaced cheeks, and bleeding notches, an expression of horrified alarm slipped out. As wounded as he was, what he was seeing with his left eye worried him much more, and her waking up didn't alleviate his terror. *Where's Jesus?* With a small twist of her head, the man who commandeered the name Jesus Christ appeared in her vision. Three feet away, he hung motionless from the red ground, neck destroyed, his eyes frozen in what Anna hoped was a perpetual sense of incompletion, his nihilistic ambition untamed, his vast plans for the future unfinished.

Turning back to Sean, her partner said, "You got Matthew too, Anna. They're all dead now, they're all dead. We're going to get you home." That last sentence seemed more like a desperate appeal than a realistic goal.

Beneath them, a swell of black burst through the clouds of the overcast and submerged the sky in darkness. Higher and higher the wave rose, nearing Anna and Sean while the daylight receded with unnatural rapidity, as if nightfall had skipped over the afternoon and dusk. Light wasn't totally lost to the land above the night, however, specks of yellow gleamed in the blackness, some of them twinkling. They were as Sean described. Stars, dozens of them though probably more, each of them a messenger, comforting Anna with the knowledge that even the largest forces in existence cannot withstand the calling of the entire universe. One day or another, everyone answers for their actions. To this, Anna was overcome by a great pacifying sensation, a blaze of contentment and freedom that only Chloe and Sean could convey. A smile spread over her as she gazed down at Sean. "I love you too," she said, and followed him into the starlight dark.

14: SEAN

Two months after the destruction of Sword of God, Sean Halley sat up on his bed in Marathon Hospital, holding a mirror in his hand. Black sheeted and warm, the bed fit with his room. Black floors, walls, and ceiling, as per the order of the Commanders, and with barely ten feet from the black exit door on his left to the window on the right, his room was cramped. However, with a latrine and shower just across the hall, heating, and meals brought to his room daily, Sean had no desire to complain. Even if those spoils weren't included in his stay at Marathon Hospital, he wouldn't have protested. He'd survived the return journey from the Aegean Valley; he was alive in New Terra, Marathon.

Directing the mirror to the left side of his face, he stared at his Carthage scars, patting the coarse skin with his free hand. Then he moved the mirror to the right side of his face and rubbed the matching scars molded by Jesus's knife. As red as the blood that leached through the wounds two months ago, as if the bleeding had left a mark of its own, the newest spider-web burned whenever he touched the mutilations. With both sides of his face malformed as they were, his appearance was, to him, a misshapen presence in the world that everybody would glare at as though he himself had carved the scars into his cheeks. But still, he preferred judgement from Marathon's citizens over the Aegean Valley.

Unable to wake Anna after she lost consciousness again, Sean realized he had to get her back to Sword of God's bunker. Forgetting about the terrorist commander's ravaged corpse, he sought out a means to carry Anna up the hills that bordered the cliffs she'd fallen from. Although he'd reset his left arm as best he could before descending to the valley floor, he had no hope of lifting Anna up and over him with both arms. The blood that draped her, painting her clothes red and oppressing all traces of their true black color, made her too slippery to grasp. Then, Sean developed an improvised method of transporting his partner. Lying on his stomach, with his right shoulder against her head, he pulled her over his back and shoulders with his right arm. Slack from unconsciousness, Anna came along rather easily, though she drenched him in Jesus's blood as he positioned her behind his head. When she was in place, he dug his boots into the snow and stood, balancing the Second-Gen barbell on his shoulders. This effort was successful—-Anna dangled from his shoulders yet didn't drop—-but it was accomplished with an expensive amount of energy from Sean's exhausted and wounded body, and an unhealthy quantity of agonized screams. As he carried her towards the hills, he knew he didn't have the strength to take her the entire way up by himself. He ignored this fact, intent on killing himself to save Anna if he had to.

The fog had lessened in the time since Anna's fall, though being able to see where he was going only hurt Sean further, showing him how far he still had to go before they reached the bunker. He'd covered less than a quarter of the distance up the steep incline when his legs, shoulder muscles, back muscles, and ribcage all surrendered at the same moment and he crumbled to the ground. Anna rolled off his shoulders and began to slide head first back down the hill, dyeing the snow dark red as she slid. Sean caught her right leg with his right hand and plowed his left hand and boots into the snow. Bellowing in pain, he clung to her, desperate, yet couldn't pull her back up as she started to drag him down the slope with her, his boots and left hand breaking from the snow. He drove his limbs back underneath the snow, only to have them resurface seconds later as he and Anna skidded several feet more. Behind him, a stampede of crunching snow emerged and descended the hill. Sean didn't have a chance to turn around before Jacob and Mia were there.

From the side, the children interrupted Anna and Sean's slide, grabbing at Anna's side and pressing their boots in the snow. Neither sibling offered a word of explanation, as their ability to communicate normally likely remained stalled by weeks of imprisonment. Conversely, Sean had no words to express his gratitude as Jacob and Mia stayed by his side, helping him carry Anna the rest of the way up the hill. He'd expected them to take off running when he left them on the hillcrest with Matthew's decapitated body, their trust in people forever lost in the nightmare their young lives had become, yet here they were, rescuing the Dragoons from the valley floor, without anticipation of reward. Jacob and Mia Holloway might've been the two most selfless people Sean had ever met.

Back through the bunker doors, the children led Sean and his comatose partner to the first room from the blackened staircase. No different than the room he'd been interrogated in, the room was stuffed with boxes that fenced a small patch of floor space in the center. Two kerosene lanterns lit the room in dark orange. They laid Anna down on her back between these lamps. It was Jacob who brought Sean the first box and opened it to show him what was inside: bandages, gauze, clotting packets, sponges, disinfection spray, rags, and gloves, among other items. Sean understood this room stored the bunker's stock of medical equipment.

They knelt around the unresponsive Anna, Sean doing so to manage the worsening pain in his bleeding back and face, broken ribs, blinded right eye, and repeatedly dislocated left arm, the children copying his motions. Starting with Anna's right shoulder, they cleaned the area around the wound with sponges and rags, coated the gunshot wound with an army of clotting-agent, sealed the dark red hole behind a bandage, and then wrapped the entire shoulder with gauze and additional bandaging. Next her upper chest, stomach, and back, where the consequences from her fall were many. On and on this went, for how long Sean didn't know, as time itself seemed to wait outside the bunker's exit, having no part in the events that occurred below ground. They dressed every wound they found. Even the wound Anna received in Athens and the self-inflicted cuts on her left arm and forehead they uncovered, scrubbed, and bandaged once more.

Sean was well aware his, Jacob, and Mia's healing attempts did not account for the throng of internal injuries Anna may or may not have been stricken by. He remembered learning during his college years in Carthage that Second-Gens were supposedly impervious to pervasive internal bleeding, their resistance to injury growing sturdier the deeper into their anatomy you went. Nonetheless, when the trio finished their work, Sean tried and again failed to stir Anna. He began to believe the Second-Gens protection from inner bleeding was either a hoax or had been exaggerated in the years following the Reform.

Anna looked to be dying. Her breathing continued but decelerated to short, aching croaks, worse than Sean's own. Her skin was ice cold, her awareness non-existent. Sean could've punched her in the gut without reaction. It was as if Anna's conscious mind had traversed over to another planet, another universe even, displacing her from the life she'd led up until this point. The people she loved weren't enough of a hook to keep her tied to the world she knew. The trauma was too immense, the outlook too grim for her to stay.

Deciding eventually he and the children had done the best that could be done with the resources they possessed, Sean gestured to Jacob and Mia, offering to treat their bulging cuts. They rebuffed him with mild shakes of their heads, uncomfortable with a stranger getting that close to them. He watched for a minute as Jacob used a new box of medical supplies to treat his little sister's wounds, Mia allowing him to do so. How close Jacob and Mia were to each other before Athens fell to Sword of God, Sean obviously had no knowledge. But he was certain this relationship between brother and sister had now mutated into something much more resilient, a lifetime bond of trust and empathy no one else could ever fully appreciate. Neither their father nor any future significant others would understand them like they understood one another.

Leaving Jacob and Mia to themselves for the time being, Sean turned back to his fading partner. The extent of bandaging and gauze she was wrapped in would've fooled anyone who walked in without prior context into thinking Anna was already dead and in the process of being preserved for some burial ritual. Sean had to lean his head in close to hers to make sure she was breathing. The cuts on his face and the hole in his back had bled whilst he'd stumbled down the hill to the valley floor, carried Anna back up, and dressed her wounds. Dark red dripped from his cheek and trickled down the back of his pants. The wooziness of blood loss had come to him and he was well overdue for his own clotting and bandages. However, he had something to say to his partner before he tended to himself.

As if she was more likely to hear him were he quiet, he whispered to Anna, "If you want to go, you can. It's okay, I understand. And Chloe will too, probably not right away, not for years, but she'll make peace with it one day. I know you think she can't survive in Missio without you, but if she's anything like you, she can. Before you go I'd like you to know something though. I died in Carthage, or so I believed. Then you showed up, irritated, angered the living shit out of me at first. You could say our missions were too distracting, but I was just too scared to let myself see what you really are, a bright star in a pitch black night. So don't worry, Commander Darius isn't here to make this decision for you. Take all the time you need."

He rotated his head around to check on the children. Jacob was almost finished treating and bandaging his sister's gashes. Mia set her hand on the box Jacob had taken supplies from, ready to do the same for her brother once he was done. Sean wondered where Joseph Holloway's children attained their skill with caring for injuries. Not only for themselves, but their help with Anna had been impressively efficient, Sean rarely having to guide them on what to do. Then, Sean reckoned that Athenian children were probably taught basic medical care from a young age, given the dangers posed by the town's location in the Aegean Valley and their limited population and resources compared to Marathon and Carthage. *Kids in the Aegean Valley don't get to be kids, same with the Cavaliers' kids. As abysmal as Marathon is, at least the kids there get to have something resembling a childhood.* He was starting to compliment Jacob and Mia's medical aptitudes, hoping to gain their trust, when he heard Anna exhale a sudden sharp breath. His heart hung low in his chest as he shut his eye, for he knew what he'd just heard was the rattle of life departing from Anna's body. Sean remained that way for ten seconds or so, facing away from her with his eye closed, as if that would save him from the reality that he was alone, once again. Amidst a throbbing breath of preparation, he looked back down at his partner.

But Anna's eyes were open. Her head tilted to the side, towards Sean, her expression pained and confused. The corners of her lips curved in a puzzled smile, her body readapting to the world. "I saw stars," she said to him, whatever that was supposed to mean. Sean was laughing, though why he didn't know or care. He also couldn't care less how much his ribs hurt as he laughed. Concern showed on Anna's face. "Sean, why're you crying?" Perhaps he had been since they brought Anna back to the bunker. Bending his head over Anna's, their lips connected in a kiss. Surprised as Anna was at the onset, she reciprocated, raising her left arm around Sean's head and running her hand through the back of his hair. And for a minute, the world no longer frightened him.

Two months later, Sean angled the mirror up from his face, modifying the view until his left eye could glimpse the right side of his head. A route of scars, as pronounced as those on the right side of his face, ran towards his right eye socket. He traced them with his fingers, arriving at the eye itself. "Didn't you say you were going to stop with the mirror?" Veering his head to the right, he gave his left eye a view of the room's second bed, between his own and the window. Anna Corday sat on this bed, alive and facing him with an expression that mixed a relaxed smile with minor apprehension.

Grinning, Sean replied, "One more hour, when we get discharged."

"That's a penalty," Anna giggled as Sean resumed his practice with the mirror. His fingers curled around his right eye, visible and free of blood. Except it wasn't his eye anymore. A glass eyeball replaced the ruined eye his skull no longer contained. "Does it still itch?"

He kept his living eye on his false eye as he said, "I'm still getting used to having it there."

"I know the feeling." Sean looked at her as she removed her glove and folded her sleeve up above her dark blue prosthetic arm. She stared at the plastic limb in reluctant acceptance, the loss of her right arm housed in mind though not cordially welcomed. "The weird thing is it feels like my arm is still there."

Sean put the mirror on the bed and shifted to sit across from Anna. Stretching out his arm, he placed his hand in her plastic hand, interlocking his fingers with her inflexible digits. "Seems pretty real to me."

Anna snickered. "I guess we made it out all right, given what we walked back from."

Sean, Anna, Jacob, and Mia stayed in that bunker for seven days. The majority of that time was expended guzzling the facility's stash of non-perishable Previous Civilization rations and water, changing the bandages on their wounds regularly, and sleeping in the bunk room, across the hall from the medical storage room. Using water and rags, they washed the blood from their bodies when they were able. Sean also found old winter gear for all of them to change into, including some in the children's sizes. However, he purposefully neglected to tell them he'd taken the clothing from a room towards the rear of the bunker that had been engulfed in the discarded garb of many a victim, though he was sure Anna suspected as much. The Dragoons attempted to interact with the liberated Athenians, but Jacob and Mia often kept to themselves, never speaking in Sean and Anna's company. Even after Sean informed them that their father was in Marathon they remained detached, not once asking about him.

Over the course of the days sheltered in the bunker, their strength rejuvenated, barely, although enough that at the end of the week they were ready to begin the trek south to friendly territory, if Marathon's territory could be called friendly. Four packs were filled with food, water, and medical supplies, and then distributed among the group. Given that Sean and Anna each had one arm lacking proper motor function, they armed themselves with pistols and several magazines of ammunition. Neither of them had the endurance to carry a complete rifle load, nor would they be able to wield the T-05s efficiently if attacked.

The discussion of whether Jacob and Mia would follow Sean and Anna to Marathon did not take place. The assumption was made by the adults, and the children didn't appear to object. The four headed south together via Fort Valley, hugging the Aegean Mountains. Their walk was slow; Sean and Anna's wounds and the poor post-storm landscape forbade their progress from reaching any further than five miles a day. Nights were spent in the valley's natural caves, around a campfire built from the bountifully available woodland debris, Jacob and Mia always isolating themselves to their own side of the fire. After three days the four of them escaped through the southern tip of the valley within a valley. On the tenth day of their long walk they passed through the junction of the Aegean and Troy Mountains, leaving the Aegean Valley. And at last, fifteen days after leaving the bunker and twenty-two days after the defeat of Sword of God, Sean,

Anna, Jacob, and Mia were rescued by a Nightwalker patrol, twenty-five miles south of the Aegean Valley.

Try as he did to stay awake, Sean was asleep before the convoy had gone ten miles down the Highway. He woke up two days later in Marathon Hospital's recovery wing, his left arm in a sling, stitches and new sturdier bandaging covering his chest and face, and a ball of glass in his right eye socket. The doctor who administered the procedure explained that his right eye had been both infected and permanently blinded. It was an unnecessary risk not to remove the eye altogether.

From there, Sean was assigned to the room he and Anna shared during their time at Marathon Hospital. Anna was already there, sewn and bandaged as he was, her right arm amputated at the shoulder and the prosthetic in place. The damage had been irreparable. The hospital staff commented that Anna would've died a month ago were she not a Second-Gen. Sean asked the staff where in the hospital Jacob and Mia were being treated, and discovered that Anna already queried about the children. Jacob and Mia weren't soldiers, thus they'd been denied treatment at Marathon Hospital and taken to Missio as immigrated citizens of Marathon. Sean didn't get much time to agonize over the children's wellbeing before learning he and his partner would soon part ways with the Black Dragoons.

"No longer medically fit for service," was how the hospital staff summarized their evaluation of Sean and Anna's conditions. With his right eye gone and her right arm amputated, disabilities that prohibited any future work in the military, Sean Halley and Anna Corday had been slated for medical discharge from the military upon their release from Marathon Hospital.

Their first two weeks at Marathon Hospital were consumed by the intrusive recovery practice the building's staff obeyed. Constantly, it seemed, they were in Sean and Anna's room, performing checkups of their vitals, adjusting their pain medication, and changing their bandages. Between these disruptions, Sean strived to comfort Anna, telling her, "Once we get to Missio, we'll look for Chloe together. We'll go street by street, barrack by barrack, bunk by bunk until we find her, her and Jacob and Mia, no matter how long it takes." But his assurances could only do so much while they were trapped in New Terra.

At the start of their third week as patients, the stay grew more tolerable. Sean's left arm came out of the sling as he regained use of the limb, the stitches taken out of his chest and lower body; the pain in his ribs, back, head, and face began to subside. In the next bed, Anna was relieved of her stitching, the bandages ripped from her frame to reveal the unscarred skin that bore no sign of her wounds from the Aegean Valley. Recuperating from her amputation was now the sole focus of her rehabilitation, a task that as a Second-Gen she would accomplish by the end of her fourth week without a right arm, months ahead of the time it would take for a human.

With Sean and Anna's improvement, the hospital staff visited less often. Nights were theirs without staff repeatedly checking in on them and without health monitors beeping at their bedsides every few minutes. Sleep wasn't abundant, however. Tossing and turning for hours, tormenting themselves with thoughts of the Aegean Valley, became their nightly routine, until the last night of their third week in Marathon Hospital. That day, Sean was taken off the heavier pain meds and had the stitches removed from his back and the side of his head. That night, as he lay on his mattress waiting for slumber, Sean heard Anna climb out of her bed. He rolled on his side and found her standing over him, her left hand resting on his arm. Like their moment of near-telepathy in the plane when she'd called him over to lie next to her without using a single word, Sean realized what Anna was asking. *Do you want to? Yes.* Almost at once, as if Sean was seeing the flash images of a dream, he and Anna shed their clothes and Sean ended up on his back, his hands clasped to Anna's hips, her body dancing over his. He wondered afterwards how the noise hadn't alerted the hospital staff.

The stitches and bandaging on Sean's face were removed in the middle of the fourth week, unveiling the throng of blood-red scars that ensnared him. The mirror given to him by the staff and stupidly never taken away was in his hand many times in the days that followed, as if he were bracing himself for the looks of quiet disdain he was bound to receive.

On the afternoon of their release, Sean and Anna sat on their respective beds, holding hands, locking eyes. It made no difference to them that one of those hands was made of plastic and one of the eyes composed of glass. Dressed in the civilian uniforms of Marathon, dark blue jackets, black pants, black boots, black socks, and black gloves that fit much like the military's recreational gear, with two black travel bags packed and sitting between their beds, they were ready for the trip to their new housing. "I guess we made it out all right, given what we walked back from."

"Yeah." Waving a hand in front of his face, Sean said, "You okay living with someone who looks like this?"

Tapping her prosthetic arm with her left hand, Anna joked, "Only if you're okay living with someone who's missing an arm."

"Okay, you got it," Sean chuckled in reply, before exchanging a kiss with his partner.

A knock from the hall disconnected them and had them standing apart at the foot of their beds when the door opened a couple seconds later. A shimmer of yellow reflected in Darius's glass eye from the overhead lights as she came in, wearing her recreational attire. Sean felt his muscles tauten throughout his recently mended body as Darius focused on him, as if snubbing the fact that Anna was in the room. "How's the eye?"

Training his head at the wall as he answered, Sean said, "It's all right ma'am, I'm still getting used to it."

"I wouldn't worry. In a few years, you'll forget it's even there."

"Thank you, ma'am."

"I have to confess Sean, I was wrong about you." Sean turned to Darius in amazed confusion, never projecting he'd hear her say, "Still fighting after losing your eye and getting your face cut up like that, you've certainly proved your worth to Marathon."

He gathered that Darius's words of praise were employed only to spite Anna. A final parting gift before Anna left the military, make Sean the champion of their mission. "Thank you, ma'am," he replied, hoping Darius stopped there.

"I wish we were keeping you around. I'd like to see what you could be after a couple more ops. But since you're leaving us today, let me express my appreciation by telling you that as of this morning your Carthage ancestry and your involvement with hostile forces during the Marathon-Carthage War have been expunged from your record. You can now live in Missio as a full-fledged citizen of Marathon."

The insult beneath Darius's gesture wasn't thoroughly hidden; Sean was convinced the Commander wanted him to find it. In the view of Marathon, his upbringing was better lost to history than kept on file. As offended as he was, all he could safely say was, "Thank you, ma'am," once again.

Darius dropped him from attention and changed her entire demeanor as she shifted to Anna. "Can't say the same for you, I'm afraid." Unabashed contempt and disappointment carried in her expression as she told her fellow Second-Gen, "I expected a lot more than two missions." Anna stood by, absorbing the Commander's verbal blows with a slight dip of her eyes towards the floor. "And I was hoping those missions would do some good. Word from the Dragoon teams I sent to scout the valley is the Face Cutters have jumped at the opportunity to take Sword of God's place. You two saw their artwork firsthand, so you can imagine the issue that creates for us."

Sean thought of the corpses hanging in the dark green of his T-05 Sniper's night vision scope, the flesh carved from their faces, but ditched the memory before it could harden. "You'll also be happy to know, Anna, Athens, the town whose people you wasted so much time pining over, surveillance from the Auroras is showing another terrorist group has squatted there, fifteen to twenty new residents as best as we can tell. They won't be staying long, of course. I just have to make sure the team I send this time actually knows what they're fighting for."

Which is?

"Yes, ma'am," Anna responded. Her voice was inert but her expression shuddered with the remorseful awareness that if any Athenians were still alive in Athens they likely continued to suffer, she and Sean together having failed to help them.

Based on what Anna told him about her conversation with Jesus, Sean was positive Marathon would be at war in Serenity and the Aegean Valley for decades. Even after they'd expanded to settlements beyond Marathon, the killing would continue. Again and again, Marathon would wipe the leading terrorist organization from the region like a coat of dirt from a countertop, only for a new layer of grime to appear within days.

"I shouldn't have to tell you both that once you're out of the service, everything you've seen, heard, and done is classified under threat of detainment and execution for treason."

"I understand, ma'am," Anna replied.

"I understand, ma'am," Sean copied.

"Very well." Darius netted Sean and Anna both in the gaze of her right eye. "Then as Commander of the Black Dragoons, I hereby dismiss Anna Corday and Sean Halley from the military forces of Marathon." An extra degree of bitterness overtook the Commander's tone, as if she was banishing them into exile rather than early retirement. "From this day forth, they'll serve Marathon as civilian workers at the factories of Ignis and citizens in the barracks of Missio."

"Thank you, ma'am," Sean and Anna rejoined in unison, mechanical and without sentiment. A quiet rage thrusted into Sean's nerves, the temptation to hit Darius quelled only by the knowledge that such action would be the death of him and Anna both. What infuriated him more, though, was the understanding that he and Anna were accomplices of Marathon's societal infidelity. And no matter how many years Sean and Anna put between their current lives and their time with the Black Dragoons, their guilt was irreversible, their place in Marathon's history forever fixed, their actions always referenceable in their memories.

They were discharged from Marathon Hospital an hour after Darius left. True to his word that time, Sean left the mirror on the bed as he and Anna grabbed their bags and followed a staff member to the hospital's exit. The Nightwalker was waiting when they walked out, the decayed frozen breeze welcoming them back after a month away. Into the backseats they climbed, Sean on the left and Anna on the right, the soldiers upfront starting and turning the vehicle towards Broad Street. Down the city highway and across the river that gave the metropolis its name, the Nightwalker drove into south Marathon. With ice and snow crunching underneath the vehicle's tracks, they traveled between the two stretches of the Inner Fence.

The neighborhoods of Missio were crowded with thousands of civilians, moving in lines amidst the black barracks and gray streets like dozens of tangled dark blue and black wires. Citizens were transferring between their homes, chow halls for dinner, showers, latrines, and whatever other services their evening schedules commanded, their movements tired and sluggish from another day in Marathon. *Is that what we'll look like tomorrow?*

The black gateway to the district came a few minutes later. Glancing out his window, Sean could see the sheets of snow, tattered and grounded by thousands of overlapping boot prints. He winced at the thought of several thousand people trying to squeeze through this tiny corridor, and the Ignis gate on the opposite side of Broad Street, every morning and afternoon. Tomorrow they would join that crowd, their boot prints invisible, even when left in plain sight.

Through the gate and onto the first patches of Missio's snow, the Nightwalker stopped and the driver asked Sean and Anna, "Where to?"

Inside Missio for the first time, Sean saw the city sub-district for what it was: a tedious strip of eastward bound streets, built with such duplicating design the blocks blurred together as he tried to account for all the roads he could see. Each row he and Anna had the choice of pointing the driver towards was comprised of a slim snow-immersed roadway, adequate for one lane of Nightwalker transport though apparently used for foot traffic the majority of the time, with barracks lined up on both edges of every road like vehicles in a parking garage. The black metal structures replicated into the horizon. Someone observing Missio without preceding knowledge of the district or the city it belonged to might think they were looking at an extravagant trick, perhaps a grander modification of the infinity mirror illusion. Sean strained his head to the right till his left eye spotted Anna in the seat beside him, hoping she would know the answer to the driver's question, because he definitely didn't.

The fear Sean endured throughout their trip to the Detention Center two months prior now appeared to have repositioned itself in Anna, quivering her figure and clenching her face in kinks of apprehension. She was gazing down the road straight in front of the Nightwalker, her childhood street, Sean gathered. Her eyes stretched wide with recognition, enabling Sean to guess that her home barrack was visible from where they were parked. To her it wasn't a decision about where to live; it was a question of whether to go back where she started from and try to start again.

"Where to?" the driver asked a second time.

Punching through the trembling pitch in her voice, Anna told him, "Barrack 804." Then she turned to Sean, as if believing she needed to explain herself. "That's where I lived, before." To that, Sean nodded and offered a supportive smile. He would follow Anna anywhere.

Anna's childhood home was indeed within sight of the gate. The Nightwalker crept down the road, the packs of citizens stepping aside to let the vehicle pass, and then carrying on with their evening as if they'd forgotten about the military transport. Past barracks 800, 801, 802, and 803, the Nightwalker stopped between 804 and 805. With a single black door at the center of the building's front, a lone window, and a dark blue identification number painted on the wall, barrack 804 was no different than the barracks that bordered it. To Anna, however, and Sean as well, the implications of this barrack were so significant the neighborhood around them seemed to withdraw behind a temporary shade of irrelevance. And for a second, there was but one barrack in Missio.

The Nightwalker backed up towards the gate as soon as Sean and Anna were standing alongside barrack 805 with their bags on their shoulders. When the vehicle was out of the way and out of mind, they walked across the street. Sean kept a step or two behind Anna, letting her set the pace. This wasn't the Serenity Hills or the Aegean Valley; he didn't know the territory like she did. Treading through the streams of people that passed by 804, Sean noticed he and Anna were drawing attention. A shot of unnerved remembrance to Anna and a disturbed glance to Sean and his scars before turning away. *At least they aren't trying to kill us, yet.*

They were ten feet from the door to 804 when it opened from inside, halting Anna and Sean in the middle of the road. The residents had undoubtedly seen them coming from the window, because a group of them rushed out of the barrack, staring at Anna in startled disbelief as they clogged the doorway. Two Previous Civilization children, a man and woman in their later sixties, two post-Reform children, a man and woman about three or four years older than Sean, and two literal children, a boy of five or six and an infant, swaddled in black cloth and held in the arms of the twenty-something man. Sean gauged these were three generations of the same family, the twenty-something-year-old woman bearing more than a coincidental resemblance to the elderly man and woman, whereas the boy's appearance was quite like that of the man carrying the baby. The older man and woman stood close together at the head of the group, the twenty-somethings and their baby behind them, and the child between the edges of the doorway, his back still inside the barrack.

The oldest man was the first to speak. "You're alive?" Incomprehension ruled his tone, as if he expected Anna to crumble into dust, a ghost fleeing at the sound of his voice.

"Yes," Anna told them, almost apologetic, as though she felt her return planted a heft of burden on this family.

"How?" the daughter of the elderly couple asked, as baffled as her father. "We heard you died in Serenity, two months ago."

Sean and Anna looked at each other in confusion, neither of them sure what to make of the apparent rumor. "I was in Marathon Hospital," Anna responded, rolling her right sleeve to show them her dark blue prosthetic. "We both were," she added with a glance to Sean.

The 804 tenants shifted to Sean, scanning his disfigurements, but kept their focus on Anna.

"We were medically discharged less than two hours ago," Anna explained, as she lowered her sleeve, resealing her prosthetic from the soiled wind gusts. "Where'd you hear I was dead?"

The man with the infant answered Anna's question, and the air seemed to rest as he did so. "Chloe told us."

Sean's eye altered between the family, as the mother of the child and the infant walked back into the barrack, her father following, and Anna, whose face swarmed with both exhilaration and panic. "Chloe's okay?" she managed at a whisper, her eyes moistening.

Standing alone now at the tip of the group, a flare of sympathy assembled in the older woman's expression. It was as though the woman and her family had been waiting for Anna to prove to them she was really here, truly home. "Chloe found her way back the night word came from New Terra you'd been killed. Her guardians told her you'd died in Serenity and she couldn't stay with them anymore. You must've done a much better job teaching her how to get home from the Community Office than you thought, because she came through the door in the middle of the night, hypothermic and crying out for you. Kept the whole street up half the night, took till dawn to get her to calm down. She's been staying with us since. That first night aside, she's the quietest kid I've ever known. Hardly says more than a word a day, but she's about as healthy as anyone can hope to be this time of the year."

Sean understood then that he and Anna had underestimated the hospitality of her neighbors. Although they may still maintain their bias against Second-Gens, it hadn't prevented them from helping and caring for Chloe. Anna's daughter was an inactive Second-Gen, genetically destined for an Awakening like her mother. Yet on the night Chloe was evicted from the Community Office, the people of barrack 804 chose to see Chloe for what she was, a scared child, grieving, in need.

Sean felt as though he had the strength to lift a Nightwalker off the ground or run a mile in less than four minutes. A smile came to him, only to lessen when he looked to Anna. Her demeanor was worsening, dread dwarfing her excitement. Anna hadn't believed she would find her daughter alive, and now that she was about to reunite with her, she was afraid of Chloe's reaction.

The older man resurfaced from the barrack, his head glimpsing over his shoulder, as if checking to see if he was being pursued. And he was. His daughter followed him through the door, her arm extended behind her back, leading someone by the hand. Then, a girl was joining the 804 residents outside. Equivalent in age to the boy who stood in the doorway, the girl's blond hair had the same shape and texture as Anna's but was several shades brighter than Anna's and Sean's dirty blond hues. This variation was marginal, however, for this child was unmistakably Anna's daughter. It was as if Anna's six-year-old self had traveled to the future for a meeting with her twenty-one-year-old self.

At the end of thirteen months of separation, Anna and Chloe Corday stared in blank shock across the eight or so feet that divided them, mother and daughter daring to accept the truth that they were back together. Anna's eyes teemed with tears, her lungs inhaled ecstatic gulps of white air, and with something that could be judged as both a cry and a laugh, she charged at her daughter.

"Mommy!" Chloe wailed in a tear-choked frenzy of joy. Crying at a rate that matched her mother, Chloe spread her arms out, clamped them around Anna's torso as Anna used her left arm to embrace her daughter for the first time in as many as four hundred days. Anna fell to her knees, planting her chin on Chloe's shoulder as the child drove her face into her mother's chest.

They were sobbing together, the noise drowning out the engines of Nightwalkers traversing adjacent streets. The torrent befell Sean's left eye, which he brushed with his glove. The adults in the 804 family had better success shielding their reactions, though Sean swore he could see the tears brimming in the corners of their eyes. In an action based on mutual understanding that required no verbal communication, they and Sean congregated together in a protective circle around Anna and Chloe.

"You were gone mommy, where did you go?" Chloe asked, instigating a round of question and answer.

To this, Anna couldn't answer honestly without committing treason and without horrifying the child. "I'm so sorry, dear. I'm sorry I left. I'm so sorry."

"Why did you go?"

"I'm so sorry, Chloe. I thought I had to. I was wrong, I'm sorry."

"Were you mad at me? Is that why you went away?"

"No." Anna raised her left hand to Chloe's eyes and wiped away the girl's tears. "Listen to me, Chloe. This was not your fault, this was not your fault. It's mine, it was all my fault, no one's but mine. Okay?"

Chloe nodded as a fresh swell of water droplets descended her cheeks. "Okay."

"Okay?"

"Okay."

"Never let yourself think you did something wrong. You did nothing wrong, you did nothing wrong. I love you and I'm so sorry I left."

"Mommy, what happened to your arm?"

Sean's real eye skimmed around the street, becoming mindful of the attention Anna and Chloe's scene was drawing from the Missio populace. Up the road in the direction of the gate, citizens were bunched outside barracks 800 through 803, fatigued and confused eyes gravitating towards the Second-Gens and their wall of humans. The residents of 805 were filing through the door, coming out to see the commotion. The crowds were larger heading east, as many as a hundred people convening between barracks 806, 807, 808, 809, and so on. Sean's vision settled upon a trio of figures that looked familiar to him.

They stood along the wall of 806, against the dark blue numbers, a man in his late forties with a shaved and lacerated skull, and burn scars that demolished his face, a boy, around ten years old with black bushy hair, and a girl, eight years old with the same hair. Joseph Holloway and his children, Jacob and Mia Holloway, dressed in the dark blue and black apparel of Marathon civilians, their wounds healed in the months since the fall of their hometown.

The astonishment provoked another trickle of tears from his left eye. He blinked and swiped at his eyelid with his glove, but when he lowered his hand the Holloways had vanished, leaving an empty barrack wall. Sean turned his eye into the observing crowds, frantic to reacquire the family before he lost them again. He took longer than he was proud of to understand he was chasing a hallucination, a mirage summoned from what he wanted to be real. A time would come when he and Anna would search for Joseph, Jacob, and Mia, but it was too late today.

"Sean," Anna called. Startled back into the circle, Sean looked down and found Anna smiling up at him, Chloe's damp but drying eyes switching between her mother and him. "Come here."

He wouldn't have described himself as afraid, despite how petrified Anna later claimed he'd appeared. In either event, Sean was uneased as he kneeled beside Anna and Chloe, who probably hadn't taken stock of his presence till now. "Chloe, this is Sean."

The girl's gaze hurtled up and down his frame, inspecting this strange person she didn't know. As expected, her eyes dilated when they studied his uneven face and false eye. The childish fright was there for a couple seconds, but then Chloe relaxed to his appearance. Offering her gloved right hand, the child said, "Nice to meet you."

Sean smiled as they shook hands. "Nice to meet you too, Chloe. Your mom's told me a lot about you. She missed you very much."

Then, Chloe asked Sean a question he never thought he'd be asked. "Do you still have both your arms?"

"Uh, yes I do," he stuttered after an awkward half-second.

"Good, because my mommy only has one now." There was nothing for the former Dragoons to do except turn to each other and laugh.

The light and the temperature both sank as nighttime loomed in the afternoon's rearview mirrors. The citizens returned to the shelter of their barracks. Sean, Anna, and Chloe stayed in that spot by the door for some time, however, caught in the introductions of their new relationship. When they did head in, Anna scooped Chloe up with her left arm and carried her through the doorway. She looked as if she would hang onto her daughter forever. Sean waited for her to signal him that he belonged here, with them, and then followed the beckoning nod from Anna.

He, Anna, and Chloe chose a vacant black bunk in the back of the barrack, one among three rows and at least forty other residents. Trips to the showers and latrine were made, their teeth cleaned with communal stores of toothpaste and swabs. Night came as they returned and the civilians of 804 settled into bed, decayed outside air and body odor cohabitating in a tense coalition. Lights out was called throughout Missio and with that, 804 descended into darkness, cold, and a swift quiet, as if everyone had been waiting all day for the occasion to sleep.

Chloe was already lying underneath the covers of the bottom bunk when Sean and Anna kissed goodnight. How much the child suspected at this point he wasn't sure, though in such close vicinity it was inevitable she would discover the scope of his and Anna's relationship. How long they had until Chloe's elation subsided and she started asking tougher questions about where her mother had been and why, he didn't know. What Anna and he would say, he had even less of an idea.

Sean took the top bunk for himself, knowing Anna needed to spend her first night back with her daughter. He removed his boots and placed them at the foot of the bed, but decided to leave the rest of his clothes on, given that he could already see the white puffs of his breath in the dark. Beneath the black blanket of his uncomfortable yet passable bed, he noted a pattering sound coming from the floor. Tilting his head over the side of the bed, he eyed a handful of tiny black furred objects scurrying between the bunk rows, scampering towards the front of the barrack. *Guess the rats come out when we turn off the lights.* Something tickled the back of his neck as it crawled in the direction of his head. He swatted away what he guessed to be a spider, certain it wasn't the sole vermin he was sharing this bed with tonight. *Wonder how long it takes for the lice to show up?* Sean might've surrendered to Missio at the thought of the multiple vermin species that infested the barrack, had he not heard another sound coming from the bunk below him, a noise that made the difficulties of his new life well deserving of the trouble.

"You know I love you."

Chloe giggled. "Yes, you loved me from the second I was born."

"From the second you were born to the second I die."

"Are you happy, mommy?"

"Yes I am, Chloe. I'm happy now. Let's go to sleep, okay?" It was as if Anna sent those words to Sean's brain, because he was down right then. And for the first time in what seemed like a hundred years, Sean fell asleep happy.

He wasn't happy when he woke in the middle of the night, he was scared. The bunk was quaking on the floor, though he soon realized that was him. An icy sweat inundated his clothes and skin, saturated the pillow and blanket. His scars were burning, the left side of his face and the right side both. Grime and sweat mixed water stung his left eye, his chest throbbed as if he'd been stabbed in the heart, and his throat sored and stiffened from overuse. Through the dark, he heard the exhausted grumblings of his neighbors, numerous curses meant for whoever it was that robbed them of a seamless night's sleep. There was a squeaking noise below him, and when he looked up and saw Anna's worried face hovering at the side of his bunk, he recognized he'd been screaming in his sleep.

From a distance of what sounded like four or more streets over, came the crack of multiple reports, semi-automatic. *Sword of God's out there!*

In a second, Sean's Dragoon mentality came biting back. He was about to leap from his bunk when Anna pressed her left hand on his shoulder, keeping him grounded. "It's okay, it's okay," she said at a soothing hush. "It's just the drug gangs going at it, nothing to do with us. You had a nightmare, you're safe."

His dream hadn't been a nightmare, it had been a reenactment. He'd had plenty since Carthage. "He cut my face with a knife," he whimpered, tears streaming from his eye.

Anna pulled her left arm back and used it to climb over the rail at the side of his bunk, joining him in his bed. Her prosthetic arm dangled from the right side of her chest. "I know, I know," she said. "But it's over now, it's all over now."

Sean rotated onto his side, facing away from her. Reaching back, he grasped and tugged at her left arm, motioning her closer. Acting on cue, Anna shifted her chest into his back, drew her arm around his trembling body, and rested her face behind his hair. Speaking into his ear as she scrubbed his eye with her left hand, Anna said, "You and I are safe and everything is going to be all right." That sentence would be reiterated thousands of times in the years that followed, whenever one of them was assaulted by a reenactment.

"I killed those kids," he said in disgrace, whispering low enough that only Anna could hear him.

"So did I," she muttered in regret.

"Did you have a bad dream?" Chloe was already scaling the side of the bunk when Sean and Anna looked over, Sean having to twist his body around to angle his left eye at her. She sat on her knees between the rail and Anna and Sean's legs, the bedframe screeching beneath her. The girl's concerned expression was indistinguishable from her mother's. It still amazed Sean how alike they were.

"Yes I did," he answered, his quiet tone trying and failing to reassure her that he was fine.

With a supportive voice, Chloe said, "My mommy likes to talk when I have bad dreams, so I feel better."

The singeing in Sean's face and head calmed, his eye and pores drained, and his chest relaxed. The understanding that he'd earned enough of Chloe's trust for her to want to help him was the consoling thought his nerves needed to cease their insurrection. Only his shaking was untamed as Anna jumped at the opportunity Chloe created. "You know what Sean did once?"

Sean smirked. Chloe leaned in, awake and excited.

"He tried to trick me into thinking there's a game where people slide around on frozen lakes and whack at each other with sticks. But he couldn't even think of a name for his fake sport."

To Chloe, her mother's story made no sense, yet the amused laughter came. She was at an age where laughter came easy. Sean's quavering stopped as he rolled his left eye in annoyance. "Like I've told your mother a dozen times Chloe, it was a real sport."

"Then what's it called?" Anna jested.

With a large grin, as if by finally recalling the name of the sport he'd accomplished something of historical significance, Sean told them, "Ice hockey."

"Ice hockey?"

"Ice hoca?" Chloe replied, stumbling with the word.

"Yep, that's what it was called."

Anna snickered. "Ice hockey's a stupid fucking name."

A second rumble of complaints echoed throughout the barrack as Sean Halley and Anna Corday, human and Second-Gen, native of Carthage and native of Marathon, a former Carthage Scout and a mother, recently discharged field agents of the Black Dragoons assassination unit and life partners, couldn't stop themselves from laughing at an unjustifiably hysterical volume, nor did they try to stop Chloe Corday from participating in their midnight commotion.

ACKNOWLEDGEMENTS

To my friends and extended family, who've provided more support and encouragement than I could ever ask for, both in writing and in general. I could write a whole other book about how you all have helped me. But for now, all I can say is thank you.

Thank you to the James River Writers club for showing me that writing doesn't have to be a totally isolating effort. Finishing the last chapter of my book at your daylong writing event will always be a favorite memory of mine. And thank you to several local Richmond authors I've had the pleasure of meeting, either through James River Writers or otherwise. The value of your advice and your encouragement cannot be measured.

Thank you to my subscribers and followers. I hope this book was to your satisfaction.

Thank you to Maggie Peyton, who took time out of her own work to design the cover for this book. Seeing the complete cover for the first time was like an out-of-body experience.

Thank you to Abbey Elliot, for leading me into the fray of social media and networking as the head of my marketing department, and its sole employee. The work you've done as my coworker and my friend has been invaluable.

A huge thank you to Jamie Fueglein. The edits, corrections, suggestions, positive reactions, and humorous comments you've given me over the past year have been vital, not only so I could shape this book into something hopefully readable, but also so I could find the confidence to go back through these chapters again and again and try to make them better.

To my godmother and guidance counselor, Wanda Fischer, I can't even begin to describe how your wisdom has benefited me throughout my upbringing and now with this book. I've been fortunate enough to have a third parent in my life. I just hope I can return the favor someday. Thank you and I love you.

Ethan Ratke, thank you for being my brother. I hope I've been there for you like you've been there for me, and I hope I can inspire you like you're always inspiring me. You're my very best friend. I love you. Oh, and I'm sorry I tried to get you sent back to the hospital when we first brought you home. That was my bad.

Last, and most important, I have to thank my parents. Without the years you spent encouraging me to try writing, without all the reinforcement and compassion you showed me once I started writing, and without the everlasting love you've given me since long before I knew what writing was, there would be no book and I would not be the person I am. Hopefully, this book doesn't give you nightmares. I love you both and thank you a million times over.

ABOUT THE WRITER

Evan Ratke was born and raised in the suburbs of Richmond, Virginia. He graduated from Longwood University with a Bachelor of Science in Sociology in the spring of 2016. Somewhere between exams, papers, and an awkward attempt at a social life, he started work on what would eventually become his first novel, Dragoon. Ratke is an active runner and continues to live in the Richmond area. He is currently in the process of writing his sophomore novel.

Made in the USA
Columbia, SC
17 January 2019